To: My Friend, John Buzzell,

Happy Trails, Pard.

Dusty Rhodes

Longhorn

Book I of the Cordell Dynasty

SUNDOWNERS
a division of
Treble Heart Books
1284 Overlook Dr.
Sierra Vista, AZ 85635-5512

Published and Printed in the U.S.A.

ISBN: 1-932695-31-1

Longhorn
by
Dusty Rhodes

Sundowners
A
Division of

Treble Heart Books

"Somebody said that it couldn't be done
But he with a chuckle replied
That maybe it couldn't, but he would be one
Who wouldn't say so till he'd tried."

—*Edgar Albert Guest*

Chapter I

Death hovered over the valley like a dark cloud. The peaceful looking little valley had been turned into a slaughterhouse.

The coppery scent of blood mingled with the acrid stench of gun power drifted up the hill on a soft April breeze and burned Buck's nose. His sorrel gelding smelled it, too, and pawed the ground nervously.

Captain, Benjamin, *Buck,* Cordell leaned wearily on his saddle horn. He squinted through the smoky haze of lingering gun smoke at the carnage below. His jaw tightened. He snatched the Confederate Cavalry hat from his head and swiped a sleeve across his sweaty brow. His long shoulder-length, wheat-colored hair fanned loosely in a breath of wind.

He sat tall in the saddle, tall and corded and lean and comfortable, like he had been born there. His square features had the hard-set look of a man far beyond his twenty-two years.

Even by Texas standards Buck Cordell was a giant of a man. He stood a full hand above six foot and weighed more than two hundred pounds.

He was a hard man, not easily shaken, the war made him so, yet the killing field below revolted even him and caused his lips to razor into a tight line. Outwardly he appeared unchanged, but inside he felt like part of him had died. Everything came with a price and learning to kill without thought or remorse was the highest price of all.

He clapped his faded Confederate Cavalry hat back on his head and allowed his pale-blue, nervous eyes to sweep the small valley below with a slow, searching gaze.

Lifeless bodies of two dozen or more Yankee soldiers lay sprawled where they fell, cut down by a deadly crossfire. The bluecoats had been escorting a single, canopy-covered Union Army wagon with a large US stenciled on the side of the canvas.

The Yanks never knew what hit them. But Captain Cordell's surprise ambush hadn't come without cost. They paid a high price for their bittersweet victory. Six of Cordell's men lay dead. Two others were critically wounded and likely wouldn't last out the day. They were cared for by two of his three surviving men.

Three men, he thought sadly, *I started out with eighteen. I've seen more death than a man's conscience can tolerate.*

Captain Cordell and his detachment were part of the infamous "Mosby's Raiders" commanded by Colonel John Singleton Mosby. His detail was one of a dozen gorilla units sent out by the colonel on *search and destroy* missions. Their orders were to disrupt and destroy the Union communications and supply lines.

They were a fast riding, hit and run calvary unit that roamed the Virginia countryside, meting out havoc and death wherever they encountered the enemy. They had been in the field more than a month on the current mission.

The war was going badly. In his heart he knew it couldn't last much longer. Anyone could see the cause was lost, at least anyone except Colonel Mosby. These raids were a *last ditch* effort on the colonel's part to turn things around, at least here in Virginia.

"Captain," Corporal Chester Colson called loudly from the back the Yankee wagon, "You best come and lookee here what I found."

Buck Cordell touched the sorrel's flanks lightly with his heels, gigging his horse down the sloping hillside.

The enlisted man stood with his head and shoulders protruding through the opening in the white canopy. His unruly red hair and freckled face gave the corporal a youthful look of an innocent schoolboy, but looks are often deceiving. Buck watched the corporal grow from a boy of seventeen into a battle-hardened veteran that, when the occasion called for it, was as tough as they come and had proved himself time and again. Some men were hard and tough, while others were dangerous; Chester Colson fell into the latter category. Like Buck, the corporal was from Texas.

"What is it, corporal?"

"Looks like we struck pay dirt, Cap'n. There's a strongbox and an official looking dispatch pouch in here. Seems we stumbled onto a quarter master wagon carrying a blue belly payroll."

"Toss it down."

"I tried to lift it. It's too heavy."

"Hold on."

Buck swung a leg across the saddle and stepped down. He ground hitched his sorrel and climbed into the wagon. Sure enough, a large metal strongbox sat near the rear of the wagon. It had a padlock on it.

"Move back. I'll toss it down."

Buck easily lifted the heavy strongbox and tossed it to the ground. Buck picked up the leather mail pouch lying nearby. It, too, had a lock on it.

Wonder why they would put a lock on a mail pouch?
They both jumped from the wagon.

"Want me to shoot that lock off, cap'n?"

"Go ahead."

Corporal Colson pulled his sidearm from a flapped holster and casually blew the lock off the strongbox as easily as pointing a finger. Colson was the best hand with a gun Buck had ever seen.

Removing the remaining hasp, Corporal Colson lifted the lid.

"Goll . . . lee!" The corporal exclaimed. "Would you look at that?"

Both Buck and the corporal stood speechless and slack-jawed, staring down at stacks and stacks of Yankee money. The Greenbacks were separated into bundles of ones, fives and tens, each wrapped with a paper band with writing on it, showing how much was in the bundle.

Underneath the bundles of paper money the strongbox was filled with small, canvas bags. Buck reached down and pulled open the drawstring of one of the bags. It was full of shiny, brand new, twenty-dollar double-eagle gold pieces.

"Reckon how much is there, cap'n?"

"More'n I ever seen."

Private Brodie and Private Simmons hurried up, drawn by the shot. They, too, took one look at what had been discovered and stood with their mouths open.

"We're rich!" Simmons shouted at the top of his voice. "We're all rich!"

"Not likely," Captain Cordell told them. "We'll turn it in."

"Turn it in?" Simmons said, wrinkling his forehead in a questioning look. "What are you talking about, captain? This is Yankee money. We found it. Now it's ours."

"It ain't ours, we'll turn it in, it will help the cause."

"That's plumb crazy, captain. Any nitwit knows the war is about over, and we lost. That money wouldn't go for no *cause,* it would just be stole by higher officers of the *cause.*"

"Best watch your mouth, private!"

"Shore is a passel of money," Private Brodie said, still unable take his gaze off the chest of money.

"How are the wounded?" Cordell asked.

"Dead."

"Both?"

"Yes, sir," Private Brodie said.

"Add their names then bury them."

"What about all the dead bluecoats, captain?"

"Leave 'em."

The three enlisted men grabbed shovels and headed up the sloping hillside. They chose a spot underneath a sprawling Oak tree and started digging graves.

Left alone, Buck stared at the chest of money again, before picking up the canvas mail pouch. He had seen Yankee mail sacks before, but never one with a padlock.

Better see what we got here, he decided. He dropped the pouch and drew his Walker Colt, took aim, and blew the lock off. Inside he found a packet of brown envelopes. Thumbing through them he discovered that each was addressed to a different general of the Union Army.

Finding the one addressed to Major General Philip Henry Sheridan, he tore open the envelope and unfolded the official-looking letter inside.

Major General Philip Henry Sheridan

Commander-Army of the Shenandoah

My dear sir:

Again, I wish to congratulate you on your outstanding display of courage and military genius in helping to bring this tragic war to a speedy and successful conclusion. With General

Lee's surrender at Appomattox on 9 April, the struggle that has separated these United States is at an end. However, your service is still vitally needed. Further orders of your new assignment as Commander of the Military Division of the Gulf will be forthcoming.

Sincerely,

General Ulysses S. Grant

General-In-Chief

United States of America

Buck re-read the letter three times, then pulled a little book from his shirt pocket and quickly turned the pages. April 17. It was April 17, 1865. The war ended been over for eight days, ago.

He stood motionless, in a trance, staring with unblinking eyes at the letter in his hand. He felt sick to his stomach. He and his men had just killed two-dozen Yankee soldiers needlessly. Eight of his squad died in the ambush, and for what? For nothing! The war was over.

What now?

The burying was done. Captain Cordell and his three men stood with hats in hand at the foot of eight fresh mounds of dirt. The proper words were said. The evening sun spent its last rays lighting a lonely hillside somewhere in central Virginia A gentle breeze fluttered the fresh, green leaves of the giant oak tree under which their comrades must rest throughout eternity.

As his men replaced their hats and turned to go, Buck stopped them.

"Got something to say."

His three men turned to face him with questioning looks.

"Ain't no easy way to say what I gotta say so I'll just come out and say it. I opened that mail pouch while you were digging the graves. Seems the war's over. General Lee surrendered eight days ago at a place called, Appomattox."

A look of shock registered on all their faces, and then shock turned to excitement, then excitement into disappointment, all within the space of a few heartbeats.

"That's the good news. The bad news is that thirty two men just died for nothing."

"But cap'n, we didn't know the war was over." Corporal Colson said, "How was we supposed to know?"

"Don't matter, dead's dead. They catch us, we'll all hang."

"But if we just explained that we didn't know, you think they would still hang us, Cap'n?"

"Yep."

"Then what are we gonna do?"

"Got no choice. We light a shuck."

"What about the money?" Simmons asked.

"What about it?"

"We shore can't turn it in now and I ain't about to just ride away and leave it lay."

"Got any better ideas, private?"

"Yeah, I got a better idea. I say we get our bite of the biscuit while we can, I say we split that money and go our separate ways."

"I agree with Simmons," Private Brodie said.

"What about you, Corporal Colson? That what you think?"

"Far as I'm concerned, you're still the captain, war or no war. Whatever you say we do, we do."

They all turned their gazes on Buck, waiting for his decision. He stared off into the growing twilight for a long minute, weighing their options.

"Reckon you're right, not much else we can do. Private

Brodie, you're best with figures, you'll be in charge of dividing up the money."

While Brodie counted the money, Corporal Colson walked over where Buck was tightening the cinch strap on his sorrel.

"Mind me asking where you'll be heading, captain?"

"Texas."

"Ain't no place like Texas. Born and raised near Tyler, my folks still live there. Mind if I ride along?"

"Do what suits you. Be proud to have you."

Buck couldn't help noticing Simmons and Brodie with their heads together talking serious-like in low voices. It was worrisome. He led his sorrel over where they were just finishing the count. Corporal Colson followed along.

"Done?" Buck asked.

Simmons and Brodie stood to their feet, as they did, they shucked their guns from their holsters and drew down on Cordell and Corporal Colson.

"Yeah, we're done," Simmons, said. "We're done with this stupid war and we're done taking orders from the likes of you. By our count there's twenty thousand Yankee dollars here. We figure that's just about enough to take care of me and Brodie for a lifetime, but not enough for four. Looks like you fellows are out of luck. We're taking it all."

"Not likely," Buck said.

As the words left his mouth, he threw his big frame into a sideways roll, dragging his Walker Colt from its holster as he did. Simmon's gun roared. Buck felt something tear at his side. A sharp pain stabbed through his body.

The Colt bucked in his hand. It turned out to be a lucky shot. The heavy .44 slug caught Simmons in the throat. Blood, flesh, and bone splayed the air like a heavy rainstorm, splattering over Private Brodie's face, blinding him temporarily. Simmons managed a loud, gurgling scream before tumbling over, dead before his body hit the ground.

Buck heard Corporal Colson's weapon bark, once, twice. Private Brodie staggered backward on his tiptoes, his gun spinning from his hand. Colson stepped forward, firing again and again into Brodie's lifeless body with each step until his gun clicked on an empty chamber.

Buck and Corporal Colson rode through the night, their horses' noses pointed southwest. For more than an hour neither man spoke. Finally, Chester reined close and broke the silence.

"I still can't believe Simmons and Brodie drew down on us like that back there. Why you reckon they did that, captain? I never did trust Simmons, but Brodie throwing in with him caught me off guard."

"That much money does strange things to a man."

"How's your side doing? Looks like that bandage I put on it is leaking again."

"It'll do."

"We might ought to keep an eye on it, don't want it to get infected. I'll look at it again next time we stop. Lucky that bullet didn't hit a bone or something."

"Simmons never could shoot worth a spit."

"I figure we'd do well to find us a hole to crawl into before light," the corporal said. "We'll be less likely to run into a Yankee patrol if we ride at night and hole up during the day."

"Makes sense," Buck agreed.

Before first light they came upon a burned-out farmhouse that set off the road a piece. They saw a small barn that was only partially burned.

"Looks like that barn might be a good place to lay low," Chester said. "Let's check it out."

Staying in the field alongside the road so as not to leave

tracks, they approached the barn. The Yankees had burned it, but all of one side and part of the front still stood.

"It'll do," Buck said.

A rope and pulley hung over a dug well and a watering trough sat nearby.

"Let's see to our horses."

Daylight crept over the Virginia countryside as they led their horses inside the burned-out barn and loosened their cinches. They slipped their rifles out of the saddle boots and untied their bedrolls from behind the saddles.

"Might be wise if one of us sleeps while the other keeps an eye peeled," Buck said. "Get some sleep."

Chester looked beat. Riding all night had worn both of them to a frazzle and he didn't argue the point. He rolled out his bedroll and fell sound asleep within minutes.

Buck settled down behind some charred timbers that gave him a good view of the main road. It lay a couple hundred yards from the barn where they were hidden. It was a clear, warm day. Birds chirped and fluttered about. A cottontail rabbit ventured from the underbrush and nibbled on the fresh, green grass. Buck had lots of time to do some thinking. He tried hard to shake off the weight of his worry. Virginia was a long way from Texas.

The hope we can travel that far without running into a Yankee patrol is too much to ask, he reasoned. *But what do we do when we are stopped? Do we run for it? Do we shoot it out? I don't cotton to killing any more Yankees, but reckon we'll do what we gotta do. One thing for sure, we can't allow ourselves to be captured and searched, they'd find the money and we'd end up swinging from the nearest tree.*

Wonder how Ma and Pa and little Cody are doing? It's been more'n a year since I got a letter, course, I've moved around a lot, maybe the mail just ain't caught up with me.

Hope they're well. Cody would be near sixteen, I reckon. Probably wouldn't know him. He was only twelve when I rode off to join the Army.

His thoughts were scattered by the familiar sound of horses. He hunkered down lower behind the timbers and eased his rifle up into both hands.

A Yankee patrol came into view. Eight troopers, led by an officer, rode down the road. The officer raised his hand and the patrol reined to a stop at the junction of the lane to the burned-out barn where Buck and Chester hid.

The officer gigged his bay up the lane, keeping his gaze glued to the ground. Buck tightened the grip on his rifle. His hands made sweat on the rifle stock.

Can I do this? If it comes right down to it can I shoot those men down? Buck swept a quick, searching gaze of the area around the barn. *No chance of running, the horses couldn't get through the timber, we'd be on foot and they'd hunt us down like rabbits.*

He was about to shake Chester awake when the officer pulled his mount to a stop. Seeing no prints, he wheeled his horse and motioned for the patrol to proceed down the main road.

Buck took a deep breath and let it out in a long sigh.

Two more patrols passed before the sun rose to noon-high. He woke Corporal Colson and explained all that had gone on during the morning.

"Yankee patrols are thicker than fleas on a dog's back," he told his saddle pard.

"I'll keep a close eye." Chester said, settling down with his rifle in the spot Buck vacated.

Dusky-dark settled in and Chester shook Buck awake. He sat up, finger-raked through his long hair, and clamped his hat in place.

"You shore was right about the Yanks," Colson told him. "Counted four more patrols while you were sawing logs."

"Give 'em a couple more hours to settle in," Buck suggested. "Guess we'll have to make do with some jerky for supper."

"I swear to my time, I've eat so much jerky in the last few months don't know if I can swallow another bite."

"Just play like it's a big, thick, juicy beef steak and it'll taste a whole lot better."

"It's been so long I done forgot what a beef steak tastes like."

"When we get back to Texas I'll buy you the biggest steak you have ever seen."

"It's just a downright shame to have as much money as we've got in our saddlebags and have to eat jerky."

They hobbled their horses behind the barn on a patch of green grass and sat down with their backs against the wall of the barn.

Darkness deepened. Somewhere a whip-o-will called. Buck flicked a look up at a quarter-moon. A million stars winked at him from a velvety-black sky.

"Think we'll make it?" Colson asked quietly.

"Maybe."

"What you plan to do if we do make it back?"

"Been thinking on it," Buck said. "Always thought I'd like to try my hand at cattle ranching, I figure with the war over there'll be a big demand for beef cattle."

"Nursing cows is all I ever done since I was knee-high to a jackrabbit," Colson said, picking up a stem of grass and chewing on it. "I reckon I could ride before I could walk."

"You grow up on a cattle ranch?"

"Well, wasn't a *ranch* exactly, more like a farm, but we had a hundred head or so. I was more interested in the cattle than I was the farming. What about you?"

"My folks were farmers, hard way to make a living."

"You shore got that right," Chester agreed.

"What you say we mosey on down the road a piece?"

"Ready when you are."

Again, they rode all night. The miles passed quickly under their horses' hooves. Twice during the night they spotted campfires up ahead and had to swing a wide half-circle through the woods to get around them.

"I'm hungry enough to try slipping into one of them Yankee camps and steal some food," Chester said softly as they rode.

"Rather my stomach be growling than leaking from a Yankee bullet."

"Yeah, when you put it that way, I reckon you're right."

They holed up the next day in a dense willow thicket along a creek bed. Again, all they had to eat was what little jerky they had left.

"We've got to find something to eat pretty soon," Chester said, as they watered their horses. "My belt buckle is scratchin' my backbone. I'd eat a bait of grub worms if I could find some. My belly ain't near as particular as it used to be."

"Something will turn up."

They were far enough off the road that they didn't have to worry about the Yankee patrols that day. They both rested and tried not to think about how hungry they were.

After good dark they mounted up and headed out again. The road was a gray ribbon of dust flung southward through thick stands of heavy timber. They had been riding a couple of hours when they spotted another burned out farmhouse in the pale moonlight.

"Looks like they got a cellar," Buck said. "We use to keep our potatoes and turnips in our cellar. Let's check it out."

Chester stood watch while Buck dismounted and walked quickly to the cellar. The slatboard door yielded in his hands and he lifted it open. Striking a match, he peered inside. Both sides of the dug cellar were lined with empty wooden shelves. Obviously, others had been here before them and picked the place clean. He was about to turn to leave when the light from his match reflected on something underneath the broken bottom shelf. He looked closer.

The edge of a fruit jar appeared when he moved the shelf. He picked it up. A thin smile curled the corner of his mouth. It was a jar of green beans.

Striking another match he rummaged around the dirt floor. He found three small, shriveled-up potatoes. Sprouts had grown from them but they still felt fairly firm. Convinced there was nothing else edible in the cellar he climbed out.

"You find anything?" Chester asked anxiously from the back of his horse.

"You like potatoes and green beans?"

"You're pulling my leg."

Buck walked over closer so his companion could see in the dim light and held up his find.

"Well, I'll be a monkey's uncle. That will shore beat jerky."

They sat down and leaned their backs against the cellar mound and opened the sealed jar of green beans. Buck sniffed them. They smelled fresh as the day they were canned. Chester was pealing the potatoes with his hunting knife. He then sliced up the good part from the bad into a tin plate from his possible bag. There wasn't much left after discarding the bad parts, but he managed to save four small slices apiece.

"Shore would be better if we could build a fire and fry those potatoes," Chester said.

"Can't risk a fire."

"Yeah, I know, but it was a good thought anyway."

They made good time that night and only had to circle one Yankee patrol that was camped beside the road. They were glad the Yankee patrols seemed to be getting fewer and farther between.

Just before dawn they guided their horses into heavy woods that lined both sides of the road they were traveling. Weaving through the thick undergrowth and pine thickets they came upon a small clearing beside a tiny fresh-running stream. The water was fresh, clear, and cold.

"Looks like a good place," Chester said.

"Yeah, let's make camp."

They watered the horses and decided to remove the saddles for the first time since they lit out two days before. They hobbled their horses on good graze beside the small stream and relaxed against their bedrolls, using their upturned saddles for pillows.

"How far you 'spect we are from getting out of Virginia," Chester asked.

"Hard to say."

"I'll be glad to get out of this state. Seems to me the whole Civil War was fought right here in Virginia."

"Matter of fact, more'n half of it was."

"Why do you suppose we lost the war, captain?"

"Money, leadership, who knows? If I had the answer to that question I'd have been a General instead of a captain."

"Shore will be glad to get back to Texas. If I'd had a lick of sense I wouldn't have joined up in the first place."

"Well, hind-sight is always perfect. I figure about all we can do is do what we think is right at the time and live with the consequences."

Both men and horses were rested and ready when full dark arrived. They made their way back to the main north-south road and headed out. They rode the night away through countryside knobby with humpbacked hills and creased with shallow valleys. They rode through forested plateaus where spring-green trees rustled in the wind. The night was mostly spent when they rounded a bend and saw lights up ahead.

"We better get into the woods and try to swing around them," Buck whispered.

They guided their horses off the road and a few hundred yards into the woods before turning back parallel to the road. That's when they discovered that a river lay before them.

"That explains all the lights," Buck said quietly. "They had a check point set up at the bridge."

"What are we gonna do?"

"We're gonna ride downriver a ways and swim across, nothing else we can do."

"Oh, well, it's been a while since I had a bath anyway."

"I noticed," Buck kidded.

Maybe a half-mile downstream they found a sloping bank on both sides of the river and heeled their horses down into the chilly water. As the water got deeper they both slid off and hung onto the horses' tails. The water was swift but the horses made it to the far bank without too much difficulty. Buck and Chester led their mounts up the bank. The horses shook themselves after climbing the bank.

"A fire to dry out shore would feel good," Chester suggested. "I'm so cold my teeth are chattering."

"You'd be colder swinging from one of those sycamore trees. We'll dry out, let's make some tracks."

On a hunch, they turned off into the field beside a small, grown-over lane just before daylight. It wound around through heavy woods for a mile or so and finally came out at a burned-out house completely ravaged by fire, the barn, however, was completely intact.

"Sheridan and his Army shore didn't make any friends in

this part of the country when he rode through and burned everything, did he?" Chester said "I can't help but wonder where all these people went after his troops burned them out?"

"Good question."

"Don't look like they even touched the barn, let's check it out."

Inside, they were surprised to find there was still hay in the loft, also they found some small nubbins of last years' corn in a tow sack. The rats had eaten most of it, but a few still had corn on them.

"Got an idea," Chester said. "I heard an old Indian telling how they put corn in water and soaked it until it got soft enough to chew, reckon we could do that?"

"It's worth a try," Buck said.

They shelled the remaining corn into one of their pans and poured water over it until the corn was covered.

"Reckon how long it will take?" Buck asked.

"Don't recollect him saying. We'll check it after a while and see how it's coming along."

They kicked some hay out of the loft into the single stall for the horses. The horses settled down to eat their fill for the first time in a long while. But both Buck and Chester were getting desperately hungry.

"Go ahead and get some sleep, captain, I'll take the first watch."

Buck climbed the ladder and settled down in the soft, sweet-smelling hay and was snoring within a few minutes.

The warm sun sifting through the cracks in the barn woke Buck. He stretched and flicked a look at his companion below.

"Sleep well?" Chester asked.

"Did—best sleep I've had in a while. See anything?"

"Nope, everything's as quiet as a church mouse."

"What time's it getting to be?"

"Sun's near noon-high."

Buck unscrewed the cap from his canteen and took a long swallow and then climbed down the ladder.

"How's the corn doing? Soft yet?"

"I checked it a little bit ago, it's still too hard to chew, but we're making progress. I think it'll be ready by late this afternoon before we pull out."

"Hope so, I could eat the south end of a north bound buffalo."

"I know how you feel, don't recall ever being this hungry before."

"Climb up and go to sleep and try not to think about it," Buck told his friend.

Buck found a comfortable spot beside the front wall with a large crack that would give him a sweeping view of the lane approaching the barn.

Whoever picked the location for the farmhouse had chosen well. It was situated in a natural clearing beside a creek. Tall sycamore trees grew on both sides of the creek and groves of pines lined the lane approaching the house place. Nearby, cleared fields spoke of past crops that flourished there. *It must have been a good life until the war came along,* he thought.

His thoughts turned to home. *Now that the war is over I'm anxious to get home. Hope Ma and Pa and little Cody are getting along well. I sure miss them. Maybe with this money I can start that cattle ranch I've always dreamed about. Buy me some land, build me a little house with a front porch, and buy some cattle. I could make a good life for me and the family. Then Pa wouldn't have to work so hard. He could sit on the front porch and smoke his pipe and watch our cattle grow.*

The sun sank behind the line of trees and he got ready to wake Chester so they could check the corn and eat before it was time to pull out at dark.

He saw them coming when they rounded the bend in the lane. There were four of them. Confederate soldiers on foot, heading home most likely, but right now they headed straight toward the barn where Buck and Chester were holed up. He hurried to the foot of the ladder and whispered loudly to his companion.

"Better get up, partner, we got company coming."

Corporal Colson shot to his feet and scooped up his rifle.

"Yankees?" Chester asked anxiously.

"Nope, Johnny Rebs, four of them, likely just looking for a place to spend the night, but stay in the loft and keep them covered just in case, I'll look them over."

Buck picked up his rifle and took up a position just inside the opening to the wide aisle of the barn, his rifle in the crook of his arm.

All four wore ragged, dirty Confederate uniforms and two-weeks' growth of whiskers. From their uniforms Buck could tell they were infantry. The one in front wore sergeant's stripes. He was a big, burly fellow, most likely straddling thirty or so. The other three were young privates.

They stopped in their tracks when they spotted Buck standing there with his rifle. It took a long minute before the sergeant recovered from his shock. He stared for a long moment, then bit off words that sounded like they came from a gristmill.

"Didn't know anybody was here."

"Big barn, no reason we can't share. Just about to pull out anyway as soon as it gets good dark."

"Why are you traveling at night?"

"Because that's when I'd rather travel, any problem with that?"

"None of my business, but I 'spect the Yank patrols might object."

"Why is that?"

"They're crawling all over, checking travel passes and making sure we ain't carrying any guns like that one you're holding."

"Man's got a right to protect himself."

"That ain't the way they see it. A Reb carrying a gun will get shot on sight, no questions asked."

"Then that answers your question why we travel at night, don't it?"

"Yeah, reckon it does at that."

"Come on in and make yourselves at home," Buck said.

The four walked forward, each man carrying a heavy-looking pack on his back. They shucked the packs along the wall inside the wide hallway.

"Couple of you boys rustle up something to build a fire," the sergeant told his companions. "I could use some coffee."

The sergeant's words sounded like music to Buck's ears, but he didn't let on that they were desperate for something to eat.

"You can come on down, corporal," Buck hollered up to the loft. "They're fellow soldiers."

The sergeant's surprised look told Buck that the man had no idea there was someone in the loft.

"You're a mighty cautious fellow," the sergeant said.

"Live longer that way."

When the coffee was done they poured each man a half-cup from the small, blackened pot and sat around the campfire behind the barn. The big sergeant blew on his coffee, and then took a careful sip.

"Don't understand how you boys got this far riding horses and toting those guns," the sergeant commented over his cup. They made all Confederates turn over their horses and guns and swear allegiance to the Union before they would issue a travel pass. Every patrol we run into checks our travel passes.

You fellows know you're taking a mighty big chance, don't you?"

"We know, but we got a long ways to go."

"And where would that be?"

"Rather not say. But we gotta be going. We're obliged for the coffee."

The four ex-soldiers eyed Buck and Chester's bulging saddlebags as they mounted up and rode away.

"Something about that sergeant that made me nervous," Chester commented as they rode down the lane.

"Yep."

They had ridden no more than a few miles down the main road when they rounded a sharp bend and ran smack-dab into a Yankee patrol. There were six blue coats in the group. The men were dismounted and sitting on a bank beside the road, smoking and laughing, their horses stood in a wad nearby. They were no more than thirty yards away.

Without hesitating Buck jammed his heels into his sorrel's flanks and leaned forward over his saddle. The gelding responded immediately and within two strides ran flat out and belly to the ground. In a breath of time they raced past the startled Yankees. Over his shoulder he heard Chester's horse pounding away in a hard gallop. Buck threw a look back and saw the blue bellies scramble to their horses and grab their rifles. By the time Buck heard the banging of Yankee rifles they were a hundred yards down the road and nearing another sharp curve. *If we can make that bend we have a chance of outrunning them,* he thought.

A bullet passed so close to his ear he could feel the heat from it. The soft *swish* was a sound, once heard, would never be forgotten. He bent lower over the sorrel's neck and called urgently, "Run you jughead, run!"

Chapter II

Aweek passed, followed by two more. Buck and Chester rode through Virginia, Tennessee, and part of Mississippi. They managed to outrun three Yankee patrols and lived on whatever they could scrounge from the countryside.

After getting into Tennessee they often went days without encountering a Union patrol. Also in Tennessee, they had found a family that sold them some food. They felt safe enough to build a fire at night to cook small game they shot and the salt pork they bought from the farm family.

But now they faced the biggest problem of their trip so far. They sat on their horses on the bank of the Mississippi River.

"That's one mighty big river, pard," Chester said.

"You got that right. No way can we swim the horses across that. We'll have to ride one way or the other until we find a ferry boat to take us across."

"Which way do we go?"

"Your guess is as good as mine, got a suggestion?"

"Yeah, I suggest we ride until we run across somebody that can tell us where the nearest ferry boat is."

"It was your suggestion. Pick which way we go."

Without another word Chester reined his horse upstream. They rode for two days before encountering a living soul. Two black men sat on the riverbank, fishing. Buck and Chester reined up a few yards away.

"Morning," Buck greeted, friendly like. "Catching anything?"

"Yes, sir," one of them said "my brother here, he catch himself a catfish this mornin.'"

"Could you fellows tell us where the nearest ferry boat is?"

"Yes, sir, it's up to Memphis. That'd be on up the river a piece."

"We're obliged."

They reined their horses around and pointed their noses upstream. It was nearing sundown when they rode into the outskirts of town. Memphis was a sprawling city.

"I've been thinking," Buck told his partner. "This might be a good time to part with these Confederate uniforms and get us some regular clothes. We haven't seen a Yankee patrol in more'n a week."

"Sounds like a good idea."

It was dusky-dark when they found a General Mercantile store and pushed through the door.

"Howdy, fellows," the storekeeper greeted. "I was just about to close."

"We need some new clothes, got time to outfit us?"

"Be glad to, my Martha can wait supper till I get home."

"We need everything from the skin out, boots, pants, shirts, hats, the works. Give us two changes apiece."

A wide smile split the storekeeper's bearded face.

"We can sure take care of that, you fellows coming back from the war?"

"Yep."

"Terrible thing, just terrible."

As they talked the storekeeper picked out clothes and held them up against the two men, measuring for fit.

"You're a mighty big fellow, don't have much call for clothes that large. Let's see what I can find that will fit you."

In less than a half-hour they both had on a complete set of brand-spanking-new clothes and another lay in a pile on the counter. They stood in front of a long mirror and looked at themselves.

"Not half-bad," Chester said.

"My partner will be needing a new gun rig," Buck told the storekeeper. "Reckon I'll hang onto my Walker Colt, kinda feel like it's grown to me."

"I have the best selection of all the latest firearms. Walk over here with me."

The storeowner smiled broadly as he lifted a brand new gun rig from a glass-fronted case.

"This is the very latest weapon manufactured by Colt Firearms. It's a Navy 1861 model. It's a .36 caliber with a seven and a half inch barrel. It's lightweight, weighing only two pounds and twelve ounces. Just feel the balance of that gun. You won't find a finer weapon anywhere."

Chester hefted it in his hand, and then laid it sideways on his outstretched finger. The weapon balanced perfectly.

"How much do you want for the Colt with a matching holster and gun belt?" Chester asked.

"I'll take fifty dollars for the Colt and I'll throw in the holster and belt as boot."

"If you'll add four boxes of ammunition you've got a deal."

"You drive a hard bargain, young man, but I suppose I could do that since you fellows have bought so much."

"Could you direct us to a good hotel and eating establishment?" Buck asked.

"Of course, the Peabody Hotel is recognized as the finest in Memphis. They also have an excellent restaurant.

"One more thing, would you know what hours the ferry boat operates?"

"Certainly, in fact, the owner and operator is a friend of mine. I believe his first crossing is at five in the morning."

"I'm much obliged. What did you say the man's name was?"

"Don't recall saying, but his name is Horace Franklin. Tell him Glenn Dobbins told you to ask for him. I'm sure it's not important to you, but there *is* an inspection post one must go through to cross the river. General Randolph is the commanding officer here in Memphis. He's very meticulous about the rules. I believe they, too, open at five. Of course, with the proper papers you will have no trouble. But if you fellows are in a hurry, you might like to know that Horace is a stickler about his business, usually gets there a full hour before his first run."

"Thank you, Mr. Dobbins, you've been a big help."

"Glad to help a couple of southern boys, if you know what I mean."

They paid for their purchases and left the store with packages under both arms. They found the Peabody Hotel and checked in, then went directly to the restaurant at the end of the lobby.

They were met by a man in a stiff-collar shirt and a tiny black jacket.

"May I help you?" The man asked in a choppy voice.

"Yeah, we want to eat," Buck said.

"Follow me, please."

They followed the man to a table near the back. It had a snow-white tablecloth and silver utensils lay beside two gold-rimmed plates. Two crystal stem glasses also sat beside each plate.

The man pulled out a chair and waited until Buck sat down, then scooted the chair closer to the table. In the meantime, Chester had scooted out his own chair and folded into it.

"A waiter will be right with you," the man said, and then turned on his heels and left.

A short, bald-headed fellow in a white shirt and black pants showed up with two white napkins folded across one arm. He shook out one napkin and handed it to Buck and then went around the table to do the same to Chester.

"What could I get for you gentlemen this evening?"

"Steaks, the biggest and best you got," Buck told him.

"Yes, sir, I'll take care of that for you right away. Could I interest you in an alcoholic beverage this evening while you wait for your steak?"

"No, but coffee would be good."

"Right away, sir."

After the waiter hurried away Chester leaned over the table and whispered.

"You sure we're in the right place, captain?"

They both laughed. The waiter brought two cups on saucers and a silver pot of coffee. He poured their cups full and retreated.

"My pa use to pour his coffee out into the saucer and then blow on it to cool it off," Chester laughed. "Reckon what they would do if I did that just for fun?"

"Most likely throw us out on our ears."

They swigged on the scalding coffee and laughed a relaxed laugh for the first time in a very long time.

"Sure a far cry from soaked corn and jerky, ain't it?"

"I *reckon* it is."

The steaks were thick, juicy, delicious, and expensive. When Buck and Chester glanced at their bill for dinner they almost choked.

"Reckon we got enough money to pay for all this?" Chester asked, still laughing.

* * *

When the ferryboat operator arrived the next morning the big clock downtown was striking four. Buck and Chester were already there waiting, their horses by their sides.

"Morning, Mr. Franklin," Buck greeted.

The man looked long at Buck, seemingly searching his memory.

"Do I know you?"

"No, sir, but Mr. Dobbins over at the store told us to ask for you."

"Ah, yes, Glenn is a good friend, we've know one another since we were boys. A finer man never walked the face of the earth. What can I do for you fellows?"

"Well, fact is, we're in an almighty hurry and we were wondering if we might get you to take us across the river."

"My first run isn't until five."

"Yes, sir, that's what Mr. Dobbins said, too, but he seemed to think you might be able to run us across earlier since we're all here and all. We'd be glad to pay extra for the trouble."

Again the ferry owner looked them over carefully. A thin, knowing smile lifted one corner of his lips.

"Well, don't see why not. Don't seem right to keep you boys waiting another hour since you're in such a hurry. Bring your horses aboard and we'll get started."

They hurriedly led their horses onto the ferry. Mr. Franklin raised the gangplank and began tugging on the heavy rope that pulled the boat across the wide river. Buck and Chester grabbed hold and helped the man. That sped the crossing considerably.

In short order the boat touched shore on the Arkansas side of the river. The man lowered the gangplank and they led their horses ashore. Buck paid Mr. Franklin the regular fare plus a generous tip.

"You young fellows take care now and watch your backsides."

"Thanks again, Mr. Franklin."

Dawn was hard-fought and slow in coming. A gray smudge on the horizon was shrouded by the dingy light of false dawn. As twilight progressed dark clouds colored the western sky and a low rumbling signaled the promise of rain.

Buck and Chester kept their horses in a fast walking gait as they made their way along the swampy-looking river bottoms. Their horses snorted frosty puffs of air in the chill of early morning. Both sides of the road were choked with thick groves of willow.

"Looks like we're in for a wet ride today, partner," Buck said.

"I'm so glad to be on my way home I'd might near swim back if I had to."

The farther south they rode the darker and more threatening the clouds became. The far off rumble now grew into loud claps of thunder. Lightening stabbed the earth and crackled with a constant display of awesome power. The horses became increasingly nervous.

"We better slip into our rain slickers," Buck suggested.

"I see a farm house up ahead, want to see if we can ride out the storm in their barn," said Chester.

"Might as well, I reckon. No use getting wet without need."

They reined their mounts off the road to a weather-beaten slatboard house with a dog run down the middle. Smoke curled from a rock chimney. Two large dogs barked their displeasure at the riders' presence and nipped at the horse's hooves.

A farmer in bib overalls appeared at the door with a single

barrel shotgun in his hands and a questioning look on his face.

Two small tow-headed children crowded close behind him to get a look at the newcomers. A frail-looking woman quickly pulled the children back inside.

"State your business or move on," the man said loudly.

"Storm coming. We were wondering if we might wait it out in your barn if you had no objections."

"It ain't much, but you're welcome to it."

"We'd be much obliged."

They turned their horses and rode to the nearby barn, the farmer was right, it wasn't much. Boards were missing in several places and lay where they had fallen. The roof had large sections of the sheet-iron curled up or blown away.

They found one corner where the roof was still intact that offered some protection from the weather and led their horses there. They unsaddled, rubbed them down with some dry straw, and settled down to relax until the storm blew over.

"What kind of farmer would let his place get so rundown? Chester asked.

"The kind that don't much care, man like that won't ever amount to a hill of beans. Pity of it is that woman and those kids we saw have to suffer because of his laziness."

"Glad it worked out so we could get across the river back there."

"Yeah, lucky we run into Mr. Dobbins, he was a big help."

"Kinda surprised the blue bellies still got inspection stations this far south."

"Well, there is a big Union presence in Memphis. We fought two major battles there. General Nathan Forrest and two thousand Confederate Cavalry attacked the Irving Block Prison trying to rescue a lot of our boys they were holding there. He failed, but managed to take a lot of Union prisoners and horses in the battle."

"I didn't know there was a battle there."

"I suppose the blue bellies that are still there have to have something to do, so they use them to inspect the comings and goings."

"Well, it was a short night in that fancy hotel room, but that shore was a good steak we ate."

"You know, Chester, I was thinking while we were chewing that thick steak what made it so good. Why you reckon it tasted so much better than most other steak?"

"You got me, why do you think it tasted different?"

"I figure it's got to be the feed that steer ate while he was alive."

"Feed's feed, ain't it?"

"No, I got a notion that some feed makes the meat tender and some makes it tough."

"So?"

"So, we figure out what feed makes the meat tender and feed our steers that and they ought to be worth more on the market."

"You said, *our* steers. What do you mean by that?"

"We'll, I've been doing some figuring. We both got a hankering to raise cattle, why not do it together? Why not pool our money and go into the ranching business as partners? That would give us enough capital to buy some land and cattle a lot quicker than if we tried to do it separately."

Chester Colson chewed on a straw and let the idea percolate for a few moments before replying.

"Sounds good to me, partner"

"I've been thinking about the brand we could use for our cattle and horses. What would you think of something like this?"

Buck picked up a stick and scratched two parallel lines in the dust, then used the leg of an L for a crossbar of the lines, making an LH. "We're gonna raise longhorns, why not call our ranch "Longhorn"?

Chester cracked a wide grin that took up most of his freckled face.

"Yeah, I like that. The Longhorn Ranch, I like it a lot."

Buck Cordell stuck out his hand. Chester took it. Both knew that a deal was a deal only after a handshake. They shook each other's hand firmly, thereby sealing a partnership that would last a lifetime.

They slept, ate from their new stock of food, and talked of the new cattle ranch they hoped to build in Texas.

"I've heard tell of thousands of longhorns that still make their home in the dense thickets along the rivers," Chester said. "They're free for the taking, providing the takers are man enough to capture and control them. They've roamed free for generations and as a result, are wilder than mustangs and meaner than wounded grizzlies."

"Yeah, I've heard those stories, too. Some say they breed like rabbits and are thicker than fleas along the Rio Grande, especially on the Mexican side of the river."

"Maybe we ought to give it a shot, captain, might give us a quick start toward stocking our ranch, after we get one of course."

"We'll look into it once we get back to Texas."

The storm blew over and the rain stopped. They saddled up and rode out by mid-afternoon. They had rode no more than a few miles when three riders appeared on the road ahead, coming toward them.

"I don't like the looks of those jaspers coming yonder," Buck said.

"Nope, they're trouble, they're riding too spread out, too deliberate."

"We better treat it serious just in case," Buck said.

Both Buck and Chester brushed their new sheep-skin coats back behind their pistols, thumbed the rawhide thong off the hammer, and lifted their pistols slightly then settled them easy in their holsters.

As the three drew nearer Buck's pale blue eyes took their measure. The rider in the middle rode easy in the saddle of a long-legged dappled gray. He held the reins loosely in his left hand, his right hand hung only inches from a tied-down Colt on his hip.

His face wore a week's worth of whiskers and a hard-set look that fixed straight ahead, squarely on Buck and Chester.

His partners on either side were also hard-looking men, men that were no strangers to trouble. They reined their mounts farther apart, a clear signal they expected gunplay.

"Afternoon," the one in the middle said, pulling the good looking dappled gray to a stop.

"Believe so," Chester said, reining down.

"Just looking at that paint you're riding. Good-looking horse."

"It'll do."

How would you trade?"

"Wouldn't."

"You ain't very sociable are you, friend?"

"I ain't your friend."

"Where you fellows headed?"

"Don't figure that's any of your concern."

"What if I make it my *concern*?"

"Then you've got a problem."

"Oh, and what would *my problem* be?"

Chester gave the man a look, a long, cold, hard look. When he spoke he pushed the words from between his teeth; they came out low, and menacing, as cold as gravestone.

"Then your problem would be figuring out how to get out of this conversation alive, because if you don't move that horse outta our way I'm gonna kill you and that's pretty much the whole of it."

The man's eyes went wide with a surprised look at Chester's words. He flicked sideways glances at his partners, and then back at Chester. He licked his lips. Chester waited.

When he saw the man squint his eyes slightly, Chester's hand moved like lightning, the Colt fisting. It belched fire and lead as the stranger's gun started its journey out of his holster. Chester fired again. The force of his two shots lifted the man from his saddle. He tumbled over backwards, dead before his body hit the ground.

Chester heard Buck's big Walker Colt blast beside him a heartbeat after his own first shot. Out of the corner of his eye he saw the man on the right reel from his saddle, drop his weapon, and grab his stomach as he fell.

The remaining would-be highwayman sawed on the reins, hauled his horse around, and pounded off at a gallop, bending low in the saddle.

Without a word Chester calmly replaced his Colt in its holster and slid his Henry Rifle from its backward saddle boot. He levered a shell, lifted the rifle to his shoulder, took aim, and feathered the trigger.

Down the road a hundred yards away the retreating rider suddenly arched his back and tumbled from his horse, his body bounced along the road for a piece before coming to a stop and laying deathly still.

"Reckon we might just as well gather those horses and weapons and take them along," Buck said, sliding his Walker Colt back into his holster. "From where I sit the horses look like good stock, but the saddles ain't worth hauling all the way to Texas."

"What do we do with the bodies?" Chester asked.

"Let's put them over yonder in that willow thicket along

with their saddles, somebody will come along and find them, but maybe it will give us a little head start before they do."

They put the three extra horses on lead ropes and rode out. By good dark they crossed what a local they encountered said was the St. Francis River. Because of the earlier events they decided to ride a while and put as many tracks between them and the shooting as possible.

"You handled that situation pretty good back there today, pardner." Buck said as they rode side-by-side in the night. "How'd you know that fellow was fixing to draw?"

"Friend of mine taught me that when I was growing up. He said to always watch a fellow's eyes instead of his gun hand. He said the eyes would signal when the man was about to draw."

"Never heard that before, but it shore worked today. You had him cold."

"You didn't do so bad yourself."

"Why'd you decide to finish off the one riding away?"

"I've got a rule I live by," the youthful-looking corporal said. "I've never killed a man who wasn't trying to kill me, but when a man tries I don't leave any loose ends, he might try again."

"You'll do to partner with," Buck said.

Feeling certain that the Union Army would have a visible presence at the Arkansas River in Little Rock, they swung east, planning on crossing the river at a place called Pine Bluff. They learned from a freighter they met on the road that the blue coats pulled out of the small town immediately after the war ended and there was, indeed, a ferry boat crossing there.

They arrived at mid-morning. Pine Bluff was built on a high bluff on the bank of the Arkansas River. It was a beautiful spot for a growing community. Apparently, for whatever reason, a high concentration of newly freed slaves huddled in makeshift shelters scattered along the river.

The Yankees boasted they had freed the slaves, but to what purpose? They were left to wander aimlessly in a war ravaged land with less than nothing. Their freedom left them homeless, helpless, and hopeless.

Buck and Chester paid the fare and led their horses aboard the large, flat boat.

Two black men with bulging muscles and deep baritone voices pulled the rope hand over hand across the wide river and sang "Swing Low Sweet Chariot" as they worked.

Soon the barge touched land and the gangplank lowered. Leading their horses ashore they quickly mounted and left the river behind.

The countryside changed rapidly. Rolling, pine covered hills choked the road on both sides. They noticed several sawmills back in Pine Bluff and now they understood why.

Pines grew straight, tall, and so thick a rider on a horse couldn't get through them.

The road they traveled swung southwest. By sundown they gained another twenty miles or so. They made camp in a small clearing surrounded by thick pine groves and stretched a rope between two trees and picketed their five horses along the line.

They hadn't seen a Yankee patrol in days so they built a fire. After putting on water to boil for coffee they sliced salt bacon and potatoes into a frying pan.

Supper was over when the sound of approaching horses reached their hearing.

Not knowing who the approaching horsemen might be, they quickly hid their saddlebags containing the money in the nearby thicket underneath some low-lying huckleberry bushes. As they remained sitting beside the fire sipping coffee a Yankee patrol reined up on the road. There were six troopers, a sergeant, and an officer.

"Let's not hurt anybody unless we have to," Buck whispered.

The lieutenant and sergeant guided their mounts into the clearing and pulled up near the campfire.

The lieutenant seemed very young, Buck guessed him to be no more than twenty. The man swept their campsite with a slow, searching gaze.

"Mind me asking where you men are headed?"

"Texas," Buck answered, staring up at the officer over the rim of his coffee cup.

"Where did you come from?" the lieutenant pressed.

"We've been to Memphis, rode up to have dinner with General Randolph. We were trying to sell him some horses for the army."

"Ah, yes, General Randolph, I've heard of him. So you are civilians then?"

"Do we look like soldiers?"

The lieutenant let his gaze crawl slowly over Buck and Chester, and then shift to the five horses tied nearby.

"No, I suppose not. Very well then, sorry we bothered you."

"No bother."

The officer and sergeant turned their horses and led their men on down the road. Buck and Chester breathed a long sigh of relief.

"You're a pretty good liar, partner," Chester said, lifting his cup in a mocking salute. "How'd you know the general's name in Memphis?"

"Mr. Dobbins mentioned it when he was telling us about the ferry."

"Well, good thing you remembered it, that lieutenant had us cold."

"Yeah, he did. Can't let that happen again, we might not be so lucky next time."

Chapter III

Buck and Chester rode into Tyler, Texas as the sun tilted to the west.

"This place shore has changed since I left," Chester said, looking in amazement at all the new stores around the town square.

"How far out of town do your folks live?" Buck asked.

"They've got a little ranch about eight miles south along the Angelina River."

They reined up in front of the tallest building in town; it was a three-story brick building with a sign out front that identified it as the Yarbrough Mercantile.

"I want to pick up a few things for my folks before I ride out."

"I see a café down the street, want to grab a bite to eat when you get through? I'll wait on you there."

"I won't be long."

Buck took the lead ropes for their three extra horses and rode down the street. He tied his horses at the hitching rail in front of the café and then stepped up onto the boardwalk and pushed inside. He was greeted by a heavy-set lady with a wide smile and an apron around her ample middle section.

"Afternoon, cowboy."

"Afternoon, ma'am."

Buck swept the room with a quick glance as he made his way to the only empty table. He scraped out a chair and settled his big frame into it. The friendly lady set a heavy, white coffee mug in front of him and poured it full from a blackened pot.

"We got beef stew and corn bread, that suit you?"

"My partner will be here directly. I'll sip coffee and wait for him."

The small café was clean, neat, and judging by what he saw on the other customer's plates, the stew looked good.

Buck sipped slowly on his steamy-hot coffee. Before long the woman came around and refilled his cup.

"Where you hail from, Cowboy?"

"Little place out in West Texas just west of San Antonio called Hondo. Ain't much, but it's where I call home."

"What are you doing in Tyler?"

"My partner's folks live about eight miles south."

"Oh, what's their name?"

"Colson."

"I know the Colsons. Sam and Kathleen are good people. What's your friend's name?"

"Chester."

"Chester Colson? I've known Chet since he was knee-high to a jackrabbit. Land-sakes, the last I heard of him he rode off to fight in the war like a lot of our young men. Glad to hear he made it back in one piece."

"Yep, lots didn't."

"That's the gospel truth. You staying around or riding on?"

"Riding on."

"Sorry to hear that, we need young folks like you to put down roots in these parts."

"Got a hankering to see my family, it's been way too long."

Chester walked up while they were talking. She saw him and set the coffee pot down.

"Chester Colson, I swear to my time!" she said, circling him with a bear hug. "When you rode off you wasn't dry behind the ears and here you are a full growed man."

"Howdy, Mrs. Tucker, how's my folks?"

"Your ma and pa stopped by just a few weeks ago when they come into town for supplies. They seem to be doing fine."

"I'm anxious to see them."

"I'm reckoning you would be. Sit yourself down," she told him as she poured him a cup of coffee. "Like I told your friend, here, I've got beef stew and corn bread and lots of it so eat your fill. I'll have it set in front of you boys before you can cool your coffee."

True to her word she brought a steaming bowl of stew and a pone of corn bread. They dug in. Three bowls later they sat back and sipped their coffee.

"Wish you'd ride out to the ranch with me, captain."

"Still got half of Texas to cross. I reckon I best be getting on, but I'm obliged for the asking. You take the bay and the roan and I'll take the dappled gray, that seem fair?"

"More'n fair."

"Then like we planned, I'll meet you in San Antonio two months from now, around the last of July."

"I'll be there."

Buck stood up and extended his hand. Chester took it and they shared a firm handshake.

Since it was already mid-afternoon when Chester rode out, Buck decided to stay in Tyler overnight and get a fresh start early the next morning. He found a livery and stabled his two horses with instructions to stall them with plenty of grain.

He slung his two heavy saddlebags over his shoulder and slid his Henry rifle from its saddle boot. After checking into the local hotel, he stiffly climbed the stairs to his room.

It was a simple room furnished only by a small bed, a nightstand with a washbasin, and a pitcher of water. A straw-backed rocking chair that looked like it would collapse should anyone dare sit in it sat near a window in front of a faded curtain.

Buck scooted the saddlebags under the bed, pried off his boots, and flopped down on the bed. He was tired. Their ride from Virginia had taken the best part of a month and he still faced a good week's ride to his home.

Outside, muffled saloon sounds filtered through the thin walls of the hotel: a tinny piano, the loud, drunken laughter of cowboys spending their hard-earned money, and the shrill playful screams of the saloon girls. None of these things held the slightest interest to Buck Cordell. His mind was saturated with thoughts of home, seeing his ma and pa and little brother.

While daylight slept somewhere in the dark depths behind the eastern horizon, Buck was in the saddle headed southwest.

The dappled gray was on a short lead behind his sorrel. Buck was pleased the gray gelding proved a good trail horse. It didn't fight the lead rope, kept pace with the sorrel, and was quick and sure-footed. Buck decided to put a saddle on the gray at their next stop and see how it rode.

The miles passed quickly under the horse's hooves. From time to time Buck encountered other travelers on the road, paused briefly to ask directions or pass the time of day, then moved on, always headed southwest. *Sure feels good to be back in Texas,* he thought.

Just before sundown of the first day after leaving Tyler, he reined up on the bank of the Trinity River. A wide sandbar backed up against an overhang in the rocky bank looked like a good place to make camp.

He kneed his sorrel down the bank and across the stretch of sand. Charred wood gave witness that other travelers used the inviting campsite before him. He swung a leg from over the saddle and stepped stiffly to the sandy ground.

Loosening the girth, he lifted the saddle and turned it upside down near where he intended to build his campfire. He led both horses to water and allowed them to slake their thirst.

Finding a small clearing in the thick growth of willow trees nearby, he hobbled his horses and allowed them to graze on a patch of thick, green grass.

He scooped out a hole in the sand and built a small campfire, then filled his coffee pot with water and dumped in a handful of coffee. While the water heated he used his new Bowie hunting knife to slice salt pork into a frying pan and potatoes in on top of it.

He settled back against his upturned saddle to wait for supper to cook.

Darkness settled over the land. Stars twinkled in an ink-black sky. Sparks from the campfire drifted lazily skyward. The peaceful feeling was interrupted abruptly.

"Hello the camp," a man's husky voice called from just beyond the ragged edge of firelight.

Buck's eyes flicked to the two bulging saddlebags lying nearby. In his rush to set up camp he had relaxed too much, neglected to hide the bags containing all his money. He quickly picked up his rifle, and as he did, threw his saddle blanket over the saddlebags.

"State your business," he called out, jacking a shell into his rifle.

"Smelled your coffee. Me and my partner shore could use a cup."

"Come on in, but keep your hands on your saddle horn."

Out of the shadows a burly man with a full beard and mustache emerged riding a tired-looking bay. His clothes were dirty and he had narrow, shifty eyes.

Another man walked his horse into the circle of light from the campfire, a smaller fellow. He wore a black, floppy hat with a rattlesnake hatband. Buck didn't like their looks.

"We mean you no harm, neighbor. My name's Rupert Stout, just thought you might spare a couple of fellow travelers a cup of coffee and some friendly conversation."

"Climb down slow. Strip those guns and holsters and hang them on your saddle horn, then you're welcome to coffee, and I'll decide how friendly the conversation's gonna be."

"Mighty cautious fellow."

"Yeah, I am."

The two men did as Buck instructed, then walked to the fire and squatted on their haunches. Buck handed them both a tin cup.

"You're welcome to coffee, then move on."

"That ain't very neighborly, friend."

"You ain't my neighbor and I ain't your friend."

Something didn't feel right to Buck. When he saw the big man flick a look over Buck's left shoulder he knew what it was; there was a third man in the bushes. As Buck whirled and threw himself to his right, a rifle blasted from the darkness.

Something slammed into his shoulder, spinning him around. He fired at the muzzle flash to his left even as he fell. A loud grunt sounded from the bushes just before Buck hit the ground.

The two men at the fire scrambled toward their horses to get their guns. Buck struggled to his knees and tried vainly to bring his rifle up. Pain stabbed at him, radiating from his left shoulder into his chest.

He tried to lever another shell. Realizing that it was no

use, he dropped the rifle and grabbed for his sidearm. Before he could get it out of its holster, a gun barked. A red blossom of flame bloomed from the bearded man's gun. The bullet knocked Buck over backwards.

His body went numb. The world around him spun like a child's top. He couldn't move. He blinked his eyes and stared into a blackening sky. The stars were getting smaller and fading. *Is this the way it ends?* Total darkness wrapped itself around him.

Pain...

As he drifted slowly back from the world of darkness his first conscious thought was of pain. He blinked his eyes to full consciousness. He struggled to move. A gnarly hand pressed against his chest.

"Jest lay right still, young fella," a gravely voice said.

Buck squinted in the direction of the voice and blinked to clear the glaze from his eyes.

"Who, who are you?"

"Name's Eli Hoyt, I happened along while the shootin' was still going on. I hid in the bushes until them two fellas pulled out. You was shot up mighty bad, had to dig a couple slugs outta you."

Buck rolled his head and gazed to where the saddlebags had been. They were gone. His heart sank. He swallowed and drew a long sigh.

"Yep, they took everything, horses, guns and all, even took your boots."

Buck looked long at the speaker. He was a small man, stoop-shouldered and weather-beaten, but his eyes were fiercely proud and alive. He wore a ragged work shirt and patched britches that, like the wearer, had been too many miles down too many roads. A black, floppy hat failed to hide the gray hair that matched his shaggy beard. He had two teeth missing in front. He wore a Walker .44 Colt in a ragged holster.

"I've got to go after them," Buck said.

"'Fraid not, sonny, you're lucky to be alive, but you shore ain't up to travelin', not by a long shot."

"But they took everything I had. I've got to get it back."

"From the sound of all their whooping and hollering about being rich you must have had a passel of money in those saddlebags."

"You said something about *two* of them pulled out?"

"Yep, the other one is deader'n a door nail. He's over yonder in the bushes."

"Did you happen to see which way they went?"

"Not that it will do you any good, but I figure they'll head for a place called Cross-roads. Ain't much there 'cepting a few saloons and fancy house fer loose women. Decent folks stay clear of the place. One thing you can know, there shore ain't nothing there to cause a visit."

"Where is this, Cross-roads?"

"It's up yonder way maybe a half-day ride or so," the old timer said, motioning with a nod of his head. "I patched you up as good as I could but I need to get you over to Palestine to see the doc. Reckon you could ride?"

"I'll make it."

"All I got is ole Shorty, my mule, she ain't much to look at, but she's better'n walkin'. I'll go fetch her."

While the old timer was gone Buck took stock of his situation and it didn't look good.

I'm all shot up. The makeshift bandages the old timer put on are already soaked with blood. He's right, I need to get to a doctor.

By the time I can get up and around the bandits will be long-gone with my money, the money Chester and I needed to start our ranch.

The thought of Chester sparked an idea.

The old timer returned with a squatty, flop-eared mule wearing a worn out saddle.

"Come on, sonny, let me hep you climb aboard. That might take some doin', you're shore nuff a big en."

He tried to sit up and cringed at the sharp stabs of pain. *How will I ever last long enough to get to the nearest town?* He gritted his teeth and allowed Eli to help him into the saddle.

"Jest hang on, young fellow, ole Shorty will have you to Palestine before you know it."

Buck was aware of only short snatches of the trip. He slipped into and out of consciousness, more out than in. His wounds were blindingly painful A cold sweat soaked his clothes wringing wet.

Just after daybreak the mule plodded into town with Eli leading Shorty to the hitching rail in front of the doctor's house and office. Buck was only vaguely aware of being lifted from the saddle and half-carried into the doctor's office. The voices seemed far away, like they were inside a barrel or something.

"Who you got there, Eli?"

"Happened by last night when some jaspers jumped this young fellow. They shot him up and took everything he had. I dug out the slugs and patched him up best I could."

"He's lost a lot of blood. Looks like you did a good job taking out those bullets. You'd make a pretty good doctor."

"Live by yourself as long as I have, you learn to make do."

"I need to clean up these wounds a little better and put some salve and bandages on them. He'll be all right, but he'll need to stay in bed for a couple of weeks."

"This young fellow's a scrapper, doc. He sent one of those

jaspers to meet his maker before the other two put hurt in him. I reckon it'll be a chore keepin' him in bed that long."

"Say, come to think of it, Widow Clark's got a room at her boarding house up the street maybe that would be a good place for him to rest up."

"I'll jest mosey up and have a talk with her."

Buck came full awake while Eli was gone. He watched the short, gray-haired old doctor as he bandaged the wounds. The doc's wire-rimmed spectacles sat on the edge of his nose.

"How'm I doing, Doc?"

"Considering what you've been through, you're doing remarkably well. Eli went up the street to make arrangements for you to stay at Widow Clark's boarding house for a couple of weeks. You'll need to stay in bed for at least that long."

"Can't."

"I'm afraid you have no choice. Right now I've been able to stop the bleeding. You've lost a lot of blood. If you get up you'll open those wounds and bleed to death."

"They took everything I own. I've got to get it back."

"On the contrary, son, they didn't take your life. Everything else is unimportant compared to that."

Eli walked back in.

"Got ye a room, sonny, say, what is your name anyway, never thought to ask?"

"Name's Buck Cordell from West Texas."

"Eli, reckon you could rustle up some fellows to help Mr. Cordell up to the widow's place? I've got a canvas stretcher you can use."

"You can lay odds on it, I won't be a minute."

True to his word, Eli returned shortly with three fellows to help him carry Buck to the boarding house.

Widow Clark turned out to be an enormous woman with an easy smile and a throaty laugh. Buck could tell right off that he was going to like her. She hovered over him like a mother hen.

"Bring him right in here," she instructed. "I'm going to put him here in the front bedroom so he can see out the window and so I can look in on him from time to time."

Doctor Seymour followed the little procession and checked the wounds again after they got Buck into his bed.

"I'll look in on you tomorrow and see how you're doing. We'll need to change those bandages every day for a while. Make sure he stays in bed," he said, directing this last set of instructions in widow Clark's direction."

"I'll see to it, Doc, don't fret yourself about that."

After everybody except Eli left the room, Buck called the old timer to his bedside.

"Got something I want to ask you."

"Ask away."

"Think you and Shorty are up for a ride?"

"Reckon so, where we headin'?"

"I need you to ride over to Tyler as fast as you can. My partner lives eight miles south along the Angelina River. His name is Chester Colson. Tell him what happened. Tell him I need him. He'll understand and make it worth your while."

"Be glad to do it, sonny, no need for pay though, ain't much I need that I don't already have. I've lived most of my life on branch water coffee and beef jerky."

"I'd be much obliged."

"You just take care of yourself, sonny. Dag nab bit, you got a way of growing on a fellow. And don't you worry none, I'll be back with this Colson fellow before you know I'm gone."

Chapter IV

It had been a tearful and happy homecoming. Kathleen Colson rushed into her son's open arms and hugged him to her breast. They both shed tears of joy. Even Chester's pa betrayed his usual business-like image and wiped tears from his tired-looking eyes.

They talked late into the night. Chester wanted to know what had happened during his four-year absence and Sam and Kathleen quizzed their son about the war and the part he played in it.

Other than the usual aches and pains that come with growing older, Chester found both of his parents in relatively good health.

After a good nights sleep in his childhood bed and a breakfast like he remembered from growing up, Chester and his pa strolled down to the corral.

"Where's all your cattle, pa?"

"I got out of the cattle business a couple years ago. Just not able to do what you have to do to make it pay. About all we grow around here now is older."

"You and ma both seem like you're doing pretty good."

"Yeah, we are at that, your mother sure is glad you're home. Got any idea what you want to do?"

"A man I rode with for more than two years was my Captain, named Buck Cordell. We rode all the way back to Texas together. We've partnered up and are gonna start a ranch somewhere in west Texas. I'm supposed to meet him in San Antonio in two months."

"I see. Your ma sure won't welcome that news. She was hoping you would settle down here on our place."

"I know, pa, but I ain't a little boy any more. I need to make my own way."

"You've grown into a man tall and fine. I'm mighty proud of you, son."

"Thanks, Pa."

Sam Colson was sitting in his rocking chair on the front porch smoking his pipe. Chester was propped against the wall in a straight-backed chair sipping coffee when they spotted a rider on a mule coming down the lane.

"Wonder who that could be?" the elder Colson asked. "Don't recognize him."

"Reckon we're about to find out," Chester said, watching the old man on the mule as he rode into the yard.

"Looking for Chester Colson."

"You found him, what can I do for you?"

"Friend of yours sent me, fellow named Buck Cordell, know him?"

Chester stood at the question.

"Your friend's been hurt. Three fellows jumped him, robbed him, took everything he had and shot him up pretty bad. He'll pull through but he's gonna be laid up a spell. He sent me to fetch you, said you'd know what to do."

"Where is he?"

"Place called Palestine, bout a day's ride."

"I'll saddle my horse. Light down and drink a cup of coffee while I get my gear."

Chester's mother had walked to the door and overheard the conversation.

"I'll pack you men some vittles for your trip," the woman said. "Sam, go saddle Chet's horse while he gathers his traveling gear."

"Pa, you still got that sawed-off double barrel you use to have?"

"Shore do, you need it?"

"Might."

"I'll fetch it and some shells."

In less than a few minutes Chester had his bedroll tied behind his saddle, told his folks good-bye, and was riding beside the old-timer's mule.

As they rode Eli explained in more detail all that had happened.

"Tell me about the place where you think these jaspers headed."

"Like I told your partner, it's a hangout for all the riff-raff east Texas's got to offer. It's a place where life is cheap and pleasure is almighty expensive. Ain't nothin there but a harlot house and saloons but it's the kind of place they'd head with jingle in their pocket."

"Which is closer, where Buck is or this place called Cross-roads?"

"Cross-roads is some closer, I reckon."

"Then that's where we're heading."

* * *

Cross-roads, Texas was a sorry excuse for a town. It was past bedtime for decent folks but Chester wondered how many decent folks would live in a place like this. A few scattered dilapidated houses hugged both sides of the road. The single, dusty street was lined with horses standing hip-shot at hitching rails.

Chester counted two saloons and a large slatboard building with a steady flow of girls and men going in and out. They reined up in front of the loudest saloon.

"Just stay out of the way, old-timer," Chester said, "I don't want you getting hurt."

"Sonny, I been in more scrapes in my time than you can count." His thin lips parted in something close to a smile. "Don't concern yourself bout me. I'll watch your backsides."

Chester broke open the double-barrel ten gauge and thumbed in two double-aught shells and then snapped it shut with a flip of his wrist.

"When we walk in see if you can spot them. If you do point them out"

Somebody at an out of tune piano was banging out an unrecognizable tune when they pushed through the swinging doors. They paused just inside and swept the room with a slow gaze.

The place was packed. Hard looking men stood shoulder-to-shoulder at a long bar. A dozen or more saloon girls worked the customers at several tables. A poker game with five players was surrounded by spectators standing two deep.

Chester gave Eli a sideways glance. The old-timer had his gaze fixed on a man at the poker table. He pointed with a nod of his head.

There were five players at the table and twice as many

men gathered around watching. One of the players was a burly-looking fellow with a full beard and mustache.

"That's the fellow I seen at the river, the one that shot your friend."

Chester held the shotgun close along one leg and walked unnoticed over to the game and shouldered through the men watching until he was standing behind the big man.

A stack of greenbacks and double-eagles lay on the table in front of the highwayman. A large pot of money was piled in the center of the table.

"I'll see your fifty and raise you another hundred," the big man said loudly, staring straight at the only other man still in the game.

They were playing five-card stud. Each player had one hole card with four cards lying face up on the table. The big man had two aces showing. His opponent across the table had three jacks and an ace lying in front of him.

The fellow with three jacks stared hard at the cards lying in front of him. Beads of sweat appeared on his forehead. The man licked his dry lips.

"Ain't no way you could have caught that other ace," the man said.

"It'll cost you another hundred to find out," the big man said, smirking.

The man across the table hesitated for a long minute before pushing another hundred dollars to the center of the table.

"You're trying to run a bluff. I call."

Letting out a big, loud laugh, the big man flipped over his hold card, the last ace in the deck. He reached both hands to rake in the large pot.

Chester raised the shotgun from beside his leg to nudge the back of the big man's head with the twin noses of the Greener. The click of two hammers being pulled back sounded loud even in the noisy room.

The piano stopped playing. Spectators around the poker table melted silently out of the way. The other four players in the game quickly left their seats, leaving the big fellow alone at the table. A hush filled the room.

"Where's your partner?" Chester asked, his voice rock steady. "Don't make me ask twice."

The big man hesitated only a couple of heartbeats.

"He, he's off somewhere with one of the girls. I don't know where. Who are you?"

"What's his name?"

"Tinker, Ross Tinker."

"Gather up your money and get up. We're going for a little walk. One wrong move and I'll blow your head clean off."

When the man stood to his feet and scooped the money from the table, Chester lifted the man's gun from his holster and stuck it under his belt. He grabbed the back of the man's collar and kept the shotgun pressed against the back of his head. In a loud voce he told everyone in the saloon, "This is none of your affair. Just stand right still and no one has to die. I'll kill the first man that moves."

As they walked slowly toward the front, Chester saw Eli standing beside the door with his big Walker Colt .44 in his fist, his gaze swept the room, watching for any movement.

At the front door Chester paused and said over his shoulder, "The first man out this door's a dead man."

Outside, Chester pushed the outlaw toward the hitching rails.

"Which one is your horse?"

The man pointed to a bay tied to the rail. Chester pulled a lariat from the saddle and dropped a loop over the man's head, cinching it tight.

"Climb on."

While the man mounted, Chester untied his own horse and

swung into the saddle. He did a half hitch around his saddle horn with the loose end of the lariat. Eli backed through the door with his weapon still in his hand. He quickly climbed aboard his mule.

Together they left Crossroads in a cloud of dust. A mile outside town they left the road and reined their horses up a rocky hillside. They pulled up and listened, but could hear no one following.

Chester jerked the man off his horse with the rope. He hit the ground with a thump. Half-dragging the big man to a large pine tree, he wrapped the rope around the outlaw, tightly pinning him to the trunk of the tree. When the rope was secure he stood facing the outlaw with his Bowie knife in his hand. Eli stood nearby watching.

"Mister, you done my partner a bad wrong, you ought not to done that. I'm gonna ask you some questions. Every time I don't like the answer I'm gonna cut something off, starting with your ear, understand? That's the first question."

"You're bluffing."

"I only bluff at poker."

The man was bug-eyed and sweating profusely. He quickly nodded his head.

"Where's the money you and your partner took from my friend a couple of nights ago?"

"I, I don't know what you're talking about."

Chester grabbed the man's right ear with his left hand and sliced it off with one sweep of his Bowie. The outlaw's scream stopped short by the bloody ear being stuffed into his open mouth.

"Wrong answer. Let's try again. Same question."

The man spat the ear out like it tasted bad. Blood dribbled from his mouth, coloring his beard a crimson red.

"I—we split part of it and hid the rest."

"Where?"

"Couple of miles up the road under a rock."

"Where are the horses you stole from him?"

"They're at the livery in town."

"What about the man's boots? Never mind, I see you got them on."

Kneeling in front of the outlaw, Chester lifted first one foot, then the other, removing Buck's boots and leaving the man bare footed.

"You're gonna take us to where you hid the money. I don't play games, mister, if it ain't where you say it is I'll kill you hard and slow, without another word, understood?"

The man nodded his head.

Untying the outlaw, Chester took a rag from his saddlebags and threw it in the man's face.

"Might hold that against your ear, you're leaking."

They headed up the road to where the outlaw indicated he hid the money. A huge boulder thrust up through the ground beside the road. A large pine tree grew beside it.

"That smaller rock there beside the pine tree," the big man said.

Eli slid off his mule and hurried over to the rock. He lifted it and turned it over. A small hole had been gouged out and two sets of saddlebags stuffed inside the hole. Eli lifted them out and opened the flaps to peer inside.

"Shore a heap of money."

"Climb down and take your clothes off," Chester told the outlaw.

"What?"

"You heard me, now do it before I change my mind and go ahead and just kill you here and now."

The man did as he was told. He stripped down to his filthy faded long johns.

"Them, too," Chester told him.

Another minute and the bearded outlaw stood naked as the day he was born. Chester removed the rope from the man's neck and tied it securely around his ankles and then threw the loose end over a sturdy limb of the pine tree. He tied the outlaw's hands behind his back and then wrapped the rope around his saddle horn and backed his horse, lifting the man four feet in the air.

Between Chester and Eli they tied the rope to another nearby tree trunk suspending the naked man upside down in the air.

"You can't leave me here like this!"

"I'm leaving you better than you left my partner."

The outlaw didn't say another word as Chester and Eli rode away, leading the outlaw's bay.

"You're goin' after the other one, too, ain'tcha?"

"Yep."

"How you gonna find him?"

"Don't know yet. We'll think of something."

The small town was still wide open and going strong as if nothing had happened. They dismounted and tied their mounts to a hitching rail. A fellow didn't have to wonder which one was the house of ill repute. Chester turned to Eli. "Stay here and keep an eye on those saddlebags."

"Won't nobody lay a finger on 'em," the old timer said, patting his .44 Walker.

Chester pushed through the front door of the establishment. A large room was lined with red velvet sofas. Gaudy paintings of half-nude women in gilded frames hung on the walls. A squirrelly-looking fellow sat at a piano and banged out a lively tune. *All this is an illusion,* Chester thought, *but fantasies keep places like this in business.*

Ladies of the night looking hollow-eyed, haggard and over painted, engaged in deep conversation, laughter, and frequent trips to the bar at one end of the room to refill their customer's glass. When the customer appeared sufficiently liquored up, the girl would escort him up the stairway.

A hard-looking woman who looked like she had made too many trips up the stairs worked the room, keeping a close eye on all that went on. Chester figured her for the proprietor of the place. She spotted him and sashayed over.

"Good evening, handsome, what's your pleasure?"

Chester slipped a twenty-dollar double-eagle into her hand. She glanced down at the gold coin and her eyes went almost as wide as the smile on her painted face.

"I'm looking for a fellow who answers to the name of Tinker. He wears a rattlesnake hatband. Slim sort of fellow. Seen anybody like that tonight."

"Maybe."

Chester dropped another gold coin in her hand. She bounced them up and down in her palm.

"He's upstairs with Maybelle, second door on the left. Don't hurt the girl."

"I'd never hurt a girl, ma'am."

He took the stairs two at a time. The narrow hallway shone brightly lit with lamps attached to both walls. He stopped outside the second door on the left and listened.

The sound of a man's drunken laughter mixed with a woman's playful squeal. Chester lifted a booted foot and kicked the door open.

Tinker and the girl lay in bed. The highwayman made a dive for his holstered sidearm hanging on a nearby chair. He was almost fast enough. Chester's Colt bucked in his fist, once, twice, three times. All three shots found their mark. Ross Tinker lay naked where he fell, his lifeless body oozing blood into a puddle on the bare plank floor.

The girl sat upright in bed, her fist tried and failed to stifle the screams. Blue gun smoke drifted in a cloud. The acrid stench of gunpowder filled the small room.

Chester picked up the man's pants from the floor and went through the pockets. The search yielded a wad of greenbacks and a handful of double-eagles. He pitched one of the gold pieces on the bed in front of the frightened girl before turning and walking calmly out of the room and down the stairs.

The crowd of curious onlookers melted out of his way. The madam simply crooked a smile as Chester walked past her and through the door. The shooting apparently hadn't even been noticed outside the house.

Eli stood beside his mule. He shook his head with wide-eyed amazement on his face and climbed into his saddle. They rode to the livery and collected Buck's sorrel and the dappled gray. Counting the bearded fellow's horse, they left Crossroads with Buck's money and led the three horses behind them.

The sun rose just shy of noon-high when Chester and Eli reined up in front of Widow Clark's boarding house. They stepped down and tied their horses to the hitching rail. The widow opened the front door to their knock and ushered them into Buck's room.

Buck lay in his long johns in a bed with clean white sheets pulled up around his chest.

"How are you, captain?" Chester greeted with a crooked grin.

"I'm slept out."

"Found some boots I think belong to you," Chester said, pitching Buck's new boots onto the bed.

Buck's eyes went wide.

"Where'd you find these?"

"Fellow that had 'em don't need them anymore. Got something else here that belongs to you," he said.

He swung the heavy saddlebags off his shoulder and laid them on the bed beside Buck.

"If we're gonna be partners you're gonna have to keep a closer eye on our money," Chester said, smiling. "Oh, and your horses are outside."

Buck stuck out a hand. Chester took it. "Thanks, partner."

"Don't mention it. Reckon we could find room on that ranch we ain't got yet for a broken down old codger like Eli?" Chester asked. "He's a man to ride the trail with. I couldn't have done it without him."

"I was thinking the same thing. What about it, Eli, think you might want to throw in with a couple of fellows like us?"

"Well, I hope to smile. If'n you youngins are offerin, I'm acceptin. To my way of thinking, you boys are a matched pair, aces high. Jest let me know where and when and I'll be there."

"We still gonna meet in San Antonio the last of July?" Chester asked.

"Don't see why not. I'll take Eli with me and we'll be there."

"Then I'll be getting back to my pa's place, they'll be worrying some, I reckon."

After Chester said his good-bye and rode off, Eli sat beside Buck's bed and told him every detail of all that happened. It took a while.

"I've seen some tough cookies in my time, I have, but this partner of yourn beats all." Eli told Buck. "He goes mad-dog crazy when he gets riled. Cool as a cucumber, he is, and meaner a den of rattlers."

"He's a good man," Buck said, shaking his head at the story.

Two weeks turned into three before Doctor Seymour allowed Buck out of bed and then only for short walks. Buck reluctantly agreed because he discovered he was weaker than he first thought.

Finally, after an entire month, he said good-bye to widow Clark and paid her handsomely for taking care of him so well.

"If you ever pass this way again I'd consider it a favor if you'd stop by," she told him.

"Count on it."

She wrapped him in a hug. Buck and Eli toed a stirrup and swung into their saddles. The widow stood on the front porch and watched them go. Buck looked back and waved. She waved back. He could have sworn he saw her brush a tear away.

A week later Buck and Eli rode into San Antonio. It had been a long and tiring trip and they were exhausted. Since it was mid-afternoon, Buck decided they should spend the night in the hotel and ride on out to his folk's place the next morning.

He made arrangements with the hostler to keep their horses. They checked into the Cattleman's Hotel, went to their rooms and washed up, then met in the restaurant just off the lobby.

"Sure will be good to sleep in a regular bed for a change," Buck said as they sipped coffee and waited for their meal to arrive.

"Yeah, these old bones are getting a mite stiff and creaky," Eli replied. "How long you been gone from home, sonny?"

"Joined up when I was seventeen. Been gone best part of four years, I reckon. I'm looking forward to seeing my folks again."

"Say you haven't heard from them in a while?"

"No, it's been about a year or so. I moved around a lot though. Reckon it was hard for mail to catch up to me."

They enjoyed a leisurely meal, visiting and agreeing to leave at first light.

"I'm gonna hit the sack," Buck said.

"Me, too, I'll be waitin' on you at the livery."

* * *

The first rooster crowed as Buck and Eli rode out of San Antonio and headed due west. Buck now led three horses on lead lines behind him.

"How far is it to your folk's place?"

"Oh, forty miles, more or less. We ought to be there before sundown."

"Say you got a younger brother?"

"Yep, his name is Cody. He's close to sixteen now, I reckon."

"How big is their farm?"

"It's a small place, only a hundred-sixty acres. They settled it under a land grant before I was born. I've lived there all my life. My folks worked from dark to dark most of their lives and never had two nickels to rub together.

"Hondo ain't really a town, ain't nothing there but a trading post. No more than a half dozen families live within twenty miles."

Just as Buck had said, the sun kissed the western horizon when they rode down the winding lane Buck knew so well.

"Another quarter mile and we'll be home," Buck said, heeling his horse into a canter.

They rounded a curve. Buck pulled his sorrel to a sudden stop.

The house was gone.

Fear clamped its sharp talons into his heart. A lump crawled up the back of his throat and lodged there. He felt his eyes go wide and blurry with tears. His breath came sharp and quivery.

For several minutes Buck sat, unmoving, stunned by what his heart was telling him.

They rode closer.

The house had been burned to the ground quite some time ago from the looks of the bushes that grew up through the ashes, maybe as long as a year. His slow gaze paused on two crosses under a giant oak tree nearby. He rode that direction.

The crosses were simple, made from two pieces of board from the small barn. Carved with a knife into the arm of each grave was an inscription.

WILLIAM T. CORDELL
Murdered by Comanche
March 12, 1864

SARAH JANE CORDELL
Murdered by Comanche
March 12, 1864

Buck felt his heart drop out of him. He stared at the markers and sunken graves for a long time. Sorrow weighed heavily on his shoulders. His eyes burned with salty tears. His heartbeat thundered in his chest. Thoughts swirled. He swallowed around the lump in his throat. Words failed. Guilt gripped his soul like a vise. *If only I had been here, maybe this wouldn't have happened. Why did I ever ride away and leave them?*

Then it hit him, *what about Cody? There's no grave for Cody. What happened to my little brother? Is he alive? Was he taken by the Comanche?*

Twilight captured the countryside. It would be dark soon. Still Buck couldn't tear himself from the gravesides.

Eli was busy watering the horses from the dug well and scouting the surrounding area for any clue of what had happened.

Full dark came before Buck finally walked away from the graves with a scar on his soul he knew would never heal.

"We'll stay in the barn tonight," Buck told Eli. "Tomorrow I want to ride over to the Johnson place and see if Luther knows what happened here."

When Buck finally walked over to the barn, Eli had a campfire built and coffee boiling. As Buck approached, Eli handed his saddle pard a tin cup and poured it full. Buck leaned back against his upturned saddle, swigged at the scalding coffee, and thought of his growing-up years with his parents.

Eli finally stoked up the fire and crawled into his bedroll. For a long time neither said anything, then, as if the old-timer could read Buck's mind, he said quietly, "You can't live in the past, Sonny, the past lives in you."

Shrouded in the gray of false dawn, Buck and Eli saddled up well before daylight. They rode west.

Just shy of noonday they arrived at the Johnson place, or at least where it use to be. It, too, was nothing but a pile of ashes. Buck decided to backtrack to the Hondo trading post, which sat only ten miles south from the Johnson place. He needed to find out what happened, he couldn't rest until he did.

The sun tilted westward as they approached the Hondo Trading post. It was still standing, located on the bank of the Hondo River.

"Reckon why the Comanche didn't bother the trading post?" Eli put words to his thoughts.

"The post is operated by an old Mexican they call Hondo. Never heard him called anything else. The name Hondo in Spanish means *deep*, describing the river at the point where the post was built," buck explained.

"Hondo trades with the Indians. It's the only place for hundreds of miles where they can trade their pelts for tobacco, dry goods, and whiskey. They may burn everything else but they won't touch the trading post."

Buck reined up in front of the small, adobe building. Pelts of every description lay stretched on boards drying in the sun. A large herd of goats milled about, munching on anything that resembled vegetation. The old Mexican appeared in the doorway. He stared blankly at the two newcomers.

"*Buenas tardes, señor*, Hondo" Buck greeted.

The old Mexican only nodded.

"I am Buck Cordell, son of William and Sarah Jane Cordell. I returned from the war and found my parents murdered and their house burned. Can you tell me what happened?"

"Comanche."

"My younger brother, Cody—do you know what happened to him? Was he killed?"

"Many killed," the man said, spreading his hands in a gesture saying he didn't know the boy's fate."

"Do you know who did this?"

"Quahadi, Quanah."

The old trader turned and went back inside, ending the conversation.

"Who is Quanah?" Eli asked.

"Quanah is the chief of the Quahadi. They're the most cruel and blood-thirsty band of the Comanche, the most war-like and feared tribe in the Comanche Nation."

Returning to San Antonio in hopes of finding someone who knew something about his younger brother, they checked back into the Cattlemen's Hotel. Buck was tired, dirty, and hungry. He walked across the street to the barbershop. The bath felt steamy-hot, just tolerable but hot enough to cut a layer of trail dust. The shave was close and smooth and the barber made him look half-civilized again.

Buck spent two days searching and asking questions, but was unable to find anyone that knew anything about Cody. In his search, however, he heard about a young Mexican attorney with a law practice in San Antonio. On a hunch, more than anything, he stopped by the lawyer's office above the store.

The sign at the foot of the steps read, MANUEL RODRIGUEZ-ATTORNEY AT LAW. Buck pushed open the door.

The man behind the desk was tall for a Mexican, tall and clean-shaven. He wore a genuine-looking smile and had friendly eyes. Buck liked him immediately.

"I'm Buck Cordell," he said, sticking out a hand.

The man took it in a firm handshake.

"How may I be of assistance, Mr. Cordell?" the lawyer asked in near perfect English.

"My partner and I are considering getting into the cattle business. We're kinda looking for some land somewhere in south Texas as close to the Rio Grande as we can get. Don't suppose you might know of something that might be available?"

"How much land are we talking about, Mr. Cordell?"

"Depends. We couldn't afford a whole lot right off, a thousand acres maybe."

"I see, so then you are looking to purchase this land?"

"I reckon."

"Would you be interested in perhaps *leasing* instead of buying?"

"Hadn't thought along those lines, but don't see why not."

"Well, I do have a strip of land such as you describe, but you probably wouldn't be interested in this one."

"Oh, why not?"

"Well, I have to be completely honest with you, Mr. Cordell.

This particular parcel of land is in the middle of the Nueces Strip."

"Don't reckon I ever heard of it."

"The Nueces Strip is the land that lies just past the Nueces River and runs all the way to the Big Bend country. It has quite a bad reputation as a haven for the outlaw element. It's also a favorite hunting ground for both the Apache and Comanche and Tonkawa Indians. That's the reason my client is willing to lease the land so cheap."

"How much land we talking about?"

"Ten thousand acres."

"And what's he asking?"

"He's willing to lease it for a period of five years for twenty-five cents an acre. It would come to twenty-five hundred dollars for the five years. Renewable providing both parties agree."

"Does it have grass and water?"

"Yes, it borders both the Rio Grande—the Mexicans call it *Rio Bravo*—and the Sycamore Rivers. I am told the grass grows belly high to a horse."

"Who owns it now?"

"An acquaintance of mine is a rather large landowner in Mexico. He also has several parcels of land in Texas, some quite large, that he obtained through Spanish land grants."

Buck mulled that over for a long minute.

"Supposing we were interested, do we get to look the land over before we make the deal?"

"Of course, in fact, one of his requirements is that he insists on meeting the interested parties before the agreement is finalized."

"Exactly where is this land?"

"I can show you on a map," he said, unrolling a large map onto the top of his desk and pointing a finger. "As I said, it's in an area called the Nueces Strip near *San Felipe del Rio,* just south of the Big Bend country.

"Let me chew on it overnight and I'll give you an answer tomorrow."

"Agreed, I'll look forward to hearing from you tomorrow then."

Buck returned to the hotel, met Eli, and went into the restaurant to have dinner. While eating he couldn't help overhearing a well-dressed fellow sitting at a nearby table discussing the cattle business with another man.

During a lull in the conversation of the neighboring men, Buck twisted around.

"Excuse me, don't mean to interrupt but I couldn't help overhearing part of your conversation. You in the cattle business?"

"Well, I'm a cattle broker from Sedalia, Missouri. G. W. Garner is my name."

"I'm Buck Cordell. I wonder if we might be able to talk when you have the time."

"Of course, we were just finishing up here. What about right now?"

"Suits me if you're sure you fellows are finished with your business."

The man sitting with the cattle broker excused himself and left. Buck turned his chair around and scooted it up to the cattleman's table.

"Say you're a cattle broker?"

"That I am, I represent Swift & Company, one of the largest meat packers in the country. I'm here in Texas to contract for cattle."

"Mind me asking what kind of price you're offering?"

"Well, that depends on the size of your herd of course, but delivered at the railhead in Sedalia, Missouri it's safe to say I could offer you somewhere in the neighborhood of Twenty dollars a head. How large is your herd?"

"Well, truth of the matter is, Mr. Garner, we don't have any cattle right now, we're just getting started in the business."

"I see, then, Mr. Cordell, it seems we have nothing more to talk about, you're wasting my time. Good evening to you, sir."

With that abrupt brush off the cattle broker from Missouri stood and hurried from the room.

Chapter V

Chester Colson rode into San Antonio on July 28th. Buck and Eli were waiting for him.

"You sure took your own sweet time," Buck said, splitting a grin at his partner. "We've been looking for you for over a week."

"It's a piece down here," Chester said, climbing stiff-legged from his paint horse.

"Yeah, but worth the ride."

The three shook hands like family.

"Any trouble on the way down?"

"None worth mentioning."

"Come on in the hotel. We've got a room and a hot bath waiting on you."

"Go ahead and get him settled in," Eli told them. "I'll take his horses down to the livery and get them put away."

After a while Buck sat with his two friends in the restaurant inside the hotel sipping coffee. They enjoyed a good meal and filled one another in on all that happened since they were together.

"Sorry to hear about your folks," Chester said.

"I appreciate that."

"Well, I'm here, partner," Chester said, quickly changing the subject. "What do we do now?"

"We go catch us some longhorns. I leased some land down near a place called San Felipe del Rio and thought we'd ride down and take a look at it come first light."

"Where is this place?"

"On the border just across the Rio Grande from Mexico."

"You mean you ain't seen the land yet?"

"Nope, the lawyer says it's got water and grass In this country that's about all a man can ask for."

"How much land we talking about?"

"Ten thousand acres, it's a land grant owned by some wealthy Mexican rancher named Antonio Rivas. He lives just north of Piedras Negras. We're supposed to visit his place to sign the papers on August twelfth.

"I'm beginning to question how I got hooked up with you in the first place. First you lose all your money and your boots, now you lease ten thousand acres of land without even seeing it. Eli, I trusted you to keep an eye on him."

"One thing for shore," Eli said, "parter'n up with you young roosters keeps life excitin'. You're both loco, so I reckon that makes us three of a kind."

They rode out at daybreak. Trailing on lead ropes behind them strode Buck's dappled- gray and Chester's extra horse he brought from home. They sold the other horses to the livery owner. They loaded with heavy packs onto the two extra horses with supplies, leaving room for anything else they hoped to purchase along the way.

"I figure to find the land we leased and look it over. After we sign the lease we'll need to build some strong corrals that can hold the longhorns we capture. I'm hoping to hire some Mexican vaqueros to help us," Buck told them as they rode.

"Is our land close to the river?"

"Yep, butts right up against the Rio Grande and runs along the Sycamore River"

"Sounds pretty good, partner," Chester said.

Buck didn't tell Chester the downside about the Indians and outlaws; he'd save that bit of news for later.

On the second day out, the country took on a drastic change in appearance. Low rolling hills dotted with live oak, red oak, and juniper trees offered sanctuary for an abundance of deer, buffalo, and turkey. No wonder the lawyer warned that the area was a favorite hunting ground for Comanche, Tonkawa, and Lipan Apache.

On the third day after leaving San Antonio they reined up in front of *Thomas B. Hammer's* General Mercantile near the small town of Uvalde. It sat on the road between San Antonio and the Rio Grande. The store was situated at the intersection where the road crossed the Sadinal River.

They reined up and tied their horses. A wagon and several saddle horses were also tied to hitching rails around the store. They climbed the steps and went inside.

A short, balding man with a white apron tied around his middle was pilling supplies onto a wide counter. A thin, sickly-looking woman in a shapeless cotton dress and sunbonnet nervously watched the pile grow. A small girl clung to her mother's dress tail.

Four hard looking men gathered close around a single table near the back, sipping coffee. They swung long, searching gazes when Buck, Chester, and Eli entered.

"I'll be with you fellows directly," the storekeeper said.

"Take your time," Buck told him. "We're in no hurry."

Eli browsed around the store gathering a few items of food they needed. Chester picked out a crosscut saw, two double-bit axes, a shovel, and post-hole diggers they would need to build the corral. Buck selected half-dozen heavy ropes and two log chains.

The woman-shopper's husband joined her and began carrying their purchases out to their wagon. The storekeeper turned to Buck's growing stack of supplies.

"Looks like you fellows are fixing to do some serious building. Are you locating in these parts?"

"Over where the Sycamore runs into the Rio Grande. Thought this might be the last place we could get supplies."

"Where the Sycamore runs into the Rio Grande, you say?" The storekeeper frowned. "That's in the strip. You laid eyes on this land yet?"

"Not yet. We're on our way to look it over."

"Well, just a word of advice, if you ain't already bought the land, save your money. Either the outlaws or Indians would burn you out. You boys wouldn't last a month."

Chester and Eli walked up in time to hear the last part of the storekeeper's comments.

"What do you mean we wouldn't last a month?" Chester wanted to know, leveling a stare at the man.

"That's the favorite hunting ground for the Comanche, Tonkawa, and Lipan Apache. They don't take kindly to folks even crossing their land, let alone settling on it. Besides that, the land we're talking about is infested with outlaws. They steal anything that ain't nailed down."

Chester cut a questioning look at Buck.

"Something you forget to tell me, pardner?"

"We'll talk about it later. I'm Buck Cordell. These are my partners, Chester Colson and Eli Hoyt."

"Pleased to make your acquaintance."

"How far you reckon it is to the Sycamore River?"

"Oh, sixty, seventy miles as the crow flies, near twice that the way you'll have to go."

"Why's that?"

"The country north of here is crisscrossed with canyons. You'll be circling around a lot."

"Any easier way?"

"Not that I know of," he said, then turned to the four men at the table near the back. "Any of you boys know how these fellows could get to the Sycamore River without circling the canyons?"

A slim, raw boned, coarse-looking fellow dressed in buckskins pushed up from the upturned nail keg and walked over. He wore a bushy mustache that matched his black, receding hairline. He also wore a cross-draw belly holster that held a bone-handled Remington.

"If them horses you're riding can sprout wings and fly, otherwise there ain't no easy way to get from here to yonder. I'm Charlie Sweet, I've rode all over this neck of the woods, ain't no way except to circle them canyons."

"Much obliged, Mr. Sweet," Buck said.

"So you boys are settling in these parts? You don't look like farmers."

"We ain't, we're gonna raise cattle."

"You don't say. Now that's interesting. There's plenty of water and good graze over near the Sycamore, shore enough."

"If you boys are ever over that way, stop by for a cup."

"We'll do that, Mr...I didn't catch your name?"

"Cordell, Buck Cordell."

"Mr. Cordell, I'll remember the name. Come on boys, we need to get moving."

His three hard-faced companions rose and tromped out the door.

The storekeeper watched them go. After they mounted and rode away, the storekeeper turned to Buck.

"A word to the wise, Mr. Cordell. None of my business, but you might better hope those jaspers don't come calling."

"Oh, why's that?"

"Charlie Sweet's a hard number. Rumor has it he's killed at least four men, not counting Indians, most likely more. He and those he rides with work the Nueces Strip, both side of the river, stealing cattle and horses. I'd steer clear of those fellows if I was you.

"Once you cross the Nueces River just to the west of here you're in the strip. It runs all the way to Big Bend country between the Nueces River and the Rio Grande. It's a lawless country with Indians, thieves, cattle rustlers, and outlaws thicker than fleas. Your land is smack-dab in the middle of it."

"Thanks for the advice. Figure up what we own you and we'll settle up."

Buck paid the storekeeper. They loaded their supplies on their packhorses and headed out.

Chester rode alongside Buck and fixed him with a sideways stare. "Is that the reason the land is so cheap?"

"Yep."

"My mama always told me that if something sounded too good to be true, it most likely was. I shoulda listened to her."

After a while Chester slipped his Henry rifle from the saddle boot, levered a shell into the chamber, and laid it across his saddle in front of him.

"Expecting trouble?" Buck asked.

"Didn't like the looks of that bunch back there, better safe than sorry."

Buck and Eli withdrew their rifles and rode with them at the ready.

Off in the distance, mountains rose majestically out of a

cactus-spiked desert that seemed to stretch endlessly. Flat-topped mesas loomed large against the distant horizon. The relentless sun baked the sandy soil and radiated upward like an oven. Prickly Pear cactus and thorny bushes grew in thick fields that tore at their pants and boots. It was a land like none other any of them had ever seen.

The sun slid steadily toward the horizon and splashed the sky with crimson. Orangey-gold rays bounced off puffy-white clouds and outlined them with bright silver. A panorama of color played out before their eyes. The vastness of the land was like a glimpse of eternity.

"Don't remember ever seeing a prettier sunset," Buck said.

"Shore is somethin', ain't it?" Eli agreed.

"Reckon we better find us a place to make camp," Buck told them.

A splotch of green trees loomed off to their right.

"Let's take a look-see over yonder," Eli said, lifting an arm to point.

They rode that way and discovered a field of rocky outcroppings pointing their fingers toward the sky. A small spring bubbled out from under a rock ledge and gave birth to a small stream of clear, cool water.

A thick stand of Juniper trees surrounded the small spring, nourished by its life-giving liquid. It was a beautiful spot and a perfect campsite. Working together, they quickly set up camp, tended the horses, and made a fire for coffee as dark settled in.

Eli had taken on the cooking chores and quickly opened two tins of beans that were already cooked. He raked them into a small pot with his hunting knife and sliced salt pork in on top. The coffee soon struck a boil and he poured them all a cup.

With supper finished and coffee poured, Buck lay back against his saddle and sipped the scalding black liquid that Eli called creek coffee.

"I'd sleep better if we post a guard tonight," he said. "I'll take the first watch."

"Wake me at midnight and I'll relieve you," Chester agreed.

The three friends talked a while until first one then the other fell silent, leaving Buck alone to keep the vigil. He stoked the fire to ward off the night chill and laid a couple more sticks of wood on it. He poured himself another cup of coffee and settled down with his rifle and his thoughts.

His memory flashed a picture of his mother before him. A picture of the last time he saw her alive floated in his mind. She stood on the front porch beside his pa, her long hair wound into a bun and pinned on the back of her head the way she always wore it.

She wore the bib apron that he seldom saw her without over a plain floor-length work dress. Her eyes were red-rimmed from crying. The memory of that moment, that one special moment, kept him going, gave him strength to survive the four terrible years of war.

She had pleaded with him not to go. Yet his overpowering belief in the cause of the Confederacy was strong enough to drive him to leave even in spite of her tears. But the war was lost. The only thing he did was lose four years of his life, four years away from his family. He rode off nothing more than a green kid of seventeen; he returned now as a man of twenty-two, going on a hundred.

As he neared the curve in the lane he had looked back one last time and lifted a wave goodbye. He saw her hand rise slowly, her head drooped, and her face buried in the hollow of pa's strong shoulder. That memory would haunt him every day for the rest of his life.

From his ma, his thoughts turned to Cody, his little brother. He was only twelve when Buck left home. He would be sixteen, maybe seventeen now. Buck questioned anyone and everyone he could think of that might have seen him, but had found no one that knew anything. He ran into a dead-end everywhere he turned.

His thoughts scattered when one of their horses snorted a deep, low alarm. It swung its head and pointed its ears in the direction of their back-trail. They had company.

Buck quickly jacked a shell into the chamber of his Henry rifle and shook Chester awake. He crossed his lips with a finger and pointed into the darkness beyond the jagged circle of light from their campfire.

Chester nodded and touched Eli awake. Buck motioned for them to take cover and hunkered down behind an upthrust rock. He strained his hearing for any sound, any movement from the darkness. His ears had to do the watching until his eyes could do the job.

From somewhere in the depth of darkness a boot dislodged a rock. Buck's pale-blue eyes pierced the blackness, flicked to and fro, his muscles stretched as tight as a rope on a lassoed steer.

He saw the muzzle-flash an instant before he heard the sound. It bloomed out of the blackness, a fiery-red splatter that spat hot lead in Buck's direction. Instinctively, his stomach muscles knotted as the slug whispered a message of death before it tore a chip from the rock only inches from his chest.

Before the sound of the attacker's rifle quieted Buck's own rifle blasted. He fired at the red glow that still lingered in the darkness. The familiar slap of a bullet hitting flesh gave witness that his shot found its target. A high-pitched scream followed, a moan, then silence.

Other rifles opened up, sending showers of lead in Buck's direction. He hunkered down and listened to the whine as the bullets ricocheted off into the night. He counted three new shooters making four attackers in all. *No doubt about it,* he thought, *it's Charley Sweet and his men.*

"Thought we'd drop by for that cup of coffee you offered," Sweet's voice called from the darkness.

"Just drank the last drop. Looks like you're plumb outta luck."

"It's the other way around. You're the ones out of luck. We want your money and horses. Send 'em out and we'll ride on, nothing personal."

"Oh it's *personal* for sure. A man tries to kill me, it's *real* personal."

"Then I reckon you'll die where you sit."

"Everybody's gotta die someplace. What you gonna do, talk us to death?"

The question met with another long volley of shots. Chester and Eli joined Buck in returning the outlaw's fire. Another loud scream ripped from the throat of one of the outlaws. *"That leaves only two,"* Buck whispered to himself.

Quietness settled in.

The sound of shod hooves on the hard-packed ground told them the remaining two outlaws had given up and high-tailed it back to wherever they came from.

Buck and his companions waited a spell just to make sure. From the darkness the voice of a wounded man called weakly.

"I'm gut-shot, somebody come help me."

"Your help just rode off and left you," Buck called back, "Don't expect help from us."

"But I'm dying," the pitiful voice pled.

"Then do it," Buck hollered back.

That was the last sound they heard.

Morning came quickly on top of the high plateau. Buck and his companions sat around the campfire and watched the eastern sky give birth to a new day. They watched the sun birthing out of the depth of the eastern horizon, watched the cloud shadows creep slowly across the plateau, and like all those who witnessed these things before them, they were awed by the display.

They checked the two wounded attackers and found both dead. Their two companions took their horses and left them to die.

"Don't expect we've seen the last of Charley Sweet," Buck said.

"Next time I see him I'll kill him," Chester said flatly.

Eli fried salt pork and potatoes for their breakfast. They ate, then broke camp and swung into their saddles. By the time they rode away, buzzards had already spotted the dead outlaws and circled overhead waiting for their next meal.

All day and the next they wound their way around deep canyons, gouged from the earth by time and persistent water. Massive cliffs with multi-colored faces towered into the air. Fields of flowering Guajilla scrubs resembled a breath-taking carpet stretched endlessly before them.

On the third day they spotted the Sycamore River. It snaked its way toward its rendezvous with the Rio Grande. They reined down and sat their horses, staring at the land that stretched out before them. Their land.

The grass was good. Mesquite and buffalo grass grew near fetlock high, giant red oak, live oak, and sycamore trees were plentiful.

"It's a good land, captain," Chester exclaimed. "Cattle will do well here."

"Never seen better," Eli agreed.

"It'll do for now," Buck commented. He wasn't ready to share with them the dream he had for their ranch, it would scare them both to death.

"What say we split up and scout around a bit and see if we can find some place to hole up for a few days?" Buck suggested. "We've still got some time before we are supposed to meet the Mexican fellow who owns this land. Let's meet back here by sundown."

All agreed and rode off in different directions. Buck chose to follow the river. In places it tumbled down from the high plateau with thundering force, cascading over house-size boulders. Other places it flowed gently in deep, wide pools of clear, cold water, which were ideal for herds of thirsty cattle.

He rode until late afternoon before turning back, disappointed that he found no shelter for them to spend a few days resting up. It was just after sundown when he arrived back at their meeting place. Chester and Eli were already there.

"Any luck?" Buck asked.

"Found the perfect place to build our cabin," Chester said. "It's up high on a flat plateau, a rock bluff protecting the back, natural spring with lots of fresh water, and plenty of timber down lower along the river."

"How far is it from here?"

"No more than a couple of miles."

"We'll check it out come daylight. What about you, Eli? Find anything?"

"Found the prettiest little cave you ever laid eyes on with water close by."

"Where is this cave?"

"'Bout three mile yonder," he said, pointing.

'Then that's where we'll rest up before heading for Mexico."

"Shore a passel of Indian signs hereabouts," Eli said.

"Yeah, I saw them, too," Buck said. "Might be wise to keep a sharp eye."

By dark they had their supplies unloaded from the

packhorses and stowed, the stock watered and hobbled on good grass, and a fire going in the spacious cave.

"All the comforts of home," Chester laughed.

"It'll do," Buck agreed, rolling out his bedroll.

"Supper's cookin', coffee's ready," Eli called. "Come day, I'll shoot us a deer fer meat."

"Be good to have something besides salt pork for a change," Chester said.

"Ye make do with what ye have, Sonny."

"I know, just joshing you, Eli. You're a mighty fine cook."

"I figure we got two days before we need to leave for Mexico," Buck told them. "I ain't exactly sure where this Mexican fellow lives so I'm allowing an extra day."

"Wonder why his lawyer in San Antonio couldn't just sign the lease papers?" Chester asked.

"I asked him that, and he said the owner was particular who he leased his land to and wanted to look us over first."

"What're we gonna do if he decides he don't like what he sees?"

"We'll cross that creek when we come to it."

The next two days they lazed around. Their horses needed the rest, too, and spent their days munching the lush, green grass.

At daylight on the third day they saddled up and headed for Mexico. Eli suggested that he remain behind, to watch out for the horses and their supplies. Buck hated to leave him behind but finally agreed it was probably best.

Buck and Chester shook hands with their old friend like he was family.

"You boys ain't what I'd call good company, but I sorta got use to the two of you. Ride careful, ye hear?"

They said their goodbyes and swung into the saddle.

Both they and their horses were rested and ready and struck a short lope for several miles. By mid-day they crossed the muddy Rio Grande and climbed the bank into Mexico.

"You ever been to Mexico, captain?"

"Nope, you?"

"Not until just now, always wanted to, though. I hear those little Mexican gals are right pretty."

"Reckon we'll find out."

"You know how to find this fellow's place?"

"The lawyer said to cross the river and ride southwest until we hit the *Salado River* and then follow it upstream to the headwater. His headquarters is supposed to be there."

"What's this fellow's name again?"

"Antonio Rivas."

All day they rode steadily. The country through which they traveled was hot, dry, and desert-like. The only vegetation was gnarly mesquite, cactus, and occasional patches of bunch grass. Deep arroyos bore witness to ancient streams that once snaked through the countryside.

The only inhabitants they encountered were a few sandal-clad goat herders in their off-white clothes, sombreros, and serapes. These Mexican peasants eyed them with both curiosity and suspicion, usually reluctant to make eye contact with the *gringos*.

By mid-afternoon they encountered the Salado River. It wasn't much to look at, just a shallow stream of surprisingly clear and cool water that struggled through the barren countryside. They took their time watering their horses before heading upstream.

They ran across a goat herder watering his charges just before sundown and tried to engage him in conversation, but discovered that communication was difficult. Finally, mentioning Antonio Rivas's name did the trick. The old man smiled a snaggle-toothed grin and raised his arm to point upstream.

The day was winding down. The bright sun ball slid behind the rolling desert-like horizon. They reined down on the bank of a dry arroyo that joined the river.

"What say we make camp and waste some time. We ain't due to arrive until tomorrow," Buck suggested.

"Fine by me, captain."

They made camp, unsaddled and watered their horses, and made coffee with water from the river. After a supper of a tin of beans, dried jerky, and a tin of peaches, they settled back to enjoy their coffee.

There was little conversation between the two friends, both being quickly caught up in the beauty of the desert night and their own thoughts. Off in the northwest the bulky dark masses of mountains loomed. A radiant moon washed over the landscape, creating an enchanting brightness like an eerie daylight. The velvety sky seemed to stretch into eternity, flooded with stars so bright it seemed one could almost reach up and touch them.

A desert owl broke the deafening silence by asking the eternal question, and then again its sound carried in the stillness of the twilight. Soft shadows of pear cactus and spiked yucca resembled approaching intruders and played tricks on their minds.

A breeze carried the subtle perfume of sweet grasses and whispered through the branches of mesquite bushes. The flames of their campfire crackled. It was a friendly, soothing sound.

After the boiling sun went down both men were surprised how quickly the night cooled off. Chester got up and laid a couple pieces of dried mesquite limbs on their small campfire.

"Want another cup, captain?"

He had to ask twice before he drew Buck from his thought world.

"Huh? Oh, yeah. Obliged."

Chester poured another cup from the smoke-blackened coffeepot that bubbled softly over the fire.

"Ever wonder why some things happen the way they do?" Buck asked absently.

"Yeah, reckon all of us wonder about things like that from time to time."

"My ma use to read to us boys from the book when we were sitting around that old pot-bellied stove at home," Buck said quietly. "Pa never was much of a believing man, but he was a good man. I remember something Ma read to us one time about all things working together for good for them that loved God. Never did understand that. Wish now I'd asked her more about it."

"I'm shore sorry about your folks, Captain. I'm lucky mine are in good health."

"Life's shore hard out here. Man works his whole life trying to scratch a living outta the ground, trying to make it a little easier for his wife and youngins. My pa was a good man. Him and Ma didn't deserve to die like they did. It seems like bad things are always happening to good people."

"That seems to be the way of things."

"Did you have any brothers or sisters?"

"No, just me. Sometimes wished I had though. Reckon the folks decided if they couldn't do no better than that, they'd just quit trying."

That brought a thin smile from Buck. He drained his cup and scooted down into his bedroll and aimed a look at the stars a while before drifting off to sleep.

Dawn broke quickly on the desert. Seemed as if one minute it was pitch dark and then the next minute it was full light. Buck and Chester ate a quick breakfast, warmed over and finished their coffee from last night, broke camp and were headed upstream shortly after the sun put in an appearance.

Sometime near mid-morning they saw a plume of dust up

ahead, it seemed to be coming their way. No living thing could move in this country without leaving dust signs above its travels. A dozen riders emerged from the dusty cloud riding fast and riding in Buck and Chester's direction.

"Shore hope that welcoming committee is the friendly sort," Chester said, slipping his rifle from its saddle boot and levering a shell.

Buck did likewise.

The approaching vaqueros were a sight to see. They all rode highbred midnight-black horses with heavily ornamented saddles and bridles. The riders wore leather chaps, large Mexican-style spurs, and wide-brimmed sombreros. Each had a gun strapped to his waist, carried a rifle in his hand, and bandoliers criss-crossed their chest.

As they drew within rifle range they reined into an open horseshoe formation that swallowed Buck and Chester up like a giant dragon. If the riders meant them harm, they wouldn't have stood a chance against the twelve. They reined up in a cloud of dust surrounding Buck and his companion.

The leader moved his prancing horse forward a few steps. He sat straight, tall, and proud in his saddle. His face was smooth and handsome. His dark eyes took Buck and Chester's measure in a searching gaze.

"*Buenos dias, señor.* Are you *Señor* Cordell?"

"I am."

"We were sent to welcome you to Don Antonio Riva's hacienda. Follow me, *por favor*."

The speaker wheeled his horse without so much as a head bobble and led out. Buck and Chester fell in behind him. The others brought up the rear.

They rode for a good hour. The landscape began to take on an entirely different look. The dry, arid desert-like country gradually became a green oasis. Trees and flowering shrubs began to appear. Thick, green grass covered the ground.

A mountain loomed in the distance, its green trees a sharp contrast to the country they passed through only a couple of hours before.

They passed herd after herd of longhorns guarded by vaqueros walking their horses slowly around the peacefully grazing cattle.

Off in the distance Buck could see a cluster of half-a-hundred adobe houses, most likely where the workers lived, he figured.

A large walled compound set apart and backed up tight against the mountain. The walls were made of adobe and looked to be at least ten feet high. A mountain stream emerged from the thick trees of the mountainside, ran alongside the compound, and formed the river they were following. The picture before them took their breath away.

The vaquero leading them rode directly toward a large opening in the wall. Inside the compound a bell sounded. Two heavy log gates stood ready to close and repel any attack or deny any intruder entrance. It was a literal fortress. Buck looked it over carefully, hoping one day to have something similar.

They passed through the opening into a large courtyard. Red-tiled paths wound through a garden filled with all sorts of flowering plants. A natural spring bubbled from underneath moss-covered rocks and trailed through the garden before emptying into a round, rock fountain. A wide, covered veranda circled the massive adobe hacienda.

The tall, dark man standing on the veranda wore a short, embroidered jacket, black pants and a red sash tied around his waist. A thin, well-trimmed mustache only partially covered his top lip. His hair was short and well groomed. He stood rigidly straight and proud.

As they reined up at a hitching rail the Mexican walked forward with long, even strides to greet them. Buck and Chester swung down from their saddles.

"Ah, Mr. Cordell, how nice to see you, and this must be Mr. Colson? I am Antonio Rivas. , Welcome to our humble hacienda."

"Nothing humble about your place that I can see. Never laid eyes on a more beautiful home."

"You are very kind, *señor.* Come in, *por favor.*"

Buck and Chester followed the man through a massive door into yet another courtyard, this one much smaller but no less impressive. Flowering baskets hung from chains. Wrought-iron benches were scattered around a brightly colored fountain.

Don Rivas ushered them across the courtyard and through another door into a large den. A floor-to-ceiling rock fireplace dominated the comfortable room. Two leather sofas sat facing on either side of the fireplace with a wrought iron and glass table in between.

A large original painting dominated the wall. It was of the most beautiful Mexican lady Buck had ever seen. He couldn't help but pause and stare.

"That is my wife, Señora Consuela Rivas," the man said proudly.

"She is very beautiful," Buck said, struck by the breathtaking beauty of the woman in the painting.

"Come, be seated, *por favor.*"

As Buck and Chester folded onto the comfortable sofa, a pretty Mexican girl entered with a silver tray holding a silver coffee pot and three white china cups. She set the tray on the glass-topped table and poured three cups of steaming coffee.

"Would you gentlemen prefer brandy?"

"Coffee would go good," Buck said.

"Again, we are honored to have you in our home. You will, of course, meet my wife at dinner. She is looking forward to meeting you. We have prepared rooms for both of you. I insist that you spend the night."

"We're obliged for your hospitality, Señor Rivas."

Following their host's lead, they picked up their cups and sipped the rich, strong coffee.

"I trust you were successful in locating the land you discussed with my attorney in San Antonio?"

"Yes, sir, it's everything he said it was and more."

"That parcel of land was but a part of twenty-eight leagues, or *sitios,* consisting of some 123,000 acres granted to my ancestors in 1765. Over the years we have disposed of all but the small strip in question. The land being considered is only 10,000 acres, I'm afraid, hardly enough to sustain a large cattle operation."

"It would be fine to get us started," Buck said, secretly taken aback by the amount of land being discussed.

"And do I understand correctly that the two of you are partners in this ranching venture?"

"Yes, sir."

"And should I decide to agree to the lease as outlined by my attorney, does the price meet with your approval?"

"Yes, sir, I believe we agreed on twenty-five cents per acre over the five year term of the lease, which would come to twenty-five hundred American dollars."

"Precisely. Very well, if that is agreeable, then I see no reason to delay this transaction any longer. I'm prepared to execute the lease agreement."

"Could I ask a question?" Chester spoke up.

"Of course," Don Rivas replied.

"You said you disposed of the rest of that land grant. Why did you decide to keep this track and why are you willing to lease it to us for that price?"

"That's a fair question. As you gentlemen may know, there is still some dispute over many of the land grants issued by the Mexican Government. Most have been recognized by the Republic of Texas. Some however, are still drawing scrutiny.

"One of the requirements of these particular grants is that they must be occupied and under improvement. Your use of the land, even under a lease agreement, legitimizes the grant so it is beyond question.

"I have no personal use for the land, I have more than enough here in Mexico and I have other grants of land, some quite large, in Texas that are not in question. I have kept the small track you are leasing more for sentimental reasons than anything. Years ago, my grandfather lived on that parcel of land. You may have come across the remains of his hacienda. I find it difficult to dispose of it.

"I'm sure you also know that there is an outlaw element that causes quite a lot of trouble along the river. The Indians also frequent the area since game is plentiful in the area your people call The Strip. Are there further questions?"

"Not from me," Chester said, crooking a grin at Buck. "I'm satisfied."

"Nor from me," Buck agreed. "I think we're ready to sign the agreement and settle up if you are."

Don Antonio produced a folded paper from an inside pocket and handed it to Buck for his inspection. Buck looked it over closely and handed it to Chester. He examined the document and nodded his head in approval.

The ranch owner handed Buck an ink quill. First Buck, then Chester signed their names on both copies and passed the lease to Don Rivas. He also signed the document.

Reaching into his pocket Buck produced a small, leather pouch and handed it to the rancher. Without bothering to count the money inside the bag he set it aside and stood. To extend his hand. Buck took the Mexican's hand in a warm handshake. Chester did likewise.

"Riding in, I couldn't help noticing your herds of longhorns," Buck said, returning to the sofa. "How many head do you run?"

"I have several locations besides this one. Together we have something over six thousand head, or at least in that neighborhood."

Buck lifted an eyebrow and shot a sideways glance at Chester.

"That's a pretty big neighborhood," Buck said. "Mind me asking where you market them?"

"Now *that,* gentlemen, is the problem, as I'm sure you are aware, the market for cattle has been stagnant for some time. Every cattle rancher that I know posseses more cattle than they know what to do with. There simply is no market for cattle in Mexico. They are there for the taking in any thicket along the *Rio Bravo.* Any peon with a reata or rifle can help himself. If I am to market my herds it has to be in your country."

"What will longhorns bring in Mexico?" Buck asked.

"Almost nothing, the way things are now. Two, perhaps three dollars a head is about all one could expect, and that only if one could find a buyer. No one is purchasing cattle.

"If the market ever opens up, one could easily get considerably more at the railhead. There again, the nearest shipping point to the eastern packing houses is in Missouri and that is a long way from Mexico. No, my friend, I'm not trying to discourage you, but now is not a good time to be in the cattle business."

Buck let that settle in his mind some length of time.

"Would it be possible to look over your operation?" Buck asked.

"Of course, I'd be happy to show you anything. Come, I'll have Pedro saddle the horses."

As on Don Antonio showed them around the vast ranching operation, both Buck and Chester were visibly impressed. They were particularly taken aback with the skill and efficiency of the Mexican vaqueros as well as with the horses they rode.

"Tell me about your horses?" Buck asked. "I notice they are all black and seem more high spirited than horses in our country."

"*Si,* they are. They are from Spanish ancestry that we breed here on our ranch. We have found them more adaptable and efficient than their American counterpart. We sell our horses all over Mexico.

"But come, we must get back to the hacienda, Señora Rivas will be expecting us for dinner."

Arriving back at the sprawling hacienda, the rancher had the pretty house girl show Buck and Chester to their upstairs rooms. They agreed to meet downstairs in the den in an hour.

Hurriedly, Buck used part of the hour to wash up and sleeve into his only clean shirt. He used his fingers to rake his long, wheat-colored hair into some kind of order, tied and knotted his blue neckerchief back around his neck, and, after checking himself in the mirror, decided he looked as presentable as he could muster.

Buck hurried to Chester's room and tapped on the door. When it opened he strode inside.

"We need to put our heads together about something, partner."

"What is it?"

They both took a seat and Buck explained about his conversation in San Antonio with the cattle broker.

"Did you catch what Don Antonio said a while ago about the price of cattle here in Mexico? He said they were going for two or three dollars a head. That's a mighty big spread between three dollars a head and twenty dollars a head."

Chester lifted his head to stare at the ceiling for a long minute.

"I see where you're headed. You're thinking we could buy some cattle here in Mexico, trail them to Missouri, and pocket the difference. How much you figure it would cost to get them to Missouri?"

"Couldn't say for sure, no more than a dollar a head I would guess."

"Then we're looking at fifteen or sixteen dollars a head profit? How come Don Antonio don't herd 'em to Missouri himself?"

"Well, first off, the meat packer that fellow represented was Swift & Company. He said they were just getting ready to open a large facility in Chicago. I doubt word has spread down this far yet. It will, sure enough, but in the meantime we could make ourselves a passel of money."

"Think we ought to fill the rancher in about the price of beef in Missouri?"

"I'd feel better about it if we did, wouldn't you?"

"Yeah, think so."

"So what do you think? Should we offer to buy us some cattle?"

"We come to south Texas to go into the cattle business didn't we? Let's fish or cut bait."

"Then let's go meet that pretty wife of his, eat some dinner, and talk some business."

They walked downstairs together. Don Antonio was already in the den when they arrived. All three men seated themselves on the sofas and talked cattle talk, but didn't mention what they had in mind.

Señora Rivas entered. The men stood to their feet. The rancher moved to meet her.

It was as if the woman in the painting stepped from it and entered the room. She was the picture of elegance. She wore a full-length black dress buttoned all the way to her neck. Her long black hair was pulled to the back of her head in a knot and held in place with a small black fan-like comb. Her soft smile looked warm and genuine.

"Gentlemen, I'd like you to meet my lovely wife, this is Señora Consuela Marquette Rivas. *Señor* Cordell, *Señor* Colson."

Buck stepped forward as their hostess extended her hand, palm down. He leaned over and lightly brushed the back of her hand with his lips. It felt unusual. It was the first time he had ever kissed a lady's hand. Chester followed Buck's lead and then took a step backwards.

"I believe dinner is served, shall we go?" The rancher said.

Gold-rimmed china place settings lay at both ends of the long dining table. A single setting occupied either side of the long table. The wife took her place behind a chair at one end of the table. Don Rivas pulled out the chair for her allowing her to be seated and then scooted the chair forward.

Dinner was unbelievable. Buck had never eaten *real* Mexican food and found that he sincerely loved the hot, spicy fare the house girl kept bringing. Some of it he had no idea what it was, but he tried to put it out of his mind and ate it anyway.

The dinner conversation was interesting and informative. He learned some of the history of the Rivas family and how Don Antonio's grandfather had been a General in the Mexican Army and awarded numerous land grants for his service.

"What about your family, *señor,*" Señora Rivas inquired.

"They were simple farmers, those you would call *peasants*. My family were murdered by the Comanche while I was away in the war. I have a younger brother, but I can't find out what happened to him."

"So," the father quickly changed the subject. "Just you and Mr. Colson will be living on the land?"

"Well, we have a side-kick, an older fellow named Eli Hoyt that will be with us. We need to build some corrals and a cabin. Mostly though, we'll be somewhere out in the thickets catching maverick longhorns."

"Shall we retire to the den and have a glass of brandy?" Don Antonio suggested.

A fire had been started in the big fireplace. They allowed Señora Rivas to be seated first on one of the sofas. The rancher sat in an upholstered armchair facing the fireplace. Buck and Chester folded into the soft leather sofa facing the lady of the house.

Two house girls brought trays, one with a single glass and a bottle of sherry, the other tray held three glasses and a bottle of brandy. After sitting the trays down on the table she poured the after-dinner drinks. Although Buck had never cared for alcoholic beverages, but he decided rather than refuse and embarrass his host, he would simply sip the drink.

"I couldn't help but notice Mr. Colson referring to you as captain from time to time," Señora Rivas commented. "Were you an officer in the army?"

"Yes, ma'am, I was a captain in the Confederate Cavalry, I served under Colonel John Mosby, mostly in Virginia. Chester Colson, here, was my corporal and my right hand. He saved my bacon, excuse my language, ma'am, more than once."

"War is a terrible thing," Don Antonio said, sipping his brandy.

"Can you gentlemen spend a few days with us?" The rancher asked. "There is so much more of the ranch you didn't have time to see."

"I'm afraid not, but we appreciate the invitation. We need to leave tomorrow."

"If you gentlemen will excuse me I think I will bid you goodnight," Señora Rivas said standing.

The men all rose to their feet and offered their appreciation for her hospility. After she left they sat again.

"Actually, I'm glad we have this time alone, Don Antonio," Buck said. "Chester and I have been talking about something you said this afternoon. If we heard you right, you said cattle brought two or three dollars a head here in Mexico, is that right?"

"It is."

"Don't know if you've heard, but cattle are bringing considerably more than that at the railhead in Missouri."

"*Si*, I am aware that my herds would be worth as much as twenty dollars a head, I believe, in Missouri."

"That's the price I heard, too. Just wondering why you don't trail your cattle to Missouri and sell them?"

"As no doubt you are aware, there are many obstacles one has to overcome to take a herd all the way to Missouri, especially cattle from Mexico. I understand several states are moving to restrict by law herds from Texas from entering their state, let alone cattle from Mexico. Some say gangs of enforcers are intercepting herds and demanding payment for allowing the herds to enter the state. Some of my friends have lost their entire herds to these bandits

"Even if I were successful in getting my cattle to Missouri, buyers and brokers are reluctant to contract for cattle from across the border. Several Mexican growers have attempted this risky adventure and failed. Some lost everything. No, señor, the risks are simply too great for Mexican growers to attempt such a thing at this time."

"Then what if we bought your cattle and drove them to the rail head, would you consider selling to us?"

"Of course, I would be happy to sell my cattle to you gentlemen. What price did you have in mind?"

Buck cut his eyes at his partner, and then down to examine the toes of his boots for a long moment before answering.

"We'll give you three dollars a head, delivered to our land in Texas."

"How many head are you interested in?"

Buck looked at Chester again then back at the Don Antonio. "What about two thousand head?"

The rancher's eyes widened. A thin smile spread across his face.

"For three dollars a head I will see that you get the very best cattle on our ranch and deliver them to your land whenever you say."

Buck and Chester stood up and stuck out their hands. Don Antonio did the same. The three shook hands thereby sealing the bargain.

"Your money will be waiting when the cattle are delivered, señor. Would the first of October be agreeable for delivery?"

"That would be splendid."

"What about horses? I believe you mentioned that you also sell your horses. Do you have horses we could buy?"

"Of course, but I'm afraid they are more expensive than the cattle. How many would you be looking for?"

"What about a hundred?"

"I could sell you a hundred of my best horses for twenty American dollars each."

"Done. Deliver them when you bring the longhorns."

"It will be done as you say."

"Now if you would excuse us, I think we will retire, it's been a long day."

"Goodnight, gentlemen, it is a pleasure to do business with honorable men."

* * *

Their horses stood saddled and ready. The morning sun crested the eastern horizon.

"I have a small gift I want to give both of you," the rancher said as he motioned to the old stable man.

The Mexican disappeared into the stable and returned leading two high-stepping geldings. Their slick, coal-black coats glistened in the early morning sun. Long-bodied, deep chested, and tall—Buck guessed them to be at least fifteen hands high—they were the most magnificent animals either Buck or Chester had ever seen.

"Please accept these as a token of our friendship," the rancher said.

"But, we can't accept such a gift," Buck told him. "They are beautiful, but it is too much."

"A gift is an expression of friendship. Friendship is the greatest gift one can give another, *Vaya con Dios, Amigos.*"

The three new friends shook hands. Buck turned to gather his reins.

Chester led the two black geldings on lead lines as they rode away. Buck twisted in his saddle to lift a hand goodbye and then heeled his sorrel into a short lope.

Chapter VI

Chester saw him first.

"Oh, NO!" he shouted, lifting an arm and pointing.

Buck swung a look.

Eli's lifeless body hung from a rope attached to a large limb of a sycamore tree.

Buck kicked his sorrel in the flanks. Chester held the two black geldings on a lead and fell behind as they raced across the wide field toward their friend.

Eli's hands were tied behind his back and his neck was crooked to one side. His whiskered face was a sickly-looking purple and his mouth hung agape in an unfinished scream. His eyes were wide open and stared off into eternity.

Buck slid to a stop and whipped out his Bowie knife as Chester reined up beside him.

"Catch him when I cut the rope."

Chester swung quickly from his saddle and gathered Eli's legs as Buck sliced the rope allowing the body to be lowered gently to the ground.

Buck swung down and fell to his knees beside their old friend. His throat was suddenly full as tears welled up and leaked from the corners of his eyes. Chester stood nearby, his face raised to the sky with his eyes closed.

Neither man spoke for several long minutes.

"I shoulda never left him here alone," Buck said. "I shoulda known better."

"It wasn't your fault. He wanted to stay."

"Still and all, we coulda figured out some other way."

"What's done is done, capt'n. Ain't no un-doing it. But somebody's gonna pay for it, you can write it down."

"Who you reckon it was that done it?"

"Most likely that Charley Sweet fellow and his bunch. That your thinking?"

"I figure. Let's get him buried."

"I'll ride on up to the cave and get some shovels. Where you figure to bury him?"

"Here under this tree is as good a place as any. We'll build a fence around it later on."

While Chester rode toward the cave, Buck hobbled the two black horses so they could graze and rode a wide circle looking for hoof prints of the ones who did the hanging. He cut the trail and stepped down to examine it more closely. For several minutes he squatted on his heels, fingering the hoof prints, reading the sign.

There were four of them. They took Chester's extra horse and Buck's dappled gray. They had even taken Eli's old mule Shorty. The trail headed south along the Rio Grande.

Chester returned with a shovel.

"They rummaged through our supplies and took most everything worth anything. They left the shovel, saws, and tools. Reckon they weren't interested in anything to do with work."

"Found their trail," Buck told him. "There was four of them. They headed south along the river."

"What's down that way?"

"Place called Eagle Pass and Fort Duncan on this side of the river, village named Piedras Negras on the Mexican side."

"I reckon they took the extra horses?"

"Yep."

"Thought so, most likely that's what they were after. How long you figure they been gone?"

"No more'n a day."

"Well, let's do what we gotta do and get after 'em," Chester said. "This ain't gonna get no easier."

They buried their old friend deep and covered the fresh mound of dirt with rocks to discourage scavengers. Chester lashed together a makeshift cross and drove it into the ground at the head of the grave. They said their good-byes with bowed heads and a long minute of silence.

"What about the two black geldings?" Chester asked. "We can't leave them here."

"Yeah, we got no choice. We'll have to take them with us."

"How about we give our own horses a rest and ride the blacks?"

"Good idea."

They transferred their saddles and tied their extra horses on lead lines. In less than an hour they had packed what supplies the killers left and were in the saddle and on the trail.

They followed the trail until darkness swallowed it up. They made dark camp on the bank of the Rio Grande.

Before the first gray of dawn touched the sky they were in the saddle and picked up the trail again. They followed it until it merged into a heavily traveled road a few miles outside Eagle Pass.

They rode circles trying to find the trail again, but to no avail.

"Before we lost it the trail was headed straight toward Eagle Pass," Buck told his partner. "Ain't no place else they could have gone. Let's ride in and have a look around."

It was only halfway to noon and already Eagle Pass, Texas was hotter than it had a right to be. The dun-colored adobe houses and sun baked false-fronted stores and saloons along the single, dusty street stood quiet and deserted in the shimmering heat waves.

Half-a-dozen nearly starved dogs yapped at the horses hooves as Buck and Chester rode past two saloons and a mercantile store before spotting a rundown looking stable. They reined up in front of the livery beside a small corral.

A whiskered old hostler limped out to meet them. He wore tattered britches, sandals, a faded, ragged shirt and an old sombrero.

He spent a long moment eyeing the black geldings they rode before lifting his squinting eyes to the men who rode them.

"Mighty fine looking horseflesh you be riding there, strangers."

Buck and Chester sat their saddles and ignored the comment.

"If a fellow had a couple of horses for sale, who would be the man to see?" Buck asked.

"That'd be Ike, he does all the buying and selling of stock in these parts. He ain't too particular about bills of sale and such, if'n you git my meaning."

"What's this fellow's last name?"

"Don't rightly know, never heard it said."

"Where can we find him?"

"'Bout four miles north you'll come to the mouth of a canyon. Ike lives up the canyon a piece. Best ride easy-like, though, less he knows you he don't take kindly to strangers ridin in."

"We're obliged," Buck said, reining his black gelding around. They headed north.

A well-traveled road branched off the main road and led

into the yawning mouth of a canyon. Buck and Chester reined up.

"I figure there'll be at least one lookout," Buck said. "That what you're thinking?"

Chester swept his hat off and sleeved the sweat from his forehead as he stared into the opening.

"Yep, likely up high among the rocks."

"Mark 'em good in case we have to leave in a hurry."

They healed their horses into a slow walk. The two extra horses trailed behind. Their searching gazes swept the sheer faces of the opening as they descended deeper. The canyon walls were a hundred feet straight up. Rocky crags offered hundreds of places for a lookout to hide.

Up ahead the opening doglegged to the left and narrowed. A brief glint of sunlight on metal caught Buck's eye.

"Up there near the top," Buck told his companion.

"Yep, I see him."

"Just hold it right there!" The lookout shouted.

They reined to a stop.

"Got some horses for sale," buck hollered, "heard Ike is the man to see."

"Who said so?"

"Fellow named Charlie Sweet."

"Ride on in," the lookout shouted, standing and waving his rifle.

Buck and Chester gigged their horses and rode on. Once around the bend, the canyon opened up into a wide valley. A spring-fed stream gave life to green grass and scattered trees before ending in a small lake. From what they could see, it was a box valley; the only way in or out was the route they took coming in.

A small herd of longhorns grazed peacefully. Buck spotted his dappled gray and Chester's Bay as well as Eli's old mule among the dozen or so head of horses that milled about in a large split-rail corral.

Smoke trailed up from the chimney of a nearby adobe cabin. Two men stepped onto the porch as Buck and Chester rode up, both held rifles in their hands.

One was a big man. Buck guessed him to weigh at least three hundred pounds. His face was mostly hidden by a long, bushy beard. His cold eyes took their measure.

The other was young, probably no more than sixteen or so.

"Looking for a fellow called, Ike." Buck said, sweeping a slow, searching gaze around the area.

Two more men emerged from the barn and were walked in their direction. Both wore pistols.

"Don't believe I know you, stranger," the big man said.

"We lost some horses a few days ago, that dappled gray and the bay yonder in your corral belong to us, them and the mule. They were stolen by Charley Sweet and his bunch. They hung our friend and stole our horses. We want 'em back."

"You'll have to take that up with Charley. He's the one I bought 'em from?"

"Oh, we aim to do that, sure enough. Where you reckon we'd find him?"

"Who knows? Most likely find him across the river in Piedras Negras, he hangs out in one of the cantinas. I understand he's sweet on some little Mexican gal that works there. No skin off my back."

"Obliged for the information, now if you'll have your boys gather up our stock we'll be on our way."

"Whoa, now, right there we got ourselves a problem. They ain't *your* horses any more, I bought them fair and square. They belong to me now."

Beside Buck, Chester eased his horse around so he faced the two wranglers that walked up from the barn and stood nearby.

Buck let his right hand settle on his leg, only inches from his Walker Colt.

"Mister, I'm gonna say this just once. When we leave our horses are gonna leave with us, one way or another. Now we can do this the easy way or the hard way, makes no difference to me, but you ain't gonna like the hard way. Something you ought to think on, is two horses and a mule worth dying over?"

Buck fixed his hard gaze on the fat man and the boy, watching for any threat, any movement, any indication that either of them were going to raise the rifles they had in their hands.

Long seconds slipped by slowly. Finally the man's shoulders sagged, the tension seemed to drain from his body.

"Go ahead, take 'em. They weren't much good, no how."

"Good decision. What say we just wait right here until your two men bring our stock, then we'll be on our way?"

"Go ahead Slim, fetch those two horses and the mule we bought from Charlie."

Buck never took his eyes off the fat man or the boy.

"Chester, you might want to tag along to make sure they get the right ones."

"I'll see to it, captain."

"Ike, I sure would feel more comfortable if you and that boy laid those rifles on the porch."

They did.

Chester returned in short order leading their two horses and Eli's mule. The two wranglers walked back to stand near the porch beside their boss.

"Chester, why don't you go on ahead? I'll be along."

Chester turned his black horse and, leading their stock, headed back the way they came in.

"Word of advice, Ike, don't buy any more stock with a Longhorn brand. Next time we have to come back we won't be as understanding." Buck said, backing his horse away from the house.

Ike and the others stood silently and watched Buck go.

The lookout only lifted his rifle and waved it in the air as they rode past him and out of the canyon.

"Where we headed, captain?"

"Let's drop off our stock at the livery, then ride across the river to *Piedras Negras,* I want this over and done with."

The old hostler came close to grinning when they rode up.

"See you fellows got your horses back."

"Yep. We'd be obliged if you'd look after them until we get back, we've got to ride across the river for a bit."

"If'n you're going after Charlie Sweet, watch your backside, he's a bad'un."

"That's what they tell me."

Chester handed the lead ropes to the old timer and reined his black gelding around. Buck joined him and they headed for Mexico.

"If we're gonna have a cattle ranch in the Nueces Strip, these rustlers and thieves gotta learn not to mess with our stock," Buck said as they waded their horses across the Rio Grande.

"Let's send 'em a message," Chester agreed.

"How we gonna do that?"

"A stout limb and a short rope works every time."

"Then you got it, partner, I'll back your play."

Piedras Negras was a beehive of activity. Heavy freight wagons, farm wagons, buggies, and people on foot and horseback went every which way.

Adobe buildings of every description lined the single dusty street. Buck and Chester rode slowly, their searching gaze examining every horse tied at hitching rails in front of the numerous cantinas.

Most had Mexican riggings with gaudy silver studding and the telltale large saddle horn the vaqueros preferred.

They rode halfway down the long street before they spotted four horses with Texas rigs.

The horses stood hip-shot, tied to a hitching rail in front of a cantina. They reined into an opening and tied their horses.

"How you want to play it?" Buck asked.

"Straight-up, I reckon."

Chester pulled the sawed-off shotgun from its saddle holster and flipped it open. He thumbed two double-aught shells into the twin openings and closed it with a flick of the wrist.

"Give me a few minutes to get around back before you go in. Maybe they will be looking at you and I can get the drop on 'em."

"Anytime you're ready."

Chester hurried around the corner of the large, adobe building. Buck's right hand raised his Colt gently in its holster then settled it back with ease. He waited a handful of minutes and stepped through the open door.

He swept the room with a quick glance. His look showed him only four men in the whole place that weren't Mexicans. Charlie Sweet and his three men sat at a table near the back. Each of the four sat with a Mexican bar girl on his lap and a drink in his hand.

Buck paused a moment to allow his eyes to adjust to the dimness of the room. That's when he saw Chester step through a curtained opening off to the outlaw's right. His partner didn't hesitate; he walked casually toward Sweet's table.

The killers were so preoccupied with the girls and the drinks in their hands they weren't even aware of Buck's presence until he lifted his gun from its holster and spoke. His voice was loud and clear.

"Charlie Sweet!"

A hush fell over the room. Sweet looked up right into Buck's fixed gaze. Recognition rounded the killer's eyes and swept across his face. His left arm was wrapped around a pretty, Mexican girl's waist. His right hand held a half-filled glass part way to his mouth.

All four of the killers froze in place. Chester used the distraction to step up directly behind the four men. He leveled the shotgun and thumbed back both hammers.

"First man that moves gets his head blowed off!"

As one, the four men twisted a look at Chester and slowly raised their hands shoulder-high. Without needing to be told, the girls quickly disentangled themselves from the mens' grasp and hurried away.

A tense hush filled the room.

"Right easy now," Chester said. "First you, Charlie. Lift that gun out with your left hand and toss it on the floor in front of my partner."

The killer hesitated for a long breath. Chester nudged the nose of the shotgun into Sweet's right ear.

"I won't say it again."

Sweet seemed to have a change of heart. He lifted his sidearm from his belly holster and tossed it at Buck's feet.

"Now you, fatso, it's your turn."

Buck glanced quickly around the room. Men stood unmoving, not daring to do anything to offer a threat.

When all the four killers were disarmed, Buck gathered up the weapons and jammed them under his belt.

"Now we're all going for a walk," Chester told them. "Anyone try anything funny and I'll blow you in half, got it?"

He marched them outside. Buck followed, backing from the room, sweeping his Colt back and forth, covering those inside. One by one Chester tied the killers' hands behind their backs with short lengths of a lariat rope from one of their saddles.

After they were tied he helped all except Charlie onto their horses. He tied their reins to another horse's tail so they would be in line. When he had them secured he turned to Charlie.

"You don't deserve to ride," Chester said, dropping a loop over Sweet and pulling it tight around his chest.

Buck watched the front door until Chester swung into his saddle and looped a half hitch around his saddle horn with the free end of Sweet's lariat. Chester gathered the reins to the lead horse and heeled his black gelding into a trot.

As Buck swung aboard his own horse he saw the slack go out of the lariat and Sweet was jerked off his feet. The killer's thrashing body plowed a furrow along the dusty street as Chester dragged the outlaw out of town.

Buck followed the procession, his gaze sweeping both sides of the street. People stopped to watch, but offered no threat. Charlie Sweet screamed his head off. A steady stream of curses filled the growing darkness.

When they reached the river Chester didn't even break stride. His horse plunged into the muddy water with hooves churning, dragging Charlie Sweet behind him. By the time they reached the Texas side of the river the killer was coughing and choking.

As the procession rode into Eagle Pass word spread quickly. Men poured out of saloons onto the boardwalks to witness the sight. Since there was no lawman in Eagle Pass except the army at the fort, which was twenty miles away. No one tried to interfere.

Chester dragged Sweet up in front of the Silver Spur Saloon before reining to a halt. He loosened the rope from his saddle horn and tossed it over the railing of the second story. Swinging off his horse, he moved the loop from around Sweet's shoulders and cinched it tight around the man's neck. He hoisted the half-conscious killer into the air and tied the loose end of the rope to a post.

Leading the three remaining outlaws' horses close to the front of the saloon, Chester dropped loops over their heads. He drew the ropes tight and tossed the free ends over the second story railing and tied them off to hitching rails.

Chester turned to face the growing crowd of spectators crowding close.

"I'm Chet Colson. That fellow there on the black horse is my partner Buck Cordell. We own the Longhorn Ranch out by the Sycamore River. This is Charlie Sweet. Him and these three men hung our partner and stole our horses.

"We want to give every rustler and thief fair warning. We hang killers, rustlers, and thieves who come onto Longhorn land to do their dirty work. No talk, no trial, just a long drop on a short rope, might want to pass the word around."

That said, Chester swatted the three outlaws' horses on the rump. The horses bolted, jerking their riders from the saddle. Their muffled screams pierced the night air before trailing off into a choking death. The onlookers stood in stunned silence.

Chester toed a stirrup and reined his black around, walking his mount toward the livery to gather their horses and mule. Buck fell in beside him.

"You said you was gonna send a message, partner," Buck told him. "I believe they got it."

"Hope so, but I reckon some will still try us now and again."

Chapter VII

On the ride back to their land they rode in silence for a ways, each reliving the hanging in their minds.

"You ever hung a man before, captain?"

"No. Sure ain't a pretty sight, bad way for a man to die."

"Don't reckon I ever seen a good way."

They arrived back at their land just before sundown. After seeing to their horses, they walked side-by-side toward the cave.

"It's less than two months before our cattle will be delivered," Buck said. "That's not much time and there's a lot to do. We've got to have some hands to help take care of that two thousand head of longhorns after they get here."

"That's a fact."

"The way I see it, one of us needs to ride into Del Rio and see about hiring some help. We're gonna need a cook, too. Those men are gonna need a bunkhouse and we can't keep living in that cave, so we're gonna have to do some building before the cattle get here. What's your thinking on the matter?"

"No doubt about it, captain, we've got a lot to do and a

short time to do it. Why don't you ride in and see what you can come up with? I'll watch after things and get started cutting some timber? What do you think about us building our operation on that flat plateau beside that natural spring we found? It would be easier to defend in case of an Indian attack, and we don't want to build where a flood like the one they had earlier this year would wipe us out. It kinda worries me some that our land borders on two rivers."

"That's good thinking."

Before the shroud of darkness lifted, Buck was in the saddle headed for Del Rio. He rode into town by mid-morning. It was his first time in the small town, even though it was by far the closest to their ranch.

San Felipe del Rio consisted of an irregular cluster of flat-roofed adobe houses huddled along a small stream that tumbled down from the nearby mountains. A single, wagon-rutted dusty was lined with several businesses.

He rode past two saloons, a barber shop, a livery and blacksmith, a café, and an undertaker's business before reining up at a busy general mercantile store.

A Short, stocky fellow that Buck guessed to be straddling fifty looked up from behind a counter where he was tallying up a bill of goods for a middle age couple.

"Howdy to you, I'll be with you in a minute, just finishing up here."

"Take your time. I'm in no hurry."

Buck browsed around the large store. It was well stocked. It looked like the store owner had a booming business.

"Don't recognize you," the storekeeper said, approaching Buck with his hand extended. "I'm John Walker, my daughter and I run the store."

"Howdy, Mr. Walker, pleased to meet you. I'm Buck Cordell. Me and my partner are starting a ranch over by the

Sycamore River called the Longhorn. We'll be needing supplies from time to time. We'd like to do business with you if it's agreeable."

"Good to meet you, Mr. Cordell. What's your partner's name?"

"Chester Colson."

"I've heard the name. You boys the ones that hung those fellows over in Eagle Pass couple nights ago?"

"Yes, sir. They hung our partner and stole our horses."

"Good riddance, I say. That Charlie Sweet and his bunch was nothing but trouble."

"Well, that's over and done with as long as those that want to do us harm stay off Longhorn land."

"Can't fault a man for protecting what's his."

"You still willing to sell us the supplies we need?"

"That's what we're here for. Be right glad to have your business. Just call me John."

"If you'll call me, Buck. I'm looking for some hands. Got any idea where I might start looking?"

"What you looking for, cow punchers?"

"Yep, could use a good cook, too. Kinda tired eating our own cooking."

The storekeeper rubbed his chin for a minute in silent contemplation.

"Might know a cook if you could talk him into it. He's kinda contrary at times, but he'd shore make you a good one. I understand he was a cook in the army."

"Where could I find this fellow?"

"He's got a little place 'bout a mile north of town. Lives there with his missus and a couple of youngins. He's a black man."

"Don't care if he's polka-dot if he can cook. What's his name?

"Washington Long, but most folks here about just call him Wash."

"I'll ride out and have a talk."

"Say you're looking for cowhands, huh? I could ask around if you like?"

"I'd be much obliged. Put the word out that we're hiring. Tell them to ride out to our place come Saturday and we'll look them over."

"I can shore do that. Calling your ranch the Longhorn, huh? Good name."

"I'll drop back by after I talk with Mr. Long."

After leaving Walker's store Buck visited both saloons and the barbershop, leaving word they were looking to hire punchers.

He headed for the small café he spotted earlier. It was a small place but so clean Buck felt like he could eat off the floor. He was greeted by an exceptionally beautiful young Mexican girl with a nice smile. Buck judged her to be in her late teens.

Buenos dias, señor."

"Good Morning."

There were only four tables. Three were occupied. Buck walked to the only empty one and slid out a chair.

"Would you like coffee, señor?"

"I sure would. Is this your place?"

"No, señor, it belongs to my mother, she is in the kitchen."

"Is she a good cook?" Buck asked with a smile.

"*Si,* my mother is a very good cook."

"Then I tell you what. Just bring me a plateful of whatever she's got back there that's good."

The young lady smiled a wide smile. It looked good on her.

"You will enjoy it, señor, it is my promise to you."

After the girl headed for the kitchen, Buck let his gaze crawl around the room at the other customers. One table was occupied by a Mexican man and woman. They were laughing and talking as they enjoyed their food. An elderly Mexican sat at a table alone, sipping coffee. Three Mexican fellows sat at the other table. They were young, most likely no older than him. Buck sized them up. They looked clean cut and from their dress Buck judged them to be vaqueros.

When the waitress returned with his coffee, Buck motioned to the three fellows with a nod of his head.

"Those fellows there, they look like vaqueros"

The girl swung a look and smiled.

"*Si,* that is true. They are very good vaqueros.*"*

"Do you know if they speak English?"

"*Si,* señor, one of them is my brother, he speaks your language, the other two are my cousins, and they do not."

"I'm Buck Cordell, me and my partner are starting a cattle ranch nearby. We're looking for hands. Would you mind asking your brother if I could talk with him?"

"*Si,* I will be happy to do that."

The girl stepped to the Mexicans' table and said something to one of them. All three men swung a look in Buck's direction. Buck lifted his coffee cup in a salute. One of the young men pushed from his chair and walked over.

He wasn't a big man, but tall for a Mexican. He was slim built, tight-waisted and clean-shaven. He walked with a springy smoothness in his step. He wore black work pants, a bright blue shirt with a wine-colored neckerchief, and a jacket of Mexican cut.

A Smith & Wesson was strapped around his waist. The young man was what most would call handsome. Buck could see it ran in the family. The easy smile on his face looked genuine.

"*Buenos dias*, señor, I am Carlos Rodriguez. My sister tells me you would like to speak with me."

"Yes, I'm Buck Cordell. Would you like to sit down?"

The young man pulled out a chair and sat. His dark eyes looked directly into Buck's. He liked that.

"Like I told your sister, my partner and I are starting a cattle ranch out where the Sycamore runs into the Rio Grande. It's called the Longhorn Ranch. We're looking for workers. Don't know if you fellows would be interested, but thought I'd ask."

"What are you looking for?"

"Well, like I said, we're just getting started. At first you'd likely be felling trees and helping build a bunkhouse and a couple of cabins. After that you'd be working cattle. We've got two thousand head being delivered in a couple of months. We're gonna be rounding up all the longhorns we can out of the thickets along the river to mix with them.

Come April we'll be trailing a herd to the railhead in Missouri. Your sister tells me you and your cousins are vaqueros?"

"*Si,* it is true. We have all worked with cattle since we were very young."

"We pay fifty a month and keep. If you want the job it's yours."

Buck saw the young man's eyes widen. His head turned for a quick glance at his two cousins.

"What about my cousins?"

"I was talking about all three of you."

"*Gracias,* you will not be sorry. When do we begin?"

"You just did. As of now, all three of you work for the Longhorn. I've got to ride out and talk to another fellow I heard about. Suppose you fellows meet me here before sundown with your gear?"

"We will be here, *señor.*"

* * *

After finishing a delicious meal of beef stew spiced with chili peppers and corn bread Buck paid for his meal and left a generous tip.

"My brother tells me that you hired him and my cousins to work on your ranch."

"Yes, they look like good men."

"*Si,* they are the best vaqueros along the Rio Grande. You will be pleased."

"I know your brother's name, what's yours?"

"I am, Selena Rodriguez," she replied, smiling and dipping slightly in an easy bow.

"Just didn't want to leave your name out when I tell my partner all about you."

"How is your partner called?"

"Chester Colson. I reckon you'll be meeting him soon enough," he said as he touched thumb and forefinger to his hat brim and turned for the door.

The small adobe shack north of town sat off the thin road a piece. A heavy-built black woman bent over a washtub scrubbing clothes and two children played in the yard.

As Buck left the road and turned up the lane toward the house, the woman gathered the two children and hurried inside. He reined up half-a-hundred yards away and sat his horse.

The black man stepped through the door carrying a shotgun was a big man, broad, slope-shouldered and solid. His black hair was tight-curled and streaked with a touch of gray. A cropped mustache covered his top lip. Dark, flashing eyes settled on Buck.

"Looking for Washington Long," Buck called.

"That'd be me. What you want?"

"I'm Buck Cordell. Me and my partner are building a cattle

ranch over by the Sycamore River. We're looking for a cook
and a woman to help around the place. The storekeeper said
you were the best cook in these parts. I'd like to talk about
hiring you and your missus."

"Ain't interested."

"Listening won't cost you nothing."

"Ride on in, light down and rest your saddle if'n your of a
mind. I'll listen."

Buck gigged his horse forward and swung to the ground.
The black man folded his big frame onto a short length of tree
trunk he used to split wood on and motioned to another. Buck
sat down.

"I hear you cooked for the army?"

"Yes, sir, nigh on twelve years."

"Mind me asking why you got out?"

"Cracked a fellow's head. Spent a year on a chain
gang fer it."

"He have it coming?"

"Thought so."

"What'd he do?"

"He said a bad word about my mama, rest her soul."

"I see. Well, we won't speak of it again. I'd like to have
you and the missus come work for us at the Longhorn Ranch.
We'll build you a cabin and pay you fifty a month. Your woman
can do woman's work around the place and we'll pay her forty
a month. Sound fair to you?"

"How many hands would I be cooking fer?"

"Couple dozen to start with, more later on. We got two
thousand head of longhorns coming in a couple of months. We'll
be trailing a herd up to Missouri come spring. We'd want you
to come along."

"When you got in mind fer us to start?"

"Reckon you could lay your hands on a chuck wagon and
team good enough to make the trip to Missouri?"

"Most likely."

"Then do it. Here's two hundred dollars for the team and wagon. I'll stop by the store and tell Mr. Walker you'll be stopping by. Stock it with all the supplies you'll need.

"When you get it done, move your family out to the ranch. Ain't nothing there now but a dream and a lot of hard work, but there will be."

The big man stared for a minute at the ten gold double-eagles Buck handed him.

"Ain't never in my life held that much money in my hand before. You trust me with all that money, mister?"

"If I didn't trust you I wouldn't have offered you the job."

"Mister Buck, you done hired yourself a cook and housekeeper."

Buck stood and stuck out his hand, then wished he hadn't. The handshake felt like it crushed his knuckles. He winced. Washington Long crooked a thin grin that showed his pearly-white teeth.

After leaving Washington's place, Buck rode back to Walker's store to tell him that the cook would be stopping by for supplies. He tied his sorrel to the hitching rail and stepped up onto the boardwalk. He swiped off his hat and used it to dust himself off. He pushed through the front door.

A small bell attached to the door announced his arrival. Buck swept the store with a glance, expecting to see the storekeeper; instead, the most beautiful lady Buck had ever seen stepped through a curtained opening to an adjoining room. He was immediately struck speechless.

He drank her beauty in like a starving man and thirsted for more. Try as he might, he couldn't tear his eyes away from her.

She had long, auburn hair the color of a winter sunset. It was gathered in the back and tied with a green satin ribbon that matched her emerald-green eyes. Her creamy-white complexion was as fresh as virgin snow and sprinkled with a generous helping of freckles.

She wore a white blouse, buttoned at the neck, and a long blue denim skirt that hung to her ankles with a white apron tied around her tiny waist.

She was short, barely over five foot and in her late teens, but no more than twenty, Buck guessed, All the round places were in all the right places.

Her beauty was breathtaking. For a short slice of eternity neither spoke, his gaze holding hers. The fresh, natural smell of her reached out and grabbed him by the nose. He had to swallow twice before he could force words past the fist-size knot in his throat.

"You must be Mr. Walker's daughter?"

"Yes, I'm Rebekah Walker. And you must be Mr. Cordell, father told me that you were in earlier."

"My friends call me Buck."

She smiled. It was like no smile he had ever seen. One corner of those perfectly shaped lips lifted in sort of a mischievous pucker. Her emerald eyes fixed on his and seemed to look directly into his very soul.

"Then that's what I will call you."

"Mighty pleased to make your acquaintance. Is your father here?"

"No, he had to deliver a load of feed. Is there something I could help you with?"

"He told me about a cook, a black man named Washington Long. Tell your father that I hired him and that he will be coming by to pick up some supplies."

"Father said you were starting a cattle ranch out near the Sycamore River?"

"Yes, ma'am."

"I've always loved cattle and dreamed of, one day, living

on a cattle ranch. Perhaps you and Mrs. Cordell would show me around your ranch sometime?"

"Afraid there ain't no Mrs. Cordell. I ain't married."

A satisfied smile wrapped around the reply she gave him.

"I see. Then I suppose you will have to be my guide."

"Of course. I'd like that. Only thing is there's not much there to see right now, we're just getting started, but there will be. Give me a little time and I'd be happy to show you around."

"I'll look forward to it."

"So will I," he said, touching thumb and finger to his hat brim.

The next few days were a beehive of activity. The three vaqueros proved to be excellent workers. Buck, Chester, and the three Mexicans worked from daylight until dark, cutting trees, trimming the limbs, and dragging them up the trail to the top of the mesa that overlooked the Sycamore River.

It was hard, backbreaking work. But as he worked Buck's mind kept flashing back to the memory of Rebekah Walker. In all his twenty-two years he had never met anyone that made such an impact on him. He kept searching for an excuse to ride into Del Rio again.

By Saturday they raised walls the up for two log cabins and put the roof poles in place. Each of the cabins consisted of two rooms, separated by a dogtrot in the middle. One side would be used for sleeping and the other for cooking and such.

By mid-morning on Saturday a dozen men showed up looking for work. Buck gathered around in the yard of one of the cabins. He and Chester stood in front of them.

"I'm Buck Cordell. This is my partner, Chet Colson. We're the owners of the Longhorn. We're obliged for you fellows riding out. We're looking for hands. We pay fifty dollars a month and keep. I know that is more than most ranches pay, but in return, we expect those we hire to ride for the brand.

"Who you were or what you did or didn't do before you rode in here is no concern of ours. What you do once you're hired, is. We expect a day's work for a day's pay. If you ain't willing to do that you best fork your horse and ride out.

"My partner handles any problems that come up so I'll ask him to say a word."

Chet took a step forward. His cold gaze fell upon each man in turn and lingered a long moment before he spoke.

"Some of you most likely heard about the hanging over in Eagle Pass a few days ago. Just so there's no misunderstanding, we don't hold with thieves or troublemakers on the Longhorn. I'm gonna say it like it is: you get caught stealing or rustling or help others do it, we'll hang you from the nearest tree.

"We're looking for men that will stand fast when trouble comes along. We ain't looking for gunslingers, but you'll need to know how to handle a gun."

That said, Chester nodded toward Buck.

"We'd like to have a word with each one of you alone before we make up our mind. One at a time, come to that big tree over yonder and we'll meet you there."

Buck and Chester turned and walked away from the wad of men and stopped under the big oak tree. They squatted on their haunches and waited.

The men looked anxiously at one another before one of them stepped from the bunch and walked toward them.

Buck and Chester took the man's measure as he walked toward them. He was a cowboy through and through. He was tall, thin, and weathered. You could see one or more like him around any chuck wagon anywhere in Texas. The man was bow-legged and wore run over boots. His denim pants, leather vest, and flat-crowned black hat looked as old as the wearer, which Buck judged to be pushing forty.

But the walnut-handled .44 hanging on his right hip looked as much a part of the man as his handlebar mustache.

"I'm Ray Ledbetter. I been nursing cows since I could walk, near 'bouts. Rode for the Lazy K up near Abilene for a handful of years. Don't mean to brag, but what I don't know about longhorn cattle ain't worth knowing. I need a job. I'll make you a good hand and ride for the brand."

"Howdy, Ray," Buck said. Looking the man straight in the eye. "Mind me asking why you left the Lazy K?"

"Caught a card shark cheating in a poker game in town. I called him on it and he pulled iron. I shot him."

"You a known man, Ray?"

"No the law said it was self-defense, but I just thought it was time to move on."

"Then you got a job. Turn your horse to graze and stow your gear. Send the next man over, will you, Ray?"

Buck saw relief wash over the cowboy's face. "Shore will, boss." The man said as he nodded and turned to walk back to the others waiting to be interviewed.

The next man to walk toward them was a Mexican. By his dress Buck took him to be a vaquero. He wore tight leather pants, a short Mexican jacket and an easy smile. He walked with a springy confidence as he approached.

"I am Pedro Sedillo. I am a vaquero, perhaps the best in all of Mexico."

"Can you use that gun you're wearing?" Chester asked.

With no warning and faster than a heartbeat the man's hand flashed to his side and came up with a .44 in his fist. The movement caught both Chester and Buck by surprise. They exchanged a quick glance of amazement.

"You're hired," Chester chuckled and told the man. "After

you stow your gear see Carlos over yonder at the cabin, he'll show you what to do."

The next man didn't look to be a man at all. He looked young enough to still be mashing pimples. Buck judged him to be no more than fifteen, if that. Yet, he saw something in the young fellow's face as he approached, something that reminded Buck of himself not many years past.

The boy wore a Colt in a tied down holster. Buck suspected he knew how to use it. "What's your name, son?" Buck asked.

"Name's Jimmy, Jimmy McCord. Heard you was hiring. I need a job real bad, mister."

"You look pretty young. Your folks know you're looking for a job?"

"Ain't got no folks. They're all dead. It's just me, has been since I was twelve."

"I see. You ever work longhorns?"

"No, sir, but I'm a fast learner and I'll give you a day's work for a day's pay."

Buck glanced at Chester. He nodded his head.

"That's all we ask, Mc Cord. You'll do, but we're gonna have to find you a set of spurs. We can't have you walking around slick-heeled."

The smile over the boy's face was worth a month's pay by itself.

As the next man approached, Chester leaned close and whispered to Buck.

"What we got here?"

The man looked to be straddling fifty. He had round shoulders and walked with a loose-jointed gait in boots that rose to his knees. He had a hawkish face that was weathered like worn saddle leather and a close-trimmed smear of mustache.

Buck immediately recognized the long rifle cradled in the crook of one elbow. The Yankees used them against the

Confederate boys during the war. It was a Spencer Carbine, a lever-action repeater .50-caliber rim fire cartridge in a tube magazine in the butt stock. It would fire seven shots just as fast as a man could work the lever.

"I be Zack Gibbs."

"You ever worked longhorns?" Buck asked.

"Sonny, if it's work, I've done it. Was chief scout for the army for three years, led two wagon trains over the trail to Oregon back in forty-six and forty-seven, worked the gold fields in California. Yes siree, I've near about done it all at one time or another."

"That's a wicked looking rifle you carry," Chester said. "Can you hit what you aim at?"

"Sonny, I can drop a buffalo in its tracks at three hundred yards. It will blow a hole in a man big enough to stick your fist through. Not many men come back for a second helping after getting a taste of ole Betsy. "

"Might be a good man to have on our side when trouble comes," Buck offered.

"We'll give you a try," Chester told the man.

As the day wore on others rode in and took their place in line. By the end of the day they had hired sixteen men and turned away only two, one an obvious drunk that smelled like a whiskey still and the other Chester suspected to be a troublemaker.

Just before sundown Washington Long and his family arrived. He was drove what looked like a brand new chuck wagon loaded down with supplies.

"'Bout time our cook showed up," Buck greeted with a wide grin. "Looks like you found us a chuck wagon."

"Yes, sir. Found it over at Fort Clark. The quarter master said they had no use fer it, so I bought it cheap."

"Well, you got here just in time. We got us a passel of hungry men with nothing to feed them."

"Mister Buck, I'd like you to meet my missus. This be Jewell, and these be my youngins, Jeremiah and Sarah."

"It's a pleasure to meet you folks," Buck said, toughing a thumb and finger to his hat brim. "We're mighty glad to have you at the longhorn."

Jewel smiled and nodded.

"So happens I shot a buck deer coming over, Washington said. "Won't take long I'll have them fat and happy in no time."

True to his word, shortly after dark, the new crew of the Longhorn sat around a campfire eating venison stew and sopping their plates with pan-fried flapjacks.

"Reminds me of my ma's cooking," one cowboy said around a mouthful.

"Well, I ain't your ma, sonny," Wash told him, "but you earned yourself another helpin' with them words."

From then on there was nothing but complimentary comments about the cooking.

Buck and Chester squatted beside the fire sipping coffee and listening.

"Appears we got ourselves a salty crew." Chester said in a low voice to his partner.

"Seems so," Buck agreed.

Within two days they had completed one cabin and were ready to put the roof on the second one. Buck insisted that Wash and his family move into the finished one. Jewel, Wash's wife beamed as they moved in.

Another day and the second cabin was ready. Buck and Chester moved their bedrolls inside as the men went to work on the bunkhouse. When finished, the long, log structure would house thirty-two men with sixteen bunks along either side. Gun ports were cut into the thick log walls and the doors in front and back were made of heavy timber. The place was a literal fortress.

Within a week the bunkhouse was finished and they started on a barn and large corral. But time was slipping by. The first of October was fast approaching. The herd of longhorns from Mexico would arrive within a few days.

Both Buck and Chester kept a close eye on their crew.

Wash woke them before daylight every morning with a loud banging on a plowshare with a hammer; it was enough to wake the dead. But the coffee was always hot and ready, and breakfast was cooking when the sleepy-eyed men rolled out of their blankets.

The work proved hard and the days were long, working from can see until can't see. But the men never complained. They knew that a good supper and a soft bunk was always waiting. After their bellies were full the men either played poker or sat around the campfire spinning yarns.

Chapter VIII

They heard them long before they could see them. The large herd of longhorns announced their arrival with a steady chorus of bawling that could be heard for miles before they reached the Sycamore River.

Buck and his crew swung into their saddles and rode to meet the herd. It was a sight he would never forget. Chester reined up beside him. They sat their saddles on a hill overlooking the river and watched as the large herd of longhorns splashed across the muddy river. Their own crew joined the Mexican vaqueros and formed a corridor across the wide river to prevent the cattle from turning downstream.

Buck saw a rider on a magnificent black horse splashing across the river and immediately recognized *Señor* Rivas flanked by four heavily armed body guards.

"Our Mexican friend is a careful man," Chester commented as they watched the riders urge their horses up the bank and onto Longhorn land.

"I'd pity the hombre that was dumb enough to tangle with

those fellows," Buck agreed.   *Señor* Rivas reined his black horse to a halt beside Buck and Chester. His four security guards pulled up a few yards away.

"*Buenos dias, señors,*" The Mexican rancher greeted with a wide smile.

"*Buenos dias*, Buck replied. "See you brought us a few longhorns."

"*Si*, I bring you two thousand of the very best cattle in all Mexico."

"What about the bulls we talked about?"

"They are following a short distance behind. My best vaqueros are in charge of them. You will be well pleased, you have my word."

"Your word is good enough for us," Buck assured him. "Let's ride on up to the house and we'll settle up over a cup of coffee. Our men know what to do with the herd."

"As you say in Texas, coffee would go good," their Mexican friend said, smiling.

By the time half the sun's golden orb was swallowed by the western horizon the cattle were separated into four smaller herds. Señor Rivas's vaqueros along with the Longhorn crew ringed the herds into tight groups and settled them down for the night.

The herd of magnificent bulls milled about in the sturdy corral built for that purpose.

All hands except the first shift of night guards gathered around a large campfire sipping coffee. Buck noticed that Wash had been expecting the Mexicans and planned well. Several large pots of bubbling spicy Mexican stew hung over the fires. Pans of sourdough bread were stacked close to keep them warm. He even made cold bread pudding for the occasion.

After everyone ate their fill and enjoyed another cup of coffee around the campfire, someone came up with a guitar and filled the night with Spanish guitar music and singing.

Every man sipped his coffee quietly, stared at the dancing flames above the campfire, listened to the lonesome sound of the music, and seemed lost in his own thoughts of home or a pretty girl somewhere.

The night was half used before the first man headed for his bedroll. It was one of those times that every man would long remember.

Señor Rivas and his crew pulled out well before first light. They left behind eight vaqueros that chose to hire on with the Longhorn.

A slight graying of the eastern sky gave promise of another hot day as Buck and Chester threw saddles on their mounts and cinched them tight for the day's work.

"With the eight new vaqueros we have thirty men on the payroll now, not counting Wash and his wife," Chester told his partner. "Think that'll do for the time being?"

"Ought to. We'll most likely pick up a few more here and there. Might think about hiring a few more before April when we start the drive."

"Yeah, I'm thinking we'll need a dozen or so to watch after the ranch and round up some more critters out of the thickets while we're gone. How long you reckon it'll take to make the drive?"

"Well, I figure it's the best part of eight hundred miles from here to Sedalia, Missouri. If we averaged twelve to fifteen miles a day it would take us at least two months to get the herd there, then another three weeks to make it back home. Reckon we best figure we'll be gone three months."

"That's a long time. We're gonna need a good man in charge of the ranch while we're gone that long," Chester said as he toed a stirrup and swung into the saddle. "Got anybody in mind?"

"Nope, not yet anyway. Let's both keep our eyes peeled for someone to emerge as a leader that we could count on. What say we ride down and take a closer look at the bulls our friend from Mexico brought us?"

They rode down to the large corral and climbed from their saddles to sit on the top rail of the fence. For long, quiet minutes their gazes examined the herd of breed bulls. Like their female counterparts, they were a mixture of various combinations of red and white and brown and white paint colors. They were long and lean with good top-line. Most were young stocker steers, but their gazes lingered longer on the older, more mature bulls that would serve as their sire bulls.

These possessed a natural thickness with a long and deep body. Their horns were unbelievable with tip-to-tip measurements in the fifty-to-sixty inch range.

"Looks like a good foundation herd of breeding bulls," Chester commented.

"Yeah, and the young stuff looks promising, too," Buck agreed.

While they were talking and looking over their herd of bulls they saw a rider coming. He rode a large, steel-gray gelding with a high-stepping gait.

They watched as he approached. At first glance he appeared to be a grizzled old timer. He wore a black floppy hat that partially covered shoulder-length, unruly hair that was mostly gray to match his full beard and mustache.

His clothes were rough-cut-cowboy covered by full-length, bull hide chaps from his waist down to his boots. He wore heavy leather leggings over his boots and a canvas duster that hung to below his boot tops. Heavy gauntlets stretched halfway up his forearms. A coiled braided rawhide reata hung from his saddle.

As he drew near, it became obvious that this was no ordinary cowboy. The way he sat his saddle, erect and alert, dark, piercing eyes that searched everything around him and a Walker model Colt cinched around his waist suggested this was a man to be reckoned with.

He reined up near the fence only a few feet away and sat his saddle for a several minutes without saying a word.

"Something we can do for you, stranger"? Buck asked.

"Maybe. We'll see. You fellows the owners?" He asked in a raspy voice.

"I'm Buck Cordell. This is my partner, Chester Colson. I didn't catch your name?"

"Folks that know me call me Pappy. The fellow over at the store in Del Rio said you boys might be needing a brush popper."

"Don't reckon I ever heard the term. What's a brush popper?"

"You boys must be new to these parts. A brush popper is a fellow who catches longhorn critters outta the thickets. I'm the best there is."

"What makes you the best?" Buck asked, fixing the man with a level-eyed stare.

"Sonny, what I don't know about longhorns ain't worth knowing. I know where they live, what they eat, when and where they water and how they think. I've chased mossy horns from the Pecos to the Rio Grande. One way or another, been making my living, such as it is, off them critters since I could fork a saddle."

"You be willing to head up a crew to drag some longhorns outta them thickets?"

"What's it pay?"

"Eighty a month and keep."

"You aiming to catch a few or a bunch?"

"As many as we can."

"Do I get to pick my crew?"

"Wouldn't have it any other way."

"Then I reckon you just hired yourself a top hand."

"Ride on up to the bunkhouse and stow your gear. We'll be along directly."

Buck and Chester followed the new man with a long gaze as he rode toward the bunkhouse.

"Reckon it's time to start catching us some longhorns," Chester said.

"Seems so," Buck agreed.

"Well, the bunkhouse, chow hall, and cabins are about finished. Couple more days ought to wind that project up. We still need to put up a couple of barns and build some more sturdy corrals for the wild stock they bring in from the thickets but a smaller crew could handle that."

Wash sounded the bell for supper. After seeing to their horses, Buck and Chester headed for the chow hall.

The aroma of pan-fried steak, fried potatoes mixed with onions, and hot biscuits filled the long building. Buck and Chester followed them in, picked up a plate and tin coffee cup, and stood last in line for supper. As the cowhands filed past the stove Wash and Jewel filled their plates to overflowing.

"Think I done died and gone to heaven," one cowboy said loudly, carrying his plate to the table.

"If ole Wash ain't the cook there, don't think I much care about goin." Another fella agreed.

"Gonna tell you boys something," Zack Gibbs spoke up around a mouthful of steak. "I been over the mountain and down the river more times than I can count and I never ate better'n this. Now if he could just learn to make coffee that's fittin' to drink, we'd have ourselves a genuine cook."

"What's wrong with my coffee?" Wash demanded.

"Well, for one thing, it's too thick to drink and too thin to slice."

Everybody laughed except Wash. He just crooked a grin that took up most of his face.

Lots of good-natured joshing between the hands kept the meals lively.

When things quieted down a bit, Chester spoke up.

"Want you boys to say howdy to a new man we just hired a while ago. This is Pappy. He'll be ramrod'n a crew to catch as many longhorns outta the thickets along the river as he can.

"We agreed to let him pick his own crew. If he picks you and you're of a mind to take on the job, it pays seventy a month. I don't have to tell you how ornery these critters are gonna be, they've likely lived their whole life in those thickets. They ain't gonna take kindly to leaving. I figure you'll have to drag most of 'em out and bring 'em back to the longhorn corrals we're building for that purpose.

"Anything you want to say, Pappy?"

"Give me a day or two to look the hands over before I decide who I want in my crew."

Over the next few days they saw Pappy talking to first one then another Longhorn cowboy. Three days passed before he sat down with Buck and Chester over a cup of coffee.

Both of the owners quickly grew accustomed to Pappy's manner and thought nothing of it when he stared silently at his coffee for a while before speaking.

"You boys have put together a pretty salty crew. If I'm any judge of men, you got some boys here that ain't afraid of work and that will ride for the brand. I've looked them over. Gonna tell you what I need to do the job you want done.

"I need five men, plus me, for herders and catchers. We'll work in two teams. We'll build a fence with the big end open sorta like a funnel that narrows down into a sturdy corral.

"I need four heavy freight wagons with a driver for each to use as dragging wagons. They won't actually drag the cattle. We'll snug 'em up on short heavy lead ropes so they have to follow along. I figure to tie four critters behind each wagon. The wagons ought to be able to make two round trips a day back to the ranch.

"By my tally, that's thirty-two critters a day. If that ain't enough to suit you boys we can always add more wagons."

Buck glanced at Chester. Both nodded agreement.

"Sounds good," Buck said. "You decided on which men you want?"

"Yep, I would like to have the vaqueros, all eleven of 'em. Every one of 'em them has been raised around longhorns. They know the breed like they know their own mama. They know how they think and act, and they're some of the best rope handlers I ever seen. Give me those eleven men and we'll bring you all the longhorns you can handle."

Again Buck and Chester agreed.

"Let's you and me ride into Del Rio tomorrow and see if we can locate some wagons," Buck said. "You can pick up whatever supplies you'll need while we're there."

A gritty, gray dawn colored the eastern sky as Buck and Pappy swung legs over their saddles and pointed their horses' nose toward Del Rio. It was only about ten miles and the small town wasn't fully awake when they rode in and tied their mounts in front of the Del Rio Café.

Selena greeted them with a wide smile. *"Buenos dias, Señors."*

"Mornin'," Buck greeted, touching thumb and finger to his hat brim.

"Coffee?" she asked, already pouring two cups at the table they were headed to.

"Yep, and keep it coming until I tell you to whoa," Buck said. "We left the ranch before breakfast so we'll need that, too."

"Your partner that you told me about still hasn't come in to try our food."

"He's been pretty busy at the ranch. I expect he'll drop by in a few days. I reckon after he sees you I won't get much work outta him."

That brought a smile that dimpled her cheeks as she turned and headed for the kitchen.

"Right pretty little thing, ain't she?" Pappy said, sipping his coffee and allowing his gaze to follow her as she left the room.

"'Comes close to being as pretty as I ever seen," Buck agreed, his thoughts suddenly flashing a picture of John Walker's daughter before him.

After they ate their fill they walked their horses up the street to Mr. Walker's mercantile store.

"Good Morning," the storekeeper greeted as they walked in.

"Mornin'," Buck replied, his sweeping gaze searching for Rebekah.

"Howdy, Pappy, are you working for Mr. Cordell now?"

"Shore am."

"I'm obliged for pointing him in our direction," Buck said, disappointed that apparently Walker's daughter wasn't in the store.

"Well, I remembered you saying you were gonna flush some longhorns' outta those thickets along the river. Ain't a man living better at that than Pappy. How long you been brush poppin', Pappy?"

"Longer'n I wanna talk about."

"Mr. Walker, we've got a need for four heavy freight

wagons and a two-hitch team of mules for each. Where you reckon we ought to start looking?" Buck asked.

"I'd talk to old Pete down at the livery. If there's anything like that in this neck of the woods he'll know where it is."

"Much obliged. Pappy will need some things. See he gets 'em."

"Shore will. Say, Pappy, you been in them thickets more'n most, you ever see that bull the Mexicans call El Toro?"

"Nope."

"What's he talking about?" Buck said.

"There's talk about a ghost bull that lives in the thickets they call, El Toro." John Walker said. "Black as the blackest midnight and half again bigger than the biggest ever captured, or so the story goes. They say his horns are wider than most men are tall.

"Anybody ever actually seen him?"

"Nobody who lived to tell about it," the storekeeper said. "What about it, Pappy, you ever seen him?"

"Nope. Spent most of my life in them thickets, but I never laid eyes on a bull like that, shore would like to, though, if there really is one. I reckon it's all just tequila talk."

"I met your daughter the last time I was in," Buck told the storekeeper.

"Yeah, she said you stopped by. Since her mother passed on a couple of years ago she's shouldered a lot of the load around here, don't know what I'd do without her."

"Well, tell her I said howdy."

"I'll do that."

"Come on, Pappy, let's mosey down to the livery and have a talk with Pete about them wagons."

As they approached the livery Buck noticed half a hundred or so mustangs milling about in the corral. They walked over to the fence and propped arms on the top rail. Buck examined the horses with a critical eye.

"Howdy, neighbor. Name's Pete" the livery man greeted with a wide smile as he walked up to fill a space beside Buck and Pappy.

"Howdy," Buck replied, swinging a look at the hostler.

He was a bear of a man with Texas-wide shoulders and a barrel chest. His arms were near as big as most men's thighs. He wore bib overalls with a leather smithy's apron that hung to his ankles. The floppy hat partially hid his long brown hair. Pete served as both blacksmith and hostler for Del Rio.

"I'm Buck Cordell. This is Pappy. I'm putting together a ranch out where the Sycamore empties into the Rio Grande. See you got a corral full of mustangs."

"Yep, bought 'em a few weeks back. You interested?"

"Might. What're you asking?"

"Good stock. Mostly unbroken fresh in off the range. Take thirty a head. Take your pick."

"How many you got?"

"Got forty head."

"Give you a thousand dollars for the lot."

"That's just twenty-five dollars a head."

"That's the way I figure it, too."

"They're worth thirty."

"Not to me."

"You drive a hard bargain, mister, but you just bought yourself some mustangs."

By noon they bought the herd of mustangs, four freight wagons and eight teams of Missouri mules and made arrangements for the hostler to deliver them to the ranch within two weeks.

The days turned into weeks all too quickly. By the end of the second week, Pappy and his crew had gathered over three hundred longhorns out of the thickets. The thickets along the river were a mixture of chaparral, mesquite, and scrub cedar. In places they were so close a man couldn't even fight his way through on foot, much less on horseback. It was hard and dangerous work.

Two new corrals were built to hold the longhorns during the gentling process. This consisted of holding them in the sturdy corrals and starving them until they became completely dependant upon their captors for both food and water.

Those that proved to be real outlaws and troublemakers were yoked to heavy oxen that outweighed the longhorn in every department. After a week or two of being dragged around by a two thousand pound ox, the troublemakers became as meek as kittens.

Gradually they started rotating out the first captured longhorns. They were mixed into the four herds brought over from Mexico. Two cowhands continually rode a circle around them, watching for bunch quitters and guarding each of the herds.

Another corral was built to hold the unbroken mustangs the liveryman delivered.

A wrangler named Jody Brown came highly recommended as the best bronc buster in Texas. Word was that he could stay aboard a tornado if it had legs. He was a short, wiry fellow who looked older than his thirty-two years. Buck and Chester decided to see what he could do before they hired him. Word spread quickly and most of the hands gathered around the bucking corral to watch the action.

A big-boned strawberry roan stallion was without a doubt the worst outlaw among the herd of horses Buck had bought in Del Rio. He stood over fifteen hands high with muscled legs and fire in his eyes. He made a habit of chasing any cowboy over the fence that ventured into the corral with him. The cowboys called the roan Red Thunder.

The stallion was the only horse in the bucking corral as the bronc buster climbed the fence and dropped to the ground.

Red Thunder tossed his head and reared up on his hind legs snorting a warning. His front hooves pawed the air. Jody walked slowly toward the outlaw mustang, playing out a loop of the lariat in his hand.

The outlaw ran back and forth, tossing his head, snorting wildly, coming closer to the bronc buster with each charge. Suddenly the stallion charged directly at Brown.

The bronc buster's arm whipped out. The throw was true. He stepped quickly out of the path of the stallion's charge and wrapped the lariat around the heavy center post in the middle of the corral. In short order he had the outlaw stallion cinched up short to the post.

He took a gunny sack from his hip pocked and tied it over the fighting stallion's eyes. The blinded horse immediately calmed down and stopped fighting the rope that held him tight against the center post.

Buck was amazed at the man's skill of handling a wild mustang. Brown motioned for a cowboy to bring the saddle blanket, halter and saddle, that hung on the fence. He spent a few minutes rubbing his hand along the stallion's neck and speaking in a soft, soothing voice.

He slipped the bridle in place and cinched the neck strap tight. He let the reins drop to the ground. He held the blanket in front of the outlaw's nose and let him sniff it before laying it gently on the horse's back. The stallion trembled when the blanket touched his back, but quickly settled down again.

The roan snorted nervously when Brown laid the saddle gently on the stallion's back. It fought against the rope for a minute before quieting down again. The bronc buster waited a minute, again rubbing the horse's neck and speaking softly as he bent and reached underneath the stallion to grasp the cinch band. He quickly threaded the latigo and snugged the rigging tight. Then he slowly loosed the lariat from the horse's neck and dropped it to the ground.

Brown hooked a boot into the stirrup and slowly lifted into the saddle. Everyone watched breathlessly as the wrangler jerked the blindfold from the stallion's eyes.

For several heartbeats the roan remained perfectly still. Suddenly the outlaw stallion exploded at both ends. Arching its back, all four feet left the ground at the same time. It landed with a bone-jarring impact and immediately swapped ends and sunfished across the corral in a series of high, bounding leaps.

Jody Brown lost his hat in the midst of a whirling twist that took the horse and cowboy high into the air. The outlaw's hind feet lashed out at the air, touching ground only long enough to leap again, twisting, spinning, whirling, and slamming the bronc buster from front to rear in the saddle.

The roan reared high, humped its back, and shook itself in midair, trying desperately to rid its back of the rider. When the red devil landed it exploded in a pounding charge around the corral.

Gradually its bucking leaps reduced to a series of stiff-legged crow hops that lacked power. It was clear to all there was no fight left in the outlaw stallion. Brown reined the roan around the corral a few times in a fast trot before reining up and stepping down from the saddle. The horse stood shaking nervously and walleyed, an outlaw no longer.

Brown led the roan over to the corral fence where Buck and Chester sat on the top rail.

"Good horse," the bronc buster said with a Texas drawl.

"Good ride," Buck replied. "You're hired."

* * *

At supper on Friday night Buck stood to his feet.

"Got something to say, boys. To our way of thinking you've done a good job. We've accomplished a lot in a short time. The place is taking shape. You've done everything asked of you and more. We couldn't be prouder. We figured you boys could use a couple of days off.

"After you've got the wrinkles out of your belly, stop by the table here and collect your pay. If you got a notion to ride into town, just keep in mind that you ride for the Longhorn. Have fun, but stay outta trouble. I'll expect you here and ready to work come Monday morning at first light.

"We'll start trail branding right after Christmas in a few more weeks. Days off will be few and far between, so enjoy it while you can. Those of you who have guard duty can go into town next Saturday."

Shouts and cowboy yells filled the room. They made short work of supper. By good dark several had already ridden out to make the trip to Del Rio.

"Chester, why don't you take a couple of days off ? I'll hang around the ranch and watch after things."

"Might just do that, I've been wanting to look Del Rio over. I'll take a ride into town tomorrow."

"While you're looking, stop in the café and take a look at Carlos's little sister, you'll like what you see."

"Might just stop and have a looksee," Chester said.

Buck heard Chester ride out early the next morning, but lingered in his bed a few more minutes before rising. He knew Wash would have the coffee pot going for the night shift guards when they got off duty, so after he washed up he headed for the chow hall.

"Mornin' Mr. Buck," the big negro greeted cheerfully as Buck entered.

"Morning, Wash. Short crew to cook for this morning."

"Yes, sir, don't hardly know how to cook for just a handful of folks."

Buck filled his plate with flapjacks and poured a generous helping of honey over them. A steaming cup of coffee rounded out his meal.

The eight night guards sat around a long table eating their breakfast. Buck carried his plate and coffee over. He found a place on the bench and joined them.

"Everything quiet last night, Smokey?" Buck asked around a bite of flapjack.

Smokey Cunningham was one of the newer hands. He was a square-built fellow with Texas-wide shoulders, slim waist, and a no-nonsense attitude. He struck Buck as being a levelheaded kind of fellow. Buck decided to keep an eye on him. He might make a good top hand down the road a piece.

"Nothing unusual. Some of the new stock from the thickets still take a notion to go back home now and then, but they'll settle in."

"Where you from, Smokey?"

"Born and raised in Alabama. Went back after the war but wasn't nothing left. Always liked cattle. Thought I'd try my hand at ranching. Figured Texas was a good place to start."

"Well, right proud you signed on with the Longhorn."

"Mr. Cordell," another cowboy spoke up. "Which hands will get to make the drive to Missouri?"

"Your name is Jimmy, ain't it son?"

"Yes, sir."

"Jimmy, when the time comes we'll look every hand over

and pick those we think will make us the best trail crew. You ever been on a trail drive?"

"No, sir, but I shore would like to go."

"Well, we'll see," Buck said, feeling somewhat sorry for the young man. "So far, you're making a good hand."

The boy's smile took up most of his face.

After breakfast Buck worked on the new corral a while just to have something to keep him busy. He was tying one of the top rails in place when a detachment of Union Army appeared in the distance. They headed in the direction of the ranch house.

Buck pulled off his work gloves and leaned against the corral. He chewed on a stem of grass and watched their approach.

A spit and polish type lieutenant sat stiff-backed and erect in a McClellan army issue saddle in front of a squad of a half dozen troopers. The officer lifted one hand shoulder high and reined up a few feet from Buck.

"I'm Lieutenant Nathaniel Reed, fourth United States Cavalry from Fort Clark. I'm looking for a Mr. Cordell. Would you know where I might find him?"

"You just did, lieutenant, I'm Buck Cordell. What can I do for you?"

"Oh, I mistook you for one of the workers. Colonel Ronald Callahan, commandant of Fort Clark would like to see you."

"Fine, tell your colonel I'll stop by in a day or two, we're kinda short-handed right now, or tell him he's welcome to ride out and see me anytime."

"No, sir, you don't understand. You are to accompany me back to the fort to see the colonel."

Anger left over from a bitter war welled up and surged through him. His face flushed and his lips clamped together like a vice. Pausing, he took a deep breath. When he spoke he bit off the words and spat them out

"No, *you* don't understand. Go back and tell your colonel

if he wants to talk to me, I'll be right here, but it don't sit well with me to be ordered around like I'm some private. I'm not in his army."

"I'm afraid I can't do that, Mr. Cordell. I have my orders. The colonel sent me to bring you back to the fort. That's what I intend to do. In chains, if need be."

Buck allowed his hand to rest on the butt of his Colt as he locked eyes with the young lieutenant

"Then you better have more men than I'm counting."

Apparently Wash saw what was happening and roused the night herders from their bunks. The big black man and eight cowhands emerged from the bunkhouse with rifles in hand and walked toward the lieutenant and his men.

The officer saw the cowhands coming and began fidgeting in his saddle. He glanced nervously from Buck to the Longhorn crew, then back toward Buck.

"You dare to raise weapons against the United States Army?" He blurted out. "Colonel Callahan will have you in irons for this."

"Now you listen, lieutenant. You came onto *my* land and *order* me to come to the fort so your colonel can talk to me. You got no authority here. Now git while the getting' is good."

For a moment the officer stared hard at Buck.

"We'll be back," he said, reining his mount around roughly. They rode away.

Buck and the Longhorn cowboys watched them go.

It was mid-afternoon on Saturday when Chester rode into San Felipe del Rio. The town was a bustling beehive of activity. *Just like back home,* Chester thought, *everybody comes to town on Saturday.*

He was hungry. He reined up at the hitching rail in front of the small café and had to admit to himself that hunger was only part of the reason he stopped at the café first. He wanted to have a look at that pretty senorita Buck went on so much about, Carlos's little sister.

Chester pushed through the door and scanned the room. Carlos, Jose, and Pablo were sitting at a table. They spotted their boss and motioned him over.

"Well, did you fellows paint the town last night?" Chester asked as he pulled out the fourth chair and settled into it.

"No," Carlos said smiling. "The other Longhorn boys took care of that."

"No problem was there?"

"Nothing serious, just the usual bruises and black eyes."

Chester felt a presence and glanced up right into the face of the most beautiful creature he had ever laid eyes on. His breath caught in a short gasp.

Slowly, so slowly it had to be obvious both to her and to her brother sitting only a few feet away, Chester's gaze took her in.

She was short, no more than five feet tall at the most. Her waist was so tiny he was certain he could encircle it with both hands. But the loose, ankle-length black skirt and white blouse drawn tight just below her shoulders couldn't hide the fact that those five feet contained a lot of woman.

Her long, coal-black hair hung straight down her back to waist-length. Her creamy-brown complexion looked flawless.

Carlos's voice broke into Chester's thoughts.

"This is one of the owners of the ranch where I work, Chester Colson. Boss, this is my little sister, Selena

Her coal-black, dancing eyes settled on his. For a long moment their gazes fixed on one another. She smiled. It was a pretty smile and Chester liked the way it looked on her.

"It is good to finally meet you," she said.

"Finally?" he asked.

"Yes, your partner told me about you and said you would be stopping in."

"Well, not sure you ought to believe all he says."

"On the contrary, he spoke very highly of you, as did my brother."

"Did they now? My partner told me the food was good. Thought I'd find out for myself."

"What would you like?"

"Surprise me."

His words brought a smile that showed her sparkling-white teeth and deep dimples. She turned and headed for the kitchen. Chester watched her go; his gaze followed her until she disappeared from view.

Chester and his three Mexican vaqueros sipped coffee and talked about cattle until Selena returned with a beef steak so large it actually hung over the edge of the platter. She sat it in front of him with great mocking fanfare, bowing and smiling widely all the while. A large, sliced, baked sweet potato with fresh butter and a pan of biscuits quickly followed.

"We are going to have a drink over at the saloon," Carlos said.

"I'll drop by after I surround this steak. It may take a while."

Carlos and his two companions left. Chester settled down and got serious about enjoying the best steak he had tasted in a long time, maybe ever. But his mind kept flashing a picture of Selena, his eyes constantly flicked toward the kitchen, hoping for her return.

"I could get use to eating like this right quick," he told her as she refilled his coffee cup for the fourth time.

"Then you will have to come back more often," she said with a smile and a lingering look. "Did you get enough to eat?"

"All I could crowd in. I might just have to take you up on that invitation."

"I will look forward to your next visit."

The Del Rio Saloon was going full blast when Chester pushed through the double doors. The place was crowded with both Texan drifters and Mexican vaqueros. He spotted Carlos, Jose, and Pablo and headed for their table.

A heavy-set bar girl arrived as he settled into a chair. He ordered a bottle for he and his men to share.

They sipped their drinks and talked a while.

Pablo leaned close and said something in Spanish to Carlos. Chester saw Carlos swing a look at a table near the back. Chester looked that direction. Five hard-looking men wearing low-slung gun belts leveled a gaze back at them.

As he looked, one of the men stood up and headed toward their table. He walked with a confident swagger. Chester had seen his kind many times before. Sensing trouble brewing, Chester thumbed the rawhide cord off the hammer of his Colt.

He judged the man to be somewhere shy of thirty: tall, lanky, and with a hard-set look about his face. He wore a tied-down Smith & Wesson on his hip in a cut-away, gunfighter holster. He stopped no more than two arms' length away.

"Your name Colson?" The man demanded in a loud voice.

"I'm Chester Colson, what can I do for you?"

"I'm Bob Bridger. You may have heard of me. Word is you're the one who hung my brother over in Eagle Pass."

"I hung four murderers and horse thieves. If your brother was one of them, then I reckon you heard right."

"You shore don't look like much. From all the talk hereabouts I was expecting you to be ten foot tall and meaner than a wounded she-bear."

"Well, you know how people talk."

"Stand up! I'm gonna kill you."

Chester held a half-filled glass of whiskey in his left hand. As he pushed up from his chair he threw the whiskey into the man's face and drew his Colt with his right hand in the same lightening motion. For the briefest instant the whiskey blinded the gunman. He hesitated. That hesitation cost him his life.

The man's weapon hadn't cleared leather before two holes punched through his chest no more than a hand span apart.

Blood blew from the holes the .38 slugs made when they exited his back, showering spectators nearby.

The man's eyes rounded in disbelief. His mouth dropped open. The unfired Smith & Wesson slipped from his grasp and fell to the wooden floor, landing with a clatter.

He staggered backward in a clumsy half step and clawed at the holes in his chest, trying vainly to stop the flow of life liquid. His knees gave way. He collapsed to the dirty saloon floor and bled his life away in a growing pool of his own blood.

Chester swung a look at the man's companions. They sat stone cold still. Stunned looks filled their faces.

"Anybody else here this fellow's kin?" Chester asked in a raised voice. His question was met with silence.

Chester's eyes flickered over the crowd as he routinely reloaded his weapon. Satisfying himself that no one else was of a mind to take up the argument, he sat back down and with shaking hands, poured another drink.

"I never see anybody so fast as you," Carlos said, clearly surprised how Chester handled the gunfighter. "The man you killed was a very bad hombre. He has another brother named Wade Bridger that has a reputation as one of the fastest gunman in all of Texas."

"Why do they all have brothers? I reckon we'll cross that creek when we come to it." Chester said. "Know anything about those fellows he was sitting with over yonder?"

"No, señor, I have never seen them before."

"Well, I'm gonna head on back to the ranch. You boys staying in town?"

"We will ride with you," Carlos said, pushing from his chair.

It was late when Chester and his companions arrived at the ranch. All the lamps had long since been put out. They unsaddled and stalled their horses before making their way to the bunkhouse and falling into their bunks. Chester didn't want to wake Buck, so he found an empty bunk and stretched out.

For a long time he lay quietly staring into the darkness. Off in the distance, cattle lowing in the night soothed his mind, that, and a half dozen cowboys snoring were the only sounds that disturbed the darkness.

He replayed the killing in his mind. The shooter backed him into a corner with no way out; it was kill or be killed. Still and all, he had taken another man's life. *How many is it now? Reckon I've lost count.*

His mind went back to the first man he ever killed. It seemed so long ago....

Chester grew up with a gun either in his hand or on his hip and he was good with it. By t time he was twelve he could draw and hit a falling leaf before it hit the ground. All the boys who lived nearby often came to the creek bottom where they knew Chester practiced with his sidearm. They stood around watching in amazement. Chester enjoyed putting on a show for his friends.

He wore his gun constantly around their ranch, but had never worn it into town, at least not until the day he turned sixteen. It was a Saturday. In Tyler, Texas everybody went to town on Saturday.

The sound of music from the barn dance drifted on a soft breeze as Chester and his friend, Billy Sawyer, rode into town. Chester and Billy had been best friends since they were small. Billy was sweet on Sally Elkins. That's all he talked about on the long ride into town.

They tied their horses to a wagon wheel of one of the dozen or so wagons and hurried inside the large barn. Billy spotted *his girl,* as he liked to call her. She was talking to a couple of her friends.

Chester headed for the lemonade table. Billy headed for Sally Elkins.

The fiddle player swung into a slow tune and Billy took his girl in his arms for a dance. That's when Sammy Riker walked in. Sammy was a grown man and the local bully around Tyler, Texas Most everyone gave Sammy a wide berth when he strutted down the street, most everyone except Chester. Chester never took backwater for anybody.

Chester watched as Sammy grabbed Billy by the arm and pulled him away from Sally, then took her in his arms to finish the dance with her. She struggled to loose herself. That's when Billy hit him.

By the time Chester rushed across the floor, Sammy had knocked Billy down and was sitting on top of him, pounding him with both fists. Chester tried to pull Sammy off his friend, but the bully was like a crazy man. He just kept driving his big fists into Billy's broken and bloody face.

Determined to stop the beating, Chester drew his weapon and swung it with all his might. The blow landed just above Sammy's right ear. Even now Chester could remember the sound, like a piece of dried wood when it breaks.

Sammy keeled over and didn't move. Someone told Chester later that the blow fractured Sammy's skull. He was dead.

Most folks in Tyler hated Sammy and the killing saddened few. No charges were brought against Chester, but his reputation was born that night and would dog his trail for the rest of his life. Not long after the incident he joined the Confederate Army.

Chester shook his head to clear his mind of the painful memory and drifted off to sleep.

* * *

At breakfast the next morning all the hands talked about the visit from the army detachment. Wash was in the process of telling Chester what he knew about it just as Buck walked into the chow hall. He poured himself a cup of coffee and sat down across the table from Chester.

"Hear you had a visit from the army while I was in town."

"Nothing to worry about. I hear you had a run-in with some jasper in town."

"Yeah, a brother of one of the men I hung decided he was gonna kill me. I convinced him otherwise."

"So I understand."

"Reckon we better ride over and have a talk with the army and explain what happened?"

"Soon as we can find time, got too much to do right now. Soon as the boys get back from town we need to start them on another corral. Our brush crews are dragging longhorns in faster than we can handle them. We need another corral to hold 'em."

"I'll get them on it first thing in the morning."

"Been watching one of the new men, Slim Hopkins. I'm thinking he might make a good man to watch after the maverick longhorns the boys are bringing in, what's your feeling on the matter?"

"Think you're right. He's a hard man to overlook. He knows cattle."

"Let's watch him a while."

"Met Carlos's little sister while I was in town."

"What'd you think?"

"She's something to write home about, sure enough. I never dreamed a girl could be so pretty."

* * *

A few of the men sported busted lips and swollen eyes, but all hands were present and accounted for come Monday morning. Breakfast was a lively affair with everyone wanting to relate their adventures in town.

After breakfast, Chester made the work assignments for the day. Every spare hand went to work building another new corral to hold the longhorns being brought in from the thickets.

Both Buck and Chester pitched in to help speed up the project.

It was just after noon when somebody spotted the approaching Column of Union Cavalry and sounded the alarm. Buck and Chester laid down the post hole diggers and picked up their rifles, just in case.

An officer wearing the bars of a full colonel led the long column of soldiers. Riding beside him was the young lieutenant Buck chased off the ranch earlier. They reined up a short distance from the corral. The officer urged his mount forward.

"I'm Colonel Ronald Callahan, Commander of the garrison at Fort Clark. Which of you would be Mr. Cordell?"

"I'm Buck Cordell. What can I do for you?"

"I wonder if I might have a word with you privately?"

"This is my partner, Chester Colson. Anything that concerns me concerns him."

"Very well, I sent my lieutenant to invite you to stop by so we could get acquainted and discuss some recent events that have come to my attention. He reported to me that you ordered him off your ranch at the point of a gun."

"Gonna tell you something, colonel, if that's what he said, your lieutenant is a liar. Weren't no *invitation* to it. Your man rode in here and *ordered* me to come with him to the fort. He said he was gonna take me back in chains if he had to. I don't take kindly to being ordered to do anything."

"I see, well, perhaps he got a little over-zealous in carrying out his assignment, but be that as it may, it's been reported to me that you and Mr. Colson, here, took it upon yourselves to hang four men over in Eagle Pass a while back. We can't have you taking the law into your own hands. That's what the army is here for."

"Where was the army when Charlie Sweet and his men hung our friend and stole our horses?"

"We can't be expected to be everywhere at the same time. But I simply won't allow you or anyone else to run around hanging people."

"And we won't allow anyone to come onto our land and hang our men and steal our horses or cattle. We'll stomp our own snakes."

"I hoped you would be reasonable about this, Mr. Cordell, but I can see you are not a reasonable man. So let me warn you, any more hangings and I will hold you personally responsible."

Buck thumbed back his hat and looked the officer straight in the eyes. When he spoke his words were harsh, stinging. "I look on warnings the same as I do orders, don't like either. I've said my say. Do what you gotta do and I'll do the same. Now that's my final word on the matter."

Buck deliberately turned his back, picked up the posthole diggers, and went to work. The colonel jerked his horse around abruptly and rode off in a huff. His men followed.

"There goes one unhappy fellow," Chester said.

Chapter IX

It was the deepest part of the night when the shots rang out. A galloping horse charged up to the bunkhouse, followed by a loud banging on the plowshare. Men poured out of the bunkhouse with rifles in hand to see what the alarm was about.

"Indians!" the nighthawk charged with guarding the remuda yelled. "They jumped us and took the horses."

"Anybody hurt?" Buck hollered as he ran up buckling on his gun belt.

"Ain't shore, Tolbert was on the other side of the herd. I hollered, but couldn't get him to answer."

"How many were there?" Chester asked.

"Couldn't tell in the dark, I saw a half-dozen or so. Could've been more though."

"Chester, how about taking half the crew and go after 'em, we need those horses. I'll stay here with the rest. I got me a gut certain hunch that raid was a diversion to draw us all away so they could attack the ranch with their main force"

"You heard him, boys," Chester hollered. "Saddle up and let's get after 'em!"

Half the cowboys ran for the corral where their mounts for the next day were kept. Wash hurriedly sacked up some trail supplies while they saddled up. In minutes Chester and his crew galloped off into the darkness.

"Wash, just to be safe, I'd feel better if you'd move your family into the bunkhouse until this is over."

"Yes, sir, Mr. Buck."

"Let's post a couple of guards outside. I'll take a turn. Keep a sharp eye, boys. The rest of you load all the rifles we have and take up positions at the gun ports. If they come at us, let's try to put some lead where it'll do the most good. Wash, how about making some coffee, it's liable to be a long night."

Buck and another lookout took up positions, one at each front corner of the bunkhouse.

Buck cradled his rifle in the crook of his arm and leaned his back against the log wall of the bunkhouse. His eyes searched the darkness, looking for any movement, listening for any sound. Minutes crept by slowly and turned into an hour, then two. Glancing up at the stars, he judged it to be no more than an hour until first light.

Maybe I was wrong. Maybe they were just after the horses. Oh well, rather be safe than sorry. Hope Chester and the boys were able to pick up the trail in the dark, we can't afford to lose all our horses.

His thoughts were interrupted by the soft swish of an arrow. It buried itself in the log wall only inches from his chest. Instinctively he dropped to one knee, bringing his rifle up to his shoulder in the same movement.

"Indians!" he yelled.

Scrambling boots on the hard-packed ground told him the other guard was already dashing for the door to the bunkhouse. He did the same.

A volley of arrows buried into the heavy door just as Buck slammed it behind him.

"Everybody inside?" he shouted.

The answer drown out by several rifles as cowboys opened fire through the gun ports.

"Take your time. Pick a target!" Buck shouted.

He found an empty gun port next to the door and poked the nose of his rifle through.

He sighted down the barrel of his rifle and saw several dark figures charging towards the bunkhouse. A clear target appeared. He squeezed the trigger. The Indian stumbled, dropped the long lance he carried, and pitched forward face down into the dirt.

Another painted warrior charged forward, raising an old .56-50 caliber Spencer carbine to his shoulder. Buck fired. The Indian stopped dead in his tracks, dropped the rifle, and clawed at a hole in his stomach. He looked down to watch bright red blood gush through the ghostly-white war paint that covered his stomach and color his clutching fingers red.

Buck swung his rifle and centered the nose on the chest of another warrior, fired, then found another and another.

Four warriors charged from the darkness into the firelight, firing their rifles as they ran a zigzag route toward the bunkhouse. Buck swung the nose of his rifle and sighted in a target.

One of the warriors stood out from the others. His face appeared painted half-black and half-white. Three eagle feathers were tied at the crown of his head into his long black hair, distinguishing him as a chief. Before Buck could finger a shot the Indian chief melted into the darkness beside the log structure.

All around him the other Longhorn men put up a fierce battle. When their rifles snapped on an empty chamber they dropped it and scooped up another loaded one and continued firing.

In the heat of the battle Buck suddenly realized that it was as light as day, not from daylight, but from firelight. The Indians torched one or both of the cabins.

The light from the flames exposed the attackers. The cowboys now gained clear shots and they took advantage of the opportunity. It was like shooting fish in a barrel. Warrior after warrior was cut down under withering fire from the cowboys.

Suddenly the shooting stopped. For a time an eerie silence hung in the air. The Indians had simply vanished. Nothing moved outside the bunkhouse. The night remained silent. Still, like the lull after a bad storm.

"Anybody hurt?" Buck asked.

"Nobody 'cept them Injuns," came the reply.

"Reckon they're gone?" Somebody asked.

"I wouldn't bet on it," Another answered.

They waited.

Chester and the eleven heavily armed men riding behind him galloped hard to where the remuda was held before they were stolen. Once there they reined down while two men rode a wide circle.

"Over here!" Zack Gibbs yelled.

The trail left by the hundred head of horses proved easy to spot, even in the dim light of a quarter moon.

"How many's herding 'em?" Chester asked.

"Hard to say just yet," the old former army scout told him. "We'll be able to tell come first light."

They rode at a fast walk with Zack in the lead, his gaze glued to the ground. Just before daylight the trail crossed the Sycamore River then swung north.

"They're headed into some rough country," Zack told Chester. "There's a whole passel of canyons up ahead that could hide the whole herd of horses. But, if they think they can give ole Zack the slip, they got another think comin'. We'll find 'em."

The trail they were followed twisted through steepening rugged hills dotted with gnarled live oaks, scrub cedar, and stunted mesquites. The only sounds heard were the creak of saddle leather and the hollow echo of shod hooves on rocky ground.

Chester swung his searching gaze from rock cluster to gully and back again. He grew nervous. The last thing they needed was to ride smack dab into an ambush.

They climbed steadily, circling deep arroyos and thick cactus fields. The blazing sun cooked into the riders and rendered their clothes wringing-wet with sweat.

Up ahead the trail led into a tight canyon opening. Zack reined up and raised his hand to halt the others. Chester rode up beside the scout.

"Don't like the looks of that canyon, boss, don't like it a tall."

"Yeah, good place for an ambush."

"You and the others sit tight, I'll check it out."

The old scout slid his Sharps from the saddle boot and jacked in a shell. He heeled his mount forward at a slow walk. His head swiveled to and fro, his searching gaze examining every rock, every bush, and every crevice for hidden danger that might lurk behind them.

Suddenly he lunged from his saddle, hitting the ground in a roll that brought him to his knees, the Sharps pressed tightly to his shoulder. The roar from the long rifle in the tight confines of the canyon was deafening.

Up high, on the right side of the canyon wall, an Indian pitched forward, his shrill scream followed his body as he tumbled end over end in midair and landed in a jumble of rocks on the canyon floor.

A rifle barked from the opposite side of the canyon. A puff of dust kicked up only inches from the scout. Chester swung the Sharps in a fluid motion and squeezed off another shot.

From behind a scrub cedar an Indian half-rose before dropping his rifle and clutching frantically at a large hole in his chest as he fell. The force from the big shell propelled him over backwards.

Chester dug his heels deep into the flanks of his paint. The animal responded and leapt forward. He could hear the rest of his crew following closely as they charged into the mouth of the canyon.

Shots rang out from both sides of the canyon. Bullets bit up dust around the cowboys. They returned fire from the backs of their galloping mounts.

Chester saw Zack take an arrow in his upper leg. Seemingly oblivious to his wound, the old scout kept firing his big Sharps.

Reining his mount to a stop, Chester dropped to one knee beside Gibbs and brought his Henry rifle to his shoulder. He searched for a target.

All around him the other cowboys had left their horses, and taken cover behind rocks, and dealt out death in a withering hail of lead. Return fire from the Indians slowly subsided, then stopped altogether.

Chester and his men waited. Nothing moved.

After a half-hour they cautiously ventured from behind their hiding places.

"Couple of you men mount up and check out things farther up the canyon. Ride careful."

Chester turned his attention to Zack's wounded leg. The old scout had already cut away his britches-leg to expose the wound. He saw an arrow had buried deep in the fleshy part of Zack's leg just above the knee. "That looks pretty deep, Pardner," Chester said.

"I've seen worse," the old timer said. "Hope you know how to use that knife."

"I've dug out bullets, but never had to dig out an arrow before."

"Same thing, just more of it. Look in my saddle bags and get that bottle of whiskey."

Chester found it and knelt beside the old scout.

"Pour some over this knife and give the rest to me," Zack instructed.

Chester did as told. The old scout turned the bottle up and gulped down several large swallows.

"Twist a piece of rawhide good and tight just above the wound to cut off the blood, then get to cutting. Run the blade in alongside the arrow as close as you can. You've got to open it up wide enough so the arrowhead will come out, understand? Whatever you do don't leave the arrowhead in there."

Chester placed the point of the razor-sharp knife right against the shaft of the arrow. He paused, took a deep breath, and gritted his teeth.

"This is gonna hurt, pardner."

"Don't worry about me, just get to cuttin'."

Zack watched throughout the whole ordeal, the only sounds to escape his lips were a few low grunts. When it was over Chester handed the bloody arrow to Zack.

"Might want to keep that for a souvenir."

"Yep, right alongside another."

Chester didn't understand the meaning until the old timer took the knife from Chester's hand and pushed to his feet. He used his rifle as a crutch to hobble over to the dead Indian whose arrowhead Zack clutched in his hand. Kneeling, he grabbed a handful of hair, deftly slit the hide along the Indian's forehead and jerked the scalp loose.

Chester had never seen a man scalped before and he hoped he never did again. His stomach protested the sight he just witnessed and threatened to empty its contents. Bitter bile lodged in his throat. He swallowed repeatedly, but couldn't get it to go away.

"Now you can douse the wound with the rest of that whiskey," Zack told Chester. "Wrap it up with some kind of bandage and I'll be fit as a fiddle."

He had just completed the task when one of the men Chester sent to explore the rest of the canyon rode back in.

"Found our horses, boss. This is a box canyon, no other way out. Bob is bringing 'em out now."

"You heard him, boys. Round 'em up and head 'em home. I'm taking Zack into Del Rio to see the doctor. Carlos, come ride with me. Tell Buck we'll be along in a while."

Zack made the ride to Del Rio as if nothing had happened. Except for the fresh blood that dripped constantly from his boot, one would never know he was wounded.

Chester and Carlos watched as the doctor removed the blood soaked bandage, cleaned the wound with alcohol, and carefully examined the gaping wound.

"Done wasted good drinking whiskey on that, doc," the scout told him.

"Might have kept it from getting infected but, I've got to sew that up. Take a swallow of this, it'll dull the pain some."

He handed a dark bottle of liquid Laudanum to the tough old scout.

"Ain't that stuff dope?" Zack asked.

"Well, it's a pain killer, but some abuse it."

"Nope. Don't want nothing like that, just get on with it."

After the doctor finished and gave Zack some extra bandages and a tin of salve, Chester paid the doctor and thanked him.

"See he keeps that wound clean. Keep that salve on it and change the bandage regularly. Doubt a little thing like an arrow could hurt that tough old codger. Don't get many patients like him."

"Well, see, doc, now that's a good thing right there," Zack told him.

It was nearing suppertime, so Chester took Zack and Carlos up the street to the café.

Selena's face brightened and a wide smile crossed her lips as Chester walked in. She hugged her brother and showed them to a table. Carlos went into the kitchen to see his mother.

"I saw you when you rode into town to Doctor Williams' office. Was someone hurt?"

"Indians raided the ranch last night and stole some horses," Chester explained as Selena poured them all coffee. "We chased them down and got our horses back. Zack took an arrow in his leg."

"How dreadful."

"Weren't nothing but a scratch," Zack said as he blew steam away from his coffee.

"Were you hurt?" she asked, leveling a concerned look squarely at Chester.

"No," he said, feeling his face grow suddenly hot. "What's your mother got cooked? We're as hungry as a bunch of she wolves"

"Our special today is beef enchiladas and brown beans, but she will gladly prepare whatever you would like."

"The special sounds good, just bring us that and lots of it."

"*Si*, as you wish." she said, looking directly at Chester and smiling sweetly.

As she left, Zack leaned close.

"That little lady's got her eyes set on you, boss."

"Naw, she's just being nice to her brother's boss, that's all."

"Last time a gal looked at me like that I woke up the next morning and found out I had a brand new wife."

Selena's mother helped her daughter bring their food to the table. Selena introduced them since Chester never actually met her.

She was an attractive woman, a little on the heavy side, but wore a pleasant smile. Chester could see where the daughter got her beauty.

"It is a pleasure to meet you, *Señora Rodriguez.*"

"My mother does not speak your language," Selena explained, and then repeated in Spanish to her mother what Chester said.

Her mother smiled, said something to her daughter in Spanish, bowed, and returned to the kitchen.

Selena blushed beet-red.

It was dark by the time they finished eating. Carlos and Zack left to get their horses while Chester paid for their meal.

"What did your mother say a while ago?" Chester asked.

"She said that you were very handsome."

It was Chester's turn to blush and he felt the heat rise in his cheeks.

"It was good to see you again," Chester said.

That brought a smile and a prolonged look. Their eyes met. Chester felt something pass between them. Impulsively he reached out and took her hand and held it for a long moment. The thrill of the touch raced directly to his heart. It felt good.

"Then come again soon."

"You can count on it. Hate to go, but we need to get Zack back to the ranch and off that leg."

It was after midnight when Chester and his two companions arrived at the ranch. They were shocked at what they saw. One of the cabins was burned to the ground; the roof of the other was badly burned but could be repaired.

A lamp still burned in the bunkhouse and Chester could smell coffee even before he opened the door. Buck and several of the hands sat around a table talking and sipping coffee. Chester poured himself a cup and joined them.

"See your hunch was right."

"Yep, they hit us just before daylight," Buck said. "You and the boys did a good job getting our horses back."

"Most of the credit goes to Zack. That's one fellow you don't want to rile."

"Hear you took an arrow." Buck said, looking at the scout.

"Nothing worth talking about. The boss cut it out. He'd make a fair hand at doctoring."

"Still and all, you'll be on light duty for the next couple of weeks till that leg heals up," Buck said. "Now I reckon we all better get some sleep. We've got some work waiting on us at first light."

A crew went to work repairing the damaged cabin. They completed the repair and Wash and his family moved back into their cabin within two days. Buck and Chester's cabin would take a week or so, they figured.

They decided that to discourage future Indian attacks they needed to provide more protection for the ranch headquarters. The decision was made to surround the living quarters of the ranch with a thick adobe wall. It would be a large undertaking. But both Buck and Chester agreed they couldn't afford another surprise attack. They might not be so lucky next time. A special crew of Mexican laborers must be hired to handle the enormous project.

They moved the horse herd nearer the compound each night and the nighthawks doubled to four. It was added work for the cowhands, but everyone agreed the extra security was necessary.

Meanwhile, the bush crew became more efficient and captured ever increasing numbers of wild longhorns with each passing day. The sturdy corrals filled to capacity and new ones had to be constructed.

Buck and Chester decided it was time for them to visit Pappy and his operation across the river. They found the place with no problem. All they had to do was follow the deep ruts of the heavy freight wagons. A dozen longhorns were penned up in the heavy log corral waiting to be transported back to the ranch.

As they rode up, two of the vaqueros lassoed a large cow. One rode close on the right side and easily tossed his reata over the wide horns. Another vaquero did the same from the other side. Tightening the slack from their ropes, they made the bucking, fighting longhorn immobile. A third vaquero then rushed in and secured a halter made from heavy rope on the animal and attached the loose end to the back of a nearby waiting wagon.

Pappy rode up as Buck and Chester watched the vaqueros.

"Looks like things are going well," Buck said.

"We sending you enough longhorns?"

"You and the boys are doing a good job. We just rode over to have ourselves a look-see."

"We got us a good crew."

"Any sign of the longhorns thinning out?" Chester asked.

"Naw, we might have to move our operation further upstream after a while, but these critters are thicker than fleas on a dog's back. Ain't no danger of us running out of longhorns."

They hung around and watched for a while then headed back to the ranch.

The following morning Buck saddled his big sorrel and headed into town. A bright, newborn sun was less than an hour old, but already making its presence known by burning away the last remaining remnants of a thick night fog. Herds of cattle munched peacefully on the damp grass and interrupted their grazing only for a moment to raise their heads and stare wide-eyed as Buck rode past.

As he rode he thought of Rebekah.

There had been several girls in Buck's growing up years, but none affected him like Rebekah. Her image consumed his mind since their first meeting. He thought of her day and night.

As he rode toward Del Rio he tried to picture how it would be.

As pretty as she is there's bound to be lots of men beating a path to her door. Did I mistake the looks she gave me? Maybe I read more into the way she looked at me than was really there. What if I do or say something really dumb?

He shook his head and rode on.

The closer he got to Del Rio the more nervous he became. He felt his heart racing inside his chest. His palms made sweat on the reins and saddle horn. He drew a shaky breath and reined up at the small hitching rail in front of the Walker's store.

He was nervous. His legs felt weak as he swung from his horse and his foot touched the ground. He clung to the saddle horn for a long moment.

Drawing a deep breath, he stepped up onto the boardwalk and pushed through the door.

Rebekah looked up from the small desk near the back where she sat tallying up some credit accounts. She had taken on the bookkeeping chores since her mother's death.

She felt a soft smile lift one corner of her lips when she saw the tall, handsome rancher. She couldn't deny that thoughts of him crept into her mind frequently since their first meeting.

He made quite an impression on her with his handsome face, pale blue, penetrating eyes, and shoulder-length hair the color of ripe wheat on a summer morning. She strongly suspected that behind his few words and almost bashful manner, lurked a giant of a man.

"Good Morning," she greeted cheerfully. "You are up awfully early this morning."

Buck touched his hat brim.

"Yes, ma'am. Never learned to sleep past daylight."

"I'm still waiting on that invitation to show me your ranch."

"Soon as we get it presentable you'll be my first visitor. Right now it's not fit for anybody to see, let alone a pretty lady."

"Why thank you, kind sir," she said, a mischievous smile lifting one corner of her mouth. "I'm going to consider that a compliment."

"Meant to be. Is John here this morning?"

"He's down at the barber shop, but I hoped you came to see me," she kidded.

"Truth is, I did. Talking to your father was the only excuse I could come up with."

"You don't need an excuse," she said, surprising herself for being so flirty.

Suddenly she felt jittery and breathless. Something swept over her. Her chest tightened, her heart thundered thick and loud beneath her ribs. A feeling of seriousness overwhelmed her.

As if her eyes had a mind of their own her gaze found his. He looked down at her for a very long time, his eyes unfathomable, and his bright gaze holding hers.

But in that moment of time she felt something beyond words pass between them, something scary yet beautiful, something sudden yet eternal. A warm shiver raced through her body. A feeling she never felt before. *Is it possible to fall in love with a man the moment your eyes touched his?* she wondered.

She saw Buck's face flush red. Somehow she knew that he felt it, too. His eyes dropped. He shuffled his feet, his eyes examining the toes of his boots.

He glanced up. Their gazes met again and held for a short slice of eternity. She got the distinct feeling that he was staring directly into her very soul, that he was reading her thoughts. She felt herself blush.

She saw Buck swallow hard, and then swallow again before he forced the words out.

"Might better mosey on down to the barber shop before I say something real dumb."

"I can't imagine you ever saying anything dumb."

"That's because you don't know me."

"Well, that's true, not yet anyway."

"I'd like to change that," he managed to say.

"So would I."

"Good,—I mean glad to hear it. Well, I better be getting on. I need to ask your father something."

"Glad you stopped in. Do it again soon?"

"Count on it. Good day," he said, again touching the brim of his hat.

As he left the store he felt light headed. He would be hard pressed to swear that his boots even touched the ground as he made his way to the barbershop.

Rebekah walked slowly to the window. Her gaze followed Buck until he entered the barbershop down the street. When he disappeared from sight she closed her eyes and waited for her heart to stop pounding in her throat, for her legs to stop quivering.

The vitality of his presence overwhelmed her like a river in flood, sweeping all caution aside, filling her with a boldness she never knew before, giving birth to impossible dreams.

Who is this gentle giant who walked into my life?

Buck found John Walker in the barber's chair getting a haircut and shave.

"Howdy, Buck. Didn't know you were in town. You met Sam Taylor yet? Sam's the best barber in town."

"What John means is that I'm the *only* barber in town."

"Morning to you, John, Mr. Taylor."

"What are you doing in town so early on Monday morning?"

"Lookin' to hire a crew of Mexican laborers that know how to make and lay adobe brick. Know anybody like that?"

"Juan Santos."

"Who's he?"

"Best in the business, at least in this neck of the woods. He can build anything that's made of adobe. What you got in mind to build?"

"Gonna build a wall around the ranch headquarters. Figure it might slow down the next Indian attack."

"Reckon it might at that. Talk is you boys sent a passel of 'em to the happy hunting ground when they hit your place the other night. Maybe they'll leave you alone."

"Not likely. Where can I find this Santos fellow?"

"I'll send him word and tell him to come see you. How many workers you looking for?"

"Whatever he needs to do the job."

"I'll tell him."

Buck left the barbershop and stopped by to see Pete, who ran the livery and also served as the town blacksmith.

"Mornin' Mr. Cordell. How's them wagons working out?"

"Good. Pappy's keeping them busy. I'm gonna need some branding irons."

"Be glad to make up whatever you want."

Buck picked up a stick and scraped three vertical lines side by side in the dirt, the first one half as long as the second two. He then attached a horizontal arm to the bottom of the first line and crossed the center of the two remaining lines with it, forming a large LH.

"Can you make me some branding Irons like that?"

"The Longhorn brand, huh? Shore can. How many you gonna need?"

"Twenty ought to do it, I reckon. When can you have them ready?"

"Few days, maybe a week."

"Fair enough. I'll pick 'em up in a week."

"Sounds like you're gonna do some brandin."

"Some."

"Obliged fer the business, I'll have 'em ready fer ye."

Buck looped the reins across his sorrel's neck and threaded a stirrup with the toe of his boot. He swung a leg over and settled in his saddle.

As he walked his horse up the street he fought desperately to deny the temptation to stop by the store again. He had only seen her twice and yet, thoughts of her had completely consumed his mind. It was as if some higher power ordained that they meet, that they be together. Somehow he believed she felt that, too. She was a spunky lady. He liked that.

He glanced at the window as he rode past hoping to get just one more glance at Rebekah. She wasn't there. He heeled his sorrel into a short lope and headed home.

It was nearing dusky-dark when Buck reined to a stop at the edge of the Sycamore River. Just across the shallow crossing lay the beginning of the Longhorn Ranch. He allowed his gelding to dip its nose in the water to slake its thirst. Casually he watched the horse drink. His mind was on Rebekah.

He was drawn back to the present by the familiar feeling that haunted him many times during the war. A presence. His sixth sense told him he was not alone.

Flicking a searching look, he saw him.

Sitting barely visible half-in and half-out of a thick stand of sycamore saplings on the far bank sat the same Comanche warrior chief he saw the night of the attack. As before, his face was painted half-white and half-black. He sat motionless atop a black and white pinto A rifle lay across his legs in front of him.

For a breathless moment both men stared at the other, making no threatening move toward a weapon.

"I Quanah, chief of Quahadi Comanche," the Indian called across the river.

An avalanche of bitter anger surged over Buck. His mind immediately flashed a picture of the graves of his mother and father. Sitting before him was the man that had slaughtered his folks and most likely kidnapped his little brother.

"You chief of white eyes that build on Comanche hunting ground. You leave or you all die."

Buck's mind raced, weighing his options. He held no hope of reaching his rifle resting in the saddle boot underneath his right leg. On the other hand the Comanche's rifle lay within easy reach only a heartbeat away.

The distance was over fifty yards, too far for an accurate handgun shot and if he tried it he would be a sitting duck for the Indian's rifle. The Comanche chief had him at a distinct disadvantage.

Suddenly, within the space of an eye blink, the Indian vanished. One second he was there, the next he had disappeared like a vapor. Buck's hand dipped to grasp the stock of his rifle and slid it free. He levered a shell and kicked his sorrel into a plunging run across the river.

He spent the next hour searching for the Comanche's tracks but, like the Indian himself, they were nowhere to be found. Darkness shrouded the land and forced him to abandon his search.

Buck was puzzled. *That Indian had me cold. He could have picked me off before I knew he was anywhere around. Wonder why he didn't?*

Chapter X

Chester sat his saddle, his leg looped casually around the saddle horn. He was inspecting one of their herds and passing the time of day with one of the hands assigned to watching out for that particular herd.

One of the drag wagons with four newly captured longhorns trailing behind lumbered toward the holding corral. Chester glanced that direction, and then looked closer. Pappy rode beside the wagon, something he never did. Pappy never came back to the ranch in the middle of the day unless something was wrong. Chester straightened in the saddle and headed for Pappy at a gallop.

As he reined up, a wide smile on Pappy's face told Chester that whatever news the brush popper had, it wasn't bad news.

"What's up, Pappy?"

"I saw him. All them stories about El Toro ain't just Tequila talk after all. I saw him with my own eyes."

"You sure?"

"Sure as snuff makes spit, I'm sure. I was herding half a

dozen critters into the funnel. All of a sudden the hair on the back of my neck stood up. I looked around. He was standing in a clearing not fifty yards from me.

"Biggest and meanest looking dang bull I ever laid eyes on. He was blacker than the blackest midnight with horns wider than my outstretched arms and big around as my leg. He just stood there staring at me and pawing the ground. Don't mind telling you he give me the creeps."

"What happened?"

"I glanced around for one of the vaqueros. When I looked back he had just vanished like a ghost or something. I rode over and found his tracks. His hoof prints were a double hand span across and deeper than a finger's length.

"I tried following him, but lost him in the thickets."

"You're gonna try to catch him, ain't you?"

"Sure as God made little green apples, I am. That's what I rode in to ask you."

"Long as you and your men can keep the count up, I got no objections."

"Never seen anything like him. I doubt there's another bull alive like this critter. Boss, if we could catch this big fellow, he'd single-handedly make your ranch the talk of Texas."

"Then what are you sitting here for? Go get after him."

Pappy let out a cowboy yell that would wake the dead. He sawed the reins and took off back the way he came at a hard gallop.

Reaching the river crossing just outside Del Rio, he urged his mount down into the muddy water. It was the only crossing for miles. The river at this point crossed a rock shelf and was wide and fairly shallow, normally belly deep to a horse. A heavy rain upstream made the river impassable.

He felt excited. The thought of capturing the legendary bull he heard stories about for years made his stomach do flip-flops.

As his horse splashed across the wide river, his mind laid out his plan. He planned to take only one vaquero with him, Pedro Sedillo. *Yep, he's the one to take,* Pappy reasoned *He's the best man with a reatas I ever seen. I'll leave Carlos in charge of the others while we're gone. He will see that the daily quota is met.*

With his plan laid, he was anxious to get to camp and set his idea in motion.

Just before good dark he gathered his vaqueros around the fire in their camp and laid it all out. News of the sighting had already spread among his men, it was all they talked about over supper.

Pappy hardly slept a wink all night. He got up and packed his saddlebags well before daylight.

By first light both he and Pedro knelt beside El Toro's huge hoof prints. Pappy reached a hand, tracing the width and depth of the prints with a gloved finger.

"If I hadn't seen that bull with my own eyes I would never believe a longhorn that big ever lived," Pappy said, shaking his head in disbelief at the size of the prints.

"What if we find him?" Pedro asked. "How are we going to capture him?"

"Just like always, we come at him from two sides, both of us get a rope on him and keep the ropes tight, keeping him between us."

Pedro only grunted, it was obvious he didn't agree with the plan, but didn't dare question his boss's decision.

They followed the tracks for a week. The trail led them through some of the roughest terrain either of them had ever seen: up deep, winding arroyos, along treacherous mountain trails that clung to the side of sheer cliffs where one misstep would plunge horse and rider a hundred feet to a rock strewn canyon below. It led through fields of thorn covered cactus and thickets of mesquite and scrub cedar so dense they sometimes had to follow the trail on hands and knees. It was as if El Toro somehow sensed it was being followed and deliberately chose the route he took.

On the eighth day the trail had come full circle. It led into the muddy water of the Rio Grande. They followed the trail for a full week and ended up within a few miles from where they started.

They rode the river for several miles in both directions but could never find where the bull had left the water; its tracks simply vanished. Frustrated and discouraged, they returned to camp.

Chester told Buck about Pappy seeing the El Toro and that he gave permission to see if they could capture the mysterious bull.

"Well, if anybody can catch him, I figure Pappy's the man who can do it."

Buck told Chester about his encounter with the Comanche chief and the threat he made.

"I expect we better hurry up that wall around the ranch complex," Buck told his partner. "I figure we'll be seeing more of that painted devil than we want to right soon."

Juan Santos, his two sons, and three other workers showed up two days later. Buck and Chester met with them, explained what they wanted built, and agreed on hiring all six for forty dollars a month and keep.

They brought all the tools and molds they needed on a small cart pulled by a donkey and went to work immediately.

The men would build a wall around the entire headquarters buildings. A spacious courtyard left inside the wall to allow for future expansion of the buildings. When completed, the wall would be twelve feet high and three feet thick. It would have a wide gate in the front and a smaller gate in the back. A wooden walkway must be attached inside the wall, six feet off the ground. This would allow the defenders inside to fire at any attackers while protected by the thick wall.

Ray Ledbetter and Smokey Cunningham were promoted to top hands and were given the responsibility for the herds. Buck or Chester, or both if possible, would meet with the two men each morning to get a report and lay out any plans.

On Friday morning all four gathered around a table in the chow hall. Buck became the last to pour his coffee and sit down.

"How are the herds coming along?" He asked.

"Herd number one is doing good," Ray said over the rim of his coffee cup. "Still got a few bunch quitters in herd number two. I put hobbles on 'em until they settle down. The boys in my crew are fat and happy."

"What about you, Smokey? Any problems?"

"Nope. Seems like my two herds have settled in. The grass along the Sycamore is holding up."

"Just a few days until Christmas," Buck said. "We'd like to give the boys a couple days off. Work out your own schedules. Just make sure everything is covered. I want double guards around the remuda. Have every man keep his rifle within easy reach. I want extra guards around the complex at night. I don't want Quanah and his men surprising us.

"I'm having the smithy in town make up some branding irons. We put a couple of hands to building a branding chute that ought to make a big job a little easier. We'll start the branding right after Christmas. Any problems or questions?"

Both of the top hands shook their heads.

"Then we're burning daylight."

As they walked out of the chow hall one of the hands down by the barn shouted, "Rider coming in!"

A bearded fellow riding a gray walked his horse toward them. He reined up a few yards away appearing nervous. He was careful to keep his hands well away from the Smith & Wesson tied to his hip.

"One of you fellows named Chester Colson?"

"Yeah, I'm Chet Colson. Who might you be?"

"Name's Rueben Gilbert. Friend of mine wants to see you."

"Who is this friend and why does he want to see me?"

"His name is Wade Bridger, I 'spect you've heard the name. He says to meet him at the cantina in Piedras Negras, said you'd know the place. Said to be there at sundown tomorrow."

"Tell him I'll be there."

The bearded man cut a grin, wheeled his horse, and rode off.

"What was that all about?" Buck asked.

"That's the brother of the fellow I killed over in Del Rio not long ago. This Wade Bridger is supposed to be some kind of famous gunfighter or something."

"I'm going with you."

"No, I got to stomp my own snakes, I'll go alone."

"You'll need back-up. You can bet your boots he'll have plenty of guns behind him."

"Stay here and take care of things at the ranch. I'll handle it."

"At least take some of the boys with you. It would make me rest easier."

"If it will make you feel better, I'll ask Pedro Sedillo and a couple of the other vaqueros to ride along. Ray, how about sending a man across the river and asking Pedro and a couple of his men to ride over tonight? Tell him what it's about. Tell him to bring only those who want to come. Tell him what's involved."

"I'd like to ride along and side you myself, boss."

"Me, too," Smokey said.

"Obliged to both of you, but I think the Mexicans might blend in better than you boys would."

"Can I say something, Chester?" Buck asked.

"Say what suits you."

"You don't have to go," Buck suggested. "He wouldn't dare come here to the ranch."

"If it was you he called out, what would *you* do?"

"I think you know."

"Then you know what I have to do. I couldn't live with myself if I turned tail. I've never crawfished from nothing in my life and don't intend to start now."

It was just about suppertime when Pedro Sedillo, Jose, Poncho, and one of the newest vaqueros named, Manual rode up to the corral.

Chester saw them and walked down. He shook hands with all four.

"Much obliged for coming. Did they tell you what this is all about?"

"*Si, señor*."

"Want to make sure you all understand this is a voluntary thing. No one will think less of you if you don't want to go."

"My only problem was picking only three. All of our vaqueros wanted to ride with you."

The words lifted a grin on Chester's face. "Let's go up to the chow hall and stretch our bellies."

Over supper Pedro filled them in on their failure to catch El Toro.

"He is like a ghost," Pedro said, his dark eyes widening. "I think no man will ever catch him."

"Well, maybe not," Buck said, "but if any man can, Pappy is the man to do it."

"Did you ever see this critter?"

"*No, señor*, Pappy is the only one to actually see him."

"So, has Pappy given up the hope of catching him?"

"Oh, no. He is even more determined than ever. He says if it is the last thing he does he will catch this El Toro."

"Then I'd lay odds on it."

* * *

Chester couldn't sleep. He tossed and turned all night. Although he had faced several men that were good with a gun, he never faced a gunfighter with a reputation like Wade Bridger.

What if he's as fast as they say he is? What if I'm not good enough? I don't want to fight this man, but I have no choice. I'd rather die than turn tail and run. I'll fight him and let the chips fall where they may.

When the first hint of gray tinted the eastern sky, Chester swung his legs over the side of the bunk to the floor. He pulled on his pants, stomped into his boots, and sleeved into a clean shirt. After washing his face in the pan of water beside the window, he clamped his hat on and swung his gun belt around his waist and buckled it in place. Leaning over, he knotted the rawhide tie down around his leg.

Pedro and his companions already sat in the chow hall sipping coffee.

"Mornin', Mr. Chester" Wash greeted, somewhat subdued.

"Morning, Wash."

Chester poured himself a cup of coffee and found a place at the table with Pedro and the others. They mostly stared into their coffee cups. Buck entered, poured a cup, and sat down at the table. An unwelcome silence hovered over the room.

This seemed like a funeral wake. It was clear to Chester that everyone in the room already counted him out. They thought he was going to lose.

"Has anyone here seen this Wade Bridger pull iron?" Chester asked.

They all looked from one to the other and slowly shook their heads.

"Then why is everybody already counting me a dead man?"

Buck put words to everyone's thoughts. "It isn't that we

don't believe in you, Chester, we do. It's just that no one knows what to say."

"What about wishing me good luck? Lord knows I'm most likely gonna need it."

That broke the ice. One after the other each man stood and shook Chester's hand and wished him good luck.

The afternoon sun still a good hour from the western horizon when Chester and his men reined up on the outskirts of Piedras Negras, just across the Rio Grande River from Eagle Pass.

It was a bustling community. A sorry collection of scattered adobe huts dotted the desert landscape surrounding the town. Flat roofed buildings lined the single, dusty street. Sandal-clad men with stooped shoulders and wide sombreros slowly made their way home from whatever work they found to scrape out a meager existence.

Tired looking horses with Mexican rigging stood hip-shot at hitching rails in front of a half dozen cantinas, swishing flies away with their tails. The only exception was the largest cantina in town. Five horses with Texas saddles stood tied there.

"They'll be in that one," Chester said, pointing a gloved finger. "At least I expect Bridger will be. Unless I miss my guess, he'll have some men on the rooftops for back-up. Is there any kind of law in this town?"

"The only law in Piedras Negras is the one a man wears on his hip," Pedro said. "Jose, take Poncho and Manual *to shoot* any ambushers you find on the roof. I will stay with the boss and watch his back."

The three vaqueros reined their mounts behind the line of buildings and disappeared from sight.

Chester and Pedro heeled their horse forward and rode slowly down the street. A Texan leaning against a post in front of the cantina suddenly threw down his half-smoked cigarette and hurried inside.

They reined into two empty spots at the hitching rail and stepped down. Then looped reins around the rail and used their hats to brush the dust off their clothes before stepping through the open door of the cantina.

The sickening smell of sour whiskey, cigarette smoke, and dirty bodies burned their noses as they stopped just inside the door to allow their eyes to adjust to the dim light.

A long plank resting across two upturned barrels served as a bar. A bearded bartender with a filthy apron tied around his bulging waist glanced up as Chester and Pedro stepped inside. Chester saw the man's eyes flick quickly to a table where three Americans sat sipping whiskey.

The three men were a contrast in appearance. One was a huge bear of a man with a barrel chest and a full beard. Long, scraggly hair pushed from under a floppy hat. The second man was tall, skinny as a rail, and sickly-looking. He wore a black bowler hat that looked out of place with his cowhand work clothes and worn out boots. He had nervous eyes and wore his gun tied low on his left hip.

But it was the third man who caught and held Chester's attention. He was a tall man, rangy and long boned. Chester guessed him to be in his late twenties, dressed nattily in a business suit and a wide, flat-crowned Stetson. His coat lay partially open, exposing a pearl handled Colt in a cross draw belly holster.

That would be Wade Bridger, Chester decided.

All three men twisted around in their chairs to stare at the two newcomers. Chester returned their look with a cold, hard stare of his own.

He felt, rather than saw, Pedro ease off to one side. The Mexican found an empty spot and stood with his back to the bar, facing the three gringos Chester was staring at.

Chester crossed the floor to within ten foot of the three men before speaking.

"I'm Chet Colson. I heard you wanted to see me."

Bridger pushed up from his chair slowly and turned to face Chester. His slow gaze searched the full length of him twice before settling upon the tied down Colt on Chester's hip.

His pale green eyes looked cold and hard and reflected a burning hatred as they fixed on Chester. Bridger's jaw muscles flexed and the veins in his neck bulged. For a long moment the two men stared at one another.

"Yeah, I want to see you. I'm Wade Bridger."

"That supposed to mean something to me?"

"You killed two of my brothers."

"One of your brothers was a murdering horse thief who hung a helpless old man and stole our horses. Your other brother fancied himself as some sort of gunfighter. Turned out he wasn't. He threw down on me and I had to kill him."

Bridger, clearly shaken, exploded in rage.

"You're a dirty rotten liar. I'm gonna kill you where you stan—"

He never got to finish his words. Faster than an eye could follow Chester's hand streaked to his Colt, drew it, and put a bullet in the center of the gunfighter's forehead. The bullet left only a small, brownish hole where it entered the gunfighter's forehead, but the back of his head exploded like a ripe watermelon where it came out. Blood splayed like a rain shower.

Bridger's hand never touched the pearl handled sidearm in his belly holster. His body flew backward. In the split second it took for Bridger's body to hit the dirt floor of the cantina, the two men at Bridger's table leaped to their feet and clawed for their guns.

Pedro stepped forward, two cocked guns pointed squarely at the two men.

"NO, *gringos!*" he shouted.

The men took one look and froze, their hands halfway to their guns.

Silence fell like a dark shroud over the cantina. Blue smoke curled up from the nose of Chester's Colt and licked his hand like a hungry serpent.

He stepped over to stand above the lifeless body of Wade Bridger and gazed down at him for a moment. "You talked too much."

Reaching down, he withdrew the pearl handled weapon from the dead gunfighter and stuffed it behind his belt.

Crossing the room, he relieved the gunfighter's two companions of their guns.

"It weren't a fair fight," the one in the bowler hat snarled. "He never went for his gun."

"Fair or not, when a man tells me he's gonna kill me, I take him at his word. Tell you boys one more thing, I ever see you again, I'll kill you where you stand. Are we clear on that?"

Both men nodded.

"Now fork your horses and make tracks fast and far."

The men scrambled across the room and through the door. In a few heartbeats the sound of galloping horses thundered through the gathering darkness.

Chester and Pedro made their way outside to their horses, mounted and walked their horses slowly down the dusty street. Men from the cantina cautiously moved outside to watch the gringos ride away. Jose, Poncho, and Manual emerged from behind the row of buildings, nodded to their companions, and reined their mounts in behind their boss.

Two days before Christmas Buck rode into Del Rio. Since his encounter with the Comanche chief at the river Buck rode with his rifle in his hand on the trip into town but his ride was uneventful.

His heart hovered in his throat as he tied his mount in front of Walker's store. He paused at the door, cleared his throat, and took a deep breath before stepping inside.

Rebekah was restocking a shelf near the front window. Her long red hair fell loose around her shoulders. The morning sun shining through the window set her hair ablaze with the light of a million candles. Her beauty took his breath away.

"Good morning, Buck."

Her lingering gaze fixed upon him and melted his heart right down into his boots.

"Good morning, Rebekah," he managed to get out.

"I'm so glad you came into town. I've been trying to figure out how to get word to you. I talked to father. We were wondering if you would consider haveing Christmas dinner with us."

Buck's heart almost leaped out of his chest. A flush of hotness crept up his neck. He couldn't believe his ears. She actually asked him to dinner, and not just dinner, *Christmas dinner*.

It took all of his strength just to catch his breath let, alone put sound to a word. He swallowed and then swallowed again.

"I'd like that."

"Then we'll expect you by twelve, but you can come earlier if you'd like."

"Twelve will be fine. Oh, almost forgot what I came for. Need a couple of Christmas gifts for Wash and Jewel's children. What do you have for a little boy who is six and a girl about five?

"Hmm, let me think a minute. We just got in a shipment of beautiful dolls not long ago, I'll see what's left."

She walked over and withdrew a black haired little doll. It had a beautiful pink dress and a matching bonnet. She handed it to Buck for his inspection.

"What about that for the girl?"

"Perfect. I'll take it."

"You're a man. What would you have liked for Christmas when you were a little boy?"

"Don't think I was ever a *little* boy."

She laughed. He liked to hear her laugh.

"Well, judging by the size you are now, I tend to agree with you."

"Say, you wouldn't by chance have a pair of chaps that would fit a six-year-old boy would you? I notice he's always hanging around the hands at the ranch."

"Matter of fact I just might. Let me look."

She searched three different boxes stacked in the corner before she found what she was looking for. She pulled out a pair of leather chaps with fringe along the legs. They looked to be the perfect size.

"Would these work?" she asked, handing them to Buck.

As she did their hands accidentally touched. That single brush of their hands raced up his arm and straight to his heart. Neither made an effort to move. As if they had a mind of their own, his fingers curled around hers.

Her eyes lifted to meet his. Time stood still. They stared deep into each other's eyes for a long moment. He saw a far-away look glaze her eyes. Her lips opened. He heard her breathing become heavy and short.

Buck felt the energy surging through his body, blazing, compelling. He took a tentative step nearer. His heart pounded like a drum. He felt her fingers squeeze his. She lifted her face. He slowly lowered his. As one, they breached the small distance between their lips.

Rebekah's head spun like a child's toy. She tingled all over. The touch of their hands had set off ripples of awareness in her. She felt dazed, as if she had suddenly been transported into another world.

Something in her mind told her this was a pivotal point in her life. If she allowed him to kiss her there would be no turning back. She would never be the same again. But she wanted, she *needed* to explore the irresistible desire that flooded through her, hot and aching and precious beyond all reason.

She felt his lips touch hers, soft and gentle and full. She became vaguely aware of his strong arm gathering her to himself. She tingled from head to toe. Her arm went around his neck and gathered a handful of his shirt where it strained across his wide shoulders. She needed to draw him closer. She closed her eyes and allowed herself to be consumed by a feeling so strong, so beautiful, a feeling she never knew existed.

Christmas Eve arrived. Somebody cut a small cedar tree and Jewel decorated it with strings of popcorn. Wash baked two large turkeys one of the cowhands had shot. Baked sweet potatoes, turnips, and fresh-baked bread rounded off the Christmas dinner.

After the delicious meal they all watched Wash and Jewel's two children open the presents Buck bought for them. It gave him a good feeling to see them so happy.

When things settled down Buck pushed to his feet and raised a hand for quiet.

"Boys, you have all done a job you can be proud of. You've worked hard. The ranch is starting to take shape. Chester and I couldn't be prouder.

"We decided to show our appreciation by giving every man a month's bonus and two days off. Tomorrow is Christmas. Take a couple of days off and enjoy yourselves. Be back here in two days, ready to go to work. We'll be starting trail branding a week from tomorrow. Merry Christmas."

* * *

A cold, icy wind moaned through the trees along the Sycamore River as Buck splashed across the ford. Even though he rode alert, his sweeping gaze searching every bush, every clump of trees, he couldn't help stifling a yawn with a gloved hand and pulling his sheepskin coat higher around his neck. He had hardly slept a wink the night before.

The events in the Walker store changed everything. Thoughts of Rebekah filled every waking moment. Whether he was brushing his horse or repairing a rail in the corral fence, whether riding out to check on the herds or sipping coffee in the chow hall, her image remained always there.

After their kiss, their embrace, the unspoken promises exchanged through their eyes, he couldn't imagine life without Rebekah being a part of it.

Then it hit him like a runaway wagon, how could he face John Walker? How could he act as if nothing happened between him and Rebekah?

It will show on my face, I know it will. One look and her father will know.

Buck was shocked to discover himself reining up at the hitching post at the Walker home. Without even realizing it he had ridden the entire ten miles thinking of nothing except Rebekah.

The Walker home was a simple frame house with a whitewashed picket fence around it, located at the edge of town no more than a half mile from their store. Smoke trailed upward from a rock chimney on one end of the house. A small barn off to one side was surrounded by a split rail corral. A beautiful palomino mare trotted to stick her head over the fence and nicker.

He was still tying his gray gelding to the hitching post when the front door opened and Rebekah stepped out onto the porch.

He felt his heart skip a few beats at the sight of her. She wore a deep green ankle length satin dress that buttoned at the neck. Her auburn hair cascaded over her shoulders and was tied with a ribbon that matched her dress.

On the ride into town he had practiced what to say, but now, after seeing her, all of his plans went right out the window. He stood speechless. All of his courage drained right down into his boots.

A wide smile lifted her lips as she hurried off the porch to greet him.

"I thought you would never get here," she said. "I've been looking for you all morning."

"Thought you said twelve o'clock."

"I did, just hoped you might get here earlier. Come on in, father is expecting you."

Reaching a hand, she threaded her fingers with his as they walked side by side to the house. It felt good. She released his hand before they stepped through the door.

Wonderful smells from the kitchen greeted his nose. "Something sure smells good."

"I hope it's good," Rebekah said. "Seems like nothing turned out the way I wanted it to."

John Walker rose from a rocking chair in front of the fireplace. He removed a pipe from his mouth and extended a hand in greeting.

"Welcome to our home, Buck. Mighty glad you could come and share Christmas dinner with us."

"Much obliged for asking."

"Have a seat," he said, motioning to a second rocker nearby.

Buck folded his big frame into the chair. It squeaked in protest of his weight.

"Tell me," Mr. Walker asked. "Did that Santos fellow and his crew ever come by? I sent word for him to come by and see what you wanted done."

"Yes, sir. We hired him and his two sons and three other workers to help. But after seeing the size of the job we had in mind, he sent for a dozen more men. They've already started on the wall and are making good progress."

"We don't hold with formalities here, son, how about just calling me John?"

"Yes, s—uh, John."

"Well, glad he's working out. I'd like to ride out one of these days and take a look at your ranch. I'll say one thing, you boys shore got a lot of sand building a ranch smack-dab in the middle of the Nueces strip.

"What with that being the favorite hunting ground for the Apache and Comanche both, not to mention the outlaw element that do whatever they take a notion to in that neck of the woods. Truth is most folks hereabouts are laying odds you won't last a year."

"Well, even that prediction is an improvement. Some said earlier we wouldn't last a month. Hope you didn't put down money against us lasting. We're here and we're gonna stay."

"I've been hinting for an invitation to see his ranch," Rebekah said from the kitchen. "He keeps putting me off."

Buck swung a look at her. She gave him one of her mischievous smiles.

"I'll be right proud to show both of you the ranch just as soon as we get something worth looking at."

"I hear tell your boys are pulling a passel of longhorns outta them thickets. Everybody in town is talking about it."

"Yeah, Pappy and the boys are doing a good job. Did you hear that he actually got a look at El Toro?"

"Yep, news like that travels fast."

"They tracked him for a week before they lost his trail."

"That's a shame. Wouldn't that be something if they could actually capture him?

"Sure would."

"There's something I've been meaning to talk with you about," Buck said. "We'll be taking some longhorns up the trail to Missouri come April. I was wondering if you knew where you could lay your hands on about forty or so .52 caliber Spencer saddle guns with a Blakeslee Quick-Loader."

"Don't see why not. Ain't that the one the Union used during the war?"

"That's the one. It fires a rim-fire cartridge as fast as a man can work the lever. It holds seven in a tube in the butt stock. The Yanks said you could load it on Monday and fire it all week. I'd need about five hundred cartridges, too."

"I'll go to work on it first thing in the morning."

"If you men can stop talking long enough, dinner is on the table," Rebekah announced.

She had gone all out. Turkey roasted to a golden brown with giblet gravy, dressing, mashed potatoes, and black-eyed peas. Hot rolls with honey, and an apple pie rounded out the meal.

"I never had finer," Buck said after he cleaned up his third plateful.

That earned him a soft smile and a lingering look.

After dinner Buck and Rebekah sat on a sofa, while John sat in his rocking chair. They visited for another hour or so. Sitting so close to her, Buck could feel the warmth of her presence. He fought the urge to take her in his arms and hold her close. Her frequent glances told him that she was feeling similar urges.

"I hate to run out on you, Buck, but I've got a pen full of chickens out behind the store I need to feed and water."

"Yeah, I better be going, Buck said, beginning to stand up.

"No, please don't go," Rebekah, said. "I've hardly had a chance to visit with you."

"By all means, Buck, stay for a while, I won't be gone long."

He sat back down.

After John left, Rebekah reached for Buck's hand. For a long moment their hands coupled, their fingers laced together. The thrill of her touch sent ripples of excitement racing through his entire being. Their gazes joined.

He reached a hand and brushed his knuckles along her soft cheek.

"So soft," he whispered. "So beautiful, so wonderful."

Rebekah's breath caught in a short gasp at the gentle touch of her cheek. She felt as if she were in a trance. Gazing deep into his eyes, she saw her own yearning mirrored in his. Ever since they had kissed in the store, she had dreamed of nothing else. She wanted more, much more, more than she had ever wanted anything in her life.

She leaned closer. Her lips parted. She raised her mouth to his. He kissed her. He kissed her long, and soft, and slowly. He kissed her with a sweet, simmering intensity that made her head swim and her bones dissolve.

They started branding on January 1.

"Counting the ones Pappy and his crew have brought in we've got over three thousand head to brand," Ray Ledbetter informed them at their regular morning meeting. "By the time we start the drive we ought to have doubled that. We'll still be branding when the drive begins."

"I've got a crazy idea," Chester said. "What would you think about taking two herds up the trail, with maybe twenty-five hundred in each bunch? We could pick out the best thousand brood cows for a foundation herd to stock the ranch with and drive the rest to market?"

All around the table their mouths dropped open. The room grew silent. For a time they all sat in silent contemplation, considering Chester's idea. Smokey was the first to speak.

"I like it. I like it a lot."

"So do I," Buck said. "Think we could make it work?"

"Don't see why not," Ray said. "No different than taking one, we just duplicate what we were gonna do."

"We'd need another chuck wagon and cook. We'd also need another crew. That'll mean hiring another twenty or so trail hands. Ray, would you and Smokey be our trail bosses for the drive? That would leave me and Chester free to watch over the entire operation."

"Be glad to, boss," Ray said.

"Me, too," Smokey agreed.

"Sounds good," Buck said excitedly. "We'll start looking to hire some more hands. We can use them to help with the branding. That will give us a chance to look them over before we start the drives."

"We might want to keep the herds separated by a day or so. It would make them easier to handle in case of a stampede. We'd still be close enough to help one another in case of trouble."

"Good idea," Chester said "We still need someone to stay here and watch out for the ranch while we're gone, Got any ideas?"

"My feeling is that one of us needs to do it," Buck said. "We've got to much going on right here to look out for. And with the Indians always watching for an opening to hit us I don't see how both of us can be gone for three months."

"You're better with the business end of the business," Chester suggested. "As bad as I'd like to make the drive, why don't you, Ray, and Smokey make the drive? I'll stay here and look after things at the ranch."

Everyone was quiet for a minute before Buck spoke. "If that's what you want to do?"

"Can't say that's what I want to do, but I feel strong that it's what we need to do. I'll take the next drive up the trail."

"Then it's decided. Let's get to it," Buck said, "Branding three thousand head of cattle is a big undertaking, it's dangerous, back-breaking work that begins while it's still too dark to see and ends when it gets too dark to see. After a long, tiring day cowboys drag themselves to the chow hall, wolf down some supper, and then fall into their bunks. Before daylight they roll out, eat breakfast, and do it all over again. But such is the life of a cowboy."

They all nodded agreement.

Buck was working the back chute pole. A mounted cowboy in the corral would drive a cow into a long, narrow chute barely wide enough to squeeze through. Buck's job was to slide a sturdy pole across the chute behind the longhorn, while Chester did the same in front of it, thereby trapping the animal.

A brander stuck a red-hot branding iron between the rails of the chute and brand the critter. Chester withdrew his pole allowing the animal to exit the chute. Buck removed his, permitting another unbranded longhorn to be driven into the chute.

Over and over, longhorn after longhorn, it seemed there was no end to it.

"Wagon coming!" somebody yelled.

Buck swung a look and immediately knew something was wrong.

Pappy and his entire crew of vaqueros accompanied the wagon. Buck and Chester dropped their chute poles and trotted to meet the wagon. Not a word was spoken as they reached the wagon. They looked inside and saw a canvas-covered body.

Buck glanced from the body to Pappy with a questioning look before reaching a hand to turn back the canvas.

It was Jose, one of Carlos's cousins. Jose's brother, Pablo sat his horse with his head lowered.

"What happened?"

Pappy took a moment to reply. Buck waited.

"He went into the thickets to flush out a couple of critters. El Toro was waiting on him. The tale of the tracks say the bull charged Jose's horse. Once he got the horse down, he gored Jose and his horse to death. As you can see, ain't much left."

Buck drew in a large inhale and let it out on a long sigh, all the while shaking his head sadly.

He swung a look to Pablo.

"You'll be needing to let your family know. See where they want him buried. We can do it here if you want. If that's what they want, you'll need to bring the family and a priest. Carlos, ride with him. Rent whatever buggies or wagons you need from the livery I'll settle up with him later."

They buried Jose the following day next to Eli under the big Oak tree. Every cowboy on the Longhorn attended the sad occasion.

Days slipped quickly by and turned into weeks, then weeks into months. Spring arrived. Mother earth gave birth to fresh, green grass and the herds of cattle thrived. They were putting on weight.

Buck and Chester hired thirty additional hands. They knew they would need twenty for the second herd they intended to take on the trail. Another ten were needed to round out the twenty men who would stay behind to protect the ranch and look after the thousand head of brood cattle.

Wash located another chuck wagon and another cook. His name was Joshua, Jewel's first cousin. It was only two more weeks before the trail drive began.

Buck and Chester kept an eye on the building of the wall

around their compound. Santos and his workers worked amazingly fast and efficiently.

Buck found time to ride into town only once since Christmas. Here it was the middle of March and in two weeks he would be leaving for at least three months. He missed Rebekah already.

At breakfast on Saturday, Buck told Chester he was riding into town. His partner lifted a grin.

"That ole love bug kinda gnaws on a fellow, don't he?"

"I reckon."

After breakfast he saddled his horse and swung aboard. He gigged his dappled gray into a fast walk and then into a ground eating short lope. By mid-morning he reined up in front of Walker's store.

Before he could get off his horse, Rebekah hurried out of the store.

"Where have you been, Buck Cordell?" she demanded. "I've about put my eyes out staring at the street, hoping to see you riding in."

She ran up to stand at his stirrup. Her face lifted up. Those emerald-green eyes fixed upon his. Her hand reached out to capture his.

"I've missed you," she said. She wasn't exactly crying, but her eyes were dampening.

He had to swallow the lump in his throat before he could get the words out.

"I . . ." Buck's words drifted off like wisps of smoke on a windy day. "I've missed you, too."

She squeezed his hand and smiled through the tears that scored trails down her cheeks.

"Come on in. Father is anxious to see you."

Buck climbed out of his saddle and tied his horse. Then, hand in hand, he and Rebekah made their way into the store.

Buck took notice that she didn't release his hand when they walked up to her father.

"Good Morning, Buck. It's been a while."

"Morning, John. Yes, sir, we've been awfully busy out at the ranch. We start our trail drive in two weeks. There's a lot to do before we leave."

"I can't even imagine. How long you expect to be gone?"

"I figure it will take at least two months to get there, maybe a little more, then three weeks or so to get back home. I reckon we'll be gone three months, more or less."

Rebekah crooked her head to give him a questioning look.

"You're going to be gone *three* months?"

"I expect."

A look of confusion on her face turned to disappointment and disappointment to fear.

"You'll forget all about me."

Buck darted a concerned look at her father. He was somewhat surprised to see him smiling.

"Not likely."

"Got time to take a walk?" she asked.

"Sure do."

"We'll be back in a while," she told her father, pulling Buck along behind her by his hand.

They walked down the boardwalk, side by side, holding hands. One of the local ladies from town approached from the opposite direction. Her eyebrows arched in disapproval of them holding hands in public.

Buck touched thumb and finger to his hat brim and flashed his sweetest smile.

"Morning, ma'am."

She lifted her chin in rebuff and hurried on past without replying.

"That's Mrs. Magee," Rebekah whispered, leaning her head close. "She's the town gossip. No telling what she will tell."

"I'm not much worried about it, are you?"

"Not in the least," she said, laughing out loud.

"I think that's the second time I've heard you laugh. It sounds good on you."

They crossed the dusty street and headed down a thin path. Tall sycamore trees crowded both sides of the trail. Thick underbrush choked the area under the trees.

"Mind telling me where you are taking me?" he asked.

"It's a surprise. You'll like it."

And she was right. The trail ended abruptly in a clearing. A small mountain stream threaded through the opening. The clear water rushed along, bubbling over small rocks as if it was in a hurry to get wherever it was going. Short green grass formed a carpet on both sides of the small stream, a beautiful spot.

She turned to face him. Without a word she tiptoed to bring her lips to his. Hers was a soft, lingering kiss. When she pulled back she looked deeply into his eyes for a time. Her hand rose to touch his face, letting her soft fingers conform to his chin and cheek and jaw. He turned his head and pressed a kiss into her open palm.

Rebekah gasped at the tingling sensation racing up her arm. She closed her eyes. Her knees turned to jelly. His lips sought hers, and found them.

She was trembling and feverish when he raised his mouth from hers. Two big strong arms wrapped gently around her, drew her to him and held her close. His hands splayed across her back, broad, rough and capable hands. Hands that felt strong, yet gentle. Hands that made her feel safe, protected, secure.

"Oh, Buck, I love you so much," she whispered softly.

The words swelled his heart. His mother was the only other woman to speak those words to him.

Unbridled emotion surged over him like a river in flood. He hadn't dreamed a man could fall so completely in love in such a short time and that he could know without a doubt that what he felt was strong enough to last a lifetime.

He repeated the term several times in his mind. The words set his skin to tingling. A flush surged throughout every fiber of his being.

He didn't say anything. Couldn't. Not just yet anyway. Words wouldn't come. Never in his life had he been touched by such an overwhelming sense of love. It was a feeling of selfless and complete giving of oneself without strings or holding back or even a hint of fear, just pure, unreserved surrendering oneself to another.

He swallowed. He swallowed again. Then in a voice that hardly seemed his own he managed to put words to the feelings of his heart. He whispered hoarsely.

"I love you, too, Rebekah. I know now that I can't live without you. I want you to be my wife. Will you marry me?"

"Oh, YES! Yes! Yes! That would make me the happiest woman in the whole world."

"I'll be back."

"I'll be praying that you will" She sighed, stroking his cheek with her fingertips. "I love you with all my heart, Buck. I hope that will be enough to bring you back to me."

"When I get back, we'll make plans."

That will be the longest three months of my life," she said, rising on her toes to kiss him again. "I'm the luckiest girl alive."

"No, I'm the lucky one."

"Will you have time to come again before you leave on the drive?"

"Wish I could, but 'fraid not, we'll be working pretty much around the clock getting things ready to go."

Rebekah melted into his arms. Her body shook with silent sobs.

"I've known this day would come and I promised myself I wouldn't cry."

"I'll come back just like I promised

I'll miss you every moment of every day you're gone," she whispered. "At night when you are far away from me, close your eyes and listen. You'll hear the whispers of my heart on a soft breeze, *I love you, Buck Cordell.*"

Maybe Buck Cordell had experienced a happier day somewhere in his short life but he sure couldn't remember one.

At their meeting after breakfast on Monday morning Buck, Chester, Ray, Smokey, and Slim Hopkins sat around the table sipping coffee.

"Chet and I talked," Buck said. "We've decided to continue the operation across the river. Pappy and his vaqueros have captured over four thousand head, so far. They can catch another couple thousand in the three months we'll be gone.

"We'll purchase four more freight wagons to take on the drive. We'll use them for storage of supplies, bedrolls, and such.

"Zack Gibbs will be our scout. He'll pull out at first light in the morning and pick the route the herds will take and mark the trail for us. He'll be blazing a new trail between here and the Red River. From there we'll strike northeast to Sedalia, Missouri, that's the nearest railhead, and word is they're buying cattle.

"Ray, we'd like you to be the trail boss of the first herd. We'd like your bunch to pull out next Monday morning. Wash will go with you. You and Smokey take turns picking your men. That's the only fair way I know to do it. Each of you will have a twenty-man crew.

"Smokey, you and your bunch will leave the next day. We want the two herds separated by one day, that way we shouldn't be more than twelve or fifteen miles apart in case there's trouble. Joshua will be your trail cook.

"Chester will be in charge of the ranch while I'm gone. What he says is the same as me saying it. Slim, we're asking that you stay here and be Chester's top hand. You'll have twenty men to help you get it done."

"As you know, we've already separated out the ones we're keeping here on the ranch for brood cattle. We'll start gathering the trail herds first thing in the morning. Let's bunch 'em in that big pasture down by the Sycamore, combine all of our herds into two bunches of twenty-five hundred each. That'll give 'em a chance to become part of a larger herd before we start the drive. Any questions?"

Buck waited. Seeing only shaking heads. "Then let's get at it. Time's wasting"

The ranch became a literal beehive of activity. There were a million details to check and double check. Wash and Joshua took two of the wagons into town to Walker's store to stock up on supplies. They returned with both wagons loaded.

"We got enough food to feed Cox's army," Wash told Buck.

"Just so you got enough to feed these hungry Longhorn cowboys."

"Don't you be worrying none, mister Buck. These boys are gonna think they eatin' high on the hog."

Darkness still held the land in its grip when Zack loaded his packhorse and slid his big Spencer carbine into the backwards saddle boot under the left saddle fender. Buck stuck out his gloved hand.

"See you up the trail, *Amigo*."

"Shore nuff," the old trail scout said, shaking Buck's hand. "All you boys gotta do is follow the trail I mark fer ya. It'll lead you and them critters right to the Red River."

"We're counting on it."

* * *

Less than a week later, on Monday morning, April 2, 1866, just as the first hint of gray tinged the eastern horizon, Buck sat his saddle on a sloping hillside overlooking the wide, sweeping valley along the Sycamore River.

Beside him, Chester, Ray Ledbetter and Smokey Cunningham gentled their prancing black horses. They gazed out across a sea of longhorns of every color: yellow, red, brindle, and some as black as midnight, many with horns that spanned over six feet.

Hardly a one weighed less than a thousand pounds and many of the bulls would top fifteen hundred pounds.

Buck swallowed a lump that gathered in his throat before he could speak. "That's quite a sight ain't it?"

"One I ain't likely to forget," Smokey said, shaking his head.

"Me either," Ray agreed.

"Well, Partner," Chester, said, extending his gloved hand and swinging a look at Buck. "We've rode a long trail together. Take care of yourself."

Buck took the offered hand and shook it firmly.

"You do the same, *Amigo*"

"Well, we're burning daylight," Buck told them. "Let's head 'em up and move 'em out."

He swiped the hat from his head and lifted it high in the air and waved it in a circle. Down in the valley cowboys let out a yell that was heard even above the five thousand bawling cattle. They rode along the edge, yelping like hungry coyotes and swatting the longhorns to their feet with coiled ropes.

A cowboy coaxed the old bell cow northward. A few followed, then others. Soon, an endless line stretched as far as the eye could see.

The drive had begun.

Chapter XI

Riding an hour or so out front of the herd, Buck kept a sharp eye out for the markers left by Zack. They consisted of either a few rocks placed in the shape of an arrow or one of a red strip of cloth. The scout stuffed a tow sack full for that purpose before he left.

At this point the markers were unnecessary because the scout's intended trail was obvious. After crossing the Sycamore River the trail turned upstream, giving the herd the benefit of both good grass and water.

Buck instructed Ray to push the herd hard for the first few days. His thinking was that a tired longhorn was less likely to try to leave the herd and turn back. Bunch quitters were a constant problem, especially to the drag riders whose responsibility, it was to prevent the cattle from turning back toward home.

It was a beautiful April morning. Buck glanced up. The sun stood near noon-high. Only a few scattered puffy-white clouds floated in a soft blue sky. His mind wandered.

Wonder what Becky is doing right now? I'm shore gonna miss her. Wish I could have gone to say goodbye. She's right, it's gonna be a long three months.

I recall ma saying once that God had someone special all picked out just for me. From the moment I saw her I knew what ma meant. It was like I had found the one God made just for me.

Can't wait until we can get married. But I want to have a proper house built to bring her to before that happens. Don't want her to live in a log cabin. She deserves the finest home money can provide.

An open valley lay before him. He stood in his stirrups and shielded his eyes from the sun with a gloved hand. The valley stretched as far as he could see. Live oak trees and thick stands of mesquite and scrub cedar dotted the landscape and gave the appearance of a vast green carpet covering the floor of the valley.

Buck rode easy in the saddle. His head swiveled from side to side, his eyes scanning every bush, every fallen log, and every auroro. His years in the cavalry, living on the edge, leading a squad of guerrilla raiders behind enemy lines taught him the best way to stay alive was to spot your enemy before he spotted you.

During one of the sweeps of his searching gaze, a glint of sunlight reflecting off a shiny object caught his eye.

Instinctively his hand swept his rifle from the saddle scabbard under his left knee even as he rolled out of his saddle. It was none too soon. The crack of a rifle sounded from a thick field of scrub cedar trees off to his left. A bullet clipped a small limb off the mesquite tree beside him.

He quickly bellied down behind a nearby fallen log just before another bullet gouged a chunk from the log only inches from his head.

Whoever this dry gulcher is, he's a fair shot.

Turning his head, he saw a shallow gully off to his right no more than twenty feet from the log he lay behind.

If I could make it to that gully I'd have more cover and I might be able to circle behind him. But that's a mighty long twenty feet.

Knowing he had no more than a couple of seconds to do what he had in mind, he jacked a shell into his rifle and took a long inhale and blew it out. Using his elbows, he pushed his head and shoulders above the top of the log for an instant and then immediately dropped belly flat. Sure enough, a shot from the ambusher singed through the space his head occupied a moment ago.

He's not just a good shot, he's fast on the trigger.

When the sound of the shot reached Buck's hearing, he was already moving. He shot to his feet, took three long strides, and dove headlong into the gully.

He landed hard, face down and flat on his belly just as another slug plowed a furrow from the sandy soil just above his head. Without pausing to catch his breath, Buck scrambled quickly on hands and knees along the gully.

For a change, his luck took a turn in his favor. The gully circled to his left. Its course should circle behind the shooter.

Halfway to his destination behind the would-be killer, Buck discovered the reason for the ambush. A dead horse with a broken leg blocked the gully. Whoever the man was, he was obviously looking to replace his dead horse with Buck's dappled gray.

Chancing a quick look above the rim of the gully he was pleased to see the back shooter crouched in a heavy clump of low-lying cedar. He swung the nose of his rifle back and forth along the gully where Buck took refuge.

Bringing his rifle to his shoulder, Buck leveled the sight squarely on the man's back.

"Don't move!" Buck called out.

The bushwhacker made the final mistake of his life, he lurched around, swinging his rifle for a snap shot.

Buck shot him.

Ray Ledbetter and one of the horse wranglers rode up at a hard gallop as Buck climbed out of the gully.

"You all right, boss?" Ray hollered, a concerned look on his face.

"Yeah, better'n that one over yonder," he said, pointing with the nose of his rifle. "Jasper tried to ambush me for my horse."

Both Ray and the wrangler dismounted and walked over to the lifeless body of the back shooter. Ray turned the body over with the toe of a boot.

"He paid a mighty high price to keep from walking," Ray said.

"Check his pockets. See if you can find a name to tell us who he was."

The horse wrangler searched through the man's pockets, but found nothing except two silver dollars and half a sack of Bull Durham tobacco and the makings.

"Nothing here, boss."

"Well then, dig a hole and plant him," Buck told them.

As dusk turned to full dark, a dog-tired crew of cowboys circled the herd and bedded them down for the night before straggling into camp. A crisp April evening, a warm campfire, and a piping-hot meal of venison stew and Dutch oven biscuits greeted them.

Wash ladled their tin plates to overflowing and then piled a half-dozen biscuits on top. A tin cup of steaming coffee leveled out the meal. They sat cross-legged around the campfire and wolfed down the supper.

"Good grub," a cowboy muttered around a mouthful of biscuit.

"Shore beats branch water and beef jerky," another commented.

Buck and Ray Ledbetter stood off to one side, sipping coffee and watching the hands as they ate.

"Long day," Buck said.

"Yeah, but a good one. I figure we made twenty miles or so today."

"Reckon you're about right."

"Want to push 'em hard again tomorrow?"

"Yep."

Draining his cup, Ray said no more and headed for the blackened coffee pot hanging over the fire.

Buck sipped his coffee and watched the golden tongues of light from the campfire that lit a jagged circle around the camp. He lifted his gaze upward to the twinkling stars in a velvety black sky. His gaze fixed on one particular star, the one he had pointed out to Rebekah.

"When I'm on the trail I'll look up at that star every night," he had her, pointing to the evening star. "If you will look at it, too, no matter how far apart we are, that star will bring us closer together." Thinking of Rebekah sent a surge of feeling coursing through him.

I don't understand what miracle brought us together, but no doubt about it, she's the best thing that has ever happened to me. When I get back I'm going to build her a home she can be proud of. When it's finished, I'm gonna make her my wife.

His mind dwelled on that thought for a time.

As he lingered over a last cup of coffee, Buck turned his attention to his crew. They were a salty bunch. They had been through a lot in the last few months and there wasn't a slacker among them. He felt lucky to have such a crew.

After wolfing down their supper, the crew usually swapped tales around the campfire while sipping a second cup. But not for long. As if by some unspoken signal the men crawled wearily into their bedrolls. They would have precious little time for sleep before Wash woke them.

The herd stood to their feet well before first light. The cowboys had already finished their breakfast and caught and saddled their first horse of the day. By the time the sun crested the eastern horizon the herd was on the move headed north.

Buck rode an hour or so in front, followed closely be the chuck wagon and two freight wagons. Behind them came the remuda of near fifty horses in the charge of two wranglers.

Every man knew his job. Two point riders led the long line of cattle. Swing riders flanked the herd, keeping them in line and watching for those that took a notion to strike off on their own. Two drag riders followed the herd, beating back bunch quitters with coiled lariats.

Mostly the days were long, tiring, and monotonous. Hour after hour, mile after mile they pushed the herd along at a plodding walk. When they came to water they allowed the cattle time to slake their thirst before forcing them to resume their trek northward.

Though they never saw Zack, they constantly saw the wisdom of his trail selection. Often his markers veered them off in a direction that would seemed questionable, but within a short time they discovered the reason behind the detour.

The old scout somehow managed to keep them close to water, yet, by some uncanny ability was able to steer them around heavy timber, which was every trail boss's nightmare.

As the days wore on and turned into weeks, Buck got increasingly concerned. The drive was going well, too well. If the war taught him anything it was to expect the unexpected. Someone smarter than him had said, if something can go wrong it most likely will.

He strongly suspected he would learn the truth of that statement before this drive was over.

Chester saw the rider walking his horse slowly toward the ranch headquarters just after full dark. When the rider got closer he recognized him in the light of a full moon to be Artie Blaine, one of the newer hands hired as a wrangler to watch over their remuda.

Trailing behind him were two horses with riders draped over their saddles instead of in them.

He trotted to intercept Blaine.

"What happened?"

"It's Lefty Brown and Ted Harper. We got hit just about dusk. We were watering the horses. They shot Lefty and Ted outta the saddle from some bushes along the river.

I was on the far flank of the remuda. They chased me, but I lost them in the heavy bushes and went back later to bring the bodies in. I'm shore sorry, boss. There just wasn't nothing I could do."

"You done right. Was it Indians?"

"No, sir. They were white as me and you."

"How many?"

"Not real sure. I counted five, but there could have been more."

Several of the hands saw what was going on and hurried up.

"Couple of you boys take Lefty and Ted down to the barn. The rest of you saddle up. We've got some killers to catch."

In a few minutes Chester led a dozen Longhorn cowboys riding hell-bent-for-leather. All were heavily armed and mad as all get out. They knew it could just as easily have been them draped over their saddles instead of Lefty and Ted.

In less than an hour they found the trail. Another hour

and they found where the rustlers drove the horse herd into the river.

"Some of you boys ride across the river and split up," Chester instructed. "Some of you ride upstream and some downstream. We'll do the same on this side. Fire one shot when you find where they came out of the water."

It didn't take long. A single shot sounded from downstream. Chester and his men spurred that direction.

They came out of the water about a mile downstream on the Texas side of the river and headed south.

"They're headed for Eagle Pass, sure as shootin'," Chester said. "Bet you a dollar to a doughnut they're headed for Ike's place."

"Who's this Ike?" Slim asked.

"He deals in stolen stock. Buck and I paid him a visit some time back. He bought some horses that belonged to us. We got 'em back."

"Oh, yeah, I heard about that clear up in east Texas. That's when you hung that Charlie Sweet fellow and his boys, wasn't it?"

"Yep."

"Think this Ike is dumb enough to buy stock with the Longhorn brand on them?"

"He ain't smart enough to pour rain outta his boots before he puts them on. He'll buy our horses if that's where they're headed."

A full moon lit the clear trail left by the horse herd and allowed them to follow throughout the night By daylight it was clear they were headed for Ike's place.

At the entrance to the canyon Chester raised his hand to signal a stop. His men reined close. Chester explained the setup.

"They keep a lookout high up on the side of the canyon. We'll never get in without him sounding the alarm. They'll have a few minutes to set up for us, so watch yourself."

All around him the Longhorn men slid rifles from their saddle boots and levered in shells. They thumbed travel loops off the hammers of their sidearms and gentled their prancing horses, waiting for a signal from their boss.

Chester glanced around, and then bobbed his head.

"Let's do it."

Thirteen men put spurs to their horses. The horses leaped into a full gallop. They boiled down the canyon. A shot sounded from the lookout, and then another. A bullet ricocheted off a rock and whined off into the air.

Chester and his men reached the opening to the valley and charged in, peeling off to the left and right. A darting glance showed Chester the stolen Longhorn horses in the corral.

Men scrambled toward the barn for cover, but were caught out in the open. Several got cut down by the Longhorn crew's withering fire.

Chester found a target and triggered a shot. The man staggered, then stumbled and fell headlong into the dirt.

As quickly as it had begun it ended. Shooting from the barn ceased. A voice from inside shouted.

"Don't shoot! We're coming out!"

First one, then another and another emerged from the barn with their hands empty and held high. Some of the Longhorn boys kept them covered with rifles as others stepped out of their saddles and quickly tied the outlaw's hands behind their backs.

Chester and Slim reined their horses toward the cabin. Ike stepped through the door with his hands held high.

"Tie him up," Chester ordered.

Slim climbed off his horse with a pigging string in hand.

The Longhorn cowboys searched the barn for any men who might be hiding. They found two and led them outside to join the others.

They led Ike down near the corral where the outlaws were lined up. Chester counted four of the rustlers dead and seven more, counting Ike, standing with their hands tied behind their backs. Chester walked his horse to stand facing them.

"Which of you jaspers work for Ike?"

Three stepped forward.

"Tie them to that corral"

Chester waited.

"Now drop a loop over Ike's head and put him on a horse."

The fat horse trader's eyes went wide. He started shaking his head frantically from side to side as the loop dropped over his head and jerked tight.

"You can't do this, it ain't right!" The fat man shouted. "I didn't steal your horses."

They lifted the screaming man onto a horse, then led over to the barn. The free end of the rope was tossed over a beam that extended out above the wide door and secured tightly.

Chester walked his horse over beside the frightened man. Great beads of sweat ran down the man's face. His eyes were wide and flicked from side to side.

"Last time we were here, we warned you not to buy Longhorn stock, remember? Too bad you didn't listen."

Chester backed his mount away, removed his hat, and swatted the stock dealer's horse on the rump. Ike's mount leaped forward, dragging the man from the saddle. He dropped toward the ground. When he hit the end of the rope his weight snapped his neck. His feet kicked twice in false life. His eyes seemed to bulge out of his head. His face turned a blackish purple. The lifeless body swung slowly back and forth.

"Get the rest of those killers on their horses They're going back to the ranch with us."

Within minutes they tied the remaining four rustlers securely on their horses. They bunched the stolen Longhorn horses, ready to head toward home.

"You ain't gonna leave us tied to this fence are you?" One of Ike's workers protested.

"You'll work yourself loose eventually. In the meantime, you best figure out a better way to make a living."

Rebekah had run the entire gamut of emotions since Buck left.

One morning she would awake so excited it seemed her body simply couldn't contain the flood of anticipation of becoming Buck's wife—Mrs. Buck Cordell.

She practiced saying the words over and over. She loved the sound of it. She loved Buck. She loved him more than she would have ever believed possible. He was all she had ever wanted and more.

She needed to belong to an honorable man bigger and stronger and wiser than herself, someone to make her laugh, someone to kiss the tears away, and someone to hold her in his arms and make the rest of the world go away.

Since her mother's death she had shouldered the heavy responsibility of taking care of her father, running their home, and helping manage the store. Circumstances forced her to grow beyond her nineteen years, to make decisions she felt inadequate to make. But she made them. She made them because she had been forced by circumstances to accept the responsibility.

Then there were mornings like today.

She jerked awake. Her first conscious thought was of Buck. Something was wrong. *Has he been hurt?* The thought shocked her, swelling the barely controlled panic lodged beneath her ribs. Fear sunk its sharp talons into her soul. A feeling of helplessness gripped her and stole her breath away.

She swung her legs over the edge of her bed and buried her face in her hands. But the feeling of fear remained and plagued her throughout the day. She jumped at every sound. Her mood heavy with memories, she wandered through the day, barely conscious of her surroundings, only vaguely aware of what went on around her.

Chapter XII

It was noon. The sun felt unusually hot for early May. Pappy sat his saddle in heavy brush and kept his gaze fixed on the waterhole. Tracks around the edge told him longhorns used this particular watering hole regularly and as recently as the day before. He waited.

Like a ghost it appeared. One second the small clearing around the watering hole looked completely empty, in the next blink of the eye the monster bull appeared.

El Toro!

Pappy blinked his eyes several times to make sure it wasn't a figment of his imagination.

Standing with only its monster-size head protruding from the bushes, there it was, bigger than belief. Pappy stared in amazement. He had never seen anything like it and never have believed it possible.

Horns that were thicker than a man's leg and wider than the length of a wagon bed. The massive head swiveled slowly from side to side. Huge black eyes constantly searched every bush, every shadow, and every movement for danger. The bull's flaring nostrils dripped a white, foamy substance.

Pappy felt as if he were staring into the face of Satan himself. A shiver worked its way up his backbone.

Slowly, so slowly it seemed as if his hand barely moved, his fixed gaze never left the bull. He inched his hand to the long, forty-foot, braided rawhide reata tied to his saddle. His fingers pulled the slipknot that held it. He felt the tallow-slick rope settle in his gloved hand.

The bull moved. It stepped cautiously into the clearing, only partially revealing the massive body before pausing again.

The head swung in Pappy's direction. He dared not move, not even to blink his eyes. He hardly breathed. It seemed those coal-black eyes were boring a hole through Pappy's very soul. He swallowed the huge lump that lodged in his throat.

For an endless minute the bull stared.

Then, one slow, cautious step after another, the bull made his way forward toward the water. Pappy waited. After another long, searching look around, El Toro lowered his giant head to the water.

Pappy's fingers inched out the loop in his reata until it touched the ground at the horse's hooves.

The bull lifted its head for another slow look around before dipping his lips once again in the water. Pappy made his move.

He gigged his mount with the large, twenty-four point Gaucho spurs he wore. His horse leaped forward. Only thirty yards separated him from the bull. His mount covered that in a few heartbeats.

Pappy's plan was to lasso the bull when it turned to bolt away. Instead, El Toro wheeled to face its attacker. Its massive head lowered for battle. Its huge hooves pawed the ground, throwing dirt into the air behind. The bull snorted loudly and let out a low, rumbling from deep inside its chest.

Pappy hauled back on the reins. His horse skidded to a stop no more than fifteen feet from the monster. Lifting his hand, Pappy twirled his reata once before his arm whipped forward.

Years of experience proved itself. The throw landed true. The wide loop circled the span of horns and jerked tight. Pappy quickly did a double half hitch of the free end around the large, Spanish style saddle horn.

El Toro hadn't moved.

When it did, it caught the old brush popper completely by surprise. Lowering its head, the bull charged directly toward Pappy.

He jerked his reins to the side and jammed his spurs deep, trying desperately to get his horse out of the line of the bull's charge.

His efforts failed.

El Toro slammed into the horse's side, bowling it and it's rider over. The horse let out something akin to a pitiful scream as it tumbled over. Pappy kicked free and hit the ground hard, rolling over and over as he landed.

The bull climbed on top of the horse, lashing out with sharp hooves again and again, goring the screaming horse with its massive head and horns. The horse didn't have a chance.

Using his feet and hands, Pappy scrambled away on his backside, trying to put as much distance between him and the raging bull as he could.

Suddenly El Toro raised its head. He fixed his evil eyes directly upon Pappy. For a moment it paused. Then, letting out a loud bellow, charged.

Pappy rolled over and scrambled to his feet. His legs churned even as his eyes searched frantically for a place of safety. Behind him he heard the beast pounding the ground with long strides, gaining ground with every leap.

A sturdy-looking cedar tree was the only possibility his

quick glance spotted, but it was another twenty yards away. He knew he would never make it.

Throwing a quick look over his shoulder, he saw the slack going out of the reata. It snapped taut. The strength of the braided rawhide reata held. El Toro's head jerked abruptly around, bringing the bull to its knees and drawing it up short.

Pappy didn't take time to look further, he raced to the safety of the cedar tree and scrambled up its trunk and settled onto a sturdy branch ten feet off the ground.

El Toto regained its footing, bellowed and pawed the ground. Again and again it lunged against the rope. Each time it moved the body of the lifeless horse a foot or so but the reata held. That gave Pappy an idea.

Withdrawing his Walker Colt, he lifted it and fired three quick shots into the air. He waited. He waited and uttered a silent prayer.

It took a while before Carlos and two other vaqueros emerged from the brush. Their horses shied sideways when they spotted the huge bull.

"Right glad to see you fellows," Pappy shouted.

After their saucer-sized eyes went back to near normal, they shifted their gaze to Pappy.

"*Si,* a bull chase you up a tree, eh?" Carlos laughed.

"Laugh all you want to, but you'd climb a tree, too, if that critter took out after you. Now stop jawing and get a couple more ropes on it before it breaks free, but be careful, that monster is some kind of mean."

It took only swift minutes before the vaqueros secured the bull with two more reatas.

At last, they had captured El Toro.

* * *

Chester and his men arrived back at the ranch at mid-afternoon the next day with their four captives in tow. Instead of heading for the ranch complex, however, they reined up under a large sycamore tree within sight of the Rio Grande River.

"This is the end of the line for you boys," Chet told them. "Gonna tell you what's fixing to happen. You killed two of my men. For that you're gonna hang. Then I'm gonna leave you hanging until the buzzards pick your bones clean. I reckon that ought to be a plain enough message for others thinking of doing what you boys did. Put some ropes on them, boys."

Several Longhorn cowboys came forward and fitted loops over the heads of the four killers. They drew the ropes tight and threw the loose end over a sturdy limb. The rope was then snugged to the trunk of the tree.

The four killers sat stone-faced and silent, seemingly accepting their fate. The Longhorn men sat their horses in a semicircle, watching silently.

Chester walked his horse behind the horses of the four outlaws.

"If your mama taught you boys to pray, you got about ten seconds to make up for all your backsliding."

One of the outlaws, an older man, turned his head, pinning Chester with a look of cold hatred.

"I'll see you in hell."

"More'n likely," Chester said, swatting the man's horse on the rump with his hat.

The animal bolted forward dragging the killer from his saddle. When the man dropped, the rope stretched tight, stopping his fall abruptly three feet from the ground. The outlaw thrashed and kicked, seemingly trying to find some solid footing, but instead found only thin air. Finally his kicking ceased.

One man cried and begged.

"This ain't no way for a man to die! Mercy! Have mercy."

"I'll give you the same mercy you gave my two men," Chester said, swatting the man's horse.

One after another the process continued until all four men hung suspended between Heaven and Hell.

"Like I said, leave them where they hang," Chester said again.

After the hanging, Chester rode down by the river to be alone for a good long while.

The next morning Chester rode through the wide gate of the newly constructed wall. He was well pleased with the progress the Mexican workers were making. The entire front wall and both side walls were complete. They were working on the back wall and had more than half of it built.

With walls twelve feet high and three feet thick, the wall was an imposing structure. It reminded Chester of a prison. In a way, he supposed it was, but one to keep intruders *out* rather than to keep someone *in*.

Broken glass was imbedded into the top to further discourage anyone from scaling the wall. A wooden walkway four feet below the top was built to allow those inside to use as a platform to fire at any intruders.

Inside the wall, two cabins, an expanded bunkhouse, a chow hall and kitchen, a barn with stalls enough to hold one horse for each ranch hand, all made of adobe, took almost half of the space. Before he left, Buck instructed that one large corner be left for a sprawling hacienda. He had met with the Mexican workers and given specific instructions as to what he wanted done.

Chester had a pretty good idea what that was about. His partner had been bitten by the love bug, and, though he hadn't said it yet, was about to take a wife. Juan and his two sons were already working on Buck's hacienda while the other workers finished the wall.

A sense of accomplishment swept over Chester as he reined up and sat his horse for a time. Together, he and Buck had created something substantial and enduring out of less than nothing.

Others said it couldn't be done, but they didn't know the Buck Cordell Chester knew. They said nobody with a lick of sense would attempt to build a cattle ranch in the middle of an outlaw infested land and the favorite hunting ground of three tribes of hostile Indians to boot.

While it was true that the whole future of the Longhorn was, even now, walking on a thousand mile trip to Missouri, Chester had complete faith in his partner that he could pull off the biggest gamble of their lives.

For the first time in his life, Chester truly felt a part of something. He felt at home here. He felt a great debt to Buck for taking him in and making him a partner of this great adventure. And if he could help it, nothing or no one was gonna stop them from making their dream a reality.

His thoughts scattered by the sound of wagons approaching. He reined his mount around and rode back through the front gate.

A hundred yards off and headed toward one of the dozen sturdy holding pens, two of the heavy freight wagons from across the river lumbered along, side by side. They were separated by twenty feet.

Between the two wagons Chester saw something he would have never thought possible.

A black bull more than twice the size of the biggest he'd ever seen. Secured tightly between the two wagons by double reatas, it still tossed his massive head and fought the ropes.

It was the legendary bull, El Toro

Pappy spotted Chester and gigged his horse forward. Chester galloped to meet him.

Pappy swiped his floppy hat from his head, waved it in the air, and let out a blood-curdling yell.

"We got him, boss!" Pappy shouted as Chester drew near.

"I see it, and I still ain't believing my eyes."

"It's him all right. Might near done me in, but we got him."

"My ma used to tell me to be careful what you wished for because you might get it. I'm wondering what we're gonna do with this monster now that we've got him. He's too mean to ever tame down enough to be useful.

"No offense intended, boss, but that's where you're wrong. I'll tame him. This big fellow is gonna make the Longhorn Ranch the most famous spread in all of Texas, just you wait and see."

"Well, I'll believe it when I see it," Chester said, leaning over and sticking out his hand.

Pappy took it.

"You done a good job, Pappy, a real good job."

They put El Toro in the sturdiest holding pen they had. Every cowboy on the ranch crowded along the fence, staring wide-eyed at the wonder.

The monster bull stood in the center of the pen, staring defiantly at its captors. It snorted, pawed the ground, and sent shivers up the spine of all of the observers.

"Now that's a lot of bull," Slim said, crowding in beside Chester.

"You got that right," Chester agreed, shaking his head. "If we can tame it we've really got something."

Pappy took personal control of the taming process. He starved the monster for a full week before he gave El Toro any food or water and then fed and watered it only once before beginning the process all over again. At the end of the second week, Pappy fed and watered the bull for two days before withholding nourishment. By the end of the first month the bull had tamed down considerably.

"Believe we're making progress," Pappy said out loud to the bull. "Before we get through you're gonna think I'm your papa."

The bull just stared at him definitely.

Each night Pappy spent considerable time working on something in the barn. He refused to talk about it or allow any of the other hands to know what he was doing.

One morning Chester stopped by the holding pen where Pappy was doing his daily feeding of the big bull, for a time he leaned on the fence and watched.

"How's the taming coming along?" Chester asked.

"He's coming along right well, I reckon," Pappy said. "But I need to be gone for a couple of days if that's all right?"

"Whatever suits you."

Pappy rode off and came back three days later leading two of the largest oxen Chester had ever seen. They looked like they would top the scales at well over two thousand pounds each.

"What are you gonna do with those things?"

"You'll see."

The next morning the vaqueros from across the river rode in. All hands gathered around El Toro's holding pen to watch the show. They couldn't wait to see what Pappy had up his sleeve.

Three vaqueros emerged from the barn carrying a strange looking contraption. It looked like a three-oxen yoke, except it was about twenty feet long.

It took a good half-hour and four vaqueros to get El Toro into the center yoke. Once that was accomplished, the two huge oxen were led into the pen and yoked, one on each side of the bull.

The vicious bull snorted and bellowed. He kicked and pawed the ground. He tugged and fought the sturdy yoke, but all of his antics didn't phase the mild-mannered oxen. They were separated far enough that the dangerous hooves of the bull couldn't reach them. They went where they wanted to go and the bull had no choice but to go along.

"You beat all," Chester told Pappy as they leaned on the fence and watched. "Where did you come up with that idea?"

"Kinda like being married, I reckon," the brush popper laughed.

"I get your meaning."

Chapter XIII

Buck sat his dappled gray on a grassy knoll overlooking the Red River.

The noonday sun was shrouded by a heavy overcast sky. Dark thunder-busters gathered in the west. It was a sweltering-hot, heat drenched day, and his throat felt parched. He licked his lips with a dry tongue.

Zack sat his horse beside him. The old scout busied himself rolling a smoke. Zack had been waiting on them at the crossing. He said he searched the river for miles both upstream and down before settling on this particular spot.

It was one of the narrowest places on the river and had a good bottom with sloping banks both entering and leaving the water. It was as close to a perfect crossing as they were likely to find, about three miles west of the junction of the north fork where it joined the Red River.

"I don't like the looks of those clouds," Buck said, sweeping a worried look.

"Nope," Zack agreed, glancing upward. "Looks like we could be in for some weather."

"Shore would like to get both herds across the Red before it hits. If we get a heavy rain, that water could get deep right fast."

With one long leg hooked around his saddlehorn, Buck watched the long line of bawling longhorns as they waded across the wide river. Most of them paused briefly to dip their mouths for a few swigs before being forced along by the cattle behind them or the drovers.

The crossing went well.

They were on the trail for more than a month, forty days to be exact. All in all the drive had been good, better than he could have dared hope for. Still, worrisome feelings gnawed at him and scribed his lips into a tight line. Once across the Red River they would be in Indian territory.

"See that mountain over yonder that looks like a teepee?" Zack said, licking along one edge of the paper he rolled into a cigarette. "We need to point the lead steer toward it. That mountain will lead us to the crossing on the north fork of the Red.

"No more'n a mile and half after that, there's a short mountain with a big grove of pecan trees on the south side and there's a big valley, maybe twelve miles wide and twenty miles long. It's got good grass. Shore would be a good place to rest the herd for a day of two."

"Sounds good, Zack. You've done a good job, I'm much obliged. Ride over and fill Ray in, and while you're at it, tell him to hurry them cattle along. Tell him to take his herd on up into the valley a ways and rest a day. I'll stay here and wait on Smokey and the second herd, I'll have them hold their herd on the short side of the valley."

The scout rode off to deliver Buck's orders.

He breathed a long sigh of relief as the last steer climbed out of the muddy-red water and the last drag rider hit dry land. He settled in the saddle and swung his boot into a stirrup and found a sycamore tree. He swung to the ground. He had a whole day before Smokey would be there with the second herd. He raised his head to glance anxiously at the clouds with little hope the storm would hold off long enough to get the second herd across before it hit. But he felt confident that Smokey would see the storm coming and would be pushing his herd as fast as he could.

Buck loosened the cinch on his saddle and allowed the gray to munch the short, sweet grass nearby. He settled himself with his back to the tree.

He had been keeping an eye on the trail and it looked like his herds were the first to make the trek this year. He hoped so. Maybe they'd get lucky and get through without a run-in with the Indians.

He had a bad case of the lonelies. When he was busy it wasn't so bad. It was at times like now that Rebekah's memory kept flashing into his mind. If he closed his eyes he could still remember every line of her face, feel the warmth of her presence in his arms, and taste her sweet kisses.

He spent the afternoon thinking about Rebekah and the drive. There were some things he noticed that he needed to talk to his two trail bosses about. He made a mental note to do that before they resumed the drive.

The rain started just shy of good dark. Buck broke out his rain slicker and shouldered into it. He sipped some left over coffee and tried unsuccessfully to stay dry. He kept an anxious eye on both the sky and the level of the river. With the moon and stars not visible, the night was blacker than black. He couldn't see his hand in front of his face. All night he hunkered under his rain slicker, his back against the tree trunk. It was a long, wet night.

It was still raining hard when Smokey and the second herd arrived about mid-morning. Buck shook hands with his trail boss and asked to be filled in on everything that happened since the last time he visited the herd.

Together they rode down to the water's edge and looked over the situation. The river had raised some, but both agreed the crossing was still doable.

After the briefing Buck commended his trail boss and gave him the go-ahead to start the crossing. By mid-afternoon the last longhorn climbed the bank into Indian territory. Both herds made the crossing without loosing a single head. Buck was very pleased.

He stayed with Smokey's herd until it got safely across the North Fork crossing and was settled down to graze in the valley before gigging his horse north He intended to bed down with the first herd that night.

It stopped raining but it was late when he rode into the lead herd camp. The camp looked settled in for the night and most of the tired drovers were already asleep in their bedrolls.

Ray Ledbetter walked over as Buck loosened the cinch strap on his saddle. He handed his boss a steaming cup of coffee. As he did, a concerned look swept across his face.

"You look beat, boss. You got worry hanging all over you."

Buck chewed on that thought before answering his trail boss.

"Reckon you're right. Been thinking. Things are going too good. The drive has become too routine, too relaxed. One of the things the war taught me is that trouble usually comes when you're least expecting it. We've got to expect the unexpected."

"Yeah, I'm *looking* for trouble. I talked to Smokey. I asked him to have his boys ride *expecting* trouble, because it's gonna come sure as shootin' We've got to be ready when it does."

"Anything in particular you got in mind?"

"No, just one of my gut feelings. We're in Indian territory. I ain't hankerin' for an Indian haircut. Have the boys ride with their Spencer carbines fully loaded and close enough to get their hands on, night and day.

"From here on, I want the night remuda saddled and picketed real close. When trouble hits us I want the boys to be able to get in the saddle in a heartbeat. It just ain't natural for a drive to go as good as this one has."

"I'll talk to the boys."

"You've done a good job, Ray. I couldn't ask for a better trail boss."

"Thanks, boss. The hands sure appreciated the day's rest. You better get some rest, too. Ole Wash rousts us out just when the sleeping gets good."

Buck took Ray's advice and fell asleep by the time his head hit the saddle he used for a pillow.

Just like Ray had warned, Wash rousted everybody from a sound sleep in the darkest part of the night. Breakfast consisted of flapjacks, fried potatoes, and coffee. The herd was up and milling about by the time the cowboys hit the saddle. The sky was still dark.

Zack caught up with them two days later. Up ahead was Cache Creek. They made the crossing without incident and plodded on. Two more days and they veered north to circle around the headwaters of Wild Horse creek and the heavily wooded Arbuckle Mountains.

Here they encountered the first Indians.

Buck, Ray, and Zack rode point. The Indians emerged from a thick stand of blackjack trees. Buck counted eight, but there could be more in the trees.

"You speak their language?" Buck asked the scout.

"A little, with the sign language maybe enough to get by," he said, raising his right hand in the universal sign of peace.

The larger Indian on a spotted paint horse heeled his mount forward but didn't lift his hand. He reined close and stopped.

He was bare-chested and wore deerskin britches covered by a breechclout. Colorful moccasins adorned his feet. His long, coal-black hair hung in braided plaits with an eagle feather tied in the end. He carried an older model Henry rifle in his right hand. His dark, piercing eyes fixed upon them and held for a long moment before speaking.

"Me Rising Star, chief of Choctaw. This Choctaw land. White-eyes bring many cows. Must pay."

"Ask him how much?" Buck instructed the scout.

The Indian didn't wait for the scout to relay the question. He obviously understood Buck's words.

Spreading the fingers of his left hand he opened and closed it ten times.

Buck shook his head emphatically.

"No. Too much. I give you five cows," Buck said, lifting his own hand and spreading fingers only once before closing his fist.

The Indian chief stared silently.

Finally the Indian again lifted his hand and opened it five times.

Buck shook his head and opened his hand twice.

"Ten cows. No more," he said emphatically. "That's my final offer."

Buck's words deepened the war chief's scowl. Finally he bobbed his head once, thereby agreeing to accept the offer.

"Zack, tell him another herd will be coming through tomorrow. I'll give him twenty cows now, ten for this herd and another ten for tomorrow's herd. Ray, have the boys cut out twenty head from the back of the herd."

Zack started the process of relaying Buck's message, but the Indian raised his right hand in the sign of peace, reined his horse around and rode away.

"Reckon he heard you," Zack chuckled.

"Ride back and explain to Smokey what happened. Tell him if he gets stopped not to give them any more cows."

Three weeks later they crossed the Canadian River and were only a few day's drive from the Missouri line. Zack returned from the second herd to report that Smokey's herd made it through without seeing neither hide nor hair of an Indian.

Even though they were running at least two weeks behind schedule, Buck was feeling better about the drive. They made camp and got the herd circled and settled down for the night. Wash served up supper and the crew enjoyed it beside the campfire.

A voice called from the darkness.

"Hello the camp!"

Buck and Ray grabbed nearby Spencer rifles and jacked a shell. Most of the longhorn crew scrambled to take up their carbines.

"Ride in, but keep your hands where we can see them," Buck called back.

From the depth of darkness four riders emerged.

The one in front reined up and sat his saddle, not dismounting until invited.

"I'm Spencer Adams from east Texas. These boys with me are all that's left of my crew. We were trailing a herd to Sedalia, Missouri, got jumped right after we crossed the Missouri Line."

"Climb down and sit if you're a mind."

"Obliged," the man said, swinging to the ground. His men did the same.

"Have a cup of coffee and tell us what happened?"

They handed cups of steaming coffee to the newcomers and the Longhorn hands gathered around to listen.

"The men wanted to cut my herd, said there was some kind of law in Missouri that didn't allow Texas cattle in Missouri, but they would let us through for a price. They wore badges but weren't lawmen. They weren't nothing but rustlers"

"How many cows did they want?" Buck asked.

"They demanded half of my herd. When I refused they just started shooting and killed most of my men and stampeded the herd."

"How many was in their bunch?"

"I counted twenty."

"What happened to your cows?"

"Don't know for shore. I'm guessing they rounded them up for themselves."

"Wash will dish you up some supper. Where you headed now?"

"Back to east Texas, I reckon. Don't see much else we can do."

"When did this bunch jump you?"

"This morning just before noon."

"How'd you like a chance to get your herd back?"

"What do you mean?"

"I've got twenty men with this herd and another twenty with another herd a ways back. If you boys want to throw in with us, we'll try to get your herd back and deal with these jaspers at the same time. Most likely we'd be next on their list anyway, might as well get it over and done with."

Adams grinned like a bear in a honey barrel. He glanced quickly at his other men who bobbed their heads enthusiastically.

"Count us in."

"Fair enough. Ray, send a man back to tell Smokey what's going on. Tell him to leave ten men with his herd and bring the rest of his men up here tonight. We'll ride at first light."

"Zack, ride on ahead. See how far ahead of us that bunch is. We'll catch up to you tomorrow."

"You got it, boss," Zack said, clearly happy with the decision.

Smokey and his men rode in just before dawn. Buck and his crew were finishing breakfast and sipping a cup of coffee, waiting for Smokey to arrive.

"Climb down and have a bite before we ride," Buck told them. "You boys have had a long night."

As they were eating Buck explained what he wanted.

"I want every man to saddle an extra horse and take it along on a lead line behind him. We're gonna switch horses every hour and keep a fresh horse under us at all times."

In less than half an hour Buck rode in front of twenty-four heavily armed men, galloping up the trail toward the Missouri line.

They rode in silence, Buck knew that every man felt a sense of pride that they were riding for the brand on their way to right a wrong. They knew if they didn't fight this bunch now on their own terms they would have to fight them later on the outlaw's terms.

A thousand longhorns leave a trail even a blind man could follow. All day they rode. It was a long hot ride. The sun set and dusk settled over the Missouri countryside by the time Zack appeared out of a stand of trees and intercepted Buck and his riders.

"They're up ahead a couple miles. Looks like they're getting ready to bed down for the night."

"What kind of campsite did they pick?" Buck asked.

"Shore ain't one I'd pick if I was on the run. It's a small clearing in a thick stand of cottonwood trees. They're camped beside a little creek. They circled the herd in a meadow not far off, and there's two nighthawks watching the herd."

"Think we could work our way into those trees around their camp?"

"Maybe, if we are quiet about it."

Buck held up his hand, calling a halt, and motioned for all the riders to gather around. He explained the situation.

"We'll wait till good dark before we move in. We'll leave our horses with one man and deer-foot into those cottonwoods around their camp. I need two men who are good with your knives to take care of the nighthawks watching the herd. When we're all set I'll give them a chance to surrender, which ain't likely. If they don't, we'll do what we gotta do."

They rode to the backside of a nearby hill and found a clearing. Someone built a small fire and made some coffee.

It was a picture-perfect night. The velvety-black sky was sprinkled with a million stars. A thin sliver of moon slid slowly overhead. Buck should have been enjoying the beautiful spring evening, but instead, he felt a sickening feeling building in his stomach because he knew men were going to die this night.

It was just shy of midnight when Buck and his men left their horses and quietly slipped into the woods not far from the outlaw's campsite.

Two men sipped coffee around the fire. Flickering shadows danced over the other sixteen men already asleep in their bedrolls.

Buck and Zack waded silently across the shallow creek, crawled quietly through the thick underbrush, and bellied down behind a thick fallen log no more than thirty yards from the campfire.

They waited.

Low voices from the two men beside the fire carried to Buck on a soft breeze. He was much closer than the other Longhorn riders and could actually hear what the two men were saying.

"Come morning I'll ride on into Sedalia and let the boss know we've got a thousand head for him. Bring the herd on up the trail and hold them at the regular place. As usual, his boys will meet you and take them from there."

"This ought to be a good payoff," the second man said.

"Yeah, but not as good as the next one. My man down the trail sent word that two big herds are coming. He figured there was maybe five thousand head altogether."

"Five thousand, huh? With that many cows they'll have a bunch of drovers, reckon we can handle 'em?"

"We'll handle em. We'll just shoot 'em down like every time before. Only this time I don't want any witnesses riding off, got it?"

"Quit telling me how to do my job. You just worry about your end. I'll take care of mine."

"Then make sure you do it right. Witnesses talk. Those cow nurses that got away this time should never have been allowed to ride off. We got a good thing going here. Let's not mess it up."

"Don't know about you, but I ain't happy with the cut we're getting outta all this. We do all the work and Bonner takes most of the money. Why do we need him anyway? Why don't we just sell the cattle we steal and keep everything for ourselves?"

"Because he's a big man in these parts, that's why. He deals in cattle every day. He can get by with selling a big herd. We couldn't. Folks around Sedalia know us. There'd be all kind of questions if Sam Watts and Carl Taggart showed up with a thousand head and tried to sell them, now wouldn't they? Don't go getting greedy. The boss wouldn't like talk like that."

Buck had heard enough.

"You fellows there by the fire! First one to move is a dead man!"

Buck decided long ago that outlaws were a few bricks shy of a full load or they wouldn't be outlaws; these were no exception. Not only did they move, they both leaped to their feet and grabbed for their pistols.

Blasts from several Spencers firing at the same time shattered the night. The heavy slugs slammed into the two men, tearing them to shreds. One of them was propelled backwards into the fire, his lifeless body sending sparks upward and lighting the clearing.

Sleepy men bolted out of their bedrolls and grabbed for rifles, only to be cut down by the deadly fire from the Longhorn riders. Buck and his men showed no mercy because the outlaws had shown none to their many victims.

It was all over in a matter of minutes.

Outlaws lay sprawled all over the campsite, some still in their bedrolls. Slowly, cautiously, the Longhorn men emerged from the darkness. They went about the camp, checking each outlaw closely. They were all dead.

Buck walked to the center of the killing field. For a long moment he stood silently, surveying his surroundings, his mind returning to other times such as this one. *I thought those times ended with the war. Guess I was wrong.*

Ray and Smokey walked up.

"Gather their weapons and horses, then bury them," Buck instructed. "Burying is all they get and that's more'n they deserve."

Spencer Adams and his three men walked up, their rifles still smoking.

"I can let you have a couple of men to help you get your herd on into Sedalia if that would help?" Buck said.

"Hate to ask. You've been so much help already, but I sure could use them if you can spare a couple."

"No trouble. Take a few of those horses if you need 'em. My men will take care of them after you get your herd to town."

Adams stuck out his hand. Buck took it.

"Shore much obliged for all you done, Mr. Cordell."

"Got a feeling you'd do the same for me if the hand had been dealt different."

Chapter XIV

T wo weeks later Buck rode into Sedalia, Missouri. Ray and Smokey would arrive with the herds in a couple of days and hold them outside town until they received word from him.

Sedalia was a bustling city of at least two thousand. He had never seen so many people.

Freight wagons with heavy loads, farm wagons with families aboard, and black topped buggies moved in lines up and down the wide, dusty street. Cowboys on horseback weaved in and out between the wagons.

Men in business suits, many in cowboy garb, and some in work clothes leaned against posts and lounged on benches along the boardwalk. Women with children in tow risked life and limb to dart across the busy street.

It was like nothing Buck had ever witnessed before.

Businesses of every imagination lined the streets. It seemed to Buck every third one was a saloon. Loud piano music, drunken mens' boisterous laughter, and the shrill giggles of saloon girls gave the town an uproarious and lawless atmosphere.

On the far end of town he could see the railroad station. It was clear to all that the Pacific Railroad was the sperm that gave birth to Sedalia. Here lay the terminus of the railroad. Untold tons of freight, agriculture products, and cattle began their journey in Sedalia to points all over the vast country.

There was no doubt in Buck's mind the railroad would soon spread its iron tentacles far and wide across the country, but right now, Sedalia or Kansas City were the closest shipping points for anything south of the Missouri line.

Adjacent to the railroad station a vast stockyard with holding pens stretched as far as the eye could see. Thousands of cattle could be held in those pens until they were loaded aboard the long line of cattle cars waiting along the tracks.

Buck saw a large, three-story hotel sitting on the next corner. The sign identified it as the Drover's Hotel. He reined his dappled gray in that direction.

After tying his horse to the hitching rail out front he slung his saddlebags over a shoulder and slipped the Spencer rifle from its saddle boot. He stepped up onto the boardwalk and pushed inside.

"Need a room," he told the baldheaded desk clerk.

"Yes, sir. Just sign the book there. How long will you be staying with us?"

"A while."

"I see. Would a room on the second floor facing the street be satisfactory?"

"We'll see."

Buck signed his name on the first empty line and couldn't help noticing the name of

Spencer Adams higher up on the page.

"Is Mr. Spencer Adams still a guest here?"

"Why, yes he is. I believe I saw him go into the dining room. You will be in room number twelve, Mr. Cordell. That's up the stairs and to your left. It's a pleasure to have you. Are you in town on business?"

"Yep. Brought two herds of longhorns up the trail."

"I see. Then you will be a popular fellow. All the cattle buyers and brokers are staying right here in the hotel. If there is anything we can do to make your stay more comfortable, just ask."

"Where can I get a bath and a shave?"

"You can get both at the barber shop just down the street in the next block."

"Where's the livery?"

"We have two, one on each end of town."

"Obliged."

Buck decided to say howdy to Spencer before he went to his room. He headed for the dining room.

Adams sat with two of his men drinking coffee when Buck walked up. His face spread in a big smile when he looked up and saw Buck. He stood quickly to his feet and stuck out his hand.

"Howdy, Buck. See you made it."

Buck shook hands all around the table before settling into the fourth chair.

"Did you get your herd sold?"

"Sure did, and you won't believe what I got for them. I was hoping to get twenty dollars a head. I got thirty-two."

Buck was stunned. He wrinkled his eyebrows and his mouth dropped open.

"Thirty-two? Why has the price jumped so much?"

"From what I can learn the country has gone crazy for beef since the war ended. Cattle prices are sky-high and climbing. Buyers from all the packinghouses are in town and they've got a bidding war going on. Wish now I had held off selling a few more days.

"With the size of your herds, no telling what you'll be able to get for your cattle. I'd say you could pretty well name your own price."

Buck felt a surge of excitement flood through him. If what Adams said proved to be true, this one drive could put the Longhorn Ranch on solid footing. He needed to get alone and do some serious thinking.

"Who are the biggest buyers?"

"I sold my herd to a fellow named Harvey Owens. He buys for Armour & Company out of Chicago. But there are several other buyers and brokers here. I don't even know who most of them are.

"One buyer I heard about named Garner buys for several packers. He's giving Armour a run for their money right now. All the buyers and brokers are staying right here in the hotel. He might be a good man to talk with."

"I doubt it. I met him down in San Antonio a while back. I better go find my room and get cleaned up. After two months on the trail, I smell kinda ripe. When are you heading back to Texas?"

"Pulling out in the morning at first light."

"Well, if I don't see you again before you leave, watch your back trail."

"Count on it. Thanks again for all you done for me. I won't be forgetting it."

Buck climbed the stairs to the second floor and found room number twelve. It looked clean but sparsely furnished. A bed, dresser, and a single overstuffed chair were the only furniture. A white porcelain water pitcher and washbowl sat on the dresser. He dropped his saddlebags on the bed and propped his rifle against the bedpost.

Walking to the single window, he pushed aside the white lace curtain and gazed down into the street. The activity seemed to have slowed somewhat, but still reminded him of a colony of ants scurrying to and fro.

Turning from the window he left the room, being careful to lock the door behind him. He found the livery stable the desk clerk mentioned and lodged his horse, instructing that the dappled gray be stalled and grain fed. On the way back he saw a mercantile store and purchased a new change of clothes before finding the barbershop.

After a shave, a long bath, and dressed in his new clothes, he didn't feel as out of place as he had in his worn and dirty trail clothes.

He decided his stomach could use a good meal since he hadn't eaten anything to speak of since leaving camp two days earlier. As he headed for the hotel the evening sun slid quickly behind the western horizon. The red fireball colored the evening sky blood red. Fiery rays shot out and touched the puffy-white clouds transforming them into great golden nuggets. This was Buck's favorite time of the day.

The dining room looked crowded.

Men in three-piece suits had their heads together, most likely talking business. Buck made his way to the only empty table and folded into the chair. A young waiter in a white shirt and string tie arrived with a white china cup and poured it full of coffee from a shiny silver pot.

"How may I help you, sir?" he asked politely.

"I'd like a good beef steak with all the trimmings, and don't let the coffee cup run dry."

"Very good, sir."

Buck was blowing the steam away to take his first sip when he felt a presence. He looked up and recognized none other than G. W. Garner, the cattle broker who gave him the brush-off in San Antonio almost a year before.

"Are you Mr. Cordell?"

"That's me."

"I'm G. W. Garner. I'm a cattle broker. The word around town is that you have some cattle for sale."

"Yep."

"Mind if I join you?"

"Do what suits you."

The cattle broker pulled out a chair and sat.

"May I ask how many head you have, Mr. Cordell?"

"Something in the neighborhood of five thousand head."

"My, my, that's a pretty big neighborhood. I'd like to discuss buying your cattle. You look somewhat familiar. Have we met before?"

"Yep. In San Antonio about a year ago."

"Oh, yes, I remember now. We spoke briefly, as I recall."

"Yep, very briefly. You weren't interested in talking to me then because I didn't have any cattle. Now I got cattle and I'm not interested in talking with you."

"But...but you haven't even heard my price yet?"

"And don't intend to. Like I said, I ain't interested."

Garner looked stunned. His face got beet red. He stuttered for words before abruptly rising and storming from the dining room.

Buck sipped his coffee.

A big man in a gray business suit sat at the next table with three other men. He turned around in his chair and spoke to Buck.

"Mr. Cordell. I'm Harvey Owens. I'm the buyer for Armour & Company of Chicago. I couldn't help overhearing your conversation with Garner. It's about time somebody put him in his place and I must say you did a good job of it."

Buck twisted around in his chair and stuck out his hand. Owens took it in a firm handshake.

"Pleased to meet you, Mr. Owens."

Harvey Owens looked like a cattle buyer. He wore a business suit, highly polished western boots, and a light gray John B. that was obviously expensive. His tanned, clean-cut face wore an easy smile and friendly eyes.

"If you have time I'd like to discuss some business with you at your convenience."

"Be glad to listen."

"Would you allow me to buy breakfast in the morning, perhaps we could talk then?"

"Don't see why not."

"Say at seven then?"

"Seven will be fine."

The waiter brought Buck's steak and refilled his coffee cup. On the second trip the young man set a plate of fried potatoes, a bowl of greens, a basket full of hot biscuits and a jar of fresh honey.

"Would there be anything else, sir?

"If I get around all this I'll be doing good."

He settled down to enjoy his meal. He was still chewing his first bite when another man approached his table.

"Excuse me."

Buck looked up at a short, balding fellow with a handlebar mustache and glasses.

"Are you Mr. Cordell?"

"I am."

"My name is Ben Harding. I'm a cattle broker. I understand you have some cattle for sale?"

Buck chewed a moment before replying, making sure he spoke loud enough for Harvey Owens at the next table to hear.

"Yeah, but right now I'm eating. Can it keep until tomorrow? I'd be glad to talk with you then."

"I didn't mean to interrupt your meal. I'll look forward to talking with you tomorrow."

With no more interruptions, he enjoyed the delicious meal. Harvey Owens finished his business with his three companions, said goodnight, and left looking somewhat concerned.

After supper Buck went to his room and stretched out on the bed. He fell asleep in minutes.

As had been his custom since childhood, he awoke before first light. He shaved and dressed then went downstairs to the dining room. He was on his third cup of coffee when Harvey Owens arrived.

"Good morning, Mr. Cordell. I trust you slept well?"

"Slept like a log."

Owens sat down and motioned for coffee. The waiter filled his cup.

"Are you gentlemen having breakfast?"

"Mr. Cordell will order first."

"Just bring me three eggs, a slice of ham, and biscuits," Buck told the waiter.

"I'll have the same," Owens said.

After the waiter left, the cattle buyer sipped his coffee in deep thought before speaking.

"Mr. Cordell, I couldn't help but notice that Ben Harding approached you last night about buying your cattle."

"Call me Buck, and yeah, I told him I'd meet with him later today."

"If you will call me Harvey, agreed?"

"Agreed."

"Buck, I'm gonna lay my cards on the table face up. I won't make any bones about it I want to buy your cattle. We have a country clamoring for beef. Armour & Company is the largest meat packing house in Chicago. We will soon be the largest in the country. We're rapidly expanding our facilities and that requires an ever-increasing number of cattle to meet the demand.

"Here it is in a nutshell, Buck I need your five thousand head and I'll pay top dollar to get them."

"Exactly what is *top dollar*"?

The cattle buyer glanced quickly around, then leaned close and lowered his voice.

"Can I speak in confidence?"

"Of course."

"I'm willing to pay forty dollars a head for your cattle, providing we can keep that price just between you and me and we can close the deal right here, right now."

Buck swallowed back the surge of excitement filling his throat. He struggled to maintain a poker face, stifling the urge to agree immediately to the unbelievable offer Harvey Owens just made. For a long moment he stared silently at his coffee cup in deep thought.

"The way I see it, it's your job to buy cattle at the cheapest price you can. It's my job to get the best price I can. How do I know Ben Harvey or some other buyer wouldn't offer more?"

"I'm the buyer for Armour because I make it my business to know what my competition is willing and able to pay. You won't get a better offer than the one I just made, you've got my word on that."

For some reason Buck believed the man. Somehow he sensed Harvey Owens was a straight shooter, a man he could trust.

"Harvey, you just bought yourself some longhorns."

He reached a hand. Owens took it. They sealed the bargain with a gentleman's handshake.

"I'll ride out and meet my herds and bring them in. I ought to have them here in two days. I'm supposing you will have someone to help with the counting."

"Yes, my man's name is Cheyenne Morgan, he's my top hand. I'll arrange for space at the stockyards. After the count I'll have bank draft or cash waiting for you, whichever you prefer."

"I'll need some cash to pay off my hands. A bank draft will be fine for the rest."

"It's a pleasure doing business with you, Buck, I'd sure like the opportunity to talk with you on any future herds you bring up the trail."

"You can count on it. One more thing, do you know a fellow here in town named Bonner?"

"Of course, Nate Bonner calls himself a cattle broker just to keep from admitting he don't have a regular job. He has an office upstairs over the Golden Nugget Saloon. Some say he's a little on the shady side, but he comes up with a good herd now and then. Maybe it's none of my business, but why would you want to talk with him? I understood we already had a deal."

"Oh, we do. It has nothing to do with selling him cattle."

"Oh, I see. Just a word to the wise Bonner has the reputation of being somewhat unscrupulous and he has some friends that are pretty unsavory."

"So I've heard."

Buck left the meeting and walked down the street to the livery to check on the gray. The elderly hostler looked up from forking hay into one of the stalls and spat a long stream of tobacco juice. He greeted Buck with a wide smile.

"Morning, young fellow."

"Morning, old timer. Thought I'd look in on my gray. I've got kinda attached to him.

"Mighty fine horse. He's eatin' me out of house and home, though." The man chuckled.

"Something me and him got in common, we both like to eat."

"Big a fellow as you are, I reckon it'd take a right smart to fill you up."

"My mama fed us boys good."

"Your gray is in one of the stalls down the aisle. He's an easy keep."

"I'll look in on him."

Buck stopped by the store and bought an apple. When he approached the stall the gray nickered and pranced It stuck its head over the railing, bobbing it up and down. Buck rubbed the horse's nose and stuck out his hand with the apple. The horse took it and gobbled it down.

"You like those, don't you big fellow?"

Buck took notice the gray had been curried and brushed, its gray coat glistened in the light of the stable. He was pleased.

On the way back to the hotel Buck noticed the Sheriff's office. He decided to stop by. He stepped up onto the boardwalk and opened the door.

The man behind the worn out desk looked lean and wiry, a tall, slope shouldered man. He had salt and pepper hair, more salt than pepper, and a handlebar mustache to match that shaded any expression on his mouth. He wore a brown leather vest with a sheriff's badge pinned on the left side and an air of authority about him.

He glanced up and pinned Buck with pale green eyes that rested in a leathery face showing every mile of tough trail and every desert dust storm the man had obviously traveled When the eyes squinted they went more than a little cold.

"You the sheriff?"

"That's me. Grady West is the name. And who might you be?"

"Buck Cordell from south Texas. I trailed two herds that's a couple of days outside town. Just sold them to Harvey Owens. I need a word with you if you got time."

"All I got is time, young fellow. What's on your mind?"

Buck told the whole story, leaving nothing out. When he finished the sheriff sat quietly, staring at Buck, clearly taking his measure. He slowly nodded his head.

"That's the second time I've heard that story. That Adams

fellow you mentioned stopped in to see me last week and told me the same thing."

"What did you do about it?"

"Nothing I could do. I talked to Bonner and he denied everything, said he had no idea what Adams was talking about. It was Adams' word against Nate Bonner's. Adams didn't have any proof. Are you right sure the name you heard was Bonner?"

"As sure as I'm sure of anything."

"Wish there was something more I could do, but without some kind of proof my hands are tied."

"Mine ain't."

"Hope you don't mean what it sounds like. I don't want any trouble in my town."

"If there's trouble it won't be of my making."

"Say your name is Cordell? There was a young fellow by that name through here not long ago. Come to think about it he looked a lot like you, big boy, sixteen or seventeen maybe. Come in with a trail drive I think."

A huge lump raced up the backside of Buck's throat and lodged there. His pulse went crazy and pumped a flush through him that set his skin to tingling. He dared not hope, still...

Could it be my little brother? Could this young fellow with the same name be Cody?

"Tell me *exactly* what the boy looked like."

"Like I say, he was big, not quite as big as you, but big for his age. He had hair like yours, too, and his eyes were pale blue just like yours. The reason I remember him so well, he spent three days in that cell over there."

"What for? What did he do?"

"He shot a fellow, a local bully that needed killing. Oh, it was self-defense by all accounts, but fast as that boy was, it was something real close to murder. Them that saw it all said he was chain lightening with that six-shooter. The local fellow didn't have a chance."

"You don't happen to remember his first name do you?"

"He called himself the Hondo Kid You know him?"

A thrill shot through Buck. He couldn't believe it. *The Hondo Kid. It has to be Cody! My little brother is actually alive!*

"What happened to him?"

"Who knows? When I turned him loose he got on his horse and rode out of town. Hope he never comes back. That young fellow's a shooter if I ever saw one."

"Did he happen to say where he was headed?"

"Nope, he didn't say and I didn't ask."

"What kind of horse was he riding?"

"A black and white pinto. Real pretty thing."

"Much obliged, sheriff. Sounds like my little brother. I thought he was killed or captured by the Comanche. We're from Hondo, Texas."

"If that's your little brother, he's hell on wheels. The one's who saw it said he was the fastest they ever seen. He'll cut a wide swath if he don't run into someone who's faster than him, though that ain't likely."

"Reckon you could do me a favor, sheriff?"

"Might."

"Could you contact the other sheriff's hereabouts and send me word if he turns up somewhere? I shore would like to find him. I'll make it worth your while."

"Reckon I could do that. I'll send some telegrams."

"I'd be obliged."

Buck left word with the sheriff how to contact him and headed for the hotel. He wanted to jump on his horse and take off after Cody, but which way would he go? He had no idea where to look.

When he walked into the hotel, he saw Ben Harding waiting. After learning what he just learned about Cody, he was in no mood to talk with the cattle buyer, but he gave his word and would stick to it.

"Mr. Cordell, I've been waiting to talk with you about buying your cattle."

"Want to talk over a cup of coffee?"

They walked into the dining room. It was all but empty this time of day. Only a man and woman sat at a table near the back. Buck and Ben chose a table and sat down. The waiter brought two cups and poured coffee.

"How many head is in your herd, Mr. Cordell?"

"Five thousand, more or less."

"That many? Oh my, that's a lot of cattle. Well, I'd like to buy them. I'm not a man to beat around the bush. I'll give you thirty-two dollars a head for the lot."

"You're not even close."

The man's eyebrows wrinkled in disbelief. He licked his dry lips.

"Very well, Mr. Cordell, you drive a hard bargain. Thirty-five five dollars a head and that's my final offer."

Buck stood up and stuck out his hand.

"'Fraid not, Mr. Harding, but I'm obliged for your time."

The cattle buyer looked frantic, confused, like he couldn't believe his offer was refused. He stood to his feet. "I can't believe I'm saying this but I'll give you Thirty-eight dollars a head, and I'm losing my shirt."

"Good day, Mr. Harding," Buck said, turning and walking out of the room.

He went to his room and hurriedly changed into his trail clothes. He intended to ride out to meet the herd and lead them into town.

He gathered his rifle and saddlebags and stopped by the desk to tell the clerk he wanted to keep his room and that he would be back in three or four days. He walked to the livery and saddled the gray.

"You leaving us already?" the hostler asked.

"I'll be back in a few days."

"You ride easy now," the old timer called as Buck swung into the saddle and heeled his horse out of the livery.

He set the dappled gray into a ground eating short lope and headed down the trail.

Fading crimson colored the western sky and dusk claimed the countryside but there was still light. The knowledge that his little brother was alive swelled his heart. *If only I could somehow find him, but how?* He rode on, his mind replaying the sheriff's words. *He'll cut a wide swath if he don't run into someone who's faster than him.* That last thought hurt his heart. He knew there was *always* someone faster.

The moon climbed slowly above the horizon, high and proud. It was a full moon, the color of a ripe pumpkin. Its light drove back the darkness and lit the trail almost like day.

The evening star, his and Rebekah's star, hung all alone and lonely in the western sky. He wondered if maybe she was looking up at their star and if she felt as lonely as he did His heart ached. The familiar knot he always felt when he thought of her formed in his stomach. *Rebekah, I love you so much.*

The pictures of her lodged in his mind rushed forward: the silvery spill of her laughter, the gleam of her flaming hair in the sunlight, the silky softness of her skin. He shivered at the memory of her fingers tracing a line along his cheek, of the birth of a curled-up-at-one-corner smile, of the hunger of her kisses.

He stored up these memories, every sight, every sound, every sensation, because if the war had taught him anything, it was that life was fleeting, unpredictable, and unyielding.

His thoughts scattered by the sound of cattle off in the distance so knew he was close. He breasted the crest of a hill and rode down into the shadows of a grassy meadow. They were there, as far as the eye could see—cattle, his cattle. They were settling down for the night.

Off in the distance he spotted the light from a campfire and heard the lonesome sound of a strumming guitar drifting on a soft wind. It was almost like coming home.

Chapter XV

T hey brought the combined herd into town on June 20, three full weeks behind Buck's first estimate. Still and all, it had been a good drive. The cattle were fat because of the slower drive.

Harvey Owens and his top hand Cheyenne Morgan sat beside Buck, Ray and Smokey on the top rail of the corral. Cheyenne and Ray were in charge of the count.

"Good looking cattle, Buck," the cattle buyer, said. "I'll take all the cattle like these you can bring me.

"Contract drovers handle most of the herds that come up the trail. All they're interested in is getting them here as fast as possible and collecting their money. They push them so hard by the time they get here they're not much more than skin and bones."

"We stay as close to water as we can and let them drift, grazing along the way," Buck explained.

"When can you bring me another herd?"

"Been thinking about that. It'll take us most of a month to get home. I figure we can put together another herd and have them on the trail in three weeks. That would put us back here somewhere around the first of November, if the grass will hold up."

"How many you figure to bring next trip?"

"Don't know yet, we'll see."

"Well, like I said, I'll take all you can bring and pay you top dollar."

They finished the count just before sundown. Both Cheyenne and Ray agreed on the total.

"Five thousand, two-hundred and ten," Cheyenne told his boss.

"Good. Buck, if you will meet me at the bank in the morning around ten we'll settle up. When will you boys be heading back?"

"Day after tomorrow at first light. We've got a long way to go."

At ten the next morning Buck walked into the Cattlemen's Bank. Harvey was already there. He sat in front of the bank president's desk They both stood to their feet to greet him.

"Buck, say howdy to A. C. Simmons, the president of this bank. Andrew, this is Buck Cordell, owner of the Longhorn Ranch in south Texas."

They shook hands and sat down.

"Mr. Owens has been telling me about you. He says you delivered him some prime beef."

"Well, they made the drive in pretty good shape"

"I understand you'll be bringing another herd in later in the year?"

"Actually my partner will be handling that drive. We've agreed to trade off."

"And what's his name?"

"Chester Colson. I reckon I'll be back again early next season."

"Well, let's all hope the lawmaker in Jefferson City get

some sense and repeal that silly law banning Texas cattle before then. Did you have any trouble getting your herds through?"

"None to speak of," Buck said.

"Well, according to the tally of five thousand, two-hundred and ten head, at forty dollars a head, the total comes to two-hundred eight thousand, four hundred dollars. How would you like that Mr. Cordell?"

For a moment Buck sat speechless. He had been so engrossed with the price per head he hadn't taken time to figure up how much money that would be Never in his wildest dreams had he ever imagined that much money.

"I'd like a hundred thousand in cash and the rest in the form of a bank draft."

"Very well. It will take only a few minutes."

The bank president summoned his assistant and issued instructions accordingly. Within minutes Buck walked out of the bank with a satchel containing more money than he dreamed possible.

He returned to the hotel and made arrangements to rent the entire dining room for that night, and instructed the manager to prepare the best steaks available with all the trimmings for his entire forty-four man crew. He then asked Ray and Smokey to have their men at the dining room by seven.

The crew looked happy and excited as they gathered in the dining room that night. The steaks were delicious. The cooks and waiters did an excellent job and there was lots of joking and laughter all around.

When the meal was finished, Buck rose to his feet and held up a hand for quiet.

"You fellows know me well enough to know I'm not much of a talker. I just wanted to say that you did a good job bringing the herds up the trail. To my way of thinking you are the best crew a man could ask for.

"Every man here's got a job at the Longhorn as long as he wants it. I've asked Ray and Smokey to set up over yonder to hand out your wages. Each man has three months' pay coming and there's a hundred dollar bonus for every one of you."

Excited cowboy yells shook the hotel building. After the noise died down Buck continued.

"After you pick up your pay, you have the rest of the night to celebrate. We pull out for the trip back home at first light tomorrow morning. Any man not saddled and ready will get left behind.

"The last thing I want to say is that we'll be starting another drive three weeks after we get home. Any man who wants to sign on for another drive is welcome. You'll have first chance. Those who would rather not make the next drive we'll replace with one of the other hands from the ranch.

"That's more words than I have put together in years. So have a good time and stay out of trouble tonight."

After the hands drew their pay and left to celebrate, Buck remembered one more thing he needed to do. He left the hotel and walked down the street to the Golden Nugget Saloon. Before stepping inside he thumbed the traveling loop from his Colt, lifted it halfway from the holster and settled it back gently.

He pushed through the doors and walked to the long mahogany bar. A full length mirror completely covered the back wall.

"What'll you have stranger?" the bartender asked.

"Is Mr. Bonner still in his office upstairs?"

"Far as I know."

Buck crossed the room. His long legs took the stairs two at a time. In the narrow hallway he watched the doors until he came to one with a sign identifying it as Bonner's office. He knocked once and pushed the door open.

Two men sat at a large desk, one on either side. The man

behind the desk was a heavyset fellow. He wore a black three-piece business suit. His close-cropped black mustache matched his slicked down hair. He chewed on a fat cigar as he looked up at Buck.

The second man was a gunman. The fact appeared written all over him. He was slim and rangy. His face was pockmarked and he had quick, shifty eyes that swung to Buck as he entered. The man stood quickly to his feet. His right hand dropped to the Colt in a cut-away holster at his side, but not fast enough.

Buck crossed the room in two long strides, lifting his own Colt as he did. The gun appeared in his hand in one sweeping motion. The same motion landed the weapon squarely on the gunman's left ear, knocking him over the chair he just vacated and out cold.

The so-called cattle broker started to rise from his chair, but settled back again as Buck swung the Walker Colt in his direction.

"I'll have a word with you, Bonner" Buck said harshly.

"Who are you?"

"Name's Cordell. Buck Cordell. I'm the man who buried Sam Watts, Carl Taggart, and eighteen of your men back down the trail a ways.

"I don't know what you're talking about. I never heard of those men."

"Don't lie to me, cause I ain't in no mood for it, no mood a'tall. You may dress like a businessman, but you're nothing but a cattle rustler in a business suit. You're through in this town, Bonner. If you're still here the next time I come to town I'll kill you, no ifs, ands or buts about it. And when your man wakes up, tell him the same goes for him."

With that said Buck turned and walked from the room.

The Longhorn crew was saddled and ready when Buck arrived at the camp just outside town. By the time the first gray of dawn touched the sky their four wagons and forty men on horseback strung out in a long line heading south.

They stayed together until they reached the Red River. Without the herds to slow them down they traveled from dark to dark and covered thirty to forty miles a day. Buck knew that without the wagons his riders on horseback could do close to twice that.

"Smokey, I'd like for you to stay with the wagons. Pick ten men to stay with you. The rest of us will ride on ahead and get started putting together the next drive. Don't figure you'll have any trouble since we're out of Indian territory, but I'll leave Zack with you just in case."

"You got it boss. Don't worry about us, we'll be along. Just save us a spot to lay our bedroll on the next drive."

"Count on it."

Heading southwest along the same trail they took on the way up, they made good time. When the terrain allowed they often rode until late in the night, grabbed a few hours sleep, then headed out again before daylight.

It was a welcome sight when they splashed across the Sycamore River onto Longhorn land. There were cattle everywhere. Herds of five hundred or so dotted the meadows. They couldn't hold back their desire to get home any longer and broke into a full gallop.

As they neared the ranch headquarters, Buck couldn't believe what his eyes were telling him.

Lying before him was the most beautiful walled complex he had ever seen. The walls were finished in a beige adobe, high, wide, and impressive. They stretched out across the flat butte like a giant fortress. A wide opening sported double gates of heavy timber with a well-used road leading into the complex.

Someone sounded the alarm. Longhorn hands dropped what they were doing and responded as they were trained to do. Chester burst from the barn with a rifle in his hand.

Recognizing Buck and the Longhorn riders, he let out an ear-splitting cowboy yell and hurried to meet his friend.

"Welcome home, partner."

"It's good to be home," Buck said, leaning over and pumping Chester's hand. Don't look like the same place I left," he said, pointing a nod with his head toward the compound.

"Changed a bit, ain't it?"

Buck swept his hat off, swabbed sweat and dust from his forehead, and continued to stare at the walled compound, shaking his head in wonderment.

"Wouldn't believe it if I wasn't looking at it with my own eyes."

"Ain't it the truth? That Juan Santos and his boys beats anything I ever saw. He can turn mud and into a castle quicker than you can say scat. That fellow's a legend in his own time. But if you think it's something from the outside, wait till you get a gander at the inside."

Buck swung a leg over the saddle and settled stiffly to the ground. He stomped feeling back into his numb feet as the two friends walked side by side toward the compound. Buck led the dappled gray behind him.

"The rest of the boys coming along behind?" Chester asked

"They'll be along in a few days."

"Well?"

"Well what?"

"Are you gonna tell me or am I supposed to guess?"

"Don't know what you mean."

"What did you get for our cattle, that's what I mean?"

Buck crooked a grin. "Oh that. Well, I hate to tell you this, partner, but here's the truth of it. I talked until I was blue in the face and couldn't get but forty a head."

Chester stopped dead in his tracks. His chin dropped, his mouth opened. He stared in silence with a puzzled look all over his face.

"*Forty dollars* a head? You got *forty dollars* a head?" Chester asked, a wide grin splitting his face. "Holy smoke! How much does that come to? I can't even count that high!"

"It comes to over two-hundred thousand American dollars. Yep. We've made it, partner. Not only that, but you're taking another herd up the trail in three weeks while the market's still strong for Texas beef."

"I'm what? *Three weeks?* How're we gonna put together a trail herd in three weeks? We don't have that many cattle."

"How many you figure we got?"

"Maybe two thousand, all told, not counting our brood herd."

"Then why don't we look across the river? Think our Mexican friend could be talked into selling us some more longhorns?"

Chester pursed his mouth.

"Might. Yes, sir, he just might at that."

They had been walking as they talked and passed through the wide entrance to the compound. Buck stopped dead in his tracks, his eyes wide at what he saw.

The place had been transformed into a paradise. The log chow hall and cooking area hand been completely replaced by an even larger adobe building with a red tile roof. A large rock chimney stood at either end of the building. Smoke trailed lazily upward from one of them.

One of the log cabins still stood. A larger adobe house replaced the previous one. Several smaller buildings, all made of adobe, lined the inside wall of the large compound.

The natural spring that bubbled an endless supply of water was channeled into a small pond in the center of the compound. A waist-high rock wall surrounded the water supply.

"Looks like we're here to stay," Buck said, still shaking his head in complete amazement.

"I had Juan go ahead and get started on your house. That's it over yonder in the corner of the compound. As you can see, it's coming along pretty good."

"Obliged. I'm anxious to look it over. Had any trouble from that Comanche Chief while I was gone?"

"Yeah, he's tried us a couple of times. I reckon he's learning that our boys shoot straight and often with those new Spencers. We see lots of signs that says they ain't far away, but haven't had any trouble out of 'em in a while."

"Hard to figure. I would have bet my saddle he wouldn't let us build that wall."

The two friends and partners talked the rest of the day and far into the night. Chester insisted that Buck give him a detailed accounting of everything that happened on the drive. When he finally finished Chester exhaled a long gust of air.

"You done good, partner. Got any idea how to go about tracking down your little brother?"

"Wish I did. This is a big country, he could be anywhere."

"You'll find him. Just a matter of time."

"On the ride home I had a lot of time to think," Buck said. "Remember that it was your idea to take two herds up the trail instead of one? Well, I got to thinking. Since cattle prices are going through the roof right now, why not strike while the iron is hot?

"This herd you and the boys are taking up the trail ought to put us in a pretty good position to do about whatever we want to do with the ranch If the country is still clamoring for beef next year and the market is still hot, what would you think about us expanding on your idea about putting multiple herds on the trail next year?"

"What are you getting at?"

"I think we ought to send as many herds up the trail to market as we can while the getting is good. I'd like to take at least two herds a month up the trail starting next April, with five thousand head in each herd, like last time, we'll split them into bunches of twenty-five hundred each and keep them a day apart."

Chester's went bug-eyed His mouth dropped open. He was stunned into silence at the enormity of what Buck proposed.

"Holy Smokes! You're talking lots of cattle. Where we gonna get that many?"

"I thought about that. Remember when we were talking to Antonio Rivas? Remember what he said about his friends in the cattle business having no market for their cattle? Well, why don't we just buy their cattle and drive them to market?

"I'd like to take Carlos with me when I go talk to our friend about buying some more of his cattle for your drive. Carlos is a good man. He's got a good head on his shoulders and he's got sand. I think he would make us a good cattle buyer to deal with Don Antonio's friends in Mexico."

"You're right about Carlos And he speaks the language. Pardner, I think you've hit on something. One thing for shore, nobody can accuse you of thinking too small."

"I'm about talked out. Let's get some coffee and I want to hear what's been going on around here."

Chester spent the next few hours bringing Buck up-to-date on the happenings on the ranch. When he got to the part about Pappy capturing El Toro Buck about split his sides laughing at the telling.

"I'd give a month's pay to see ole Pappy up that tree with that big bull trying to get to him," Buck said.

"Me, too."

"Where you got El Toro now?"

"We built a special lot for him. He's might near calmed

down. Pappy's a sight. You outta see him working with that big monster, he treats him like a puppy dog."

"If he can get him tamed down enough to use as a breed bull, we ought to have ourselves something special."

"Yeah, that's what Pappy says. He figures news about El Toro will be the talk of Texas for a long time to come."

"I reckon he's right. You given any thought to giving Pappy a bigger crew so he could up the ante on the number of longhorns he's bringing out of the thickets?"

"No, but we could do that mighty easy. We're getting a steady stream of vaqueros as well as Texas cowboys looking for work."

"Talk to Pappy. If it's all right with him, let's double his crew and dragging wagons. I'll ride over and have a talk with Don Antonio and see what we can work out about some cattle to take up the trail. I'll stop by and pick Carlos up on the way. I'll leave at first light. Shouldn't be gone more'n three or four days."

"Think you can wait that long to see that pretty redhead in Del Rio?"

"Does it show that much?"

"Yep."

"Don't mind telling you, Chester, she ain't ever far from my mind."

"Can't say I blame you, partner, she's shore a pretty thing. Every time I go in the store all she wants to talk about is you."

"I've waited three months, I reckon I can wait a few more days."

Everyone else had long since gone to bed when Buck and Chester finally blew out the lamp and crawled into their bunks.

* * *

The soul-deep sear of agonizing loneliness was close to unbearable. During the day Rebekah did her best to mask the throbbing ache in her heart. But at night the tug of tears was too strong to hold them back. They spilled out and wet her pillow.

Why did a love so beautiful, so encompassing, so warm and tender have to hurt so much?

She closed her tear-stained eyes and hugged her pillow until welcome sleep brought the return of the reoccurring dream of how their life together would be.

It would be a house of love and laughter and indescribable joy. It would be a marriage filled with times of tenderness, and times of passion, and times of quiet talks and long walks.

It would be one of understanding the other's deepest longings and questions and hurts without a word being said. And when the tears came they would be kissed away.

Children? Of course. At least three. Miracles of their love that would perpetuate their

Love throughout all eternity. Is this only a dream? Maybe, but a dream is nothing but a longing of the heart. Maybe someday, maybe someday.

Chapter XVI

Buck stopped by Pappy's camp and asked Carlos to accompany him to see Antonio Rivas, but didn't explain why. They rode steady all day and stopped that night beside the Salado River at the same spot he and Chester camped on their earlier trip.

They saw to their horses, made camp, and cooked supper. Afterward they relaxed with a cup of coffee around the fire.

"You speak our language real good, Carlos. Where'd you grow up?"

"Our father brought us to your country when I was very small. We didn't know it at the time but he knew he was very sick and had only a short time to live. He wanted us to grow up in the United States. He believed we had no future in Mexico. My father died when I was seven.

"My mother worked very hard. She washed clothes, scrubbed floors, and cooked in the small café in San Felipe del Rio. She put away every extra penny. It took many years but finally she was able to buy the small café.

My father and mother insisted that both Selena and I learn your language and attend school. My father was a wise man."

"I think both of us were very fortunate to have parents so willing to sacrifice themselves so their children could enjoy a better life. I have always been a goal setter. I found that if I have a clear picture of where I want to go or what I want to accomplish, it's easier for me to recognize the paths to those things when they appear.

"I'm curious, Carlos, where do you want to go in your life? What do you want to accomplish?"

"I have thought much about those things. All I have known since an early age was working with cattle. As a young boy I dreamed of being a vaquero. I still enjoy what I do, but I must confess that now I find myself dreaming of other things."

"What *other things?*"

"Those have not yet been revealed to me."

"I see."

Buck poured himself another cup of coffee and refilled the cup for his friend.

"Do you remember the man we are going to see, Don Antonio Rivas?"

"*Si,* I saw him when he and his vaqueros brought the cattle, but I did not meet him."

"Well, you'll get to meet him tomorrow. He's a good man, a man of his word. It's important to do business with men like that. Reckon we better get some shut-eye. We'll be heading back as soon as we finish our business with Mr. Rivas.

They rose and got in the saddle while the pre-dawn darkness still gripped the desert. They rode mostly in silence. Buck liked his young traveling companion. Though he wasn't ready to mention his plans just yet, secretly he hoped what he had in mind worked out.

The morning broke clear and hot. The sun rose and wasted no time going to work at its endless task of cooking the desert unmercifully. No breeze stirred the air. The stifling air was so hot it burned a man's insides just to breathe. It looked to be a real humdinger of a day.

By mid-morning their presence had came to the attention of Señor Rivas's outriders. Off in the distance a plume of dust rose from the desert.

"Here comes our welcoming committee," Buck said.

"What do you mean?"

"Don Antonio is a careful fellow. He employes a security force that is top-notch. If a man travels this close to his ranch, he'd better have a good reason."

A dozen heavily armed horsemen emerged from the dust cloud and galloped to intercept Buck and Carlos In mere minutes the outriders had closed the horseshoe formation and surrounded the two newcomers.

Fortunately, the same security man who met Buck and Chester on their previous trip recognized Buck.

"Ah, Mr. Cordell, it is you. Don Antonio did not tell me you were coming."

"He didn't know. I need to see him on business, if he is available."

"*Si, señor,* he will be very pleased that you are here."

In short order Buck and Carlos were escorted to the sprawling walled hacienda. They rode through the gate into the courtyard and dismounted. Don Antonio emerged from the house and greeted them with a wide smile.

"*Señor* Cordell, *mi amigo!* How good it is to see you again."

The two friends shook hands warmly.

"Don Antonio, I'd like you to meet my friend, Carlos Rodriguez.

"Welcome to my *casa,*" the host said, extending his hand. "A friend of Señor Cordell is my friend as well." Carlos and Don Antonio shook hands.

"Come, let us go inside."

They were ushered into the same large den Buck visited before. After they were seated a servant brought a tray of coffee and poured each man a cup.

"I trust your cattle drive was successful?"

"Yes, in fact, it is why we are here. We're putting together another herd that will head out in three weeks. It's kinda late in the year to start a drive, but we think we can make it work. We have about twenty-five hundred head. I need to buy another twenty-five hundred. Do you have that many you would be able to sell?"

The rancher listened intently and then sat in silent thought for a long moment before replying.

"I could spare another two thousand. Beyond that, it would require selling my brood cattle. I am sorry, but that is all I could sell at this time."

"I understand. I certainly wouldn't expect you to run yourself short. I'd like to buy the two thousand head. What price would you want?

"Would the same price you paid before be acceptable? Three dollars a head, I believe?"

"The cattle market is strong right now. I want to be fair. I'll give you five dollars a head."

Don Antonio raised his eyebrows in surprise.

"Five dollars a head is much more than fair, when do you want your cattle delivered?"

"Would two weeks from today be possible?"

"It will be done."

"Like before, your money will be waiting on you when delivery is made. When we were here before you mentioned other Mexican cattle growers. Do you think some of them might have cattle they would be willing to sell?"

"*Si,* I am sure many of them would be happy to sell their

cattle to you. But to contact them and arrange for the purchase and get them delivered in such a short time, I'm afraid it would not be possible."

"I understand. I wasn't thinking of this drive. My plans are to take a number of herds up the trail next season, perhaps as many as ten. That means I would need upward of fifty thousand head, maybe more.

"These friends of yours who might have cattle to sell, do you think they would be willing to sell to me?"

"*Si,* for five dollars a head you could buy all the cattle in Mexico."

"How would we know who these ranchers are and where their ranches are located?"

"I would be more than happy to provide a list and a letter of introduction. I would be doing them a great favor."

"I am be much obliged. Just give the information to Carlos. He's going to be my cattle buyer."

Buck slanted a glance at his friend. Carlos did a double take before his eyes opened wide, obviously unable to believe what he just heard.

Buck cut a grin at him.

"You will be able to stay the night won't you?"

"Afraid not. We've got to head right on back."

"Then if you will excuse me, I will prepare the list and the letter of introduction right away. It should only take a few minutes."

Don Antonio left the room to prepare the papers.

"Sorry to spring your new assignment on you like that, Carlos, but I had to be sure things would work out on this end before I could lay it all out.

"In a nutshell, I would like for you to contact the names on the list he's preparing and line up cattle for next year's drives. We'll talk more about numbers and the timing of the deliveries later on. Right now what I need to hear from you is if you will accept the job?"

"I am deeply honored that you would even consider me for such an important assignment. If you believe I am capable of this responsibility, I will gladly accept and pledge to do my very best. *Gracias, señor* I will not let you down."

"Then the job is yours. It pays two hundred a month. Is that satisfactory?"

"It is very generous, *señor.*"

"Good. Then let me be the first to congratulate you on your new job."

Buck stuck out his hand. They shared a firm handshake, sealing the agreement.

Señor Rivas returned with a brown leather folder containing the two handwritten documents. He handed the folder to Carlos. "All of the Mexican cattle growers of any size are listed there along with where they are located. Just show them my letter of introduction and I'm sure you will not have any trouble."

Buck and Carlos stood and shook hands with the rancher.

"Thank you for your help, Don Antonio," Carlos said.

"I am sorry that you could not stay overnight with us, *Señora* Rivas will be disappointed."

"Please apologize for us. Will you be accompanying the vaqueros when they deliver the cattle?" Buck asked.

"*Si,* I would not miss it."

"Then we'll see you in two weeks."

"*Vaya con Dios, mi amigos*"

Buck and Carlos rode the afternoon away. The boiling-hot sun cooked into the desert sand and radiated heat like an oven. Both horses and riders were drenched with perspiration. There was no shade where they could seek shelter, so they were forced to keep moving. Finally, the sun sank slowly behind the western horizon and shadows lengthened.

As dusk settled over the desert they reined into a dry arroyo that opened into the Salado River. Buck built a supper fire while Carlos watered the horses. After their meal of salt pork and beans they relaxed against their upturned saddles with a steaming cup of coffee.

"Chester and I had a meeting and decided to double Pappy's crew. That ought to produce seventy more longhorns a day. At that rate, we ought to pull five thousand out of the thickets between now and April.

"But that's only enough for the first drive. We want to take ten thousand head a month up the trail between April and September, that's sixty thousand head.

"We need a steady supply of ten thousand head a month delivered, starting in March. That's a tall order, but I believe you can handle it."

"I think I need to get on the road right away to see what is available."

"I agree. Soon as we get back I think you need to start contacting the Mexican ranchers and setting up the contracts. That's an awful lot of cattle."

After the extreme heat of the day, nighttime in the desert can be a shocking contrast. As darkness deepened a chill swept across the desert on a soft breeze. Buck added a few sticks of dry mesquite to the fire and pulled his sheepskin coat tighter around his neck.

They sipped coffee and talked cattle talk until the position of the stars told them it was near midnight. They crawled into their blankets.

Buck still lay awake, if only barely, when the black gelding whinnied deep in its chest. Buck came instantly alert. His hand closed over the Spencer carbine lying at his side. He levered a shell into the chamber and touched Carlos awake.

"We've got company," Buck whispered.

Both men rolled quietly from their blankets and hurriedly bunched them to resemble a sleeping man. They bellied quickly to the edge of the wash and found concealment among some low-growing mesquite bushes.

They waited.

Soft, crunching sounds of booted feet in the sand told them the intruders weren't Indians. The metallic click of three rifles being levered reached their hearing.

Buck squinted into the darkness. A dim silhouette crouched on the bank overlooking their waning campfire.

A shot shattered the stillness of the night, then another and yet another.

Buck squeezed the trigger of his carbine. The explosion slammed into his shoulder. Up on the bank, one of the attackers let out a muffled grunt and doubled over as the heavy .50 caliber shell tore into him. He pitched headlong over the bank and landed in the campsite.

Beside Buck, Carlos's rifle blasted. A long, piercing scream died away into stillness broken only by running footsteps.

Buck scrambled from his hiding place and up the embankment. The shadowy form of a retreating figure was highlighted against the starry sky. Buck threw his rifle to his shoulder and fired. The man arched backward, and then fell face down in the sand.

Cautiously, they checked the three attackers.

"Banditos," Carlos called to Buck.

"They likely have some horses stashed nearby. There might be another one. Let's check it out."

They found the horses in a nearby dry wash. They also found a boy.

He lay huddled in the sand, in the fetal position, He was barefooted. His clothes were nothing but tattered rags clinging to his body. His hands were tied behind his back and a strip of dirty cloth around his mouth. A rope was cinched around his neck and secured to the saddlehorn of one of the horses.

Carlos quickly untied the Mexican boy. In the dim light Buck judged him to be no more than ten-years old. He looked to be half-starved and bruises on his face testified that he had been recently beaten. He cringed at Carlos's touch and cowed away.

Carlos spoke softly in Spanish. The boy looked at him with terror reflected in his eyes.

Unbridled anger welled up inside Buck. That grown men could treat a young boy the way this one had obviously been treated made Buck want to unload his carbine into the lifeless bodies of the scum that lay nearby. No telling what other acts of brutality they were responsible for. An overwhelming sense of compassion and responsibility surged through him.

As Carlos continued to speak gently, the boy softened. He helped the boy to his feet and together they walked to the fire. On the way the boy saw the lifeless bodies of the bandits. He shied away, afraid even to walk near them.

Buck stoked the fire to life and poured more water into the coffee pot. He took a blanket from his bedroll and wrapped it around the boy's shoulders as Carlos continued talking to the boy.

By the time the coffee came to a boil they learned that the young man's name was Christopher Lopez. They learned that the bandits murdered his mama and papa and burned their house. The bad men had even slaughtered the few goats the family owned.

Though Buck couldn't understand what the boy was saying, Carlos repeated enough that Buck's heart went out to Christopher.

"We'll take him with us. It's so close to first light we might just as well hit the trail. I'll gather their horses. From the looks of his feet, it appears they made him walk. It's about time he rode."

By the time they arrived at the ranch headquarters Christopher opened up to Carlos and told him in detail all that had happened. He had overheard the bandits say they were going to sell him to a wealthy landowner they knew.

Buck turned the boy over to Jewel. The large black woman loved children. She was like a mother hen, and would doctor Christopher's wounds and see to his every need.

By the time Buck took a bath, shaved, and climbed into a clean change of clothes the day was mostly spent. As he dressed, all he could think of was Rebekah. He had been gone over three and a half months.

What if she has second thoughts about our marriage? What if she met someone else? What if something bad happened to her while I was away?

These and a hundred other thoughts sent wave after wave of fear racing through him. A huge lump climbed up the back of his throat and lodged there. He swallowed again and again but the lump refused to go down.

He toed a stirrup and swung a leg over the saddle even as his dappled gray danced in place, anxious to get on the trail after its long inactivity.

Buck let the gelding have its head. The gray stretched out in a long-legged gallop that covered the trip to town in record time, almost as if the horse could somehow sense his master's anticipation.

The sun slipped behind the western horizon and darkness

deepened as Buck rode into Del Rio. Lamplight seeped through dirty windows and painted square patches of orange light in the dusty street.

The tinny sound of an out-of-tune piano drifted on a soft chilly breeze through the open door of a saloon. Buck paid it no mind. His gaze remained fixed on the darkened window of Walker's store.

He heeled his mount into a short lope and rode toward the white house with a picket fence at the far end of town. His heart beat faster as he saw a light in the window.

He reined up at the hitching post.

"Hello the house!" he called loudly.

It took only a few heartbeats before the front door jerked open. Rebekah stood there.

It was obvious she was ready for bed, standing there barefooted and wearing only a white nightgown. Her red hair hung loose down her back to waist length. For an instant her image was silhouetted in the doorway with the lamplight behind her. The sight took Buck's breath away.

"Hey, pretty Lady!"

"Hey, cowboy," she replied before letting out a small scream and racing across the porch. She leaped into his open arms.

Happy tears welled up and wet his shoulder. They clung tightly to one another. For a long slice of time they were the only people in the world. Nothing else, no one else, mattered. They were in their own private world, a world that consisted of just two people, two people totally in love with one another.

Rebekah tried to choke back the sobs, but they would not be denied. They gushed out in a body-shaking burst of emotion.

"Please don't cry," Buck whispered into her neck.

"I'm just so glad you're home safe," she choked out between sobs. "I was so worried. I missed you so much."

She felt his strong arms draw her even tighter. She melted into him. She wanted him to just hold her, to never let her go.

"I missed you, too, Rebekah. I thought about you every day."

"You two lovebirds better come in the house," her father said from the porch. "You're liable to catch your death of cold out there in the night air."

Neither of them had been aware of his presence. They turned and, arm in arm, walked slowly into the house.

John Walker opened the door to the pot-bellied stove and stoked the fire with a poker.

"I'll put on some coffee," Rebekah said, still unable to take her eyes off of Buck.

"I 'spect we could all use a cup," John said, adding two sticks of wood to the fire.

"Coffee would be good," Buck said.

"Have a seat," Mr. Walker invited. "Glad you're back. You've been gone quite a spell. Becky's been moping around like a sick calf ever since you left."

"Oh, Father," Rebekah said from the kitchen.

Buck sat down on the sofa that faced the stove.

"How was the drive? Any trouble along the way?" John Walker asked.

"None to speak of. We'll be taking another five thousand head up the trail in three weeks."

Buck and John Walker jerked their heads around to a loud noise from the kitchen. Rebekah had dropped the coffee pot full of water. She stood, staring wide-eyed at Buck with both open hands covering her mouth.

Realizing that she had misunderstood his last statement, he hastened to explain. "No, I didn't mean that *I* was taking a herd, Chester will be ramrodding this one."

Rebekah let out a loud sigh of relief.

Mr. Walker sat down in a rocking chair and picked up his pipe from a nearby table. He opened the drawstring tobacco sack and carefully packed the pipe. Leaning forward he struck a match against the hot stove and put the flame to his pipe. A cloud of sweet-smelling blue smoke boiled from his mouth before he spoke.

"Not trying to pry, mind you, but sounds like you got a fair price for your cattle or you wouldn't be trailing another herd so soon."

"Yep. Cattle prices are good right now."

Rebekah walked over to stand behind Buck. Her hand rested gently on his shoulder.

"We're planning on taking quite a few up the trail come April, but I won't be going anymore until then. We've got a lot of work to do around the ranch."

Buck felt a soft squeeze on his shoulder.

"A detachment of bluecoats rode into town a couple of weeks ago. Colonel Callahan stopped in to see me. He was asking a lot of questions. Thought you'd be wanting to know."

"What kind of questions?" Buck asked.

"Said he's heard about some hangings out at your place. Wanted to know if I knew anything about it?"

"What'd you tell him?"

"Didn't know nothing to tell him and wouldn't if I did. I told him he ought to talk to you if he wanted to know the truth of it."

"Yeah, we've had some words."

"How'd the Spencer carbines work for you?" Walker asked.

"That's some rifle. It's no wonder the Yankees won the war. That reminds me, can you lay your hands on about fifty heavy sheep-lined coats in a hurry? My men might run into some nasty weather before this next drive is over. So I'll need fifty more blankets."

"I'll go to work on it first thing in the morning."

"Coffee's ready," Rebekah said, handing Buck and her

father a steaming cup and then sitting down on the sofa beside Buck.

She was only a hair breadth away. He could feel the warmth of her radiating against his leg. Just the nearness of her sent his mind spinning. The conversation might be about cattle and Indians and outlaws, but his thoughts were about having Rebekah in his arms, about her sweet kisses, about their future together.

Finally, her father yawned and rose from his chair.

"Hope you young folks will excuse me, I've got a big day tomorrow. Glad you're home, Buck. It ain't the same without you around."

"Thanks, Mr. Walker. It's shore good to be back."

After her father left the room and closed the door to his bedroom Rebekah lifted a searching gaze into Buck's eyes. Her hand rose and feathered her fingers along Buck's cheek while staring at him.

"He's right, you know, I was a mess all the time you were gone I could think of nothing else but you. I woke up every morning wondering where you were or what you were doing, needing to tell you what I was thinking or feeling. I must have stared out that window at the store half the time you were gone, searching the road, hoping to see you riding up.

"I lay in bed at night and just before I drifted off to sleep I wondered if you were thinking about me, and us, and our future together. I prayed for your safety and that God would bring you back to me. It's so good to have you home."

She slowly lifted her lips to his in a long, tender kiss. Buck's arms encircled her and drew her to him. She felt his lips come soft and full upon hers. The strength of his embrace was incompatible with the tenderness of his mouth.

He tasted of loneliness, and yearning, and need, and temptation. His energy seemed blazing and enveloped her, consumed her, and sent tingles dancing along her skin from head to toe.

It was as if she was lifted from her body and transferred into another world, a world she could never have imagined, a world of softness, and beauty, and love. She laid her head on his wide shoulder and cuddled close into the curve of his neck.

The soft crackling of the wood in the stove became the only sound that disturbed the silence.

It was well after midnight when Buck approached the walled ranch headquarters.

"Hold it right there," a sentry's voice challenged from the darkened watchtower. "Who are you and what's your business?"

"It's Buck Cordell."

"Oh, sorry Mr. Cordell, didn't recognize you in the dark. Just a minute and I'll open the gate."

Buck was glad to see the extra security. The heavy gate swung open and he rode through.

"Everything quiet?" Buck asked.

"Yes, sir, quiet as a church mouse and that's the way we like it."

Buck reined his gray to the barn and unsaddled, taking time to stall and dump a bucket of grain in the feed bin before walking across the courtyard to his cabin. Long after he shucked his clothes and stretched out on his bunk he lay awake, staring up into the darkness.

His mind replayed every word, every whispered promise, every embrace he and Rebekah had shared. There was no doubt about it, Chester was right; the love bug had bitten him real good. Tomorrow he would have Pablo and his workers begin work on the hacienda Buck wanted to build for Rebekah.

* * *

Wranglers were already trouping into the chow hall for breakfast when Buck joined them. He swept the room with a look and saw several faces he didn't recognize. He poured a cup of steaming coffee and accepted a plate of steak and eggs from Jewel. "Wash and the others ought to be pulling in a day or two," he told her.

That news brought a wide smile on the woman's face.

"Will he be going back with the next drive, Mr. Buck?"

"Only if he wants to. That'll be up to him."

Buck found a place at a table and stepped over the attached bench and sat down. He took his first mouthful as Chester sat down beside him.

"How's it feel to be home, Buck?"

"Feels good. It's a far piece to Missouri and back."

"Reckon I'm about to find out for myself. How's Rebekah?"

"Better than this cowboy deserves. She's a fine woman, Chester. Don't know if you know or not, but after her ma died she shouldered a heavy load, what with helping John run the store, their home, and taking care of her father. She's a strong woman. She'll make me a good wife."

"I don't doubt that for a minute."

"You and Selena have any thoughts along those lines?"

"I go to see her from time to time, we're getting there."

"She's a fine woman. A man could do a whole lot worse than that little Mexican gal."

"Have you been down to take a look at Pappy's bull since you got home?"

"No, can't wait to see that critter though."

"You ain't gonna believe your eyes, it's like nothing you ever laid eyes on before."

"Has Pappy made any headway in taming it down?"

"Oh, yeah, that man is something else, it's like he took El Toro as a personal challenge. He's determined to tame that monster."

While they were eating breakfast and talking, Carlos walked in and sat down at the table.

"Buenas dias," he greeted.

"Good Morning," both Buck and Chester said.

"As you suggested, Mr. Buck, I will be taking Pedro and Pablo with me to visit the rancheros in Mexico. We will be leave this morning."

"Good. I know you will do well. Find us lots of longhorns. We're gonna need 'em."

"I will do my very best, *señor.*"

"I've been thinking about something, partner," Chester said. "After I get back from the drive, what would you think about me going up to Tyler to get my folks? They're getting on in years. Pa ain't able to do much anymore and I'd like to have them closer so I can look after them."

"I think that's a mighty good idea. We need to get the workers started on a house for them right here in the compound."

"That'd be good. Reckon I need to ride into town in a day or two and tell Selena goodbye, too."

The next two weeks seemed to sprout wings and fly by. The rest of Buck's trail crew made it back and jumped right into the task of getting the next drive ready to leave in less than a week. Every hand on the ranch worked from dark till dark.

"Think I'll ride into town this morning," Chester told Buck at their breakfast meeting. "Need to tell Selena goodbye. I ought to be back before dark."

"Give her my regards."

The ride to Del Rio only took a couple of hours and he soon reined up in front of the little café. He noticed several horses with U. S. Army riggings tied at the hitching rail in front of Walker's store, but thought little of it.

Selena saw him ride up and ran out to meet him as he swung down.

"I thought you would never come," she said, pursing her lips in a pouting smile.

"Couldn't ride off to Missouri without saying goodbye to my gal."

"You better not, if you know what's good for you."

"I know what's good for me," he said, circling an arm around her waist.

"Oh, you do, do you? And just what would that be?"

"Not what, *who*, and what's good for me is you."

She circled her own arm around his waist and hugged him close as they walked inside.

After saying hello to Selena's mother they enjoyed a leisurely cup of coffee together. The door opened. Chester glanced around.

The spit and polish lieutenant and half a dozen troopers walked in. The lieutenant had his weapon drawn. The six troopers carried rifles in their hands pointed directly at Chester.

The officer walked up to stand beside Chester's table.

"Are you Chester Colson?"

"I am. What can I do for you?"

"Mr. Colson, I'm placing you under arrest for the hanging of Ike Sawyer over near Eagle Pass a while back. Sergeant, take this man's weapon. Place him in irons and bring him along."

Chester was faced with a decision.

Do I give up my gun and go along with them or do I fight? With seven guns pointed at me I don't stand a chance. Reckon it's best that I go along for now.

"Get word to Buck. Tell him what's happened," he told Selena.

The lieutenant had come prepared. He seemed to take delight in securing the handcuff and leg irons on Chester. When the job was finished, the young officer stood up and gave Chester a smirking smile.

"You ain't such a big, bad man without that gun are you?"

Chester just gave him a hard look.

As two troopers boosted Chester into the saddle Selena was racing toward the livery.

"I need to borrow a fast horse!" She told the liveryman hurriedly. "Please hurry."

"Yes Ma'am," Pete told her, sensing the urgency in her voice. "It won't take but a minute."

True to his word, a fine looking bay was quickly saddled and trotted forward. She swung into the saddle and heeled the bay into a hard gallop out of town.

Chapter XVII

With his hands and feet shackled and the lieutenant leading his horse, Chester was helpless. Troopers rode closely on both sides and behind him as they made the trip to Fort Clark, it took them most of the day.

When they arrived, they led Chester into the large headquarters building and into Colonel Callahan's office. Chester shuffled across the room, forced along by a guard on either side of him. The colonel sat behind his desk smoking a fat cigar. For a long moment the officer just stared at Chester, saying nothing.

The lieutenant stood off to one side, a satisfied smile on his lips.

"So, Mr. Colson, we finally meet. I'm Colonel Callahan, commandant of Fort Clark."

"I know who you are. Why am I under arrest?"

"You are accused of hanging a livestock dealer named Ike Sawyer over near Eagle Pass. We have witnesses who will testify they saw you commit the offense. You will be tried, and if found guilty, you will hang."

"That so called, livestock dealer dealt in stolen stock. Those horses wore our Longhorn brand. A blind man could tell they were stolen horses."

"You best save your story for the trial. Take him away."

The grinning lieutenant motioned to the two guards with a nod of his head. They roughly grabbed both of Chester's arms and led him from the office. The leg shackles around his ankles made it difficult to walk. He stumbled often as they crossed the parade ground.

The lieutenant opened the door of a large, low building and stood aside for the guards to bring Chester inside.

"Who you got for us, lieutenant?" A big, burly sergeant asked, rising from his chair behind the desk.

"Got a smart-mouth who thinks he's better than anybody wearing blue. I'd say he's a no good Reb coward."

"A Reb, huh," the big sergeant said, walking over to stand in front of Chester. "I hate Red bellies worse'n I hate skunks. We know how to deal with your kind, mister Bring him on back to the jail. I got a special cell just waiting on him."

The master at arms half-dragged Chester down the hallway and into the solitary cell. He unlocked Chester's ankle chain and fed the free end through a large iron ring fitted into the wall high above the floor. Using the chains, the master at arms and lieutenant hoisted Chester into the air, suspending him from by his wrists. His weight caused the shackles to dig deep into his wrists.

Pain radiated down his arms. Chester gritted his teeth against it and clamped his lips tight, refusing to make a sound.

"He's a tough one," the big sergeant said. "Most are screaming their heads off by now."

He accented his comments by driving a huge, balled fist into Chester's ribs. Chester felt something snap. A sharp pain shot through him. He knew the blow had broken a rib. Still he refused to cry out.

The sergeant grabbed a handful of Chester's shirt and ripped it from his body. He yanked off Chester's boots and britches, leaving him stark naked.

"He won't be so tough when I get through with him." The sergeant laughed.

A long, heavy nightstick hung by a leather cord from his belt. He hefted it in his hand, slapping it against his open palm and staring up at his helpless prisoner. A cruel smile curled his lips.

"Now comes the part I like. If you don't wantta watch, lieutenant, you best mosey on along. Me and this Reb are gonna come to an understanding about who won the war."

"I want to see it," the lieutenant said, his voice taking on a sadistic sound.

Chester saw the blow coming. He tried to roll his head to prevent the club from hitting him directly in the face, but it didn't help. An explosion of pain went off in his head. A million pinpoints of light twinkled before his eyes. A hot flush surged through him just before a black shroud of darkness settled over him.

Buck sat sipping a cup of coffee and talking with Pablo about the layout for Rebekah's house when he lookout called out that a rider was galloping toward the compound. "It's a woman, and she's in a powerful hurry," the man called from the watch tower. Buck trotted toward the gate and recognized Selena and knew immediately that something bad happened.

She rode through the gate at a gallop and reined the horse in Buck's direction. Buck hurried to meet her.

"It's Chester," the girl said breathlessly. "The army arrested him. They put chains on him and took him away."

"Manuel!" Buck shouted to the hostler who had walked out from the inside stable. "Saddle my horse and hurry!"

Ray and Smokey trotted up to see what was going on. Buck explained while he waited on his horse.

"Want us to ride with you?"

"No, I'll handle it. Keep them boys busy getting the herds ready for the trail drive. We ain't got much time left. Selena, go on back to town. I'll get this straightened out."

"No, *señor,* I'm going with you."

"Be better if you'd go on back to town and let me handle it."

"No, Mr. Buck, Chester is my man and I'm going with you!"

"Then you'll need a fresh horse. That one is lathered up and winded. Manuel throw a saddle on another horse for this lady."

In minutes Buck and Selena galloped side by side toward Fort Clark. It was forty miles to Fort Clark and would take them the rest of the day to get there.

They alternated between a gallop and a fast walk. Still, they were forced to stop occasionally to rest the horses. During one of those stops Buck looked long at the pretty Mexican girl. Her expression told him she was worried sick.

"You love him don't you?"

"Si, señor, with my whole heart."

"He's a good man. Doubt you'd find a better."

"Miss Rebekah and I have talked. We both think we're the luckiest two ladies in the world to have you and Chester."

"I'd say we are the lucky ones. We better get moving, I want to get there before dark."

The sun set in the distance as Buck and Selena rode through the gate of the sprawling fort. Buck asked the sentry on the gate for directions to the colonel's office and the man pointed to a large adobe building.

The regimental headquarters building sat just off the parade ground. Two flags waved in a stiff, hot breeze atop the headquarters building: the flag of the United States and the flag of the 3rd Cavalry.

Selena followed Buck closely as they stepped through the door into the orderly room. A burly sergeant with striped covering his sleeves sat at a desk positioned to guard another door. He looked up as they entered.

"Can I help you folks?"

"We'd like to see Colonel Callahan. I'm Buck Cordell. This is Selena Rodriguez."

"One moment, please."

The sergeant rose and tapped on the nearby door and then opened it and stepped inside. He was gone only a minute before he swung the door open and stepped aside.

"Colonel Callahan will see you now."

Buck and Selena walked briskly through the door. The Colonel was sitting behind a large desk. He was leaned back and smoking a long, fat cigar. His squinting gaze fixed upon Buck and held for a moment.

"Something I can do for you, Mr. Cordell?"

"I understand you arrested my partner, Chester Colson?"

A thin, smirking smile curled his lips. He took a long pull on the cigar and blew the blue smoke toward the ceiling before he responded. "Yes, indeed, you understand correctly, Mr. Colson is under arrest."

"On what charge?"

"I have tried unsuccessfully to tell you that you can't just go around hanging people whenever you feel like it. It seems your Mr. Colson didn't get the message."

"Those men he hung killed one of our men and stole our remuda of horses. Last I heard, both those things were a hanging offense."

"By authorized law enforcement officials, not by you and your partner."

"We stomp our own snakes. When a man comes onto *our* property, kills *our* men, and steals *our* horses, what are we supposed to do, ride down here, fill out a report in triplicate, and wait for you and the army to do nothing?"

"Well, this time your partner went too far."

"What do you intend to do?"

"Unlike the men he hung, he'll receive a fair trial. If he is convicted he'll most likely hang."

"Chester did nothing any self-respecting man wouldn't do. I want to see him."

"I suppose there would be no harm in that. Sergeant Briscoe will escort you to the brig. Now if there is nothing else?"

"Oh, there is something else, sure enough. This ain't over by a long shot. I want to see my partner and I want to see him now."

"Sergeant!" the colonel called loudly.

The sergeant opened the door almost immediately.

"Escort Mr. Cordell and the young lady over to the guardhouse. Inform the master at arms that I have given permission for them to see the prisoner, Chester Colson."

The sergeant saluted and stood aside for Buck and Selena to pass through. They followed him across the parade ground and into a low, stone building. Bars covered all the windows.

The sergeant opened a door that gave them entrance to a small office where a hard looking NCO sat behind a small desk.

"The colonel gave these folks permission to visit with prisoner Colson."

The master at arms settled a critical look on Buck.

"That boy's a hard case," the big NCO said. "Had to truss him up to control him. He ain't feeling like having visitors. Come back tomorrow."

"We ain't coming back tomorrow," Buck said emphatically. "We're gonna see him now, right now or I'll march back to your colonel's office and bring him over here with me."

The big master at arms pinned Buck with a long gaze before he struggled his large frame out of the chair and trudged slowly to a heavy wooden door. He took a lantern from a peg on the wall and lit it. Buck wondered what the lantern was for. The sergeant selected a key from a large key ring and opened the door into a long hallway with cells on both sides. Buck and Selena followed past several cells holding mostly Mexicans and a few army prisoners.

The prisoners stared hard at the visitors through the bars of their cells. Their glassy eyes conveyed a look of hopelessness.

The jailer walked to the far end of the hall and stopped in front of a solid steel door at the end of the hallway. He inserted a key and swung the door open. The space inside was totally dark, no window to offer either light or ventilation. Only the sparse light from the hallway filtered in and lit the solitary cell with a shadowy dimness.

A sickening waft of stale air rushed out through the open door. The smell of body odor, urine, and excrement forced Buck take a step backwards.

"Good Lord, man!" he exclaimed. "Surely you don't keep a human being in there!"

"That's where we keep our troublemakers," the jailer replied with a smirking smile.

Handing the lantern to Buck, the sergeant stood aside. Buck held his nose and took a step inside.

What he saw turned his stomach and his face boiled with anger.

Chester hung stripped naked. His hands shackled to two heavy iron rings high up on the wall, suspended him a foot off the floor. His face was a swollen mass of cuts and bruises.

Obviously he had been beaten while he hung helplessly suspended in the air. His head hung lifelessly against his chest.

"Sergeant!" Buck screamed. "Get this man down from there! Do it now!"

"'Fraid I can't do that. My orders were to let you visit him. Didn't say nothing about setting him loose."

"We'll see about that," Buck spat the words out.

He turned on his heels and pushed through the door, shoving the sergeant aside as he went through.

"Come on, Selena, you don't want to see what I just saw."

Buck's long strides carried him quickly from the building and across the parade ground. Selena hurried along behind him, unable to keep pace. Buck shoved through the door of the headquarters building. The sergeant leaped to his feet, but was unable to block Buck's path to the colonel's office door.

He slammed open the door. The colonel jerked up from some papers as Buck stomped across the room. He stopped in front of the officer's desk and leaned across it, his doubled fists on top of the desk supporting his weight.

"What's the meaning of this?" The colonel demanded, shooting to his feet.

"Are you aware of what's going on over there in your guardhouse?"

"I don't know what you're talking about."

"I found my partner hanging naked from the ceiling, his hands shackled. He has been beaten to a pulp. I want him down and I want a doctor to tend to him. You're gonna be hearing plenty about this, colonel. I expect my friend, General Sheridan, will have some tough questions he'll want answers to."

"You know General Sheridan?" The officer questioned with disbelief showing clearly on his face.

"Philip Henry and I go back a ways. We were in West Point together. I believe he's your superior officer here in Texas, is he not?"

Colonel Callahan suddenly appeared very nervous. Sweat popped out on his forehead. He licked dry lips.

"Uh, yes. Yes he is. I wasn't aware you served in the war."

"Apparently there are lots of things you aren't aware of, colonel, one of them being what's going on over there in your guardhouse Now get my partner down from there and get him a doctor."

The colonel strode quickly from the office.

"Follow me, sergeant," he ordered his aide as he past the sergeant's desk.

Buck, the sergeant, and Selena followed the officer across the parade ground. The colonel shoved through the door to the master at arm's office. The man leaped to his feet and saluted.

"Take me to prisoner Colson's cell," he ordered.

"But...but..." the big sergeant stammered.

"That's an order, sergeant!"

"Yes, sir."

The man fumbled to again light the lantern and open the heavy door leading into the cell block. The little procession walked quickly past the barred cells to the steel door at the end of the hallway.

"Why is the prisoner being held in solitary?" The colonel demanded.

"He, he was causing trouble."

"Get this door open and do it now."

The sergeant clearly didn't want to open the door, but he had no choice. He inserted the key and swung the door open. The colonel stepped backward when the smell billowed out from the room. His hand flew to cover his nose and mouth.

He snatched the lantern from the sergeant's hand and held it high as he stepped cautiously into the cell.

Buck, Selena and the sergeant remained outside.

"Sergeant!" The colonel bellowed from inside the cell. "Get this man down from here!"

With the help of Buck and the colonel's aide, they loosed the shackles and carried Chester out of the cell and lay him on the hallway floor.

"Send for the doctor," the officer ordered his aide. "Escort the young lady into the outer office. She shouldn't have to see this. And bring a blanket to cover this man."

Chester lay unconscious. Buck dropped to his knees beside his friend. He bent to listen for a heartbeat. There was one but it was weak, erratic. He raised his face and pinned the colonel with a hard gaze. The officer looked quickly away in shame.

Within minutes the doctor arrived and knelt beside Chester. He used a stethoscope to search for a heartbeat. A concerned look wrinkled his brow. He moved the instrument back and forth slowly, listening intently. Finally, he removed the earpieces from his ears and looked up at the colonel.

"He's alive, but barely. This man has been beaten half to death. Get him over to the hospital. Don't know if I can save him, but I'll do my best."

The colonel's aide had reappeared with two troopers and a stretcher. They lifted Chester and placed on the stretcher then carried him out. The doctor followed.

The rest of them started to follow. The colonel's hand shot out and gathered a handful of the master at arm's shirt. He pulled the man's face within inches of his own.

"If that prisoner dies I'll have you court martialed and hung. Now get in there!"

The officer shoved the sergeant into the stinking solitary cell just vacated by Chester. He slammed the door shut and turned toward his aide.

"See that door is locked. It is *not* to be unlocked until I say so, understood?"

"Yes, sir," said the sergeant.

The colonel turned to Buck. "Stop by my office after you've seen to your friend, maybe we need to talk."

Buck didn't bother to reply; he turned and followed the men carrying Chester. Buck and Selena waited anxiously in a small waiting area next to the operating room.

Buck learned the post doctor was named Dixon. He was most likely nearing retirement age. He had friendly eyes and snow-white hair.

Time crept by slowly. An hour became two, then three. Buck tried to comfort Selena as best he could. She sat silently, twisting the hem of her skirt and crying softly.

Finally the doctor came out. He looked tired. Buck searched the doctor's face for some sign, some indication that would tell him Chester's condition.

"He's hurt bad, real bad. He has several broken ribs, a broken nose, and most likely a concussion, though I won't know for sure until he wakes up. It's possible he has internal injuries to some vital organs as well, but again, we won't know that for some time."

"Can we see him, doctor?" Buck asked.

"Of course, but I'm afraid he won't be aware of your presence."

"How long is he likely to be unconscious?"

"No way of knowing, a few hours maybe, maybe a few days or even weeks. With a concussion or perhaps multiple concussions it's impossible to predict. Then there's the possibility..."

Buck lowered his eyebrows in concern and shot a quick glance at Selena. At the doctor's words she drew a sharp gasp of breath and covered her mouth with a hand.

"The possibility of what?"

"I have no way of knowing, of course, but it's entirely possible he may never regain consciousness, though let's not concern ourselves with that at this point. We've moved him down the hall to a private room. He'll receive the best care possible. Come, I'll show you to his room."

Buck and Selena followed the doctor down the hall where he stopped just outside a door.

"If you need anything, anything at all, just ask. An orderly is on duty at the desk at the end of the hall day and night. I'll stop in several times a day and keep a close watch on him."

"Much obliged, Doctor."

Buck and Selena slipped quietly into the room. Chester lay in a single bed. A white sheet covered him up to his neck. His face and head were almost completely covered with bandages with openings for his eyes and holes to allow him to breath through his nose and mouth. His eyes were closed.

Selena choked off a sob and moved quickly to his bedside. Tears invaded her eyes and scored trails downward across her cheeks. Buck circled her shoulders with a comforting arm.

"He's tough," he whispered, trying hard to sound more confident than he felt. "He'll pull through."

Selena only nodded, clearly struggling not to break down completely.

They sat beside Chester's bedside throughout the night. Their gazes fixed on his face, watching intently for some movement, some sign of consciousness. Conversation was sparse and muted, only a few whispered words from time to time, mostly they did nothing more than watch and wait.

Several times during the night an orderly came in to check on the patient and asked if Buck or Selena needed anything. They requested coffee and it was delivered in only minutes.

Morning came slowly. Doctor Dixon came by just before sunup.

"Good Morning, Mr. Cordell, Miss Rodriguez. Did either of you see any movement at all last night?"

"No, sir," Buck said

The doctor spent several minutes examining Chester.

"His pulse is still very weak. I can't detect any

responsiveness yet, but I'll keep a close watch on him. You folks need to get some rest. I'm sure Colonel Callahan can find an extra bunk in the officers' quarters. My wife and I have a spare bedroom. We'd be pleased if Miss Rodriguez would stay with us until Mr. Colson recovers."

"We're obliged for your hospitality. We'll talk about our plans and let you know later today."

Colonel Callahan stopped by just as the doctor was leaving. The doctor gave him a brief whispered update in the hallway on Chester's condition. When they finished talking the officer stepped into Chester's room.

"After further review of the events surrounding the charges against Mr. Colson, I find they are not warranted and all charges will be dropped.

"On behalf of the army, I want to apologize for the treatment Mr. Colson received while being detained. What Sergeant Hogan did was despicable. He will answer for his conduct.

"The full hospitality of Fort Clark is available to you and Miss Rodriguez for as long as it takes to bring Mr. Colson back to full health. This is the least we can do in light of the cruel and inhumane treatment he received while in our care.

"I'm afraid I have misjudged you, Mr. Cordell. Please accept my sincere apology."

The colonel extended his hand. Buck took it and the two men shook hands.

After the officer left Buck turned to Selena. "I have to return to the ranch and tie up some loose ends, but I'll be back no later that the day after tomorrow. Can you stay here with Chester until I get back?"

"I will not leave his side until he recovers."

"I'll send one of the men to tell your mother of your decision."

Buck gathered her in his arms and hugged her close.

"Chester is a fortunate man to have someone like you to love him."

It was coming dark when Buck rode into the Longhorn compound. Word had spread of Chester's arrest and everyone was anxious to hear what happened. Buck gathered his top hands together in the chow hall before supper. As he looked around the room he saw concern written on their faces.

"I know you have all heard by now that while Chester was in town he was arrested by the army. They charged him with murder for hanging Ike Sawyer over at Eagle Pass a while back.

"He was placed in the guardhouse. The sergeant in charge obviously had an ax to grind against all those who fought for the south during the war. He decided to take it out on Chester.

"They put him in solitary confinement, chained him to the wall, and beat him until he was unconscious. He's alive, but still unconscious. The doctor says he could be that way for some time.

Glancing around the room, Buck saw the men looking from one to the other in clear bitterness at Chester's treatment by the army.

"I'm going back to Fort Clark at first light tomorrow. Don't know when I'll be back. In the meantime, I'm gonna be depending on your fellows to keep things running here at the ranch. Go ahead with the gather. I want the trail herd put together and headed north right on schedule, just like we planned.

"I'm putting Ray Ledbetter in charge of the drive. He'll be the new Segundo, our *boss of bosses*. What he says goes. He'll lead the first herd. Smokey Cunningham will lead the second herd. I'm asking Slim Hopkins and Link Stone to go along as their top hands. Zack Gibbs will be our scout again for this drive. You boys will be glad to hear that Wash and Joshua have both decided to be your cooks for this drive.

Ray, have somebody that speaks Spanish take a wagon into town and tell Selena's mother what has happened and that her daughter will be staying at Fort Clark until Chester recovers. Then have him pick up some coats and blankets I ordered from Walker's store.

"Also, I need you to pick four good men. Send them up to Tyler, Texas. Tell Chester's folks what has happened and that Chester wanted them to move down here with him. Give the boys you pick enough money to purchase wagons and teams and whatever else they need to move them down."

Ray sipped his coffee and thought for a long minute before replying. "Think I'll ask Lyle Starbuck, Art Meadows, Vance Langley, and Gus Wilson. They've all got sand and a good head on their shoulders to boot. They're crack shots and good with side arms. They'll be able to handle any problem that might come up."

"Sounds good. Reckon that's all I can think of right now. Anybody got any questions?"

Buck paused for a couple of minutes to give them time to ask whatever was on their minds.

Smokey lifted a hand and spoke up. "We're hearing talk about plans to take a whole string of herds up the trail next year, any truth to that?"

"Yep, you heard right. Plans are to take two herds a month up the trail every month, starting in April, with five thousand head in each herd. They'll be split into two bunches of twenty-five hundred each, traveling a day apart just like last time."

"Where we gonna get that many critters?" Slim Hopkins asked.

"We've sent Carlos, Pedro, and Pablo to make the rounds of several Mexican ranches and contract to buy Mexican cattle.

Between what they can buy, and the ones Pappy and his crew are catching out of the thickets, ought to give us enough to make the drives. It's shaping up to be a busy year and that's a fact."

All over the room heads nodded and wide smiles filled every face. Excitement was so thick one could almost cut it with a knife.

"If there are no more questions, let's stretch our bellies. Jewel's got supper hot."

After supper Buck poured himself another cup of coffee and walked outside, needing to be alone. A livid moon hung high in an overcast sky. Stars played hide and seek with the slow-drifting clouds. Out of the north, a chill wind swept across the land and sent a shiver down his backbone. Buck pulled his coat collar up around his neck and sipped the steaming coffee.

Rebekah was restless and worried. She had heard about Chester's arrest and saw the troopers as they rode out of town with Chester in chains. From the front window of their store she witnessed Selena riding at a hard gallop out of town to carry the news to Buck at the ranch.

She knew the kind of man Buck Cordell was and that he wouldn't accept his partner's arrest. He would do whatever he had to do to set Chester free.

She worried all day. She wanted and needed to be by Buck's side. She felt so helpless. That night she tossed and turned, unable to sleep.

All the next day she kept her gaze peeled on the street. At every sound from the street she ran to the front window, hoping it was Buck, only to be disappointed again and again. That night, once again, sleep evaded her. She paced the floor until the wee hours of the morning.

Finally stoking the fire, she set the coffee pot on the stove to warm and poured a cup. Wrapping a quilt about her shoulders, she walked out into the chilly night and stared up at their star.

Buck, my love, please be safe. I couldn't stand it if something should happen to you.

Selena sat by Chester's bedside. She couldn't bear to leave.

The orderlies heard, of course, what happened to Chester in the guardhouse and knew the injustice of it. They went out of their way to provide him with the best care possible, even to the point of bringing Selena meals and coffee. They placed a cot for her in his room for her, but she refused to leave his bedside.

Doctor Dixon came regularly to check Chester's condition. Each time he reported there was no change. Even the colonel's attitude seemed to change, whether it was genuine concern for Chester or for his own career, he nonetheless went to great lengths to see that both Chester and Selena were well cared for.

Selena spent long hours sitting by Chester's bedside, holding his hand, staring at his face. She prayed constantly, begging for Chester's recovery, bargaining with God, and making all kinds of promises. Still there was no movement, no sign of consciousness.

Well before the first tinge of grayness colored the eastern horizon, Buck stepped into the stirrups, and swung into the saddle of the black gelding. His dappled gray stood close on a tight lead line. He intended to ride hard to Fort Clark and switch horses frequently.

He worried about Chester. Doctor Dixon's words kept coming back to haunt him.

It's entirely possible he may never regain consciousness...

Dawn broke clear and cold. A northern wind picked up, and the early morning chill caused him to pull up the collar of his sheep-skin coat.

Puffs of steam billowed from his mount's nostrils with each galloping stride. The dappled gray trailed behind with easy strides to match those of the black. Buck settled in his saddle and allowed his body to match the rhythm of the horse's motion.

The miles passed quickly under the horse's pounding hooves and soon the Fort came into view. Buck bore a huge lump of worry lodged in his throat that he couldn't swallow down. The sentry either recognized him or expected him because he passed him on through the gate without a challenge. Buck reined his mount toward the post hospital and tied his horses to a hitching rail.

Hurrying inside, his long steps carried him quickly to Chester's room. His heart quickened. *What if . . ?* He shook his head to rid his mind of such thoughts . . . and eased open the door.

Chester lay in the bed exactly as Buck had left him. Selena was kneeling on the floor with her fingers steepled in front of her in prayer. Her gaze was fixed intently upon a small crucifix attached to the wall. Buck quietly backed out the door, feeling as if he had intruded on a very private moment. He waited in the hallway.

Minutes passed before the door pushed open quietly and Selena slipped into Buck's open arms. He pulled her close in a comforting hug. Tears dampened his shoulder.

"I love him," she whispered.

Buck nodded. "I know," he said quietly. "So do I."

Chapter XVIII

Carlos, Pablo, and Pedro followed the Rio Bravo River downstream for three days before reaching the small Mexican village of Nuevo Laredo. It wasn't much.

A cluster of small, mostly one-room, adobe huts scattered along a single dusty street seemed to be the sum total. People stopped to stare for a brief moment at the three vaqueros riding slowly through town and leading two packhorses on lead lines. Little plumes of dust puffed away from their horses' hooves, swept away quickly by a hot eastern wind. Layers of dust clung to their horses' sweat-soaked hides. The spectators' interest quickly faded as the three riders walked their horses on down the street and reined up in front of the village's lone cantina.

"We'll stop here a while and let our horses blow before we move on," Carlos said. "Might as well wash down some trail dust while we're at it."

"How far is this ranch we're headed for?" Pedro asked as they swung down and looped their reins around the hitching rail.

"*Señor* Antonio's directions say from Nuevo Laredo we should go southwest until we hit the Rio Salado River, then follow it downstream to the ranchero. It is known as the Silver Spur rancho.

The pungent smells of stale tequila, boy odor, and sweat greeted them as they stepped into the cantina. When their eyes adjusted to the dimness of the room they saw a short, squat man with two weeks' worth of whiskers either sleeping or passed out with his head resting on folded arms across the bar.

Carlos walked over and punched the man with a finger. He raised his head. Sleepy eyes blinked open and a forced smile showed a mouthful of rotted teeth.

Buenos noches, señors"

Carlos and his two companions only nodded and took a seat at a nearby table.

"Tequila," Carlos said.

The barkeep brought a bottle and three glasses. Carlos paid the man and poured drinks for his companions and himself.

"The boss sure thinks big doesn't he?" Pablo said, sipping his drink. "I never heard of anybody driving that many longhorns up the trail."

"Far as I know, it's never been done before." Carlos said. "But if Buck Cordell says we're going to do it, I'd bet my saddle on it."

"Think we can find that many longhorns in all of Mexico?"

"We'll find them. We'll wash down the dust and move on," Carlos told them. "I'd like to make it as far as the Rio Salado before dark. We should make it to the ranchero tomorrow."

Carlos had just emptied his glass when a sound from the direction of the front door caused him to swing a look.

A bearded giant stepped through the opening and stopped just inside. Close on his heels, four more tough-looking Mexicans crowded inside. All five wore two pistols each strapped around their waists and a pair of criss-crossed bandoliers across their chests.

The leader was a huge fellow with a black beard. A long, blue knife scar ran from his left eye and disappeared behind the shaggy beard. The man swept the room and settled a hard stare on Carlos and his two companions.

Without wavering his hard stare his black beard parted, revealing yellowed teeth with a gold one showing prominently in the front.

"Tequila," his deep, raspy voice snarled wickedly.

The barkeep grabbed two bottles by the neck and rushed to deliver them as the five folded into chairs at the only other table in the room.

"We better be moving on," Carlos told his companions in a low voice as he stood up. Pablo and Pedro swallowed the last of their drinks and pushed up from their chairs.

"Hey, Amigos, why you leave so soon?" the bearded giant asked.

"We've got a long ride," Carlos answered.

"We are brothers," the big man pressed. "We sit down and we have a drink together."

"Afraid we can't, we've got to be going."

The giant unlimbered from his chair. Tequila dribbled from his mouth into his black beard as he took the bottle away from his lips. His evil-looking eyes fixed an angry stare at Carlos as he began stalking across the floor toward Carlos.

"I invite you to have another drink, *Amigo*," the giant said, spitting out the words like they tasted bad. "You do not refuse Juan Cortez."

The obvious challenge ignited a spark of anger in Carlos's eyes. He knew a fight was brewing. He flicked a quick glance at Pablo and Pedro. They knew a fight was coming and stopped and squared around to face the hard cases.

Without a word Pablo closed the space between him and the giant in two quick steps. His left hand shot out and fisted a handful of the giant's shirtfront and jerked him forward. They suddenly stood nose to nose. Pablo's sudden move caught the giant completely off guard. A weapon appeared in Pablo's right hand as if by magic. The nose buried deep in the big man's fat belly. The weapon exploded once, twice within the space of two heartbeats. The big man reeled backwards, but Pablo held him close, using the giant body as a shield.

The giant's companions flashed their guns out, but stood in limbo, obviously reluctant to fire for fear of hitting their leader.

Pablo didn't hesitate. His gun snaked around the badly wounded bandit and barked again and again. Two more of the bandits blew over backwards before they returned a shot. Bullets from the remaining two bandits smacked into their leader's back and lodged somewhere inside the giant body.

Carlos and Pedro opened up and cut down the remaining two men in a hail of bullets.

Pablo stepped backward and turned the giant loose. The man's huge body fell forward on his face to the dirt floor.

Thick smoke and the acrid stench of gunpowder filled the small room and burned Carlos's nose. Pablo stepped to check all the downed bandits before holstering his weapon. They were all dead.

Time seemed to crawl by at a snail's pace. Minutes stretched into hours and hours into days. A week passed, then two. Still Chester remained unconscious.

As the days wore on Buck became more and more concerned. Selena rarely left Chester's bedside except to bathe and freshen up. Their meals were brought to the room by an orderly.

During these long days and nights Buck and Selena spent long hours talking. They both shared their past as well as their dreams for the future. Buck became even more convinced that Selena was the perfect soul mate for his partner.

"I need to go check on things at the ranch," Buck told her. "I'll be leaving at first light. I won't be gone more than a few days. Will you watch after things here while I'm gone?"

"Of course."

"Try not to worry," Buck said, trying to sound more confident than he felt. "He's tougher than a boot. He's gonna best this thing."

Selena only nodded her head.

Buck saddled his black by lantern light and tied the dappled gray on a short lead. It was still the darkest part of the night and the fort was still asleep when he gigged the black through the front gate. He struck a short lope. The gray fell into the rhythm behind the long-legged black. By the time the rosy dawn swallowed the darkness of night, he had left the fort several miles behind.

As he rode, worry about Chester rode with him. He knew all that could be done was being done. The rest was up to the Man upstairs.

His mind jumped from one thing to another. He knew it was almost time for the drive to begin. He had the utmost confidence in his men, but still a nagging concern hovered close.

He wondered about Carlos and his men and how they were received by the Mexican cattle ranchers. All of their plans for next years' multiple drives hinged upon being able to contract for enough cattle to make it happen.

He calculated in his mind when the men would be back with Chester's folks. If all went well he figured they should be on their way back by now.

His mind flashed to his brother. Was there something more he could do to locate him?

It's a big country, he thought. *He could be anywhere. I guess all I can do is wait and hope.*

Even with all that was happening, Rebekah was never far from his thoughts. As her picture flashed into his mind, a warm feeling settled over him. He longed for her. He felt like half a person when they were apart. He closed his eyes and imagined how her fingers felt as they trailed along his cheek. The sweetness of her soft lips on his sent tingles along his backbone. She was everything he ever dreamed of, and more than he could have ever hoped for.

Miles passed quickly beneath the black's steady gait. Thought his mind remained lost in deep thought, cautious instinct kept his gaze sweeping both sides of the trail, searching for signs of danger.

Something—call it intuition—that mysterious feeling one gets when something isn't right. For whatever reason, he swung a look over his shoulder at his back trail. What he saw made the hair on the back of his neck stand up.

At least a dozen Indians were hot on his trail, not more than a quarter-mile behind him, led by an Indian on a black and white pinto. Quanah.

Buck dug heels into the black's ribs and leaned forward over the horse's neck. He knew his only hope was to outrun them.

With the outcome depending solely on superior horseflesh, he wasn't worried. There was no way the mustangs the Indians rode could match the speed and endurance of his two horses.

The black gelding responded. Within the space of two leaps he ran full out and belly to the ground. The dappled gray matched the black, stride for stride. Buck bent low synchronizing the movement of his body with the rhythm of the black's long strides.

Glancing back occasionally, he felt pride that his horses were lengthening the distance between him and the Indians. Barring any surprises, he should be able to leave them far behind.

But the black stepped into a hole and its foreleg doubled under him. Buck felt the leg give way, heard the sickening snap of bone as it broke. He immediately kicked loose of the stirrups, throwing himself from the saddle as the black let out a pitiful scream and somersaulted into the dirt.

Buck landed on his right shoulder and tumbled along the ground, finally coming to a stop in a clump of mesquite bushes. He lay stunned. A sharp pain stabbed his right shoulder. He gritted his teeth against the pain, and, with a supreme effort, pushed heavily to his hands and knees. Everything seemed to work. He shook his head to clear his vision.

A quick glance at the black told him what he already knew. The gelding was done for. The horse kicked and thrashed on the ground, one leg bent double. The gray stood quivering near the downed black, the lead line still in place.

Buck swung a worried look at his back trail. The Indians were closing fast. They were yelped and whooped, obviously sure they were swooping in for a kill.

Buck pushed unsteadily to his feet. In a staggering run he hurried to the downed horse. Luckily, the saddle boot containing his Spencer saddle rifle was on the upside of the downed horse. He jerked it clear, felt for his sidearm, and found it still in his holster.

Another look told him he was running out of time. The Indians boiled along the trail in a cloud of dust no more than a hundred yards away.

He rushed to the gray and grabbed the reins with his left hand that held his rifle. His right hand swept the Bowie from his belt scabbard and slashed the lead line.

He swung a leg over the gray's bare back and slapped the horse on the hip with the barrel of his rifle. Shots rang out. Bullets singed the air around his head. He bent low over the gray's neck and buried his heels into the horse's flanks. The dappled gray leapt into a run.

* * *

Carlos and his companions arrived at the Silver Spur Ranchero before noon the day after the shooting incident at Nuevo Laredo.

The ranchero lay in a fertile river valley and the lush green grass grew hock-high to the grazing herds of fat cattle they passed on the way in. The vaqueros were met by a heavily armed security force and escorted to the sprawling hacienda.

A tall, slim Mexican dressed in tight-fitting black pants and an elaborately embroidered waist-length jacket met them as they dismounted.

"Welcome to my casa," he greeted. "I am Antonio Lopez."

"I am Carlos Rodriguez. These are my *compadre's,* Pedro Sedillo and Pablo Rodriguez. We have come on a mission of some importance. We represent our employer, Señor Buck Cordell, owner of the Longhorn Ranch, just across the Rio Bravo in Texas."

"*Por favor*, let us go inside where we can talk more comfortably."

They were ushered into a large, elaborately furnished den. After they took a seat the ranch owner inquired as to their mission.

"How can I be of service to you?"

Carlos withdrew the letter of introduction from Don Antonio Rivas and handed it to Señor Lopez. He took a few minutes to study the document carefully.

"Aw, yes, Antonio Rivas is well respected throughout all Mexico. Precisely what do you have in mind, señors?"

"We are here to purchase cattle. We have seen the quality of your herds as we rode in. Would you be interested in contracting to sell us your cattle?"

"How many cattle are you interested in buying?"

"As many as you are willing to sell."

"What are you offering?"

"We are authorized to offer you four dollars a head, delivered to the Longhorn Ranch, on fifteen, March of next year. Allow me to stress the importance of timely delivery. It is critically important that your herd arrive precisely on your appointed day. To encourage delivery in a timely manner we will pay a delivery bonus of an additional one dollar per head, making your price five dollars a head.

"However, should you be late delivering your herd, fifty cents per head, per day will be deducted from your payment. Is this arrangement acceptable?"

The ranch owner was silent for a long moment obviously considering Carlos's terms. "I can see nothing in the arrangement that is not acceptable."

"Splendid." Carlos said. "Then how many head are we talking about?"

"I believe I could deliver five thousand head on the date you specified."

"Excellent." Carlos said, withdrawing another piece of paper from his leather case. "I have taken the liberty of drawing up a contract with the terms discussed." Carlos quickly filled in the quantity of cattle and the delivery date agreed upon and handed the paper to the ranch owner. "Look the contract over and if you find it acceptable simply sign it and we have an agreement."

The ranch owner again read the contract carefully before signing his name on both copies and handing one of them back to Carlos.

Carlos stood up and extended his hand. Antonio rose and took the offered hand, thereby sealing the agreement.

"It will be done as we have agreed," the ranch owner said.

"It is a pleasure to do business with an honorable man, *Señor* Lopez."

* * *

It took only minutes to leave the pursuing Indians far behind. Their smaller mustangs were no match for Buck's long-legged dappled gray.

He felt badly that he had no time to care for the injured black gelding or at least to put it out of its misery, but like his pa had always told him, "A man's gotta do what a man's gotta do."

After another mile or so he slowed his mount to a trot.

He arrived at the compound just before sundown. The hands were drifting inside after a long day. They greeted him and, to a man, inquired about Chester.

"No change," he told them sadly. "He's still unconscious."

Ray Ledbetter and Smokey Cunningham were waiting at the stable. Buck swung to the ground and handed the reins of the gray to Juan, the stable man.

"How's Chester, boss?" Ray inquired.

Buck shook his head.

"He's still unconscious, but holding his own. How are things here?"

"The lead herd pulls out at first light. The second herd leaves day after tomorrow. Far as we can tell, everything that needs done is done."

"Good job. Let's get a cup of coffee and you can fill me in."

As they sipped their coffee and talked, Ray told Buck that young Jimmy McCord asked if he could come along on the drive.

"The boy's a hard worker," Ray said. "I know he's still young and still a little wet behind the ears but to my way of thinking he's earned the right. It's all he talks about."

"You're the trail boss. If you think he's ready it's fine by me."

* * *

The whole ranch was up and busy well before first light. Buck climbed in the saddle and rode beside Ray, Smokey, and Zack Gibbs. They arrived at the gathering point near the Sycamore River just as the eastern sky began lightening up with a rosy glow. They reined up on a hill overlooking the herd of longhorns.

Slim Hopkins and Link Stone, their newly appointed top hands, spotted them on the hill and rode up to meet them.

"The boys have the first herd separated out and ready to move when you give the signal," Slim told Ray Ledbetter.

"I'll let the boss do the honors."

As the sun peeked over the distant horizon and filled the eastern sky with a golden hue, Buck allowed a slow gaze to slide over the vast sea of cattle. It was a hodge-podge mixture of every color under the sun. Their long horns glistened in the early morning light. The sight still took his breath away. For a long moment they soaked it up.

"Doubt you'll ever see anything prettier in this lifetime," Buck said.

Ray agreed.

Buck reached a gloved hand. First Ray, then Smokey, Slim, Link, and finally Zack Gibbs took his hand in a firm handshake.

"Good Luck, boys. Ride careful."

Swiping his hat from his head he raised it high in the air and circled it. Down below the sound of cowboy yips and yells echoed across the wide valley. A swat on the backside with coiled lariats, coaxed grazing longhorns into forward movement. Buck's chest swelled with pride as he watched the herd begin to move.

"Reckon we better hit the trail, boss," Ray told Buck. "We got a long day ahead of us. I plan to keep 'em moving until well after dark for a few days to walk some of the sap out of them."

Ray and his top hand, Slim Hopkins, lifted a hand in goodbye and rode to join their herd.

Buck, Smokey, and Link Stone sat their saddles and watched until the herd plodded out of sight.

"Got the second herd ready to pull out in the morning?" Buck asked.

"Ready and waiting," Smokey replied. "We've got some green longhorns that ain't lost all their wild nature yet and I expect we'll have some bunch quitters among em but I plan to double up on my drag crew until they settle in."

"Good thinking." Buck said.

"Wish I could have made the drive with you boys, but there's no way I could go off with Chester like he is."

"I know. We'll do fine."

"Not a doubt in my mind."

After Buck rode back to the ranch compound he met with one of the new top hands at the ranch, a newcomer named Rowdy Sloan.

"Got everything covered Rowdy?"

"Yes, sir, I put each of the new men with one of our older hands until they learn how we do things here on the Longhorn. They'll settle in real fast. They're all seasoned cowboys."

"How long you been with us now?"

"A little over a month."

"Ray tells me you were a top hand over at the King Ranch."

"Yes, sir, I spent two years there."

"Mind telling me why you decided to leave?"

"I couldn't see any chance of bettering myself there. From what I see, I figure the Longhorn is gonna grow and grow fast. I wanna grow with it."

"Well, you're the kind of man we're looking for. Good to have you with us."

"Much obliged, boss. It's good to be here."

Buck spent most of the day at his desk doing paperwork. He would much rather have been out making the rounds on the ranch, but he had a lot of loose ends he needed to catch up on.

Jewel brought him a pot of fresh coffee sometime in mid-afternoon. He poured himself a cup and paced the floor. He couldn't get Chester off his mind.

He was worried. His friend and partner remained unconscious too long. Doubts that Chester would ever regain consciousness began to creep into his mind. That possibility hit him like a charging longhorn. He couldn't bare the thought of losing his longtime friend.

Someone tapped on the door.

"Come in."

It was Juan Santos, the builder. He timidly opened the door and stepped inside with his large sombrero in his hands.

"*Por favor, señor*. When you have time I have a question about how to proceed you're your hacienda."

"I'll come with you now. I need to take a look-see. How it's coming along?"

Buck walked with the builder across the large compound to his and Rebekah's future home.

It was a sprawling structure. An outside wall surrounded the main house. An opening in the outside wall was guarded by a wrought iron gate. Pushing open the gate, Buck and Pablo entered a small courtyard that surrounded the house.

A walkway of red tile led across the courtyard, past a bubbling fountain, and under a veranda that ran along the entire front of the house. Heavy, double oval-topped doors opened into a long hallway that ran through the center of the house.

Three doors on either side of the hallway led into six large rooms. They turned right through the first door and entered a large den. One of Luis's two sons and another worker were working on building a large fireplace of flat stones.

"We are ready to install a mantle over the fireplace," Pablo said. "What would you like?"

"You're the builder. You and your men have done a good job. What would you suggest we put there?"

"I thought we could use a single piece of thick, oiled wood and put a set of longhorns over it."

"Sounds good. Do it."

"Another question, *Por favor*?"

"Let's hear it?"

"Come."

Together they went back into the hallway and walked to the very end before turning left at the last door into the large master bedroom. A small, adjoining room was set apart from the main bedroom.

"We have built this private room for bathing. As you can see, *señor*, we have dug down and built a small pool and lined it with smooth stones. We have coated it with a special mixture so that it will hold water for bathing. It is our gift to the lady of the house."

Buck had never seen anything like it. He couldn't wait to see Rebekah's face when she saw the pool was looking at. It was absolutely beautiful.

"*Gracias, Juan*. I know she will love it. How long before the house will be finished?"

"One month, perhaps two."

"*Señor*, do you already have someone to build your furniture?"

"No, don't reckon. Guess I hadn't thought that far ahead yet."

"I know a man who is the best in all of Mexico. There is no finer furniture maker to be found."

"Where does this man live?"

"He lives in Monterrey."

"Go ahead and send for him, but maybe I ought to let the lady of the house tell him what furniture she wants. I'll talk with her about it."

After leaving Juan and his workers, Buck went to the corral where they kept the extra black horses they bought from Don Antonio Rivas. After looking them over he selected a midnight black gelding with a white star in the center of its forehead. The horse long legged, deep-chested, with bulging muscles and friendly eyes.

Buck took a lariat from a corral post and roped the black. After slipping a bridle and saddle on him, Buck rubbed the gelding's nose and spoke to it in soft, soothing tones.

"Reckon we might as well get acquainted, seeing as how we're gonna be spending some time together. You're right pretty with that star on your forehead. Might be a good name for you, how does that sound?"

The gelding looked at Buck with those big, friendly eyes and snorted.

"I take that as a yes. Star it is then. Let's you and me take a ride and see what you got."

Buck toed a stirrup and swung into the saddle. The big black gelding danced in place, lifting its front hooves high. Buck reined his new mount through the corral gate and out of the compound.

It was immediately clear the gelding had been trained well and Buck was pleasantly surprised to discover that the black was natural-gaited. He settled himself in the saddle and let his big frame adjust to the rhythm of the black's short lope.

"Yes, sir, big fellow. You and me are gonna get along just fine."

He rode out to the gathering of the second herd. Smokey and Link saw him coming and rode to meet him.

"You boys ready?"

"More'n ready," Smokey told his boss.

"Just restless. Thought I'd ride out and limber up this new mount."

"He sure is a picture."

"You boys see any Indian signs hereabouts?"

"Saw some signs, but no Indians."

"Keep a sharp eye. By the time you actually see an Indian it's usually too late. I just can't figure why they haven't already hit us."

"Maybe, they got burned so bad last time, they're still licking their wounds."

"Maybe, but don't count on it."

Buck reined the black around and rode back to the compound. The sun started dipping out of sight when he turned Star over to the stable man and walked to the chow hall.

Several hands already gathered for supper. Buck joined them. Pappy brought his plate of food to the table and took a bench across from Buck.

"How's El Toro coming along?"

"He's coming along. I figure another couple of weeks and he'll be ready for some female companionship."

"That soon, huh?"

"He's still got a little mean streak, but, yeah, he'll be ready."

"You did a good job gentling him down, I never would have believed it possible."

"Most anything's possible if you want it bad enough," Pappy grinned. "I've done set my mind to it, this bull is gonna be the talk of Texas."

Carlos and his companions had visited three ranches so far. They were well received at each one. They were able to contract for cattle at each of the three. He had found the Mexican ranchers more than willing to sell their cattle for the prices the Longhorn offered.

"How many cattle have we bought?" Pablo asked as the rode.

"So far, we have contracted for twelve thousand head, which is not nearly enough."

"Where are we headed now?"

"There is a very large ranchero near the coast at a place called San Carlos. It's in the San Fernando River valley. We should be there in two days."

They rode for the next two days without incident and arrived at the ranch at mid-day. They were all amazed at the beauty of the place. The San Fernando River meandered through the desert country and created a cattleman's paradise. Thick, green grass grew knee high to their horses. Herd after herd of fat longhorns grazed contentedly and barely raised their heads when Carlos and his two companions rode past.

The ranch headquarters appeared as a sprawling collection of adobe huts with happy children running and playing, women washing and going about their daily chores, while their husbands took care of the herds of grazing cattle.

A large hacienda surrounded by a high wall sat off to one side of the village. Carlos and his friends headed that way.

Two security guards stopped them at the gate and inquired as to the nature of their business.

"We wish to see *señor* Manuel San Carlos. We are here with a letter of introduction from Don Antonio Rivas."

"Wait here, *por favor*."

Within minutes they were escorted into the hacienda. The ranch owner waited for them in a large, elaborately furnished sitting room. He stepped forward and extended his hand.

"Welcome to our home. A friend of Don Rivas is always welcome at San Carlos."

"Thank you for receiving us," Carlos said, shaking the ranch owner's hand and handing the letter of introduction to him.

It took him only a moment to read the letter and hand it back to Carlos.

"How may I be of service to you?"

"We are here representing our employer of the Longhorn Ranch just across the Rio Bravos River near Del Rio, Texas. We are looking to purchase cattle. *Señor* Rivas has already delivered two herds of two thousand head to the Longhorn Ranch. In addition, we have contracted with several other Mexican ranchers for their herds. Do you have cattle you would sell?"

"How many cattle do you wish to buy?"

"We saw your herds as we rode in. Your cattle seem to be in excellent condition. We will purchase as many as you are willing to sell."

"What price are you offering?"

"As with the others, we will contract to pay four dollars a head, delivered to the Longhorn Ranch on the date we specify. Time is of the essence. Therefore we will pay an additional dollar a head delivery bonus if you deliver your cattle on the exact date you are given. On the other hand, should you be late with delivery, fifty cents a head will be deducted for each two days you are late."

"Then am I to understand that, when I deliver the agreed number of cattle on the specified date, that I will be paid immediately the contracted price?"

"Absolutely."

"That being the case, I could sell you ten thousand head."

"Excellent. If that is agreeable, I will draw up the contract."

Within less than an hour Carlos carried a signed contract for ten thousand head to be delivered on April 15th of the following year.

* * *

Well before first light Buck was up and in the saddle. He arrived at the wide meadow where the second herd began getting to their feet. The longhorn cowboys took their places around the milling sea of longhorns. Smokey spotted Buck and rode to meet him.

"Mornin', boss."

"Morning. 'Bout ready to head 'em out?"

"Waiting on you to give the word."

Across the valley every eye was peeled upon the tall rider on the hilltop sitting his saddle on the coal-black gelding. For a long moment Buck's eyes swept the vast herd in the valley below. Then, without a word, he swept his hat from his head and circled it in the air.

A chorus of cowboy yells split the early morning air. The lead riders led the way and the longhorns took their first steps of a thousand mile journey.

Buck watched them go with a lump in his throat. He knew Smoky and his men faced a long and difficult trip But he also knew the longhorn riders were a salty bunch. Whatever difficulty confronted them they would face squarely. That's just the kind of men they were.

Riding back to the ranch, all he could think about was Rebekah. He decided after checking on things at the ranch he would ride into town and see her. It had been way too long and he was missing her terribly.

After checking in with Rowdy Sloan, his new top hand around the ranch, and being assured that everything was under control, Buck lit out for Del Rio.

* * *

Rebekah paced the floor. She was beside herself. Worry gnawed at her stomach. At every sound from the street outside she jerked a look, hoping, praying that it was Buck—only to be disappointed time and again.

She went about her tasks in the store as if in a trance.

"Pardon my saying so," Mrs. Jacobson said with a concerned look on her face. "Are you not feeling well?"

It took a minute before the words settled into Rebekah's mind. "Uh...yes, I'm feeling fine. Why do you ask?"

"Well, I asked for a sack of sugar, and instead, you put a sack of salt on the counter. I ordered five pounds of salt pork and you cut off a pound. I've known you since you were a little girl. This just isn't like you."

"I'm sorry, Mrs. Jacobson. I've...I've had a lot on my mind lately."

After Mrs. Jacobson left, Rebekah stood in front of the large store window, staring out at nothing. Her heart hurt. Her mind whirled. She felt a huge knot in the pit of her stomach.

Where is he? Has something terrible happened to him? Why haven't I heard from him?

Large tears seeped from the corners of her eyes and trailed down her cheeks. She swiped them away with the back of a hand. She closed her eyes and breathed a silent prayer.

A sound from the street jerked her eyes open. He was there! A small scream escaped her throat. She bolted out the door.

Buck had just looped the reins to his black gelding around the hitching rail when Rebekah raced across the boardwalk and leaped into his arms. Her arms wrapped tightly around his neck and her face buried into the hollow of his big shoulder. She clung suspended there, her feet a foot off the ground.

"Hey, pretty lady."

"Oh, Buck, I was so worried. I was afraid something bad happened to you."

"You worry too much. I'm fine."

"How's Chester?"

"About the same. He's still unconscious. I'm riding back to the fort tomorrow."

"I'm going with you."

"Be better if you didn't. It's a long ride."

"I'm going. I need to be with Selena."

Placing his hands on either side of her waist he lifted her to the ground and gazed deep into her teary eyes.

"I missed you," he said.

"I missed you, too. Buck, I can't stand it when we are apart."

"I know. I feel the same way. It won't be much longer. Three years, maybe," he kidded.

She doubled a fist and punched him in the ribs. That brought a chuckle from him.

"I'm not waiting three years to marry you. Today is August twelfth. I've made up my mind. We're getting married on Christmas day. No if, and, or buts about it."

"Well, I reckon if you feel that strong about it I'll just have to go along."

"Do you mean it? Can we *really?*"

"Don't see why not. I talked to Juan this morning. He said our house ought to be ready by then."

Her arm was around his waist as they walked into the store. She squeezed him tight, leaned close, and whispered. "You won't be sorry, I promise. I'm going to make you the happiest man in Texas."

"What are you two love birds whispering about?" Her father asked from behind the counter as they walked into the store.

"We're going to be married on Christmas day," Rebekah blurted out.

"*If* that's all right with *you*," Buck quickly added.

"Son, I couldn't be more pleased about it," Walker said, sticking out his hand.

Buck took the offered hand and shook it.

"I reckon we'll be needing to order some furniture for our house. Do you have a catalogue or something?"

"I've already been looking at it," Rebekah said. "I've got some picked out I want you to see."

"If it suits you, it suits me," Buck said. "Juan said he knew a fellow that makes the finest furniture in Mexico. I asked Juan to send for him and told him that you would want to tell him what kind of furniture you want."

"Father, I'm riding to Fort Clark with Buck in the morning."

"I tried to talk her out of it, John."

"Might as well talk to a fence post, son. She's just like her mother, God rest her soul. Once she sets her mind to something there ain't no changing it."

"I'll keep that in mind," Buck said, slanting a grin at Rebekah.

"How is your partner doing?"

"He's still unconscious."

"The fellow that done it ought to be horsewhipped before they hang him."

"I need to walk over to the café and talk to Mrs. Rodriguez," Buck said. "Any chance of you and Rebekah coming along and having supper with me while we're there?"

"Don't see why not. It's getting on to closing time anyway. You two go on ahead and I'll close up and be right along."

Buck and Rebekah walked hand in hand across the street toward the café. They met several people who looked long at them holding hands on a public street. Buck felt uneasy about it, but Rebekah only smiled happily at them as they passed.

Mrs. Rodriguez smiled widely and nodded a greeting as they entered the café. She hurried to pour coffee as they slid out chairs and sat down. It was early for supper and they were the only customers.

A young girl Buck guessed to be no more than twelve or thirteen hurried to their table.

"I am Nita," she said, in near perfect English with only a slight hint of an accent. "I am Selena's cousin. I am helping while my cousin is away. *Señora* Rodriguez does not speak English. May I help you?"

"Tell the *señora* that her daughter is well and is staying at Chester's bedside until he recovers. It is her wish."

The young girl repeated Buck's words in Spanish to Mrs. Rodriguez. The woman nodded and smiled.

"Mr. Walker will be joining us for supper," Buck told the young girl. "We'll sip our coffee until he gets here."

After the girl left, Rebekah gave Buck a concerned look.

"Do you think Chester is going to be all right?"

"No way of knowing. He was hurt awfully bad. He's been unconscious a long time. I'm still hoping, but I won't deny that I'm worried. I've sent for his folks. They should be getting here pretty soon."

"It's just awful."

"Yep."

"I think I'd like to talk to that man who makes furniture you mentioned."

"Good, we'll have Pablo send for him."

"But wouldn't it cost quite a lot?"

Buck just smiled. "I think we can afford it."

"I wish I could see the house before I decide about the furniture."

"If you are dead set on going to the fort with me, we could stop by the ranch tomorrow. You could take a look at the house then."

"Oh, Buck Could we really?"

"Don't see why not."

Rebekah reached and took his hand and squeezed it. Their eyes met. Buck saw love reflected there.

John Walker pushed open the door and took a chair at their table. Nita appeared and poured coffee.

"What do you have for supper?" He asked the girl. "I'm hungry enough to eat a buffalo."

The girl smiled sweetly. "We don't have buffalo, Mr. Walker, but we have beef stew and corn bread."

"Just what I had in mind," he said. Bring us three of them."

"Something I've been wanting to talk over, John," Buck said, sipping his fresh-poured coffee. "Del Rio seems to be growing. I see several new businesses moving in. I've been thinking we need a bank. What's your feeling on the matter?"

"Glory be," Walker said excitedly. "You know, I've been thinking the same thing. What have you got in mind?"

"Well, if things go the way I expect them to go, next year the Longhorn is gonna have some extra cash we'll be needing to put somewhere. I was thinking maybe we could start a bank right here in town, maybe help some folks need a hand up."

"I think that's a great idea," John said, his excitement showing. "We've been needing one for a long time."

"Of course, with the town growing like it is, we're gonna need a local lawman. Any ideas along those lines?" Buck asked.

"Why don't I talk to some of the other businessmen in town, maybe form some sort of town council or something?" The storekeeper suggested.

"Does Del Rio have any funds to work with?"

"Don't reckon, at least not that I know anything about."

"A town council can't do much without some money. If the businessmen decide to organize, I'll donate a thousand dollars to help kick things off."

"That's mighty generous, Buck, that ought to get the ball rolling sure enough. I'll talk to the other businessmen tomorrow."

"One more thing on a different subject. I need to increase the weekly feed shipments my men pick up. I'd like to start picking up a hundred sacks a week instead of the fifty you are supplying us now. See any problem doing that?"

"Not if you will give me a couple of weeks to increase my incoming shipments."

"Then let's do it."

Nita brought their food. They visited as they ate.

"I'm excited about seeing our house"

"Hope you like it."

"I'll love it, I know I will. When do you want to leave?"

"First thing in the morning, I reckon. I'll bunk down in the loft of the livery tonight."

"You won't do any such thing," Rebekah said emphatically. "You'll stay at our house. It's too cold to sleep in the livery. I'll make you a pallet in the living room."

"I couldn't do that. What would people think?"

"If they think something that's their problem."

"We won't hear of you sleeping in the barn, John agreed."

After supper they all three walked together to the Walker home.

"I'll just see to my horse and be right in," Buck told them.

He stalled his black gelding in the one next to Rebekah's palomino mare. The two seemed to hit it off almost as well as their two owners.

Rebekah was busy in the kitchen when Buck got to the house. John sat in his rocking chair in front of the fireplace, filling his pipe.

"Have a seat here in front of the fire, Buck" Walker told him.

"I'm making a fresh pot of coffee," Rebekah said from the kitchen.

"You still planning on taking a herd up the trail every month next year, Buck?" John asked.

"Yep. Planning on taking two herds a month if we can find

enough cattle. I sent three of my men to talk to the Mexican ranchers. They're making the rounds of all the big cattle ranchers now."

"Never heard of anything like that. How many you plan for each herd?"

"About twenty-five hundred in each separated by a day, that's five thousand head. We'll do that twice a month."

"That's thinking mighty big."

"Never was much good at thinking small."

"Say, Buck," John Walker said. "Have you met the Elton Burris yet?"

"Don't reckon, who's he?"

He just moved to town and is starting a local newspaper. I was telling him about you boys capturing El Toro. He said he would like to do a story about it if you wouldn't mind."

"Don't see why not. Ask him to ride out to the ranch anytime and talk to Pappy."

Rebekah brought coffee and they spent the next two hours visiting and sipping coffee.

"Well, I've had a hard day," John told them. "Reckon I'll call it a day and turn in."

After Walker disappeared into his bedroom, Rebekah brought quilts and made a pallet in front of the fire. Buck and Rebekah sat side by side on the sofa. Buck sipped his coffee and stared at the leaping flames in the fireplace.

"Does our home have a fireplace?"

"Yep, a big one."

"After we're married can we make a pallet and sleep in front of it sometime?

"We can do whatever makes you happy," he said, encircling her shoulders with an arm.

"I'd like that." she leaned her head on his shoulder.

Chapter XIX

Kathleen Colson was tired. It had been a long and uneventful journey.

She glanced sideways at her husband on the wagon seat beside her and studied his face for a long time There was something different about him. He seemed to have more energy than she could remember him having in years. He must have sensed her looking at him, because he glanced at her and smiled.

"Get up in there, Zeke!" He called, urging the matched pair of big brown Missouri mules to a quicker pace. "I think this move is a good thing for us, Kathleen."

"Why do you think that, Sam?"

"I don't know. It just seemed like both of us had lost our reason for living. Chester is all we have. It's good to see him doing so good."

They rode in the second of two wagons that held their belongings. The lead wagon in front of them was driven by Vance Langley. He was a short, raw-boned fellow with an easy smile. He was one of the four men sent to move them to the Longhorn Ranch

Both wagons were heavily loaded with furniture and household items. Kathleen found it hard to leave the only home she had known since she and Sam were married. It was even harder to leave behind friends and memories collected over those thirty-four years.

But her son was hurt and needed her and his father. Leaving their home in Tyler behind was a small price to pay.

Thirty yards or so in front of the lead wagon, her gaze fell on the leader of the group, a man named Lyle Starbuck. It struck Kathleen that Starbuck was a man who took his job even more seriously than the other three.

For a time she studied him. His searching gaze crawled slowly over a line of low-lying hills that hugged close along their trail. His rifle lay across his saddle in front of him and she suspected he would be very good with it.

Another of the four, Gus Wilson, rode a Chestnut mare off on the right wing. He rested the butt of his Spencer carbine against his right hip, like the others, ready for any problem that might arise.

The fourth man, a tall, skinny fellow named Art Meadows brought up the rear; his job was to watch their back trail. All four men were friendly and respectful, yet it was clear they all took their assignment very seriously.

The four men had arrived at the Colson home the most part of two weeks ago. They had explained that they worked for the Longhorn Ranch. They asked to speak with Sam privately and explained what happened to Chester. But Kathleen suspected her husband had told her only part of it. She couldn't understand why her son had been beaten or why he lay in a hospital unconscious. It was all so confusing.

They hurriedly loaded their belongings and had been on the trail more than a week. Mr. Starbuck told them this morning they should get to Fort Clark in another day's time. She could hardly wait.

The mid-day sun had slipped halfway toward the western horizon. They traveled through open country, the flat, sandy landscape broken only by the numerous patches of scrub mesquite and cedar. The only variation in the terrain was a line of low hills off to their right.

Kathleen saw Lyle Starbuck suddenly wheel his horse around.

"Indians!" he shouted, pointing his rifle toward the hills.

Kathleen jerked her head in the direction he pointed. A wad of dark-skinned Indians boiled over the crest of the hill headed directly toward the wagons.

The man named Meadows spurred his horse alongside their wagon. Leaning far out, he grabbed the mules' harness and guided the wagon alongside the lead wagon, leaving only a narrow space between the two.

Lyle Starbuck galloped up. "You folks get between the two wagons and stay down!"

Sam and Kathleen climbed down quickly from the wagon and huddled together between the two wagons. Sam levered a shell into his Henry rifle. Kathleen could see the oncoming Indians clearly. She estimated their number to be near twenty. A tall warrior led them, whose face was painted half-white and half-black.

The four longhorn riders left their saddles and knelt on the ground. Each held a rifle snugged tight against his shoulder and waited for the attackers to get within range of their Spencer carbines.

A spiraling cloud of dust rose from the pounding hooves of the Indians' horses and drew steadily closer. The four longhorn cowboys waited. It seemed to Kathleen they were going to allow the savages to overrun them.

Suddenly the longhorn men opened up. The cowboys laid down a hailstorm of bullets that tore several of the Indians from their horses in the first volley.

Kathleen saw a galloping pinto charging directly toward the wagons. A large warrior on the pinto's back threw his rifle to his shoulder to fire. One of the cowboys swung the nose of his Spencer in the Indian's direction and fired. A long finger of flame burst from the cowboy's rifle. The brown body spun crazily from the back of the pinto, twirling in midair, arms and legs askew. The body landed at the cowboy's feet as the horse charged past.

Volley after volley the longhorn men fired, levered more shells, and fired again and again.

Somehow the Indian leader with the painted face survived the deadly onslaught. Kathleen saw him lift an arm over his head and swipe it forward. The few warriors who were left alive turned their mounts and hurried back the way they had come.

The attack had been repelled.

Buck awoke early. The fire in the fireplace was reduced to smoldering stubs of wood that emitted a dull red glow in the darkened room.

He rose quietly, not wanting to wake John or Rebekah in the adjoining rooms. He stirred the red coals and added a few sticks of wood. The flames leaped to life. Moving barefooted into the kitchen, he lit a coal oil lamp and built a fire in the cook stove before setting the remainder of last night's left over coffee on the stove.

"Good morning," Rebekah said as she emerged from her bedroom.

"Good morning, pretty lady."

She sleeved into a robe and pulled a sash tight as she padded barefooted across the room toward him. Her red hair hung loose and long down her back and framed a face that glowed, even in the dim light. Buck drew a deep breath, overwhelmed by her beauty.

"I'm sure I look a sight this early in the morning," she said, wrapping her arms around his waist and hugging him close.

Buck's arms encircled her, drawing her in, hugging her tightly. The magic of the moment took his breath away and left him unable to speak for a long moment. Swallowing hard, he whispered. "You look like my special angel."

He felt a shiver surge through her body and she squeezed him even tighter as she lifted her face. He lowered his head. Their lips found each others in a long, sweet, expression of love.

For long minutes they stood there, holding one another, savoring the warmth of the embrace, capturing a memory that would last a lifetime.

"Oh Buck, I love you so much."

Finally, slowly, reluctantly, the embrace ended, but the deep emotions created in those moments lingered long.

The coffee was boiling. Rebekah poured them both a cup. They sat at the dining room table and shared coffee and conversation until John Walker came in from his bedroom pulling his suspenders over his shoulders.

"Good Morning," he said.

Buck and Rebekah both greeted him. Rebekah rose to pour her father a cup of coffee.

"How did you and that pallet make out last night?" John asked, pulling out a chair and sitting down.

"Slept like a log," Buck said, taking a long swig from his cup. "Shore obliged for your hospitality."

"How long you expect you young folks will be at Fort Clark?"

"I'll be there until Chester gets well," Rebekah put in. "I don't want Selena to be alone."

"Take however much time you need," John told her. "I'll get Elvira Towson to fill in for you until you get back."

"And you'll be hoping I never get back," Rebekah kidded, grinning. "I think you're sweet on Elvira."

"She's a fine woman. She's been a widow a long time."

"You men folk drink your coffee. I'll go gather the eggs and milk the cow."

"I'll help you," Buck offered, standing.

"Was hoping you might." Smiling.

She slipped on her shoes and they sleeved into their coats. Rebekah grabbed the milk bucket as they walked out the door.

It was a frosty morning. The chill morning greeted them. Hand in hand they made their way to the barn.

"Make you a deal," Buck told her. "I'll milk the cow if you will gather the eggs?"

"Mister, you just made yourself a bargain," she said, again smiling and tossing the milk bucket to him.

He caught it and dipped a half-bucket of water from the trough and then headed for the stall he spotted the cow in the night before.

He found a milk stool on the straw floor outside the cow's stall. He unlatched the gate and stepped inside. The Jersey milk cow twisted her head around to see who had invaded her territory, and then went back to munching on some hay.

Buck patted her and set the stool down and straddled it. He washed her with the water from his bucket and dumped the rest. Setting the bucket on the floor of the stall he went to work.

Rebekah walked to the stall and leaned on the gate, watching him with admiration. "That's amazing," she said.

"What's amazing, that I know how to milk a cow? I grew up on a farm."

"She never stands that still for me when I milk her."

"Maybe she just likes a man's touch."

"Seems so." Rebekah laughed.

The bucket was almost full when he finished milking. Together they walked back to the house laughing and talking.

Rebekah dressed and prepared a hearty breakfast of ham, eggs, and hot biscuits. The sun was peeking over the horizon when they finished the dishes, packed her saddlebags, and told her father goodbye.

In minutes they were in the saddle and riding side by side. With Rebekah beside him, the ride to the ranch passed quickly. Buck was a happy man.

As they splashed across the Sycamore River onto the Longhorn Ranch property, herds of longhorn cattle began to appear. They passed herd after herd of grazing cattle tended by longhorn riders. The riders lifted their hats in greeting. Buck and Rebekah waved back at them.

"I thought you just sent all your cattle up the trail to Missouri?" Rebekah said.

"Those were the trail herds. The cattle you see here are our brood stock. They are the best of the best. We won't sell those."

"Oh, I see."

As they rode within sight of the walled ranch complex she seemed overwhelmed by the vastness of it.

"I had no idea the ranch was this big," she said, shaking her head in amazement. "It's like a town inside the walls."

"That's pretty much what it is. We had to do that for protection from the Indians."

The sentry waved at them from the watchtower as they rode through the wide gate. Jewel's children were running and playing happily and ran to meet them. Buck and Rebekah dismounted. They looped the reins to their horses around the hitching rail.

"I'd like for you to meet my friends. This is Jeremiah and this pretty little lady is Sarah. Kids, this is Rebekah. Pretty soon she will be coming to live with us here on the ranch."

Both children looked long at Rebekah and smiled before running off to play.

"I can't get over how large the compound is," Rebekah said again.

"Well, if everybody was here at once we would have close to two hundred folks living inside the compound. Our bunkhouses alone sleep almost that many."

"Then you have that many who work here on the ranch?"

"Yep, at one time or another, like I said, we have almost two hundred on the payroll at last count."

"That large hacienda over there, is that ours?"

"That's your future home."

Rebekah's eyes went wide in obvious shock. Her hand flew to cover her open mouth. She jerked alternating looks between Buck and the large hacienda.

"*That*...that is *our* home?"

"Yep, come on, I'll show you around."

Rebekah was clearly in a state of shock as they walked toward the sprawling hacienda. An adobe wall surrounded the main house. As they walked through the wrought iron gate they entered a small courtyard. A red-tile walkway led past a colorful, bubbling fountain surrounded by green plants. A wide, red-tilled veranda spanned the entire front of the house. Hanging baskets of flowers were spaced every few feet.

As they entered the house through wide double doors, they stepped into a wide hallway.

"There are six rooms in the house," Buck explained.

They turned through the first door on their right into the large den and sitting room. The room was completely bare of furniture. Buck took note that the fireplace was now completed. A thick mantle of oiled wood spanned the rock facing of the giant fireplace. Above the mantle hung a set of longhorns that looked to be as big around as a man's leg and with a span of at least six feet.

"Buck, I absolutely love it. But I can see right now the

kind of furniture I was going to order wouldn't fit in this house at all."

"Come on, there's a lot more to see."

Next they visited the large dining room, then the kitchen, then two bedrooms. When they approached the last door, Buck paused.

"This is the main bedroom, our room."

"Buck, could we *not* look at this one until we are married?"

"Of course, whatever you want."

"I want it to be special, our special place."

"Then that's how it will be. Come on, I want to show you around the ranch before supper. We'll stay here tonight and leave for Fort Clark at first light."

They went outside and mounted. Leaving the compound, Buck led her to a series of corrals.

"I want to show you a sight you will never forget," he told her, riding up to an extra stout pen. "That is El Toro, the legendary killer bull, or so folks say."

Rebekah's eyes went wide. Her mouth flew open.

"Oh, my goodness!" She exclaimed. "I've never seen anything like it! That's the scariest bull I've ever seen."

"For a fact."

The monster bull swung its massive head to stare at them. He snorted and pawed the ground, sending dirt flying. Rebekah pulled back on the reins of her mare, backing it away from the fence.

"He's about as tame as he's gonna get, I reckon," Buck told her. "We're gonna put some select cows with him pretty quick and let him start earning his keep."

"I feel sorry for the cows," she said, shaking her head in amazement.

"If it goes the way we're hoping, that big fellow is gonna produce some mighty fine calves come spring."

As they were riding away from the pen Buck saw Rebekah glance quickly over a shoulder. A grin crooked its way across his face.

They rode the ranch until dusky dark.

"Reckon we best head back to the compound, Jewel will have supper hot and waiting."

It was well after dark when they turned their horses over to the stable man and walked to the chow hall.

Sure enough, the big black lady gave him what for when they walked in.

"'Bout time you two showed up," she said smiling. "I was getting ready to slop the hogs with the left-overs."

"Now, Jewel, settle down and show some manners in front of my wife-to-be," Buck kidded.

"Lordy sakes alive, I needs to have me a sit down talk with this pretty lady."

"I reckon not," Buck said, lifting a grin.

A Fried beef steak, mashed potatoes with flour gravy, boiled cabbage, and hot baked bread was piled high on their plates. Buck and Rebekah found a place at a long table and sat down. Jewel brought a pot of hot coffee and poured them both a cup.

"Do all the men on the ranch eat like this every day?" Rebekah asked the woman.

"Yes, ma'am, pretty much. We try to keep their bellies full and that keeps them happy. "Your man ain't no different."

"Ask one of the hands to build a fire in the fireplace in Chester's cabin," Buck said to Jewel. "Miss Walker will be spending the night."

"I'll sure see to it, Mr. Buck."

Jewel left to see that the fire was built. Her helpers got

busy cleaning the kitchen and chow hall. Buck and Rebekah spent the next hour sipping coffee and talking.

"I can't believe all you have accomplished in such a short time," she told him.

"I've had a lot of help."

"I'm sure that's true, but you arrived only a year ago. All this in one year is quite an achievement."

"Well, I try to think more where we're going instead of where we've been. Nothing I can do about the past, but I figure the future is pretty much what we make it."

She looked long at him. He sensed her looking his way and lifted his gaze from his coffee cup. Their gazes mingled.

"You're a remarkable man, Buck Cordell."

"And you are the most wonderful lady I have ever known."

They rose and made their way across the compound to the comfortable adobe house that replaced the log cabin the Indians burned down. Buck pushed the door open and stepped inside. A lamp had already been lit. The orange light spilled through the open door and made a square patch on the board porch.

"Looks like Jewel has been here," Buck said. "The fire's already going. Come on in and make yourself at home."

Rebekah stepped inside. Flames from a roaring fire licked upward, spreading light and warmth through the cozy room. A sofa sat crossways in front of the fireplace. A straw-backed rocking chair sat beside it.

The door to an adjoining room stood open. She walked over and peeked inside. A comfortable-looking bed appeared freshly made and the covers turned back.

"That Jewel is a marvel," Rebekah said, returning to the sofa where Buck was already seated. "Is she the cook or housekeeper?"

"Lots of both," he replied. "She kinda oversees most things around here. Don't know what we would do without her."

Rebekah sat down beside him. They spent a quiet few moments staring at the fire.

"Buck, I absolutely love our home. I can't wait to get it furnished."

"I've already asked Pablo to send for the furniture maker."

"Yes, I think that would be good. The furniture in the catalogue at the store definitely wouldn't fit in *that* house. It's so big."

"I figure we'll fill it up with our children."

"How many children would you like?"

"At least a dozen."

"Oh, my, I hope you are joking."

"Yeah, more like two, maybe three."

"Now *that* I can handle," she said, snuggling close and laying her head on his shoulder.

"Buck, I'm going to make you the happiest man in Texas."

Buck lay half asleep, but he heard the loud ringing of the bell. Jewel announced another day. All around him the forty or so cowhands in the bunkhouse where Buck slept started rolling out of their bunks.

For a moment he lay there, remembering the night before. He and Rebekah had talked until past midnight before he kissed her goodnight and made his way to the bunkhouse. He still found it hard to believe they would soon be husband and wife.

He swung his feet to the floor and pulled on his pants. He stomped on his boots and sleeved into a fresh shirt before strapping on his gun belt.

He stopped at the line of wash basins and washed up and then shrugged into his sheep-lined coat. Pushing through the door, he was struck by the early morning chill in the air. It was still dark, a good hour until daylight, but the ranch was already awake and getting ready for the day. Cowboys hurried toward the chow hall. Buck headed toward Chester's cabin.

A lamp shone through the single window, so Buck knew Rebekah was already up. Just to make sure, though, he knocked on the door.

"If that's a tall, handsome cowboy knocking on my door, then come on in," came her voice came from inside.

"What if it's a short, ugly one?"

"I don't know any like that."

Buck opened the door. Rebekah was already dressed and ready to go.

"Morning, pretty lady." Buck greeted.

"Good Morning, husband-to-be."

"Ready for some breakfast?"

"After seeing what Jewel served for supper, I can't wait to see what she has in store for breakfast."

"You'll like it."

By the time they entered the chow hall most of the longhorn hands were already eating. Buck and Rebekah moved through the line. Jewel and her workers filled their plates to overflowing with scrambled eggs, fried potatoes, ham, and hot biscuits.

They took a seat and began eating. A young Mexican girl came around and filled their coffee cups.

"No wonder your men seem so happy here," Rebekah said.

"Yeah, and the trail hands eat this good, too," Buck said around a mouthful of biscuit and honey. "That blond haired fellow over yonder is Rowdy Sloan, our new top hand here on the ranch. After breakfast he will meet with three of our other lead men and go over the work assignments for today. They meet every morning."

"Do you need to be there?" she asked.

"No, he can handle things. We need to get on the trail right after breakfast. We've got a long ride ahead of us."

"I'm ready when you are."

* * *

The two wagons carrying Sam and Kathleen Colson arrived at Fort Clark just before sundown. After Lyle Starbuck explained to the sentry their business they were admitted and pulled their wagons through the wide gate.

By the time they got their wagons stopped near the livery stable, they saw an officer and a sergeant crossing the parade ground toward them.

"I'm Colonel Ronald Callahan, Commandant of the fort."

"I'm Sam Colson. This is my wife, Kathleen. I understand our son is here in the hospital?"

"Yes, he is. I'll take you to him."

Sam and Kathleen followed the officer to the hospital and to Chester's room. Kathleen took a deep breath and pushed open the door.

Her gaze fell upon her son lying motionless in the bed. A white sheet was pulled up to his chest. His face looked fresh-shaven. He seemed peaceful, as if he had just gone to sleep.

A nice-looking Mexican girl sat in a chair beside his bed. She looked up as Kathleen and Sam entered and rose quickly to her feet.

"You must be Chester's mother and father?" the girl asked. "I am Selena."

Sam stepped close to the girl and shook her hand.

"Yes, I am Sam Colson. This is my wife, Kathleen."

"It is very nice to meet you," Selena said.

Chester's mother looked long into the girls face as she stepped forward and shook her hand. She saw something in the young girl's eyes that held her gaze for a long moment. Love, she saw love in Selena's eyes. This girl was in love with her son. Kathleen placed her left hand over the girl's hand and squeezed it. They shared a soft, knowing smile before Kathleen's gaze went back to Chester's face. "How is my son?" Kathleen asked softly.

"He has been in a coma for over three weeks now. The doctor comes every day to check him, but there has been no change."

"Have you been here alone the whole time?"

"No, ma'am. *Señor* Cordell has stayed here with me most of the time. He had to return to the ranch a few days ago. I expect him back right away."

"Is he my son's partner in this ranch?"

"Yes, ma'am."

"I see."

Kathleen reached a hand and pressed her work-worn fingers to Chester's cheek. She stared long into her son's peaceful-looking face.

"The doctor says that he is in no pain. He says his organs are operating normally, but he is just asleep."

"Does he...?" Kathleen bit off her question, not sure she was ready for the answer. She took a long, deep breath and mouthed the words. "Does the doctor say when he might wake up?"

"No, ma'am. He will only say there is no way to know."

Sam spoke up. "Does he need anything? Is there something that needs to be done?"

"No, sir. The commander of the base and his men are very helpful. They have provided everything Chester needs."

A soft knock was heard on the door before it pushed open slowly. Colonel Callahan and a sergeant stepped in quietly. The officer looked at Chester for a minute before swinging his gaze to Sam Colson.

"If there is anything we can do to make your stay more comfortable, all you need do is send me word. We have prepared an empty room in the officers' quarters for the two of you. It will be at your disposal for as long as you care to stay. You may take your meals in the officer's mess hall or here in your son's room, whichever you prefer."

"That's very nice of you, colonel, we're obliged."

"The doctor should be around shortly. I'm sure he will be glad to speak to you about your son's condition."

Sam nodded his head. The colonel and his sergeant excused themselves and left.

"Seems like a nice sort of fellow," Sam commented.

"Yes, since the...incident, he has been very helpful. Before that he was very bitter toward *señor* Cordell and Chester. I suspect the change has more to do with his fear of what *señor* Cordell will do than his desire to be helpful."

"Why was the colonel bitter toward my son?"

"*Señor* Cordell can explain it better than I. Perhaps it would be best to ask him your question."

"I'll do that."

"Mrs. Colson," Selena said. "Sit there in the chair beside the bed. I need to stand for a while."

Kathleen bent to place her cheek against Chester's.

"This is mother, Chester. I'm here, son."

Large tears escaped her eyes and dripped onto her son's face. She reached a hand and took Chester's in hers and held it as she sat down in the chair beside the bed.

The door pushed open again. An older, grey haired man in a white doctor's coat stepped into the room. His quick sweep of the people in the room was followed by a long look at his patient.

"I'm Doctor Henry Dixon, the post doctor."

"We are Chester's folks. We just arrived."

The doctor stepped over to Chester's bedside. He pulled a stethoscope from around his neck and fitted the earpieces into his ears. The other end he placed against Chester's chest and listened. He moved the instrument around, listening closely.

Finally, he removed the earpieces from his ears and hung the instrument around his neck. His experienced hands moved over Chester's body, pressing, feeling, examining. Carefully, gently, he lifted Chester's eyelids and shined a small light into each one. Finally he straightened.

"Wish I could tell you there's a change in his condition but I'm afraid I don't find any."

"What, exactly *is* his condition, doctor?" Sam asked.

"Your son is in a state of semi-unconsciousness. His brain damaged to some unknown extent by the beating he incurred. As far as I can tell, all of his vital organs are working normally.

"Most likely he can hear what is being said, but is unable to respond. I would encourage you to continue to speak to him. Encourage him, express your positive feelings toward him. That sometimes aids in a patient regaining consciousness.

"Be assured we are doing everything in our power to help your son recover."

"How long will he be unconscious?"

"There is no way of knowing. It's like I told Mr. Cordell earlier, maybe days, maybe weeks. Let's just do everything we can and trust the good Lord to work it out."

"We're obliged, doctor."

The doctor shook hands with Sam and left the room.

"I've been talking to him constantly ever since he was hurt," Selena said quietly.

Kathleen swung a soft look at her "You love him don't you?"

Salena nodded.

"Yes, ma'am, I love him very much."

"It shows, child. I saw it in your eyes when we first met."

She reached a hand and squeezed Selena's. They both smiled a small smile.

From that moment on, one of them talked to Chester. They

spoke in soft, soothing, positive tones, assuring him of their presence, their love, and that everything was going to work out.

Buck and Rebekah arrived just after good dark. He introduced himself and Rebekah to Chester's folks. Rebekah wrapped Selena in a hug that lasted for a long time.

Buck stepped over to the bedside of his friend and partner. For a time he stared down into Chester's face. "Has the doctor been in?" Buck asked.

"Yes," Selena replied. "There is no change."

Buck jerked a nod.

"I saw the colonel as we rode in. He said you folks need to come over to the officer's mess hall and eat something."

"Why don't all of you go on," Rebekah suggested. "Buck and I will stay here with Chester."

"Might be good," Sam said. "It's been a while since we ate. We got jumped by a bunch of Apaches about a day back. We were afraid to build a fire to cook a meal after that."

"Yeah, my men told me all about it when I saw them just now."

"Those boys you sent sure knew what they were doing. Hadn't been for them we would have been goners for sure."

"They're good men.

"Well, come on, Kathleen, Selena. Let's go take the colonel up on his offer for supper."

After they left, Buck and Rebekah stood on either side of Chester's bed, staring down at him.

"Hold on, partner," Buck said. "We've fought lots of battles together. Just hang on, don't quit on me now. You're gonna whip this thing."

Chapter XX

Ray Ledbetter squatted on his haunches and swigged the scalding coffee as his gaze swept slowly around the campfire. They had been on the trail three days. He and his men pushed the herd hard, averaging over twenty-five miles each day. Ray's purpose was to trail-break the herd, tiring them out in order to reduce their natural tendency to return to their home range. But the men were as tired as the cattle, maybe more.

The demanding pace had accomplished its purpose; the herd was so tired out they could hardly stay on their feet to graze, let alone try to turn back. The drag riders reported they had few bunch quitters today. *Should I push them hard one more day just to make sure, or ease off and give the boys a rest?*

He pondered the question for a few minutes. All around the campfire the boys sat quietly, their heads lowered. Missing was the usual campfire chatter and joking around with one another. That made up his mind.

"We'll drive a short day starting tomorrow," he said.

All around the campfire cowboy heads jerked up. The mood changed immediately. Heads bobbed. Ray saw a scattering of sideways looks and half-grins.

"Now let's get some sleep. There's thunder busters building back in the west. If it turns into a full-fledged storm, we'll be up and in the saddle before it hits. We don't want them cows running all the way to Missouri."

After making one last round of the herd and the remuda, Ray shook out his bedroll and crawled under his blankets. For several minutes he stared up at a blackening, overcast sky. The distant grumble of thunder sounded off in the distance. He could see the dim flash of lightening far off in the west. He closed his eyes and went asleep in minutes.

Sometime in the middle of the night a loud clap of thunder jerked Ray instantly awake. A steady drumbeat rumbled across the pitch black sky. Only the constant lightning off in the distance lit the thick thunderheads rolling in from the west. The storm would be upon them in a matter of minutes.

Ray rolled quickly from his blankets and stomped on his boots.

"Roll out!" he yelled. "Hit the saddles!"

Each cowboy kept a saddled mount on the rope picket line nearby. Within minutes they shrugged on their rain slickers and mounted, and heading for the herd. The rising wind was whipped the first raindrops into their faces before they reached the herd. The drops stung like blowing sand. Suddenly the full force of the storm burst upon them as if poured from a giant bucket in the black sky.

The herd was on its feet, bawling nervously. Ray knew the least little unexpected thing would set them off. The unexpected thing came in the form of a jagged lightening bolt that struck a dead tree not a hundred yards from the herd. It split the tree from top to bottom with a deafening noise that shook the ground underneath the hooves of their horses. The splintered tree trunk burst into flames, an eerie torch in the storm-swept darkness.

The herd bolted. They took off and running like they were shot out of a cannon.

Ray jammed spurs into his roan's flanks, bending low in the saddle, and galloped hell-bent for leather to reach the front of the stampeding herd.

The earth shook under the pounding hooves of twenty-five hundred stampeding cattle. Ray swung his gelding wide of the mass of cattle on the left side, careful to keep a distance between him and the cattle. The danger in getting too close was having his horse stumble or step in a prairie dog hole. A downed horse and rider in front of a stampeding herd rarely lived to tell about it.

During the lightening flashes he could see the silhouette of other Longhorn riders racing along the other side of the herd, dead-set on reaching the lead steers and turning them into a circle, the only way to stop a stampeding herd.

Ray crooked a quick look over his shoulder. He saw Slim Hopkins on his familiar paint gelding only a few leaps behind him. Ray slapped the loose ends of his reins against the roan's neck, demanding more speed.

The wind howled, swelling to a deafening pitch and driving sheets of rain before it. It tore at them, slashing torrents of water from the sky so heavy one could barely see. Still the longhorns hurtled onward, driven by a blind fury and the spider web shafts of lightening from above. Nothing known to man could stop a stampeding herd while the storm raged. Their only hope lay in somehow keeping the herd together.

"We've got to turn them!" Ray shouted to Slim, but the wind snatched his words and flung them away.

Maybe five miles, and what seemed a lifetime later, Ray breasted the lead runners. He angled his mount to the right, closing the distance between him and the front of the herd. Out of the corner of his eye he sensed, rather than saw, Slim following his lead.

Still at a hard gallop, Ray loosed the coiled lariat with his right hand and reined his mount against the lead steers. He swatted first one, then another in the face with the coiled rope, crowding them to the right. Behind him Slim did the same.

A quarter-mile later, the steers at the point began a gradual, sweeping curve to their right, forced by Ray and Slim into a tighter curl. They began doubling back on themselves. The herd slowed, having nowhere to go since their leaders were now blocking their way. The herd became a mass of bawling, milling cattle.

All around the herd, cowboys were yipping and swinging lariat ropes, beating back the scared cattle that still wanted to take off on their own. It took a while. Finally the herd settled down, completely exhausted by their run. Slim rode up beside Ray.

"Good job," Ray told his top hand. "Anybody get hurt?"

"Don't know yet. Thought I saw a rider go down behind me during the run. I'll go check it out." After a bit Slim returned.

"We lost one of our hands. Young Jimmy McCord. Can't rightly tell what happened. Looks like he got too close to the herd and his horse went down. Ain't much left to bury."

Ray dropped his head. He felt a lump in his throat. His chest got tight. His head shook sadly.

"Sure hate that. He wanted so bad to come along on a trail drive. Do the best you can and wrap him in a blanket. We'll bury him later today."

"It could have happened to any of us."

"The rains about stopped. It's getting light. Let's hold the herd here today and let 'em settle down and graze. Likely it'll take a day or two to round up the strays. I'll ride back and tell Wash to move the camp up closer."

Slim touched the brim of his hat and reined his paint around to pass along Ray's orders. Ray headed back to camp. Down the trail a couple of miles he met the horse wrangler and nighthawk with the remuda.

"Figured you'd be wantin' us to bring the remuda on up," Buster Keene, the wrangler told him. "Wash is coming with the chuck wagon a ways back, too."

"That's good thinking," Ray told him.

He sat his tired horse and waited for the chuck wagon to catch up.

Ray, Kathleen, and Selena returned from eating supper. Buck and Rebekah stood and moved back to allow Chester's mother the seat beside the bed. She took her son's hand in hers and patted it gently.

"How was supper?" Buck asked.

"It was good, real good, as a matter of fact. These folks are sure bending over backwards to be helpful."

Buck lifted a small grin. "Good to have you folks here. Chester wanted to move you down so he could be closer to you. He's gonna build you folks a house inside our compound."

Sam looked at him and wrinkled an eyebrow.

"Compound?" Sam asked. "Don't reckon I know what you mean."

"We have a wall built around the headquarters of the ranch. Everybody on the ranch lives inside the compound. The Indians are on the prod and outlaws cause trouble from time to time. Our folks are safer inside the walls."

"Ain't there no town nearby?"

"Del Rio ain't too far away."

"I see."

"He moved!" Chester's mother suddenly said. "I felt it. Sam, I felt his hand move," she said excitedly.

They all crowded close. Every eye in the room fixed upon Chester's face. Buck thought he saw an eyelid quiver. But then for several long minutes there was nothing.

Then an eyelid flickered, and then blinked open. Chester licked dry lips and opened his eyes. Kathleen leaped to her feet and bent over her son, kissing his cheek.

"Oh, thank the good Lord!" She cried with teary eyes. "My son is awake."

Buck saw Chester swallow, and then swallow again.

"Howdy ma," he whispered hoarsely.

"Gad you're back, son," Sam said, reaching a hand to touch his son's face. "You gave us quite a scare."

Buck saw Chester's eyes scan the room and come to rest upon Selena. He slowly lifted a weakened hand. She took it and pressed it to her lips.

"Where . . . where am I? What happened?"

"You're in the hospital at Fort Carter," buck told him. "We'll talk about what happened when you're feeling better."

"How long have I been here?"

"Over three weeks. You've been unconscious the whole time."

"Three weeks?" Chester questioned, a confused look washing over his face.

"You're gonna be okay now," Selena told him softly.

During the next hour there was lots of hugging and excited conversation. Chester drifted in and out of sleep, sometimes drifting off right in the middle of saying something.

"Might be good if you folks got some sleep," Buck said. "The colonel said he had designated a room for you. I'll stay here with Chester until morning. Selena, you need to go rest. He's gonna be fine now."

"I'll stay here with you," Rebekah said.

Reluctantly, they gave in and left to find their rooms. Selena kissed Chester's cheek and told him she would see him come morning. They hugged a long goodnight.

After the others left Buck and Rebekah talked a while, making plans for their marriage and their future together. Finally the conversation slowed and Rebekah drifted off to sleep in the chair. Buck stood beside Chester's bed, wetting a rag to moisten dry lips, giving him small sips of water throughout the night.

Doctor Dixon came early the next morning. He had heard the news from one of the orderlies about Chester waking up and came by to check on him. He examined him thoroughly.

"What do you think, Doc?" Chester asked.

"I think you are doing fine. Can't find anything that ain't working the way it's supposed to."

"Then when can I go home?"

"Let's give it another day or two before we talk about that. I'd like to keep an eye on you for a couple of days just to make sure."

After the doctor left, Chester asked what happened to him. Buck began to explain when the door opened and the colonel walked in.

"I'm pleased to see you doing so well," he told Chester. "Doctor Dixon tells me you will be able to travel in a day or two. As commander of Fort Clark allow me to offer my sincere apologies for what happened to you. There was no excuse for sergeant Hogan's actions. Rest assured he will be punished severely."

Chester said nothing. But Buck knew his partner well enough to know he was about to bust a gut.

Over the course of the next two days, Buck filled Chester in on all the details surrounding his beating and being unconscious, as well as an update on the ranch activities. Chester was furious about the beating. He remembered little after being arrested and taken to the guardhouse.

"If the army don't settle things with that fellow, you can bet your boots I will."

"I'm convinced the colonel will handle it," Buck told him.

Two days later they all left the fort together. Chester and Selena rode in one wagon and the Colson's rode in the other. Buck and Rebekah rode alongside Chester's wagon with two of the longhorn men leading the way and two riding behind.

The trip went without incident and they arrived at the ranch shortly after dark.

"Shore is good to be home," Chester said as they pulled through the gate to the compound.

They buried Jimmy McCord come daylight. The whole crew gathered around the fresh-dug grave with their hats in hand. What was left of Jimmy was wrapped in a blanket and held together with a short lariat. Four of his friends lowered the body into the grave using ropes.

Ray cleared his throat and took a deep breath. "The Longhorn lost a good man today. Jimmy McCord was only sixteen years old, but to my way of thinking, he was a full growed man. Not many men, I reckon, live long enough to do what they set out to do in life Jimmy did. His biggest dream was coming along on a cattle drive. He had a way about him that made others like him. We'll miss him. Adios, partner."

After the burying they drank a cup of coffee before climbing back into their saddles. For the next two days they searched for strays from daylight to dark. The second herd caught up to them, held a mile or so back.

Ray, Smokey, and their two top hands squatted around the fire sipping coffee.

"The herd scattered from here to yonder. We've found most of the strays, but we're still missing fifty head," he said, glancing at the faces around the fire. "We've lost too much time already. We'll take our losses and move on. We'll move the first herd out at first light. Then we'll drive dark-to-dark for the next few days to make up for the time we lost.

"Smokey, hold your herd another day, and then move 'em out. It's still a long way to Missouri."

The cowboys were still dead tired when Wash rousted them from their bedrolls the next morning well before light. After a hurried breakfast, the nighthawk arrived with fresh mounts from the remuda. They saddled up and started what would be another very long day.

Dawn broke clear and cold. By the gray of first light the herd was on their feet, well rested after the two days of grazing. By sunup they herd headed north.

As usual, the trail scout led the way, followed closely by the chuck wagon. Close behind came the wrangler, his nighthawk, and the remuda consisting of some sixty horses.

The herd trailed a mile or so behind the remuda strung out in a long, thin line. Two point men rode in front of the herd. Their job was to keep the herd headed in a northerly direction set by the scout.

Off to the side, swing and flank riders kept the cattle in line and discouraged any that took a notion to strike out on their own with a good swat from their coiled lariats. To the rear, several drag riders turned back any bunch quitters and kept the herd moving along.

Ray and Slim constantly circled the herd, watchful for any

problems. The days became long and tiring. By Ray's orders, they would be in the saddle from early morning until after dark with only a brief stop at noon to grab a quick bite before heading out again.

The next several days went well. They crossed the Red River at the crossing chosen by Zack without losing a single head. Ray was pleased. They were averaging thirty to thirty-five miles a day for several days. That night after supper he announced that, starting the next morning, they would cut back to shorter days.

"You boys have done everything I've asked of you. Starting tomorrow we'll let the herd trail-graze till mid-morning, then drive them till noon. After lunch we'll drive them hard until sundown."

It was a happy bunch of cowboys who crawled into their bedrolls that night. The weather had turned off colder and Wash issued an extra blanket for every hand. It turned out to be another short night.

Rebekah and Selena bedded down on pallets in Chester's cabin. Chester slept in the bunkhouse in the bunk next to Buck's. They talked until the wee hours of the morning before finally going to sleep.

After breakfast they asked Lyle Starbuck and his three-man crew to escort Rebekah and Selena to Del Rio after Buck and Chester promised they would ride in that weekend.

After the ladies left, the two partners sat at a table in the chow hall and made plans.

"Has your pa been a farmer all his life?" Buck asked.

"Pretty much, I reckon. Why do you ask?"

"I talked with John Walker a few days back. We both agree

Del Rio needs a bank. The way things are going the Longhorn's gonna need someplace closer that San Antonio to keep its money."

"Yeah, so?"

"So, what would you think about us starting our own bank right here in Del Rio?"

Chester shrugged.

"What's that got to do with my pa?"

"We'd need somebody we could trust to run it. I was wondering if maybe your pa might be interested."

"My pa? A banker? I can't picture my pa as a banker."

"Think about it. He's gonna need something to do besides sit here in a rocking chair. He's somebody we could trust. He could relate to the little man, and that's the type of folks we'd mostly be doing business with."

Chester was quiet for several minutes. He sipped his coffee in contemplation.

"You know, might not be a bad idea. Don't know what pa would think about it, but, yeah, I think it might just be a good thing."

"Let's give it some time before we say anything. We need to make sure our plans for multiple drives are gonna work out. We won't know that until Carlos gets back."

"Rebekah and I decided to get married on Christmas day. Well, truth is she decided and I went along with it."

Chester reached a hand across the table and shook Buck's.

"Congratulations, partner. She's a fine lady. Might near as pretty as Selena, too." Chester joked.

"Speaking of Selena, that girl loves you, you know. She never left your bedside all the time you were unconscious."

"Somehow I just knew she was there."

"Juan and his crew are about finished with my house. They'll be ready to start on yours pretty quick."

"Between you and me and the fence post, after I get my house done, I've already decided I'm gonna ask Selena to marry me if she'll have me."

"She's quite a girl. She will make you a good wife."

"I talked to Pappy the other day. He thinks El Toro is ready for breeding. He wants to turn some selected cows in with him and see how it goes."

"If Pappy says he's ready, he's ready."

"Yeah, that's what I thought, too. I told him to go ahead."

"I sent Carlos, Pablo, and Pedro to make the rounds of the big cattle ranchers in Mexico. They're trying to line up cattle for next springs drives."

"What price are we offering?"

"Five dollars a head if they deliver on time."

"Gonna be an interesting year."

"That it is. That it is."

Over the next few days, Buck insisted that Chester be on light duty.

"Rest and give yourself time to regain your strength."

"Bad as I hate to say it, reckon you're right, still feeling pretty weak in the knees."

They did ride down to the corral together and watch Pappy turn some cows in with El Toro. The monster bull didn't waste time.

"One thing for shore," Chester said. "We're gonna have us a good calf crop come spring."

Saturday came slowly. Buck and Chester left for Del Rio about noon. They figured the girls would be busy in the store and café most of the day and planned to have dinner with them Saturday night.

When they rode into town, the streets were unusually quiet for a Saturday.

"Wonder what's going on?" Buck said. "Never seen Del Rio this quiet on Saturday before."

"I figure we're about to find out. Here comes Mr. Walker."

The storeowner hurried out of his store toward them, casting quick, nervous glances over his shoulder toward the saloon.

"Shore glad to see you boys. We've got trouble."

Buck and Chester reined up in the middle of the street.

"What's wrong?" Buck asked.

"A gang of no-goods rode into town last night. Their leader is a fellow who calls himself Dawson. He's got four others with him who look to be as bad as he is. They've been terrorizing the whole town.

"One of 'em, a gun slick called Utah, pistol-whipped poor ole Sam, the bartender. He's hurt bad. Doc says he may not pull through."

"Where are they now?" Chester wanted to know.

"Same place they been since they rode in, over at the saloon. A decent woman ain't safe with them around. They went to the café for breakfast this morning and give Selena a hard time, put their hands on her I hear tell."

Chester's face flushed red. His jaw set. His lips scribed a hard line. His eyes flashed anger. Buck had seen that look before and knew its meaning. Chester had a mad on and He reined his mount toward the café Buck followed.

They stepped to the ground in front of Selena's café and looped their reins around the hitching rail. Chester strode to the front door and pushed inside. The café was empty except for Selena. She was wiping off the tables and glanced up. Her eyes were red and were filled with momentary fright. When she saw Chester she dropped the rag and ran into his arms crying.

"Did they hurt you," he asked, hugging her tightly.

She just shook her lowered head. Then he saw the bruises on her arm. He took her arm and looked closer. Clear fingerprints made deep purple bruises on her arm.

"Who done it?" he demanded.

"The young one called Utah. I was pouring them coffee and he put his hands on me. When I tried to pull away, he grabbed my arm."

"Stay inside," he said, spinning and heading for the door. Buck followed.

As the passed their horses, Chester paused and retrieved the sawed off, double-barreled shotgun that always hung on a loop from his saddle horn. He dug a handful of shells from his saddlebags.

They crossed the street and headed for the saloon. Chester broke open the shotgun and thumbed two shells into the barrels and closed it with a flip of his wrist. The street was deserted. Worried faces peeked through windows, but not a soul was on the street.

Carrying the shotgun in his left hand, his right hand thumbed off the traveling thong from the hammer of his Colt and lifted it slightly, settling it back in the holster gently.

They walked side-by-side down the dusty street. Little puffs of dust followed their steps, swept quickly away by a soft wind. Their long, deliberate strides quickly carried them to the saloon. Chester shoved through the swinging batwing doors. Buck stayed right behind him, his Walker Colt in his hand. Chester eared back the twin hammers of his shotgun.

The place was deserted except for five men. One stood behind the bar helping himself to the bottles that lined the back shelf. Four others sat around a table drinking and playing cards. They jerked a look as Chester and Buck entered.

Buck swung his gun to cover the man behind the bar. His eyes rounded and he slowly raised his empty hands.

The four men at the table started to their feet. Chester raised the shotgun. They stopped halfway to standing.

"First man who twitches, I'll blow the whole bunch to kingdom come. Who's the leader of this pack of rats," Chester asked, already suspecting the answer to his question.

"One of the four spoke up, I'm Clayton Dawson."

He was tall, wide shouldered, and narrow at the hips. His face was deeply pock-marked and hard-looking. His pale green eyes were narrow and evil looking. He wore a Colt .44 in a cross-draw belly holster.

"These are my men. What's this all about?"

"We took a vote. You and your men ain't welcome in Del Rio. You're gonna leave and you're gonna do it now."

"Who is this *we* that took a vote?"

"Me and my partner over yonder. Now I'm gonna ask you fellows real nice-like to lift those guns with a thumb and finger and drop 'em on the floor, one at a time, starting with you."

The leader flicked his gaze to the right and left, clearly trying to decide whether to try a draw or do as Chester said.

"I won't ask again." Chester said quietly.

The leader withdrew his Colt using only his thumb and finger and dropped it on the floor in front of him.

"Smart fellow. Now kick it away from you."

He did.

A big man with a face full of whiskers was next. Chester aimed the twin noses of his shotgun at him and motioned with it. The man complied and kicked his weapon across the room toward Chester.

The third man was a hollow-faced fellow who looked sickly. He had bug eyes and a long neck. His Adams apple protruded and bobbed when he swallowed, which he did often.

He did as Chester ordered.

The fourth man was the one Chester guessed to be the one

called Utah. Chester judged him to be no more than twenty, if that. His black John B. hung down his back, held by a rawhide cord. His sand-colored hair was long, stringy, and dirty looking. Some folks might call him handsome. To Chester he just looked like a killer.

"Are you the one called Utah?"

"Some call me that," the man said in a cold, sarcastic voice.

"Step over here."

The man still had his pearl-handled Colt in its low-slung, tied-down holster on his left leg. He walked slowly to stand directly in front of Chester.

The shotgun in Chester's hand lashed out and upward, the handle catching the gun-slick under the chin with a bone-crushing blow, propelling him over backwards.

Utah lay motionless for several moments before he shook his head and lifted to one elbow, glaring at Chester.

"Get up."

The man climbed unsteadily to his feet, shaking his head again, trying to clear his vision after the stunning blow from Chester's shotgun.

"Buck, how about bringing your man over to join the others?"

Buck escorted the fifth man over, removing the fellow's gun on the way. Chester handed his partner the shotgun without taking his gaze off Utah.

"Be right careful, partner, those are hair triggers. We don't want all these fellows to get shot accidentally."

Chester squared off to face Utah.

"You put your hands on my girl over at the café this morning. You ought not to have done that. No man touches my girl and lives to brag about."

Utah glared at Chester. His eyes widened. He dropped into a gunfighter stance: feet apart, knees slightly bent, shoulders straight, eyes straight ahead.

"You got a gun," Chester spat at him, "use it."

For a few heartbeats the gunfighter hesitated. Then his hand dipped to grasp the pearl handle of his Colt. Before it cleared the holster Chester's gun barked, once, twice, three times.

Utah's eyes rounded in shock. His face took on a puzzled look, like he couldn't believe what just happened to him. He staggered backwards in a dance of death.

His hand flew to his chest, clawing desperately to stop the flow of life-giving blood that spurted from three holes he could cover with one hand. First one, then the other knee buckled under him, allowing him to collapse on the floor. His booted feet jerked once, and then went still, deathly still.

Blue smoke curled like an angry snake from the nose of Chester's Colt as he replaced it in his holster.

"The rest of you shuck those boots off. Do it right now!" Chester ordered.

He didn't have to ask twice. They sat down in a chair and pried of their boots.

"Now the britches."

They hesitated at that order until Chester turned to Buck and said, "Then just go ahead and shoot 'em where they stand."

That seemed to change their minds. They unbuckled their belts and dropped their pants.

"Now the shirts."

In short minutes the four stood in dirty-looking long johns and bare feet. Chester reached to take the shotgun from his partner.

"Buck, how about stripping those saddle bags off their horses tied out front? Might want to remove any rifles, too."

Buck left to do as Chester asked. They waited.

"Outside," Chester ordered.

He marched the gang through the swinging doors, across the boardwalk, and stopped them beside their horses. Buck stood nearby with one of the rifles he had confiscated in his hand and a pile of saddlebags beside him.

"Like I told you before," Chester told them. "You ain't welcome in this town. Climb on your horses and hit the trail. If we ever see you in Del Rio again we'll shoot you on sight, no questions asked, understood?"

"This ain't over," Dawson said bitterly. "We'll meet again."

"Then maybe we ought to just go ahead and shoot you all now and get it over and done."

Without another word, all four reined their horses around and galloped out of town.

Townspeople poured from their stores and houses onto the street, looking long at the cloud of dust trailing the four bad men, laughing at the sight the men made.

John walker hurried up, followed closely by Rebekah.

"Reckon it'll be a while before that bunch comes to Del Rio again," he said. "You boys shore showed 'em how the cow ate the cabbage."

"Chester handled it," Buck said. "All I did was watch his back."

Chester said nothing. He turned and walked to the Café.

Chapter XXI

Ray left their double herd a couple of miles outside town, under the watchful eyes of Slim and Link. He rode beside Smokey into Sedalia, Missouri on October 24, 1866.

Their sweeping gazes took in everything around them.

"Can't see nothing that has changed since we were here last," Ray said.

"Not many cattle in the pens," Smokey said.

"Late in the season, not many as crazy as we are, bringing a herd up the trail in winter."

They reined up in front of the Drover's Hotel and tied their horses. Inside, they placed their saddlebags on the counter. A short, bald-headed man emerged from a back room.

"How can I help you gentlemen?"

"Need two rooms," Ray told him. "Where do we find Harvey Owens?"

"Mr. Owens's office is two doors down, right next to the barber shop."

"Convenient," Smokey said, grinning. "We can kill two birds with one stone."

The desk clerks eyes went wide at Smokey's words. Realizing the man had took his words wrong, Smokey hastened to add. "I didn't mean it like that. I was just joshing."

The man relaxed and produced a nervous smile. He handed them two keys. "You will be in rooms seven and eight, top of the stairs on your right."

They found their rooms and stashed their gear. Careful to lock their doors they went down the stairs and onto the boardwalk.

"Don't know about you, but I could sure use a hot bath and a shave before we look up this Owens fellow," Smokey said.

"You're reading my mind"

They walked to the barbershop and stepped inside.

"Howdy gents," the barber greeted cheerfully. "What can I do for you fellows today?"

"We both need a hot bath, a haircut and shave," Smokey told him.

"We can handle that. The bath stalls are right out back, all hot and ready for you. Come on back in when you get through and we'll spruce up you fellows You boys in town for business or pleasure?"

"Business," Ray said, turning for the back door.

A half hour later they walked back into the barbershop feeling clean as a fresh-licked calf. Another half hour and they emerged from the barbershop a site lighter after losing two months' worth of hair.

"You clean up pretty good," Smokey joshed.

"Wish I could say the same for you," Ray bent a grin.

They walked next door to an office with Harvey Owen's name on the sign out front. They opened the door and stepped inside. Harvey Owens looked up from a stack of papers on his desk and recognized Ray and Smokey. He rose quickly to his feet and hurried forward with his hand extended.

"Ray, Smokey, it's good to see you, wasn't expecting you fellows for another week or so."

"We understood you were expecting us around the first of November."

"Have any trouble getting through?"

"Nope."

"Anyway, I'm sure glad to see you."

"We've got close to five thousand head waiting about two miles out of town. You buying?"

"You bet, like I promised Buck, I'll pay top dollar."

"How much?"

"Give you forty-two dollars a head."

"They're yours then. When do you want 'em brought in for the count?"

"Sooner the better. You remember my top hand, Cheyenne?

"Sure do."

"I'll have him and some of my boys ride out and help bring them in for the count. Soon as we get them counted, we'll settle up. Oh, and tell Buck I'm moving my operation to Abilene, Kansas after next year."

"Kansas? How come?"

A fellow named McCoy is opening a big operation there. He's got some kind of legal loophole worked out so the Texas cattlemen can bring their herds through without being hassled. I'll fill you in on all the details later. It's still another year away, I understand. Talk around the Longhorn is we're trailing two herds a month of five thousand head in each herd come spring."

Harvey's eyes rounded. He whistled. A wide smile pushed a notch closer to his ears.

"That's ten thousand head a month. Tell Buck I'd sure like to work a deal with him to take them all."

"He'll be glad to hear that."

By late afternoon of the following day the herds had been

moved to the holding pens, counted, and the final tally agreed on. Ray and Smokey met Harvey Owens at the bank where he handed them a certified bank draft in the amount of two-hundred-ten thousand dollars.

"It's a real pleasure doing business with the Longhorn," the cattle buyer told them. I'll be looking forward to seeing you fellows in Abilene come spring."

"I figure we'll be there come hell or high water," Ray told him. "The boss is dead-set on making those drives happen."

They shook hands all around and said their goodbyes. Ray and Smokey toes stirrups and
headed out of town.

"Got one more stop before we head out," Ray said, reining over to the sheriff's office.

They looped reins around the hitching rail and went inside. Grady West looked up from a stack of paperwork as they entered.

"I'm Ray Ledbetter. This is Smokey Cunningham. We work for Buck Cordell of the Longhorn Ranch in south Texas."

"Don't believe I've met you boys, but I shore remember your boss. I'm Grady West."

"We just delivered a herd of cattle. Harvey Owens bought them. We're headed back to Texas. Buck told us he talked to you about his little brother. Wondering if you've heard any more about him?"

"Can't say I have. Like I told Mr. Cordell last time I saw him, the young man was riding out of town headed north."

"I see, well, much obliged anyway. Thought we'd check in case you'd heard something more."

"No, but like I told your boss, if I hear anything I'll send him a telegram."

They both shook hands with the sheriff and rode out of town to join their crew and head to Texas.

* * *

Carlos, Pablo, and Pedro had been on the trail for two and a half months. They traveled throughout Mexico, visiting all the larger cattle ranches they could learn about, contracting for cattle.

They arranged to buy just over forty thousand head. Each rancher who signed a contract was given an exact date when they were required to deliver their cattle to the Longhorn Ranch in Texas. Each understood that failure to meet their agreed delivery date would result in a significant reduction in their price. It was time to head home.

They spent the previous night in Guadalajara, over six hundred miles from home. They faced a long, hot ride, one filled with danger at every turn. Banditos roved the countryside, watching for travelers to rob, kill, and leave for the buzzards to pick their bones clean.

"Let's ride with our rifles handy," Carlos told his companions.

Early November in southern Mexico was like the middle of summer in south Texas. Temperatures soared to well above one hundred degrees during the day. Nights in the desert were chilly, requiring a fire to stay comfortable. In some vast stretches of Mexico the landscape is desert. In these areas water is even a greater problem than Banditos. The searing sun sapped the strength of both men and animals. Nothing survived in the desert without water, and finding water was their highest priority.

That is why their hired Anjou.

Anjou was a half-breed: half Yacci Indian and half Mexican. The last rancher they bought cattle from recommended him highly as a guide through the desert areas.

"He knows where every water hole is," the rancher said. "I would not move a herd of cattle through the desert without Anjou as my guide."

That was good enough for Carlos; he figured it was worth the price they paid him just to guide them through the desert. Anjou rode a flop-eared donkey.

The four riders plodded along, leading their three packhorses on lead-lines behind them. The first day out of Guadalajara they made good time and crossed the de Santiago River at mid-afternoon. The area they rode through was beautiful and heavily populated. It was near perfect cattle country.

Within three days the countryside changed drastically. The further north they rode, the more desert-like the country became. On their third night out of Guadalajara they stopped in a tiny place called Guadalupe.

It was a sleepy little village with only a scattering of low-roofed adobe huts. Carlos figured that if a man rode straight through at a slow walk, the journey would take him about two minutes.

There was only one two-story building in town. It turned out to be a cantina. The only occupant of the cantina was a heavy-set Mexican woman. She greeted them with a snaggle-toothed smile. Carlos ordered a bottle of tequila and three glasses. He also asked her to bring them a plateful of tortillas and beans he saw on a stove near the bar. When the woman brought their bottle and food, he asked if she had rooms to rent.

She said nothing, but pointed a stubby finger at the stairway and went on about her business, which seemed to be swatting flies.

Halfway through their bottle and food a short, hard-looking Mexican walked through the open door. He spotted Carlos and his friends. The man stared hard at them for a long time before walking to the bar and ordering mescal. He downed it in a single gulp, whispered something to the woman, and left quickly.

"Wonder what that was about?" Carlos asked his companions.

"I expect we'll have visitors either tonight or tomorrow on the trail," Pablo replied.

"You might be right. I saw a small livery on the way in. We'll leave our stock there for the night."

"I'd feel better if one of us stays with our horses and packs. I sure didn't like the way that fellow eyed us."

"Good idea, we'll take turns. I'll take the first watch. I'll take One of you can spell me after a while. You boys get some sleep."

Pablo and Pedro climbed the stairs. Carlos paid the woman, then he and Anjou went outside to gather the reins to their horses.

They led them down the narrow, dusty street toward the livery. Darkness had settled in. Only a thin sliver of moon and a splattering of stars hung in a velvety sky. The streets were deserted. Here and there a dim lamplight showed through an open doorway and drew a long patch of yellow in the dust.

A worn-out old timer carrying a lantern hobbled out to meet them at the livery and pointed to a small corral made of broken mesquite limbs. Carlos pressed two coins in the man's hand.

"We'll unsaddle and stow our gear in that corner over yonder. We'll stay here with our stock tonight."

The old man just shrugged and disappeared into a small lean-to behind the livery that undoubtedly he called home.

They spread their bedrolls and used their saddles for pillows. Carlos fell asleep in mere minutes.

Sometime later, Anjou gently touched Carlos awake. The half-breed pressed a finger across his lips in the thick darkness and pointed toward the wide-open front door Carlos lifted his Spencer saddle gun beside him and thumbed back the hammer.

A soft crunching sound, like careful footsteps in thick dust, reached the hearing of both Carlos and Anjou. They scrambled quietly away from their saddles and took refuge behind a pile of nearby hay.

The silhouette of two intruders outlined themselves against in the doorway. Both held guns in their hands. Carlos watched as the two crept silently toward the three packsaddles piled together nearby.

Lifting his rifle to his shoulder, Carlos centered the nose of the barrel on the nearest thief and feathered the trigger. A ribbon of fire stabbed through the darkness and lifted the intruder off his feet. A muffled scream pierced the night.

Even as Carlos levered another shell, the second man turned on his heels and fled back through the door. His retreating footsteps pounded off into the night.

Buck and Rebekah joined Chester and Selena in the café. Selena was still wrapped in Chester's consoling arms.

"Don't reckon we'll see those jaspers again," Buck said, pulling out a chair for Rebekah.

"I wouldn't bet on it. That Dawson fellow didn't strike me as the kind to forget easy"

Chester released Selena.

Rebekah offered her a consoling hug. "I'm so sorry that man put his hands on you," Rebekah told her.

"He won't do that ever again," Buck assured them.

"What do you mean?" Selena asked.

"Chester shot him. He's dead."

"He was a bad man," Selena said.

Selena's mother brought a pot of coffee and four cups. They sipped the coffee and shared conversation. Rebekah and Selena talked excitedly about the upcoming wedding.

"That reminds me," Buck said. "Pablo said he expects the furniture maker to get here within a week or so."

"Good," Rebekah said. "The wedding day will be here before we know it. We've got less than two months."

"I am very excited for you," Selena told her friend.

"Sure wish we knew how Ray and Smokey and the boys are doing." Buck said. "They should be in Missouri by now."

Chester took a long swig of coffee. "They're good men. They'll do what they have to do, I reckon."

Señora Rodriguez and Selena's young niece brought their supper. They ate, laughed, and enjoyed one another's company. Long after the meal was over, they sipped coffee and talked.

"Let's all walk down to my house," Rebekah suggested. "We'll pop some popcorn and plan the wedding."

They all agreed that was a good idea. The weather had turned off colder. They pulled their coats tighter. Rebekah shivered. Buck wrapped his arm around her and pulled her close as they walked. Out of the corner of his eye, he saw Chester do the same with Selena.

Ray and Smokey rode in the lead. Behind them, forty Longhorn riders rode easy in their saddles. The remuda of over a hundred horses, under the watchful care of the wranglers and their helpers, followed close. Two chuck wagons and two supply wagons brought up the rear.

Among the cowboys there was lots of laughing and joshing one another. It was a festive mood. They were headed home.

At sundown they stopped for the night. After a good supper the entire crew sat around the campfire eating plum pudding and sipping coffee.

"It was a hard drive," Smokey said, sipping his coffee.

"Yep, but the boss will be pleased with the price we got for the cattle."

"Can't even imagine that much money," Smokey said. "My thinking only goes as high as fifty a month and found."

"I know what you mean."

Pablo and Pedro came running with their rifles in hands.

Carlos had lit the lantern. He and Anjou and the old livery man stood over the dead thief as their two companions hurried up.

"We heard shots," Pablo said. "Are you okay?"

"We're okay, this fellow ain't. He tried to steal our packs and most likely do us in while they were at it. There was another one with him. He got away."

Several villagers approached cautiously, careful to keep their distance.

"Anybody here know this man?" Carlos asked.

"*Si*," the livery man said. "I know him. His name is Jose Torres. His brother is Juan. They live not many miles south of here. They are bad men."

"Not anymore," Pablo commented. "At least this one ain't."

"Well, let's get some sleep," Carlos said. "We've got a long way to ride come morning."

"You may want to bed down here in the stable," Pablo told him. "It don't smell as bad as the room."

Pablo stood guard, just in case the brother decided to return. The other three bedded down on soft straw in the corner of the livery. The rest of the night passed without incident.

Before the sky grayed they saddled and rode north.

For the next several days, Anjou earned the reputation the cattle rancher had attached to him. The green country they were passing through changed into pure desert.

During a brief stop Carlos swept his hat off, swabbed sweat from his dripping forehead, and stared at the endless desert that lay before them. The only vegetation was scattered cactus and occasionally a scrawny mesquite tree. He couldn't imagine there being water in country like this.

"How far is it across this?" Carlos asked the half-breed.

"Four, five days."

"Is there water?"

"We find water."

True to his word, near sundown of the first day in the desert, the guide diverted them from their northward course and swung due east. Just before good dark he led them into a shallow canyon.

"We find water here," Anjou promised.

Just when Carlos was beginning to doubt his word, they rounded a cutback and came upon a wide, clear, pool of fresh water, Carlos just shook his head in amazement.

They watered their stock and filled their canteens.

"We not stay here," the guide told them.

"Why not?" Carlos wanted to know.

"If I know about water banditos know. We find other place to spend night."

They rode another two hours and made dry camp in a deep ravine.

A week later they arrived at the Rio Grande River a few miles upstream from Nuevo Laredo.

"I go back now," Anjou said.

Carlos paid the half-breed the agreed price and gave him extra.

"You done a good job," Carlos told him, shaking his hand. "If we ever need your services again we'll look you up."

They watched the guide until his donkey carried him out of sight.

"Couple of more days and we'll be home," Carlos told his two companions.

They reined their mounts upstream.

* * *

Luis Salazar arrived at the Longhorn Ranch the third week of November. Juan Santos met him and they spent two hours going through Buck and Rebekah's new house. As the two men examined each room, the furniture builder busied himself sketching on a large pad he carried.

When they finished they found Buck down by the corral.

After the introductions they all walked back to the chow hall. Over a cup of coffee, the furniture builder showed Buck the sketches and explained his proposals. Buck listened patiently.

"Could you spend a couple days here at the ranch?" Buck asked. "I'd like to send for my future wife and let you tell her what you have in mind."

They agreed, and Buck sent Lyle Starbuck and his three men to Del Rio to ask Rebekah to return to the ranch with them.

The four longhorn men returned the next day with Rebekah. Buck walked out to meet her as she rode in.

"Hey, pretty lady," he greeted as he helped her down from her palomino.

"Hey cowboy," she said, smiling. "Rebekah Walker reporting for duty, sir."

Buck wrapped her in his arms in a long hug. "The furniture builder I told you about is here. He's got some sketches to show you."

"Good, I'm anxious to meet him."

They walked arm-in-arm to the new house. Luis Salazar was there, his ever-present sketch pad in hand, still putting his ideas on paper.

"*Señor* Salazar, I'd like for you to meet my future wife and mistress of the house. This is Rebekah Walker."

Luis Salazar took her offered hand and brushed the back of it with his lips, "It is a distinct pleasure, Miss Walker. May I say that in all my years of decorating homes all over Mexico, this is one of the most beautiful I have ever seen."

Rebekah's eyes flicked a quick look at Buck before a thin smile lifted one corner of her lips.

"Thank you," *Señor* Salazar. My fiancé and *Señor* Santos have done a remarkable job designing and building it."

"I took the liberty of making some sketches. I'd like for you to go over them with me if you have time"

"Of course. Buck, do you have time to look at them with me?"

"I've already seen them. I'll leave all that up to you. Order whatever suits your fancy."

Buck excused himself. As he left, the furniture builder was already showing Rebekah sketches and explaining his suggestions for furnishing their home.

Rebekah spent the rest of the day with the furniture maker.

"Oh, Buck, that man is amazing," she told him over supper. "If he can build the furniture he is showing me on the sketches, our home will be the most beautiful in all of Texas."

"Then did you order what you wanted?"

She shrugged her shoulders embarrassedly.

"Yes."

"Can he have it built by our wedding?"

"Oh, no, not even close. But he promised to have our bed finished," she said, grinning sheepishly. "I figured that was the most important."

Buck just smiled. "Smart lady."

Rebekah returned to Del Rio escorted by, what had become, The Longhorn's security detail, Lyle Starbuck and his boys.

* * *

Carlos, Pedro, and Pablo rode through the gates of the Longhorn the following day. Buck heard the alert and hurried out to see who had arrived. When he recognized Carlos and his men, he hurried to meet them.

"Welcome back, boys," he said, shaking hands with all three. "You been gone a while."

"Feels like we've ridden all over Mexico," Carlos said.

"Hope you brought back good news."

"We think you'll be pleased."

"Come on in. I'm anxious to hear all about it."

Over coffee they gave a quick recap of where all they had been before sharing their results.

"You gonna make me ask, I reckon?"

"We've got signed contracts for just over forty thousand head."

Buck's eyes widened. He cracked a smile that went from ear-to-ear. He pumped a fist into the air.

"Forty thousand!" He shouted.

"And with firm delivery dates just like you and I talked about. There'll be ten thousand head splashing across the Rio Grande every month, starting in March."

Buck again shook hands with the three men.

"You boys did a good job, I'm obliged."

"Is this going to be an ongoing thing, or just for the coming year?" Carlos asked.

"Wish I could answer that. It all depends on the way cattle prices go. If they hold up we'll keep trailing 'em."

"Several of the ranchers asked me."

"We'll know before long. You boys take off a week or so and rest up. You've earned it."

"Thanks, boss," they said in unison.

Chapter XXII

"How's the breeding coming along?" Buck asked, leaning against the holding pen housing El Toro.

"Couldn't be better," Pappy told him, walking over to join buck as the watched the activities in the pen. "I've chosen the biggest, strongest cows in our brood herd. Come April, you're gonna see 'em dropping the finest calves in Texas."

"Oh, by the way, some newspaper fellow over in Del Rio told John Walker he wanted to do a story about El Toro. I told him to talk with you. Heard anything from him?"

"Yep, he rode out a few days ago. I told him the whole story. He said he was gonna write about it."

"That bull is still hard to believe. You've done a good job with him, Pappy. How are the men doing over across the river?"

"Still meeting quota, I was over there yesterday. They're bringing near eighty head a day out of them breaks along the river. They tell me the Longhorns are still as plentiful as they ever were."

"Come spring we're gonna need every longhorn we can find."

His thoughts scattered by something he saw off in the distance. He shielded his eyes against the glare of the sun. It was Ray and his entire crew. They were back from Missouri.

Buck grabbed the reins to his horse and sprang into the saddle. In two leaps his black gelding galloped full out, heading to meet Ray and the Longhorn crew. They spotted him coming and began to wave. He closed the distance between them in moments and pulled to a sliding stop.

He reached across the remaining space and shook each of their hands, welcoming them home. "Can't wait to hear all about your trip," he told Ray and Smokey.

"Shore is good to be back," Ray said. "Think my backside is grown to this saddle."

As they continued toward the ranch compound, Buck rode between Ray and Smokey. Somehow Buck sensed that his top hands were holding back, purposely avoiding telling him something. He feared the worse, but didn't press them. He knew they would shoot straight with him when the time came.

That time came in the chow hall, over coffee a short time later. Buck and Chester sat with their two top hands.

We got something to tell you," Ray said softly.

"Just spit it out. Is it good or bad?" Buck asked.

"Some of both," Ray told his boss. "We lost young Jimmy McCord."

Buck dropped his head and went silent for several moments. "How'd it happen?"

"There was a stampede. From what we could tell, he got too close to the herd and his horse fell. We buried him on a small hill beside the trail."

Again Buck fell silent. He sipped his coffee and stared off at nothing, lost deep in his thoughts. Ray and Smokey waited.

"It could have happened to any one of you, Buck finally said

"That's the way we figure it, too."

"Don't think he had any folks to notify" Buck said. "From what he told us, the Longhorn was the closest thing to family he had."

"Yeah, that's what I understood. Shore took a liking to that young fellow."

"We all did. He had a way about him."

"We lost about five hundred head in the stampede. Took us two days to round up the strays, other than that the drive went tolerable."

Chester said, "Is the price holding?"

Ray withdrew a small, leather pouch from his pocket, reached inside, and handed Chester the folded certified bank draft. Chester flicked a quick glance at Ray, Smokey, and Buck before unfolding it. He looked at the amount. Without reaction he handed it to Buck.

Buck cut a wide grin and pumped a hand.

"That's even more than the first drive," Buck said excitedly. "How much a head?"

"Forty-two," Ray told them, beaming. "Harvey says the market is strong and growing."

"That means our plans for next year's drives are still on, Buck said. "Carlos and his boys lined up forty thousand head of longhorns from the ranchers in Mexico."

"I told him how many you were planning on bringing up the trail and he wants 'em all, says he'll pay you top dollar just like before." Ray told his bosses.

"Fellows, sounds like we're in business," Buck told them. "We've got a lot of work to do before March. How many more hands you figuring we'll need to pull this off?"

"Let me and Smokey get our heads together. We'll let you know what we come up with."

"I know you men are worn to a frazzle. We need to settle

up with the boys. Tell them there's an extra month's pay bonus coming to 'em. Then you and your crew take a week off and rest up."

That set well with Ray and Smokey.

"Thanks, boss, the boys will be much obliged."

After they left to give their crew the good news, Buck and Chester sat alone.

"We've still got the bank draft from the first herd, plus this one that we need to turn into cash. We'll need cash money to pay the ranchers when they deliver their cattle in the spring. We're gonna need money to hire all those extra hands, too. That's an awful lot of money."

"This draft is drawn on the bank in San Antonio," Chester said. "Looks like one of us needs to ride over and do some serious banking. I think you're the man to do it."

"Then I'll leave at first light. I'll take Lyle Starbuck and his three men, the same ones that did such a good job of getting your folks back safe. They've proved themselves. Carrying that much money, I'd feel better having them along."

Buck, Lyle Starbuck and his three heavily armed companions rode out before daylight. Behind them they trailed five of the fastest horses on the ranch, along with a packhorse with their trail supplies. Buck had learned the importance of an extra horse in his earlier run-in with Chief Quanah.

It was only a two-day ride, as the crow flies, but the way they had to detour around the canyons it was at least twice that. They made the trip without incident.

The sun rose noon-high when they reined their horses up to the hotel and tied them off. Vance Langley stayed with the horses. The rest of them walked into the hotel.

I need five rooms," Buck told the desk clerk. "You got five upstairs and side-by-side?"

"Yes, sir, just sign the book. How long will you fellows be staying with us?"

"Hadn't decided yet, we'll let you know."

The clerk handed Buck five keys and glanced at the register. "Good to have you with us Mr. Cordell."

Buck nodded and picked up the keys.

"You boys go on up and get settled, I'll ask Vance to take our horses down to the livery and stall 'em. I'm gonna walk over to the bank."

After arranging for Vance to take care of their horses Buck strode down the street toward the bank. On the way, he spotted a black and white pinto just like the one the sheriff in Sedalia, Missouri described. His little brother rode a black and white pinto.

Buck's heart leaped inside his chest. The rider was still a ways off. Buck stepped quickly into the street to intercept him. But as the rider came closer, Buck saw that it was a middle-age fellow. It wasn't Cody.

Buck opened the door to the bank and stepped inside. A young man with slicked-back hair and a white shirt greeted him.

"May I help you, sir?"

"I'd like to see the man in charge."

"That would be Mr. Seymour. May I tell him your name?"

"Buck Cordell."

The young man disappeared through a closed door with Seymour's name on it. Buck waited. The young man returned.

"Mr. Seymour will see you now."

Buck opened the door to Seymour's office and stepped inside. The man behind the wide, highly polished desk had a fleshy face and was heavy-jowled. His hair looked thin on top and he wore wire-rimmed glasses that sat on the tip of his nose. He puffed on a fat cigar and didn't bother to stand.

"Have a seat, Mr. Cordell," he said, removing the cigar and pointing it at a chair in front of his desk. "What can I do for you?"

"I've got a couple of certified bank drafts I'd like to cash," Buck said, laying the two papers on the desk.

Seymour picked them up and glanced at them casually. His eyes went wide. His cigar drooped when his mouth dropped open. He sat upright in his chair, stammered and stuttered before he could get a word out.

"This is for two hundred-ten thousand dollars. The other one is for one hundred thousand dollars. That's three hundred-ten thousand dollars!"

"That's what I come up with, too."

"Where... how did come by *that* much money?"

"I'm in the cattle business. I drive longhorns to market in Sedalia, Missouri. As you can see, those drafts are issued by the bank in Sedalia."

"I, yes, I can see they are."

"They *are* good aren't they?"

"They look genuine. I'd have to send a telegram and get verification, of course, but yes, they seem in order."

"Then there will be no problem cashing them, right?"

"Surely you don't mean you want *cash?*"

"Yes, sir, cash. I buy and sell cattle. I need cash to pay for the cattle I buy and to pay those who work for me."

"What is the name of your ranch?"

"The Longhorn."

"And exactly where is this ranch?"

"It's southeast of here where the Sycamore River runs into the Rio Grande."

"That's the one in the newspaper story. You just captured the legendary El Toro, I believe. I've got the newspaper right here, as a matter of fact. You can have it if you wish."

Buck was dumfounded. He hadn't seen any article in the newspaper. What was it doing in the newspaper way over here in San Antonio? He'd have to look into that.

"Cash money, you say?"

"Cash."

"Well, you realize that we don't keep that kind of money on hand. It will take a few days to have it brought in, after we verify these, of course."

"Certainly, how long will it take to get the money brought in?"

"It will have to be brought in by special coach from Austin. I'd say two, maybe three days."

"Then please do what you need to do to verify those and get the money here. I'm staying over at the hotel. I'll be back in three days."

Buck stood. The banker also stood this time, and stuck out his hand. Buck took it and they exchanged a handshake.

"I'm obliged, Mr. Seymour."

"It's my pleasure to meet you, Mr. Cordell. I had no idea there was an operation of this magnitude in all of Texas."

"Like I said, I'll be back in three days."

He couldn't wait to get back to his room so he could read the story about El Toro. As he left, he thought about the black and white pinto he had seen earlier. A thought struck him and he veered across the street to the attorney's office that had worked out the lease on their land. He climbed the stairs and knocked on the door to his office. From inside Buck heard the invitation to enter. He opened the door and stepped inside.

"You may not remember me, I — "

"Of course I remember you," the attorney said. "Mr. Cordell, as I recall. How is the cattle business working out?"

"It's doing well, thanks."

"I heard from my friend, Antonio Rivas not long ago. He is very pleased with the lease arrangement. He also said that he has been selling you large herds of cattle."

"Yes, he is a good man."

"Are you in town on business or pleasure?"

"Actually, I've got a problem and I thought you might know someone who could help."

"Of course. How can I be of assistance?"

Buck told him the story of returning from the war and finding his parents massacred by the Comanche and about not being able to find what had happened to his little brother. He also told him about the incident in Sedalia, Missouri and that he was certain the one who called himself the Hondo Kid was, in reality, his younger brother Cody Cordell.

"It's eating my insides not knowing what happened and that my brother might be running around out there somewhere. I've got to find him."

Manuel Rodriguez scribbled a name on a piece of paper and scooted it across the desk.

"Go see that man."

"Who is he?

"He's the local agent for the Pinkerton Detective Agency. They are the best at what they do and what they do is find people like your younger brother."

"I never knew there was such a thing."

"Up until the war they operated mostly in the Chicago area. Since the war ended they have branched out. The agency is headed by a man named Allan Pinkerton. I think you will find this man will be able to help you."

"Where do I find him?"

"His office is next door to the telegraph office, up the street on your left."

Buck stood and took the man's outstretched warmly in his own.

"I'm obliged, Mr. Rodriguez."

Buck found the office. On the wall beside the door was a sign with a picture of a large eye with the slogan, *WE NEVER*

SLEEP. He opened the door. A tall man wearing a dark business suit and a handlebar mustache sat behind a desk. Buck judged him to be somewhere on either side of forty. He had a square jaw and dark, penetrating eyes. A bulge in his coat told Buck the man carried a gun in a shoulder holster underneath his jacket. He stood up when buck stepped inside.

"I'm Mel Sloan," the man said, offering a hand.

"I'm Buck Cordell. Manual Rodriguez recommended you."

"Ah, yes, my friend the attorney. How can I help you, Mr. Cordell?

Buck told him the story, all of it. When the telling was over, the detective sat silent for a minute before commenting.

"I'll be honest with you, Mr. Cordell, our primary interest lies in the criminal arena, not locating missing persons. Having said that, however, your case intrigues me. You realize that finding your brother could take a considerable amount of time and expense?"

"Yes, sir, as long as you get results I won't complain about the price."

"If we take your case I assure you we *will* find your brother. We require a retainer fee of one thousand dollars, in advance. Additional charges may be required as they are incurred."

"I understand. If you will meet me at the bank in three days we will settle up. I reckon the only question left is will you take the case?"

The man considered the question for a minute before slowly nodding his head.

"Yes, Mr. Cordell, I will accept your case. How can I reach you?"

"Just telegram me at Del Rio, Texas. They will get the message to me."

On the way back to the hotel, Buck had a longing to visit his parents' graves. With nothing to do for the next three days he had the time.

Finding his four men in the restaurant, he told them his plans.

"Want us to ride along?" Lyle asked.

"Naw, not necessary, you boys take the three days and rest up. You've earned it."

Buck rode out before sunrise. It was only a half-day ride to their old home place. As he rode down the lane toward the house memories flooded his mind. He reined over to the graves of his mother and father. As he swung from the saddle and stepped to the ground, he suddenly stopped.

Two tin cans had been half-buried, one at the head of each grave. In each can was a handful of wild flowers.

Buck quickly scanned the ground around the graves. A single set of hoof prints led to and away from the graves. The imprint of several boot prints and the imprint of someone's knees as they knelt to bury the tin cans showed clearly in the soft dirt.

There's only one person that would do something like that, he reasoned. *Cody has been here.*

Kneeling, he examined the flowers closely. They weren't wilted. That meant they had been placed there no more than a day before. His heart raced. He jerked a quick look around. Leaning close, he fingered the hoof prints. They were fresh.

Leading his horse he followed the tracks on foot. They led back up the lane. He quickly swung into the saddle and leaned far over, following the tracks with his intense gaze.

Buck's heart was in his throat. Thoughts buzzed and swirled in his head. A ripple of excitement raced along the length of his spine. Just the thought that his brother was close, likely no more than a few miles away, sent hope soaring through him.

The trail headed due west. Buck knew the Frio River lay some twenty miles in that direction, beyond that was nothing for miles except barren, desolate country. The small community of Uvalde lay to the southwest, and further on in that direction, lay his own Longhorn Ranch but it was clear that was not Cody's destination.

He rode as long as daylight permitted. Finally he was forced to stop and make camp; he couldn't follow the trail in the darkness.

Before building his campfire he slowly scanned the western horizon, hoping against hope to see the red glow of a distant campfire. His heart sank when there was none.

Sitting alone at his small fire, he sipped coffee and tried to collect his fractured thoughts. He was determined to follow the tracks as long as there was any hope of overtaking his brother.

Finally, exhausted and fatigue overcame him. He pulled a thin blanket over him and went to sleep.

He didn't know how long he had been asleep, perhaps a couple of hours, but he was awakened by a strong wind out of the west. He bolted upright. The worst thing that could possibly happen was happening. The wind would wipe the desert clean. Any tracks left would be gone by morning. He closed his eyes and bowed his head in frustration.

The light of early morning told him what he already knew; the tracks were gone, swept away in the night by the wind. To go on would be a waste of time. He had to fight himself to rein his black gelding east, back toward San Antonio.

Just short of sundown Buck rode into San Antonio. He went directly to the Pinkerton office. He breathed a sigh of relief when he found Detective Sloan still in his office. He told him what had happened.

"Say the tracks were headed directly west?"

"Yep."

Sloan walked to a large map on one wall of his office. He studied the map for several minutes.

"There ain't much in that direction. He could be heading for the Big Bend country, although I tend to doubt it. He's got to have supplies sooner or later. The only place in that direction is Fort Stockton. We've got a man there. I'll send him a telegram and ask him to be on the lookout for him."

"You'll let me know when something turns up won't you?"

"You can count on it, Mr. Cordell."

The following morning, Buck rose early and met his men in the hotel dining room for breakfast.

"We'll be leaving tomorrow as soon as the bank gets that shipment of money," he told Lyle Starbuck. "I want to stop by the mercantile and pick up a few things. I'll catch up with you boys later on today."

Buck left his men and headed for the store, the heels of his boots sounding loud on the wooden boardwalk. He touched thumb and finger to his hat and shook a nod as a lady approached, going the opposite direction.

He was almost to the mercantile store when he saw them.

Six men rode slowly up the street. They rode bunched, so there was no doubt they were together. All six were hard-looking men with low-slung guns tied to their legs and rifles in their saddle boots. The leader of the group was none other than Clayton Dawson, the fellow he and Chester had braced over in Del Rio. If Dawson recognized Buck he gave no indication. The bunch reined up at the saloon.

For a moment, Buck considered following Dawson to the saloon and confronting him. But then he remembered what his mission was in coming to San Antonio. He couldn't allow anything to interfere with that. He walked on to the store.

The storekeeper was the friendly sort and greeted Buck with a wide smile.

"You got any wedding rings?" Buck asked.

"Certainly, we have a large selection. Step right over here."

For the next half-hour, he examined most every ring the man kept in stock. He finally chose a matching set, engagement and wedding ring.

"An excellent choice," the owner said. "That's the finest I have."

Buck was surprised when the man told him the price, he had never bought a ring in his life and had no idea they were that expensive. He left the store with his purchase and was walked back toward the hotel when a commotion drew his attention.

A stagecoach pulled by a two-hitch team rolled down the street. Surrounding the coach were ten heavily armed guards with rifles propped butt-end against their legs. As the coach rolled past, Buck could see more guards riding inside.

All along the street people stopped to witness the arrival of the money coach. Curious townspeople poured out of the businesses. The saloons were no exception, Buck saw Clayton Dawson and his companions crowding the boardwalk to witness the event.

The coach rolled to a stop in front of the bank. The guards quickly dismounted and formed two lines, standing back-to-back with a corridor between them. Their rifles clutched in their hands, ready for anyone who might be tempted to interfere with the delivery of their cargo. Two heavy-looking locked canvas satchels were removed from the coach and carried into the bank. It suddenly dawned on Buck that his money had arrived.

Just after daybreak the next morning, Buck walked out of the San Antonio bank carrying the same canvas satchels that arrived with such fanfare the previous day The satchels contained three-hundred-ten thousand dollars, *a King's ransom,* Buck thought.

His Longhorn escort was mounted and waiting in front of the bank. As he loaded the satchels on a special packhorse, Buck swept a searching gaze along the street. Few people were up and about that early and he could find no suspicious onlooker.

By sunup they were well on their way. They rode cautiously,

alert for anything or anyone that looked suspicious or out of place. Whenever possible they avoided places that would be an inviting place for an ambush. The miles passed quickly under the horses' pounding hooves.

Maybe we got lucky, Buck thought, as his head swiveled from side to side. *Maybe we got out of town unobserved.*

No sooner had the thought passed through his head than a barrage of shots shattered the stillness of the road. Gus Wilson toppled from his horse in the first of several volleys. The shots came from a scattering of rocks that hugged the side of the road.

As one, the longhorn riders jammed spurs to their mounts. The horses responded and leaped into a dead run. Buck leaned low in his saddle and crooked a look over his shoulder.

Riders boiled out from among the rocks behind them, firing as they came. Hot lead plowed furrows in the dirt all around them. A screaming slug singed the air only inches from Buck's head. Bullets ricocheted off rocks along the road and whined off into the air.

Behind him, Buck saw Lyle Starbuck twist his body in the saddle and bring his Spencer carbine to his shoulder. The .52 caliber exploded. One of their pursuers was suddenly swept from his saddle as if by some unseen hand. His body tumbled along the dusty ground.

The other Longhorn riders now followed Starbuck's lead. Buck saw another of the pursuers spin crazily from his saddle, twirling as he fell, arms and legs treading air.

The horses underneath them proved their breeding. Buck and his companions steadily pulled away from their pursuers, leaving them in a rolling cloud of dust. The rattle of gunfire died away. Still they held their pace at a hard gallop for a ways to put distance between them and their attackers.

Finally Buck raised his hand and slowed his mount to a trot. His three companions did the same.

"We lost Gus," Lyle said.

Buck nodded. "I saw him go down. Hated to leave him but there wasn't time to stop."

"He was done for," Vance Langley told them. "He got hit square in the head."

"Who were those jaspers?" Lyle asked.

"Clayton Dawson and his gang," Buck told them. "They tried to buffalo Del Rio a few days back. Chester killed one of 'em and stripped the others down to their long johns and chased 'em out of town. We most likely should have killed them while we had the chance."

"Shore feel bad about Gus," said Lyle.

The others nodded their agreement.

Excitement was building on the Longhorn Ranch. Ray and Smokey were busy daily interviewing and hiring new hands, getting ready for the spring trail drives. Washington Long scoured the countryside looking to hire six trail cooks and locate six more chuck wagons.

The newspaper article caused quite a stir on the ranch. As it turned out, Burris had run the article in his local newspaper and it had been picked up my newspapers all across the country. Pappy was right, El Toro was making the Longhorn Ranch know far and wide.

Juan Santos and his building crew completed Buck and Rebekah's house and were now busy on Chester's. Sam and Kathleen Colson were settling into Chester's old house and adjusting to their new life on the Longhorn.

Pappy and his catching crew were bringing in longhorns faster than the pens could hold them, and El Toro was doing his job. Life was good on the Longhorn.

At breakfast one morning, Buck sat down across the table from Sam Colson.

"How's it going, Sam?"

"You boys have quite a place here. Kathleen and I are amazed at how much you and Chester have accomplished in such a short time."

"Have you been a farmer and cattleman all your life?"

"Pretty much, my father was a farmer and I guess I just kind of inherited the trade. I've always been more interested in cattle that farming, though."

"Ever thought about trying something else?"

"Oh, yeah, I reckon most of us think about trying new things from time to time. Guess I'm too old to think about starting over."

"Mind me asking how old you are?"

"Not at all, I'll be forty-six come January. Chester was born when I was twenty-three."

"Tell you why I'm asking all these questions, Sam. Chester and I have got something we'd like for you to mull over.

"Del Rio is the closest town to the ranch. It's about ten miles east. Del Rio is growing. It's had several new businesses open up in just the last year. It needs a bank. Chester and I would like to open one, but we need somebody we can trust to run it. That's where you come in. We'd like you to think about running it for us."

Sam Colson's eyebrows expressed his disbelief. "Me, a banker? I've never done anything like that in my life"

"Far as we're concerned you're the ideal person for the job. You know farming. You know the cattle business. Most importantly, you're somebody we can trust."

For long moments Sam stared hard at the dregs of coffee in the bottom of his cup and said nothing.

"I'll give it some thought," he finally said.

"Fair enough."

* * *

It was only two weeks until the wedding. Rebekah and Selena both spent most of their time at the ranch making plans for Rebekah's wedding. On those occasions, when they did have to make the trip into Del Rio, Buck insisted the security squad accompany them. A new hand named Jordan Dyer was picked to replace Gus Wilson since his death.

Rebekah decided the wedding should be held in the living room of their new home in front of the fireplace. Selena would be her maid of honor and Chester would serve as best man.

"I'd like to have everyone attend," she told Buck, "but we'll have to limit the number by how many we can squeeze into the living room.

"The rest of the hands will understand," he assured her.

"The furniture maker promised that at least part of our new furniture would be delivered in time for the wedding, but I'm worried about it," she told him.

"You worry too much," he kidded. "If it ain't, it ain't. We'll make do."

"Selena and I would like to ride into Del Rio tomorrow and see if some of the things we ordered have arrived," Rebekah told Buck.

"That'll be fine, just make sure Starbuck and his boys are with you.

Late that afternoon a rider appeared at the gate of the compound. After learning his business, the guard brought the man directly to Buck.

"I'm Bill Parsons," the man said. "I work for the Pinkerton Agency. I've been assigned to locate your brother. We had a sighting over in Fort Stockton a few days back. We have been able to confirm that it was him. However, before we could make contact with him he disappeared again. I wanted to bring you the report in person."

"Come on in and tell me in detail about it."

They walked to the dining hall and, over coffee, the agent gave Buck a detailed report.

"We're just not sure where he headed from Fort Stockton but we'll stay on his trail. We'll find him."

Rebekah and Selena headed for Del Rio shortly after breakfast. Lyle Starbuck and the security detail rode with them, two in front and two behind. They crossed the Sycamore River and headed along the, now well-worn trail to town.

They had made the ten-mile ride many times in the last few months and were relaxed and talking excitedly about the upcoming wedding.

The security detail rode as they usually did with their Spencer saddle guns riding propped upright against their upper legs. Their heads pivoted constantly from side to side, alert for any danger.

The trail passed through a wide field of stunted cedar that hugged the trail on both sides. In places the cedar grew so thick and close together it would be difficult for a horse and rider to pass through the dense growth.

Rebekah happened to be looking toward the left of the trail when suddenly she saw a cloud of arrows emerge from the cedar trees. The arrows hissed through the air like a swarm of angry bees. For half-a-heartbeat she was stunned into silence, then screamed a warning but it was too late.

She saw Vance Langley topple from the saddle with half-a-dozen arrows protruding from his body. Lyle Starbuck got hit hard with several arrows, but managed to hang on to his rifle with one hand and the saddle horn with the other. He swung his rifle toward the cluster of cedars, one-handed, and fire blindly before slumping out of his saddle and tumbling to the ground.

A second volley of the deadly arrows flew from the underbrush on the opposite side of the trail. Rebekah heard a shot from behind her. She twisted a quick look. The new man, Jordan Dyer, already lay on the ground, mortally wounded with several arrows. Art Meadows took an arrow in his side, and one protruded from his upper leg, but he fired his Spencer, struggled mightily to lever another shell, and fired again before a dozen arrows swept him from the saddle.

It all happened within a matter of seconds.

"Let's ride!" She screamed to Selena, even as she jammed heels into her palomino's flanks.

But it was too late. Indians surrounded them. They grabbed their horses' bridles preventing any escape. Rebekah and Selena were pulled from their horses and held securely by the half-naked savages. Their hands were quickly tied in front of them with strips of rawhide. Another was jammed between their lips and tied tightly behind their neck, muffling their screams.

A tall Indian emerged from the growth of cedars and walked slowly, deliberately, toward them. His face was painted half-white and half-black. He stopped only a step from the two girls. For a time he stood motionless, staring at them.

His coal-black eyes settled on Rebekah and crawled slowly the length of her and back again. His look bored into her and made her skin crawl. Suddenly she knew—knew what horror lay in wait for her and Selena. The thought shocked her, swelled the barely controlled panic lodged beneath her ribs. As if he read her thoughts he curled his lips in a cruel, knowing smile.

Abruptly, he swung away from them lifted a muscled arm toward the dead and dying longhorn riders. He said something in a language Rebekah could not understand.

He stood over one of the Longhorn men, Lyle Starbuck. Rebekah saw Starbuck blink open his eyes and lick dry lips.

The painted Indian curled evil lips in a cruel smile. He withdrew a long knife from a sheath on his belt and bent over the dying cowboy. Rebekah's stifled scream forced itself past the knotted rawhide cutting into both sides of her mouth. She couldn't bare to watch the horror and slammed her eyes shut.

Buck and Chester used up most of the following day riding their ranch, inspecting their brood herds and visiting with the hands charged with watching over them. They sat their saddles chatting with Ben Wheeler, their horse wrangler when Ray came riding at a hard gallop.

"Come quick," he hollered as he drew close. "Starbuck's horse just showed up. Hate to tell you, boss, but there was blood on the saddle."

Buck's heart shredded. A huge lump knotted in his throat. *Starbuck and his boys were with Rebekah and Selena.*

"Get Zack and some of the boys," Buck shouted as he dug spurs into the black gelding's flanks. "Tell them to head toward Del Rio."

The black responded. In two jumps the gelding ran full out and belly to the ground. Chester stayed right on his heels.

As they rode, fear twisted inside Buck's stomach like a snake. His mind swirled, weighing the possibilities, none of which were good.

They found the men beside the trail. It wasn't a pretty sight. Lyle Starbuck and his three men lay spread-eagled and staked to the ground. Their stomachs were split open and their intestines stretched across the ground like long snakes, a favorite Comanche game.

Buck and Chester searched frantically, but found no sign of either Rebekah or Selena.

"Reckon they got away?" Chester wondered aloud, knowing the answer before he asked the question.

"Not likely," Buck replied through gritting teeth. "I'm afraid it's Quanah, that Comanche chief, he's most likely taken the girls."

"But why?"

Buck was silent. He wasn't ready to deal with the answer to Chester's question let alone put it into words.

"We've got to get after them!" Chester shouted as the answer to his own question dawned on him.

"Best we not go off half-cocked. We need Zack for tracking them. We'd lose the trail within half a mile."

Chester hung his head, shaking it from side-to-side, obviously feeling as helpless as Buck did.

They waited.

In less than half an hour fifty longhorn riders galloped up led by Zack and Ray. Their eyes took in the sickening scene in a glance.

"The tracks," Buck said quickly, even before Zack's foot had touched the ground. "Which way did they go?"

The old tracker kneed the ground, his slow gaze reading the story of what happened as easily as most would read the newspaper. His head turned, his gaze following the tracks as they led off to the north. He raised an arm and pointed before swinging to his horse's back.

"Slim, take three of the boys and go back to the ranch. Bring a wagon and some blankets. No telling when we'll be back so go ahead and bury them."

Zack followed the trail at a trot. The others fell in behind him.

"How many you figure?" Buck asked.

"I count twenty," Zack told him.

An hour later they found Rebekah and Salena's horses grazing beside the trail. They had been abandoned.

"Why would they leave their horses behind?" Chester asked.

"Those horses are shod, easier to track. The women have been put on unshod Indian ponies," Zack explained.

A few minutes later the trail split off in three directions.

"That explains why they left the horses behind," Buck said.

"How do we know which way the girls went?" Ray asked.

Zack followed each of the three trails on foot for several yards, kneeling beside the trail to examine the tracks closely before pointing.

"This one." He said, remounting. "The women are in this bunch. See how much shallower those two sets of hoof prints are?"

"Not doubting you Zack," Buck said, "but just in case, let's follow all three trails. Ray, take a dozen men and follow the trail headed east. Chester, take another dozen and follow the trail going northwest. Zack and I'll take the rest of the men and stay with the bunch headed north."

The line of rocky hills off to the west quickly swallowed the sun. Shadows lengthened Buck knew tracking would get nigh on impossible after darkness set in. A feeling of desperation gripped him. Somehow they had to catch them before dark. The thought of Rebekah and Selena having to spend the night with those savages was unbearable.

Buck rode alongside the tracker.

"Any chance of overtaking them before dark?" he asked, his voice on the edge of panic.

"Doubt it, boss, I'd say we are still an hour behind, maybe a little more."

Zack's words confirmed what he already suspected but refused to accept. In his heart he knew if they lost the trail in the darkness their chances of ever finding the girls were slim and none. He knew the Indians would likely travel all night. By morning they would be so far behind they would never catch them.

On the other hand, if they got too close, he had little doubt Rebekah and Selena's fate would be the same as Lyle Starbuck and his men. *But what else can we do?*

"Then let's ride them down, Buck shouted, as he dug heels into his horse's flanks. We've got to catch them before we lose their trail in the dark."

For the next hour, they galloped hard, pushing their horses as hard as they could. Another half hour and the trail would be obscured by darkness.

"Up ahead," Zack said, lifting an arm to point at a thin tendril of dust, off in the distance, lifting and curling in the soft breeze. "It's them."

"Indians!" One of the longhorn riders screamed from behind Buck.

The words no more than left the cowboy's lips before he grabbed at the long shaft of an arrow protruding from his throat. Other deadly messengers of death whispered through the deepening darkness. Another cowboy toppled from his saddle. The ambush was silent and deadly.

"Take cover!" Buck hollered, his sweeping gaze searching for the nearest cover.

The attack came from a jumble of rocks off to their left. Buck and his men spurred toward a ravine that lay twenty yards to their right.

They made it to the cover of the ravine without losing another man. They jumped quickly from their saddles, with rifles in hand, and took cover against the bank of the gully and waited for the expected attack.

Silence settled in. It came full dark. They waited.

* * *

The dozen Indians who had separated from them earlier in the afternoon were waiting when they rounded a bend in the shallow canyon. The leader with the painted face spoke quietly with the rest of his band and they rode away, leaving only the leader behind. He gathered the reins to Rebekah and Selana's horses and led them farther into the canyon.

The depth of the canyon looked pitch-black. Rebekah couldn't see a thing. Only the click of the horses' hooves against the rocks disturbed the silence.

They rode, for what seemed like an hour, before the horses stopped. She heard the Indian slide from his horse and heard the soft crunching of moccasins in the sand as they disappeared from hearing.

A faint, glowing light appeared a short way ahead. The Indian leader returned and pulled Rebekah and Selena from their horses. His vice-like grip dug into her arm as he dragged them toward the light. It was a cave.

Light from a small fire cast an amber glow and bounced off the ceiling of the large cavern. The Indian shoved Selena roughly to the floor of the cave but held Rebekah's arm in a tight grip. His dark, hungry eyes fixed upon hers. Her mind screamed a warning. His intentions mirrored in his gaze and sent waves of revulsion rushing through her. She had to do something to stop him—but what?

She lashed out with a booted foot that landed exactly where she intended. He let out a deep groan and doubled over in pain, but held tightly to her arm. When he straightened, his long, muscled arm lashed out with a sweeping blow, striking her alongside her head.

Excruciating pain exploded along her cheek ad jaw. Her head snapped sideways. Stars flared bright before her eyes. Her legs buckled. She collapsed in a heap on the rock floor.

When she woke, the Indian was gone. Her head rested in Selena's lap. She sat upright and reached her bound hands to clasp Selena's. Somehow they drew strength from each other.

Buck felt like a fool. Lying there in the darkness against the bank of the ravine, it suddenly dawned on him what happened. Quanah had outsmarted him. He had deliberately split his band into three groups back down the trail in hopes Buck would do the same, thereby reducing his fighting force. It had worked. Buck fell for it hook, line, and sinker.

Now, he'd bet his boots the two groups of warriors had lost Ray and Chester and their men in the darkness and had rejoined Quanah. That would explain why there seemed to be so many Indians surrounding them. The other Longhorn men would never find Buck and his men in the darkness, at least until it was too late.

Buck scooted over to Zack's side and, in soft whispers, explained his thoughts. Zack nodded agreement. "No way of knowing how far away Chester and Ray are, but a few shots won't matter none."

With that said Buck pointed his rifle toward the moon and fired three shots into the air.

The Indians attacked in mass. One group boiled down the darkened ravine on horseback from both directions. At the same instant, dark shaped poured over the edge of the banks, their dark forms highlighted against the gray sky.

Buck swung the nose of his Spencer upward at a dark shape hurtling over the edge toward him and fired pointblank. The Spencer bucked in his hands. The warrior crumpled at his feet. All around him he heard firing from the Longhorn men mixed with screams of the wounded.

Beside him, Zack shot a dark figure that dove from the bank, and then swung his rifle to shoot another. An Indian on horseback charged past. Buck jerked a look at the sound in time to seethe warrior hurtle from his horse's back in a headlong dive toward him. Light glinted off a long blade in the savage's hand.

Instinctively, Buck threw his rifle up in both hands, blocking the thrust of the deadly blade, at the same time he swept the butt of his rifle in an arch, catching the Indian alongside his head. The stunned attacker tried to scramble to his feet. Buck reversed the rifle and shot him in the chest. The sound of many galloping horses sent chills of fear up Buck's spine. He knew he and his men would be overrun with another attack. Gunfire exploded all around him.

"It's Chester!" A familiar voice shouted. "Don't shoot!"

"Over here!" Buck shouted.

It took a few more minutes for the scattered shooting to cease. After they tallied up the dead and wounded, Chester gave Buck a report. "We lost four Longhorn riders. Two more are wounded but will recover. We count eighteen dead Indians. Quanah wasn't among them. If Zack's count was right from the tracks he saw earlier, only two escaped.

"But we have no idea where the girls are."

Ray and his crew rode up as they were talking. "We heard the shooting and got here as quick as we could. Looks like we missed all the action."

"Yep," Buck said. "It got pretty hairy there for a time."

"Did you find the ladies?"

"Nope. Looks like Quanah's still got them, we just don't know where."

* * *

Rebekah and Selena huddled together beside the small fire throughout the long, horrifying night. From time to time they added a stick or two from a small pile nearby. The fire kept them warm from the chilly night, but more importantly, it gave light. They couldn't bear the thought of darkness.

They tensed at every sound, expecting the painted-faced Indian to return at any moment. A slight sound from outside the cave sent shivers of dread racing up Rebekah's spine. Was it the evil Indian savage returning, or maybe a cougar or some other animal? She drew a shaky breath and waited for her heart to stop pounding in her throat and her legs to stop quivering. It took a good long while.

She could sense Selena's panic spiraling. Rebekah squeezed her friend's hand and groped for reassuring words.

"We're going to be all right," she whispered through swollen lips, wishing she believed her own words.

Dawn's first grayness crept through the entrance to the cave. But with the dawn, the Indian returned. A look of concern shrouded his face. He jerked them roughly to their feet and led them outside. Another Indian waited beside four horses.

Rebekah and Selena were lifted onto the backs of the unsaddled ponies. The painted-faced Indian led the way. The second Indian gathered the reins of the girls' horses and followed.

Her jaw hurt. She reached her bound hands to touch her cheek. It was badly swollen. But she figured a swollen jaw was a small price to pay compared to that could have been. She shuddered at the thought.

All morning they rode, weaving among vast fields of scrub cedar and mesquite, dipping into dry gullies and ravines, circling hills, careful not to skyline themselves. Rebekah noticed that both Indians continually glanced over their shoulders at their back trail. They were clearly worried about being followed. That thought gave her a glimmer of hope.

Even though the weather was chilly, the ever-present sun beat down relentlessly upon them. They had been without food or water for most of two days. Rebekah's mouth was dry. Her lips were cracked. She couldn't even lick her lips for the rawhide throng.

The sun dipped past noon-high when the painted-faced leader pulled his horse to a stop beside a large barrel cactus. He withdrew that awful knife and sliced off a small piece of the plant. He jabbed the point of the knife into the yellowish meat of the cactus several times and then placed it to his mouth and sucked the liquid. His companion did the same.

After they quenched their thirst, they sliced off another piece and brought them to Rebekah and Selena. The Indians cut the rawhide throng from both their hands and mouth and handed the girls the piece of cactus.

Rebekah brought the cactus to her lips and sucked thirstily. The liquid had a salty, sour taste, but it was wet. It burned her cracked lips. She grimaced at the pain but devoured every drop and gnawed at the meat of the plant as they rode.

"Where do you think they are taking us?" Selena mumbled through cracked lips.

"I don't know, but wherever it is Buck and Chester will find us."

By first light, the Longhorn men were in the saddle. They rode an ever-widening circle until they picked up the trail. Just after sunup, they found where the rest of Quanah's band had rejoined him and rode off again to carry out the ambush of the night before.

Just before noon they found the cave and their trail when they left.

"There ain't but two Indians with the ladies now," Zack informed Buck and Chester after inspecting the tracks closer. "They ain't more than an hour ahead of us."

The sandy terrain had changed to a crusted white alkali. When stepped upon, it gave off a white powdery dust that stung the eyes and sent large puffs floating into the air. Up ahead, a small white cloud lifted toward an azure-blue sky.

"We ought to catch up to them by early afternoon," Zack assured them.

Don't reckon there's a chance to flank them and lay an ambush?" Buck asked.

"Not much. The dust would give us away."

"Then I don't see we have a choice but to ride them down."

"That's the way I see it, too," The old guide agreed.

"Then let's do it," Buck said, as he heeled his black gelding into a ground-eating gallop. In half-an-hour they could make out the riders up ahead, no more than tiny specks off in the distance. They asked their tired mounts for more speed and got it.

Both Rebekah and Selena were exhausted. Two days without food or water and a night without a wink of sleep had taken its toll. Glancing over at her friend, Rebekah saw Selena slumped over on the pony she rode, clutching desperately to a handful of mane to keep from falling.

Rebekah's throat felt as dry as the country they rode through. Her tongue was thick and swollen. She gulped long gasps of air and let it out in a sigh, refusing to give up. She had too much to live for. She had to be strong.

She noticed the two Indians twisted on their horses, looking at their back trail more frequently. Suddenly they kicked their ponies into a hard gallop. She followed their gazes with her own. A huge white cloud of white dust billowed up behind them. She squinted. She could barely make out horses and riders. Her heart leaped inside her chest. It was Buck and Chester! She knew they would come.

For several minutes she watched anxiously. She saw the Longhorn riders galloping hard to overtake them, but were still a mile of more away. If only she could slow the two Indians down some way. She searched for an answer.

Unlike westerners, Indians used a single rein to guide their ponies. She noticed that both reins for her and Selena's mounts were held in the Indian's left hand, down near the very end of the reins. If only—

She held onto her pony's long mane with her right hand and leaned forward as far as she could over the horse's neck. She stretched her left arm forward. Her hand grasped the single rein tightly. She gritted her teeth and jerked with all her might.

Both reins tore from the Indian's grasp and fell free. Rebekah dug her knee into her mount's right side. The pony swerved to the left into Selena's horse. The rein to Rebekah's mount trailed along the ground beside the galloping horse. Leaning over, she snatched the rein up with her left hand, shifted it to her right hand, and grabbed Selena's loose rein.

Using her knees and the single rein she managed to turn her mount and head it back toward the trailing Longhorn cowboys, pulling Selena's pony along behind. She crooked a look over her shoulder. The Indian leading their horses turned his mount to come after them.

The distance between them and Buck's men closed quickly. A shot sounded. Rebekah looked back in time to see the pursuing Indian somersault over the back of his horse. He tumbled along the dusty ground. The Longhorn riders raced past her, obviously dead set on capturing or killing the painted-faced leader.

Suddenly Buck reined up beside her. He stilled the frightened Indian pony and gently lifted her to the ground. His strong arms came around her, holding her, comforting her. She melted into his embrace.

Nearby, Chester held Selena close.

After quenching their thirst, the four of them rode back to the ranch together. The Longhorn cowboys trailed along behind them with the painted-faced Quanah bound and gagged.

After delivering Rebekah and Selena into the care of Jewel, Buck and Chester rode down to the hanging tree. Quanah sat astraddle his horse with his hands tied behind his back and a noose around his neck.

Buck reined up before him. For a short space of time the gazes of the two enemies locked. Then, reining his black gelding behind the Quanah's pony, Buck spoke.

"This is for my ma and pa."

He slapped the Indian pony on the rump. It leaped forward, dragging the painted-faced one from its back. For several minutes they watched as Quanah's body swung back and forth. His felt kicked in false life, and then went still.

Buck Cordell and Rebekah Walker were married on Christmas Day, 1866. Family, friends, and top hands of the Longhorn Ranch crowded into the spacious den of their new home to witness the happy occasion. Chester and Selena stood beside them as best man and maid of honor.

Washington and Jewel outdone themselves with a lavish meal. Music, dancing, and laughter, and congratulations lasted far into the night.

Later, alone in their bedroom for the first time, he held her close and gazed into her eyes.

"I can't believe you are here," he whispered. "I don't know

what miracle made you love me, but I swear as long as I live I will do my best to make you happy."

She raised her head and saw her own yearning mirrored in his eyes. Barely breathing, she shifted nearer and raised her lips to his.

~End of Book I~

Don't miss the exciting continuation
Of the Cordell dynasty in
Longhorn Book II
"The Hondo Kid"

About the Author

I was born and raised in eastern Oklahoma—formerly known as the Indian Territory. My home was only a half-day's ride by horseback from old historic Fort Smith, Arkansas, home of Judge Isaac C. Parker, who became famous as "The Hanging Judge."

As a young boy I rode the same trails once ridden by the likes of the James, Younger, and Dalton gangs. The infamous "Bandit Queen," Belle Starr's home and grave were only thirty miles from my own home. I grew up listening to stories of lawmen and outlaws.

For as long as I can remember I love to read, and the more I read the more I wanted to write. Hundreds of poems, songs, and short stories only partially satisfied my love of writing. Dozens of stories of the Old West gathered dust on the shelves of my mind. When I retired I began to take down those stories, dust them off, and do what I had dreamed of doing ever since I was a small boy—writing historical western novels.

Dusty Rhodes loves to hear from his many fans.